Code 6

ALSO BY JAMES GRIPPANDO

Twenty★

The Big Lie★

The Girl in the Glass Box★

A Death in Live Oak★

Most Dangerous Place★

Gone Again★

Cash Landing

Cane and Abe

Black Horizon★

Blood Money★

Need You Now

Afraid of the Dark★

Money to Burn

Intent to Kill

Born to Run★

Last Call★

Lying with Strangers

When Darkness Falls★

Got the Look★

Hear No Evil★

Last to Die★

Beyond Suspicion★

A King's Ransom

Under Cover of Darkness

Found Money

The Abduction

The Informant

The Pardon★

Other Fiction

The Penny Jumper:
A Novella

Leapholes: A Novel for
Young Adults

Dramatic Plays

With L

Watson

★ A Jack Swyteck novel

Code 6

A Novel

James Grippando

HARPER LARGE PRINT

An Imprint of HarperCollins*Publishers*

CODE 6. All rights reserved. Printed in the United States of America. No part of this book may be used or reproduced in any manner whatsoever without written permission except in the case of brief quotations embodied in critical articles and reviews. For information, address HarperCollins Publishers, 195 Broadway, New York, NY 10007.

HarperCollins books may be purchased for educational, business, or sales promotional use. For information, please e-mail the Special Markets Department at SPsales@harpercollins.com.

FIRST HARPER LARGE PRINT EDITION

ISBN: 978-0-06-329708-1

Library of Congress Cataloging-in-Publication Data is available upon request.

22 23 24 25 26 LBC 5 4 3 2 1

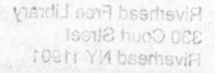

It will be found very generally that the persons called upon to give information will do so without objection or delay.

Chapter 1

"Kate Gamble!" the silver-haired director shouted from his seat in the fifth row of the auditorium.

It startled Kate to hear her name called, even if she had been waiting nearly an hour for her brief moment onstage. She was an aspiring playwright, emphasis on "aspiring." More than four hundred contestants nationwide had submitted spec scripts to win the honor of a live critique from Tony Award–winning Broadway director Irving Bass. The "Bass Workshop," as it was immodestly billed, included public readings, though it mostly drew friends and family of the winning contestants. Kate's hope was not to wow the audience, but merely to take the stage, face the spotlight, and read her opening scene aloud without her knees buckling.

"Gamble! You're up!"

Kate was seated in Row J, almost hiding behind one of nine white columns that supported the dress circle above. The famous Ford's Theatre, site of Lincoln's assassination, was still a living and working playhouse, and just being there made her feel sorry for anyone who didn't "get" the excitement of live theater. Kate was a child when her father had taken her there to see *A Raisin in the Sun*, a transformative experience that had sparked her dream of picking up the pen. It took more than inspiration to return, years later, and present her own work. Courage was essential. A touch of insanity didn't hurt. After countless hours of rehearsal in front of her bedroom mirror, Kate could probably have recited her play by heart. But stage fright could strike at any moment. She gathered up her script like a safety blanket and hurried up the steps at stage left.

"I see your play is untitled," said Bass.

Kate walked tentatively to center stage, shielding her eyes from the bright spotlight. She was five foot six in flats, but just the sound of the director's voice made her feel much smaller. Bass was in the aisle seat, a talking silhouette.

"I hope that's not a problem."

"Why would that be a problem? By all means, if you're at a loss for words, become a writer."

Kate wasn't sure if she should laugh it off or disappear through the trap door, if there was one.

"How long have you been working on your script?"

Kate hesitated. In a way, she'd been researching this story her entire life, mostly at the family dinner table. Her father was Christian Gamble, CEO of Buck Technologies International, a private data-integration company whose clients included the CIA, the NSA, and virtually every counterterrorism organization in the Western world. Kate's father adored her, and a play about the dark side of Big Data would have been the ultimate betrayal in his eyes. So Kate had worked in secret, telling precious few that her story was about the processing of personal information, and telling absolutely no one that her inspiration was the data-integration software her father had licensed to the federal government.

"I've been at this a very long time," said Kate.

Bass's assistant brought another liter of vodka and placed it next to the pitcher of orange juice on the tray table in the aisle. Bass poured the vodka into his tall glass, seemed to consider the need for more OJ, and then thought better of it. He added only ice.

"Haven't got all day," said the director. "Let's hear the best you've got."

Kate did the nervous head jerk that she'd told herself

not to do, tossing her copper-brown hair over her left shoulder and then her right. She collected herself and began by setting the scene. "June 1890. We are in the common dining area on the ground floor of a Lower East Side tenement building. There is a simple wood table with two chairs that don't match. Seated at the table is a young mother, Shayna Fine, breast-feeding a newborn.

"At rise: Enter Hans Albrecht, a young man dressed in a summer suit and flat-brimmed straw hat. A portfolio labeled 'U.S. Census' is tucked under his arm."

"Hold, please," said Bass.

"Excuse me?"

"You're a playwright, not a costume designer. I don't give a shit what you think Hans Albrecht is wearing. Understood?"

"Yes. Sorry."

"Proceed."

Kate feared she'd already lost him. "Let me skip ahead to the good part. Albrecht is a census taker and he is asking Shayna, the young mother, the series of questions he is required by law to ask." She shifted to her Albrecht voice, responding as Shayna:

"'Ma'am, what is your race?'"

"Jewish."

"That is not one of the choices. Not sure why that is. I should mention it to my superintendent. White, black, mulatto, quadroon, octoroon, Chinese, Japanese, or Indian?"

"Qua-what?"

"Quadroon. One-quarter African and three-quarters European ancestry. Octoroon is one-eighth African and—" Kate paused for effect, conveying the census taker's realization that the ancestral fractions were lost on Shayna. "Let me ask it this way: Are you and your children the descendants of slaves?"

"Sir, my children are Jewish. Have you never read the Book of Exodus?"

"Hold, please," said Bass, groaning.

Kate looked up. "I was just getting to the good part."

"That's what you said five minutes ago. You can't begin a play in the Gay Nineties talking about kangaroos and macaroons."

"Quadroons and octoroons. The terms are outdated and offensive. I get it. But that question is verbatim from the 1890 census. I researched it."

"The cutting room floor is smothered in research." Bass tore the page from the script, crushed it into a ball, and pitched it into the aisle. He might as well have ripped Kate's heart from her chest.

"But this is a critical point," she said. "The census of 1890 is the first time the U.S. Census office used electromechanical tabulating machines."

"So what?"

"Our government got its first taste of technology—and it couldn't help but turn it against its own people. Suddenly, the Census Bureau could nail down the name and address of every single American with a drop of African blood in his or her body. This is *1890.* The possibilities are so much scarier now. This goes to the heart of my theme."

"What theme?"

"Technology and the abuse of personal information."

Bass poured more vodka. "Ms. Gamble, this is a playwriting competition for scripts about women's health and sexuality. We're looking for the next *Vagina Monologues* or *Menopause: The Musical.* Not the next *Snowden* or *Oslo.*"

Kate blinked hard, confused. Bass definitely should not have started that second liter of vodka. His assistant corrected him gently, his voice carrying.

"Mr. Bass, the women's festival is *next* week."

"Well, even so. Ms. Gamble, you can't write a historical play that isn't historically accurate. What kind of tabulating technology even existed in 1890?"

"Hollerith machines," said Kate. "The old punch-card technology that predated computers. It was invented in the nineteenth century by Henry Hollerith."

"Which your audience couldn't care less about."

"They should care. I wrote a short scene to explain. It starts at page eight."

"And it runs to what page?"

"Twelve."

Bass yanked the pages from the notebook and tossed them into the aisle.

He might as well have grabbed Kate by the throat and thrown her across the stage. "You're just awful," she said.

Bass closed the notebook on what was left of her tattered script. "*This* is awful."

With a snap of the director's fingers, his assistant summoned the next victim.

"Contestant two-oh-nine, Esther Baldwin."

"That's it?" asked Kate. "I'm done?"

A young woman hurried down the aisle, script in hand.

Bass shot one final dismissive glance in Kate's direction. "If your name is not Esther Baldwin, then yes, you are done."

Kate stepped away, and Ms. Baldwin took her place at center stage. The polite response would have been to find a seat and wait for all the contestants to finish. Kate wasn't feeling it. She hurried off the stage and headed straight for the rear exit, taking the side aisle farthest away from Bass. The door creaked on her way out, barely audible, but Bass was incapable of letting anything slide.

"Quiet!"

Kate continued through the empty lobby, past the will-call window, and out the main doors. There was a trash can at the curb outside the theater. She shoved the script into the receptacle with all the anger, disappointment, and embarrassment she was feeling, never looking back on her way to the Metro station. She caught the train as the doors were closing and took a seat by the window.

What a jerk, she thought, as the train entered the dark tunnel, but she actually pitied him. She wanted to admire a director of his talent for "paying it forward" and holding contests for aspiring playwrights, but maybe the rumors were true: he was a drunk who could no longer find work on Broadway, and he simply needed the money. Alcoholism is a scourge. Kate's mother struggled with it. She'd been sober for nearly two years, but even at her lowest point she was classified as "high-functioning." Bass was the same, which meant that while his words wounded, all too often it was only because the truth hurt. Still, he could have been nicer about it. The words of John Wilkes Booth as he leapt from the president's box to the stage on the night of April 14, 1865—"*Sic semper tyrannis!*"—had no application to Lincoln but seemed to foreshadow the arrival of Irving Bass more than one hundred fifty years later:

"Thus always to tyrants."

Squealing brakes brought the Metro train to a gradual stop, and the mechanical voice announced Kate's arrival at Tysons Corner station. Kate exited to the elevated outdoor platform, converging with dozens of other late-afternoon commuters, a human funnel that emptied into the downward escalator. Kate pushed through the turnstile at the station exit. The sidewalk was still wet from a summer shower that had passed through earlier. September was the tail end of the hot and muggy season in northern Virginia, but a late-afternoon or early-evening shower was still common. A limo was waiting for her at the pickup circle, beaded raindrops glistening in the twilight. Kate could see her parents' penthouse apartment from the station. It was less than a half mile away. Kate enjoyed long walks, and she'd told her mother not to send the driver. But Kate knew she wouldn't listen; she never did. As the family counselor often reminded her, "No point arguing over the small stuff."

The mother-daughter arguments had been epic, starting with the time Kate had bravely called her out on a daily routine that was poisoning her body. Her mother started each morning at the club around

11:00 a.m., when her tennis friends came off the court for a round of Bloody Marys. The server was under a standing order to bring Kate's mother a double. After the tennis players left, the first wave of golfers rolled in from the ninth tee around noon, which meant wine with lunch, lunch optional. Some of her friends played eighteen holes, slightly more serious about golf than chardonnay, and Mrs. Gamble met them for afternoon cocktails until it was time for happy hour. On rainy days she'd settle for the card room, an older group of women who were generally so lit up by lunchtime that it didn't matter who actually knew how to play. Through it all, she managed to remain in total control of her daughter, if not her own faculties.

At least Cooper was happy to see her. "Coop," as Kate called him, had been the family driver as long as she could remember. He hopped out of the car and hobbled around to the passenger side as quickly as his seventy-year-old bones would carry him.

"Looking lovely as always, Miss Kate," said Cooper as he opened the door for her.

Twilight was quickly fading to darkness, and Kate felt a raindrop. Another band of showers was passing. Maybe her mother had been right, after all, about not walking from the station, though Uber would have been just fine.

"Thanks, Coop," she said, as she climbed into the backseat.

"There's bottled water in the beverage bin, if you like."

Cooper was ever loyal to Kate's mother. It was his way of saying, "Go ahead, check. You won't find any vodka in that bin. Your mother has changed."

"I'm fine, thanks," said Kate, and the car pulled away from the station.

Tysons Corner was regarded by many city planners as the quintessential "edge city," a term popularized by a *Washington Post* reporter to describe the transformation of what was once the quiet suburbs into a more intense concentration of business, shopping, and entertainment outside a traditional downtown. Technically speaking, Tysons Corner was a "census-designated place"—more research for the cutting room floor—situated along the Capital Beltway in Fairfax County. The tech industry fueled much of the growth, and Kate's father had been years ahead of the trend by picking up his family when Kate was a little girl and moving the headquarters of Buck Technologies from Silicon Valley. One of Kate's earliest memories of her new hometown was waiting in line with friends for the opening of the world's first Apple store at Tysons Corner Center, one of two super-regional malls that were the city's retail crown jewels.

"Looks like we got ourselves a bit of a traffic jam," said Cooper, as the limo came to a complete stop.

They were in the center lane of a busy three-lane boulevard. For the next several minutes, they didn't move an inch. Cars to either side of them were frozen in place. Kate peered ahead, through the windshield at the long line of red taillights. No sign of movement. Not even a flashing brake light. Hundreds of vehicles all seemed to be stuck in PARK.

"I think I'm going to walk," she said.

The wipers squeaked across the windshield. The accumulation had been growing steadily with each sweep of the intermittent cycle, as if to forecast the imminent transition from sprinkles to downpour. Cooper handed her the umbrella he kept in the front seat.

"Be careful, Miss Kate."

She promised she would and popped the umbrella as she climbed out and shut the door behind her. The *pop-pop-pop* of raindrops bounced off the Buck Technologies logo as she wended her way between stopped vehicles to the sidewalk.

Up ahead, the red and orange swirl of emergency beacons caught her eye. Two ambulances were on the scene. A line of squad cars stretched across the east- and westbound lanes, stopping traffic on both sides of the long, skinny island of grass, trees, and flowers that bisected the boulevard. Kate walked faster and stopped at the yellow police tape that closed off the street and crosswalk. She was still two blocks from the flashing emergency vehicles. A pair of perimeter-control officers stood on the business side of the tape, their orange rain ponchos soaked and glistening beneath the glowing streetlights.

"What's going on?" asked Kate.

"Street's blocked," said the officer, stating the obvious.

"I'm trying to get to Tysons Tower," she said, indicating the high-rise building straight ahead.

"The detour starts here. Follow the crowd."

"Was there an accident?" asked Kate.

The officer didn't respond. Several bystanders had joined Kate at the police tape. An older man spoke up. "I'm told a pedestrian got run over. A woman."

"Please," said the officer, "everyone just move along."

A local television news team came up quickly behind Kate. A cameraman nudged her out of the way, gently at first, and then not so gently, as if it were imperative that he have her exact spot on the sidewalk. The reporter began pleading her case for closer access, but the perimeter control officers were not budging. Kate turned away and followed the line of pedestrians up the cross street, dialing her mother's cellphone as she continued on the detour. The rain was falling harder, which made the unanswered rings sound even lonelier. The call went to voicemail. Kate left a message.

"Mom, I'm in a huge traffic jam. I'll be there in five minutes. Call me if you get this message."

The detour curved around the public park to the north, which was generally in the direction of Tysons Tower. Kate was trying not to worry, but she wished the old man at the intersection had not volunteered that the pedestrian was "a woman." Kate would never forget that night during her junior year of high school, the night of the biggest argument she'd ever seen between her parents, when her mother had announced that she was leaving, that she would rather sleep in the park than sleep in the same bed as "that man." A speeding van had come within six inches of killing her as she'd staggered across the street in her nightgown.

Kate dialed building security at the front desk. "Hi, it's Kate. Did my mother leave the building anytime recently?"

"Not since I came on at two. Everything okay, Miss Gamble?"

"I think so. She didn't answer her phone."

"Would you like me to check on her?"

"No, no need. I'll be right there."

The call ended. Kate picked up the pace, passing one person after another along the detour. Tysons Tower was a mixed-use complex of residential, retail, and office space. Its massive footprint covered an entire city block, with streets on all four sides. The street closure was on the other side of the building, opposite the main residential entrance. The sidewalk was the preferred route in the falling rain, but Kate opted for the jogging path, which would shave about sixty seconds off the detour. She did her best to dodge the mud puddles along the way. Mindful of the ambulances on the other side of the building, she looked both ways before crossing the street, and then hurried up the granite steps to the revolving glass entrance door. A janitor was mopping up the trail of wet footprints that cut across the polished granite floor to the bank of elevators.

"Watch your step," said the security guard from behind the desk.

Kate said she would, even though she was walking in the opposite direction, the clean and dry path to the private penthouse elevator. The touchpad on the wall recognized her fingerprint, the chrome doors opened, and she stepped into the car. There were no buttons to push on the inside panel.

"Close," said Kate. The algorithm obeyed her command, and the express elevator sped upward like a launched missile. Kate checked her cell quickly. The ride lasted only slightly longer than it took for Kate to confirm that her mother still had not responded to her voicemail message. The doors parted, and Kate entered the cherrywood-paneled private lobby to the penthouse. One of her father's bodyguards was standing outside the closed double-entrance doors, which startled Kate. She had thought her father was out of town.

"Is my father back?"

"No. Yesterday the company went on high alert."

Kate's father had a bodyguard twenty-four/seven, but her mother put up with one only when Buck Technologies was on "high-alert" status. It could have meant anything from rumors of a planned assassination of the CEO by a foreign government, to anonymous postings on the internet that rose to the level of a "credible threat." Kate and her mother were never privy to the reason why the company was on high alert.

"Have you seen my mother today?"

"Once. There was a flower delivery this morning. Building security brought them up."

Fresh-cut flowers were a must in the Gamble apartment, and her mother had a standing order for daily delivery. Kate went inside. The flowers were right on the credenza in the foyer. Calla lilies. Kate's favorite. And unlike the standing order, this delivery came with a card: "Congratulations on your first play! Love always, Mom."

It was far from her "first." Like any aspiring writer, Kate's unseen efforts measured into the gigabytes. But the flowers and the sentiment still made her smile.

"Mom?"

There was no response. Kate continued around the corner to the great room and stopped. A wall of sliding glass doors led to a wraparound terrace. The mountain views were gorgeous at sunset, but there wasn't much to see on a rainy night. Something else, however, had stopped Kate in her tracks. One of the doors was open, and the fringe on the silk area rug was soaked from the windblown rain. Kate had a vision of the bad old days, her mother standing out on the terrace in the pouring rain. Alone. And drunk.

"Mom, it's me."

Kate walked tentatively toward the open door. The rising glow of emergency beacons flashed from street level, twenty stories below. Another vision popped into Kate's head: drunk *and rubbernecking* from the pent-house terrace.

Kate continued across the room, feeling the cold, misty spray of windblown rain on her face as she neared the open door. She stopped in the opening and checked the terrace.

Her mother was not there.

A wave of panic came over her. Kate ran to the

kitchen, to the master bedroom, to the library, to the billiard room—from room to room, calling for her mother.

"Mom! Where are you?"

She was nowhere to be found.

Kate ran to the foyer, flung open the door, and called for the bodyguard. He drew his weapon, hurried inside, and followed Kate to the terrace. She was talking fast, explaining the situation to him, but her mind was in so many different places that she felt like she was speaking in tongues. She stepped out onto the terrace, but before she could force herself to look out over the railing, she saw as much as she needed to see.

On the rail, hooked by a pointed brass finial, a torn strip of clothing was blowing in the wet breeze. Kate recognized the fabric. It was the dress she had picked out for her mother the last time they'd gone shopping together. Part of her wanted to scream at the top of her voice. Part of her had been preparing for this nightmare for a very long time.

"Oh, my God, Mom. What have you done?"

Chapter 2

C hristian Gamble raised his sword toward the setting sun. The orange ball on the horizon rested atop the glistening tip like an olive on a toothpick.

The CEO of Buck Technologies was in Chicago to finalize the acquisition of a much smaller competitor in the data-integration industry. It was an important strategic transaction, but not important enough to interrupt his daily tai chi routine. Gamble and his bodyguard staked out a spot on the Great Lawn in Millennial Park, near the famous music pavilion. The sculptures, water features, and other forms of public art were popular with tourists, but September was beyond peak season, making the lawn one of the most serene expanses of greenspace within the city limits. Gamble executed a series of elegant tai chi and qigong moves, shifting the pebbles gently under his feet as he twisted and turned. A yoga class moved with equal grace at the other end of the lawn. Joggers, walkers, and the occasional surrey bike passed along the path behind him. A group of teenagers stopped to watch the strange dude in the kimono slashing his sword through the air. The bodyguard stepped toward them, which was enough to make any bystander move along, though one of the boys let Gamble know how he felt about it.

"Hey, old man, your guard is an asshole!"

Gamble didn't think of himself as an "old man," but the kid's parting shot was otherwise spot-on. Despite Gamble's regular performance of his skill outdoors, not a single unauthorized photo of him had ever appeared on social media—or, if posted, had never remained long enough for anyone to know it had ever existed.

Gamble finished his last series of moves and walked to the bench at the edge of the lawn. He wiped the sword clean and placed it in a case that a passerby might think belonged to one of the many musicians who performed in the park. His bodyguard locked it with a key.

"Sir, will you be needing this for tomorrow's negotiations?" he asked, joking.

Gamble smiled, but slicing and dicing the owner of a target company was not what made him tick. Before Buck was listed on the NASDAQ, he was known for "win-win" deals in which the *real* winner was technology. But, as CEO of a publicly traded company, he now reported to the board of directors and its chairman, and the "betterment of humankind" was not on their list of reasons to approve a proposed acquisition, no matter how badly the CEO wanted it.

"All for the greater good," said Gamble.

His bodyguard chuckled, but Gamble truly did see the growth of his company as essential to the "greater good." Its patented software programs gathered and processed vast quantities of data in order to identify connections, patterns, and trends that eluded most human analysts. The accepted goal of "data integration" was to help organizations make better decisions, and many of Buck's customers regarded its technology as indispensable. Gamble spoke more nobly of his objectives. "We built our company to support the West," he'd once told the *New York Times.* To that end, Buck proudly touted its claim that it refused to do business with countries that it deemed adversarial to the U.S. and its allies, namely China and Russia.

Gamble took a seat on the bench, grabbed a non-alcoholic beer from the bin, and cracked it open. The sunset glistened in the glass towers of the city skyline. He loved Chicago. He sometimes wished he'd moved his headquarters there instead of Tysons Corner, less for business reasons than for personal: Would Elizabeth's drinking have gotten out of hand if they'd moved to Illinois? It was the kind of metaphysical, chain-of-causation question that could make a person crazy. What if we'd stayed in Silicon Valley? What if we'd moved somewhere other than Virginia? What if we'd simply waited another month to move? What if we'd taken a connecting flight instead of the nonstop to Reagan National? What if I'd chosen the fish instead of the chicken on the in-flight meal?

What if I'd never met "that woman," as Elizabeth called her?

The mere mention of her name could trigger Elizabeth. He'd told her countless times that Sandra Levy was a trusted advisor, nothing more, but Elizabeth would never accept it. As things turned out, the point was moot.

Sandra wasn't even eligible for parole yet.

"Sir, your daughter is on the line."

Gamble put down his beverage and took the phone. "Hi, Kate. What's up?"

Her voice was filled with urgency. "It's Mom. You need to come home. Right away."

Chapter 3

B y ten o'clock, Kate could cry no more. She dabbed the corner of her eye, and the tissue came up dry. Emotionally, she could have wept till dawn, but her tear ducts had shut down, as if to say, *Pull yourself together, kiddo.*

A forensic and criminal investigation team from the Fairfax County Police Department had taken over the penthouse, so Kate had gone downstairs with one of the detectives on the scene to answer questions. She didn't live in Tysons Tower, but technically she owned an apartment there. Kate was in her third year of law school—she was quite realistic about the odds of making it as a playwright—and her father had purchased a one-bedroom unit in her name in the hope that, after graduation, Kate might return to Tysons Corner and work in the legal department at Buck Technologies. Kate had other ideas, and being her father's neighbor and employee was not even on her list of remote possibilities. The police interview was actually the first time she'd seen the apartment furnished. It reflected her mother's tastes, which didn't help, given the circumstances.

"I'm sorry I'm not being much help," said Kate.

She was seated at the dining room table with Detective Anderson of the Major Crimes Division of the Criminal Investigation Bureau. He was a large man, undoubtedly muscle-bound in his younger years, simply thick in middle age. He wore a necktie with the top button of his shirt unbuttoned, not to be casual but because the jowls made it impossible to button it. Another detective and a uniformed officer were also in the room but seated off to the side. Kate had been answering questions for nearly an hour.

"You're doing just fine," said Anderson.

Kate knew he was being kind. His questions weren't difficult. *Was your mother upset about anything recently? Had she stopped calling her friends or stopped going out? Any changes in her daily routine?* A daughter who claimed to be close to her mother probably should have been more helpful. Yet Kate found herself answering "I don't know" far too often, which only lent credence to the very accusations that had precipitated Kate's visit that night. *You never come see me anymore, Kate. You never call.*

"Did your mother use drugs or alcohol?" asked the detective.

That question she could answer. "My mother is—was—an alcoholic."

"You say 'was' because she used to drink?"

"She's been sober for a long time. But once you're an alcoholic, you're always an alcoholic. I said 'was' because—she's gone now."

"Understood. How bad was she?"

Kate could have told stories. But what was the point? Police reports had been known to find their way to the media.

"My father can speak to that better than I can."

As if on cue, the doorbell chimed. Kate immediately pushed away from the table and answered it. Her father embraced her on sight. As complicated as their relationship had been over the years, Kate needed the hug.

"I came as fast as I could," he said, releasing her.

She gave him credit for that. Ninety minutes from Chicago to Washington was fast, even on the company jet.

"I'm sorry—" he started to say, and then he paused.

Kate waited. Maybe he wasn't quite sure if he had anything to apologize for; or maybe he couldn't decide which of so many things he was most sorry about.

"I'm sorry this happened while I was away. You don't deserve this."

Kate hadn't been looking for an apology—definitely not of this sort. "That's nobody's fault."

Detective Anderson politely interrupted and handed Gamble a business card. "I'm with Major Crimes," he added.

"Is suicide a major crime?"

"We do have certain steps and procedures that have to be followed. Your daughter has been a tremendous help."

"I hope you have everything you need," he said.

"Almost," said the detective. "I'd like to ask you a few questions, if it's not too much trouble."

"I'd prefer to spend some time alone with my daughter."

"It's okay," said Kate. The phone call to her father in Millennial Park had continued through the half-way point of his flight home, which was immediately followed by the detective's interrogation. "I've been talking nonstop for the last two hours. I could use a moment to myself."

"You sure?"

"Yes. It's better for you, too, to just get this over with. I'll wait in the kitchen."

Her father didn't argue. Kate went to the kitchen and sat on one of the barstools, which looked like a director's chair, which made her think of Irving Bass—which didn't help matters. She wasn't trying to eavesdrop, but she couldn't help but overhear the voices from the dining room.

"First, I want to say how sorry I am for your loss, Mr. Gamble."

Kate's mind wandered as the detective ran through the same litany of questions she'd just endured. Her gaze drifted toward the terrace, which she would never use. The thought of stepping out there, walking to the rail, and looking down gave her chills, even though the street had been cleared. Or so she'd been told. She hadn't actually looked—not even from the penthouse; not even at the moment of discovery. The torn dress told her all she needed to know. She'd stood in the open doorway, frozen, and dialed 911. "What is your emergency?" the dispatcher had asked. There was none, really. It was too late. The deed was done. Rather than look over the rail and sear the nightmare into her memory forever, Kate, in her mind's eye, had traveled back to her undergraduate course on the history of photography and retrieved the iconic black-and-white photograph of Evelyn McHale, who, in 1947, had leapt from the Empire State Building's eighty-sixth-floor observation deck and landed on the roof of a United Nations limousine parked on the street below. The crushed car top had cushioned her fall, so that the young and pretty Evelyn lay on her back as if sleeping. *Life* magazine had captioned her death "the most beautiful suicide."

Kate wondered how beautiful it had been to Evelyn's family.

Her attention shifted back to Detective Anderson's questions, which seemed to be annoying her father.

"Mr. Gamble, pardon my digression, but I read somewhere that your company was actually involved in tracking down Osama bin Laden. Is that true?"

"I can only tell you what I tell everyone else: if we were involved, it would not be among our most impressive accomplishments."

"The old 'neither confirm nor deny' routine, eh?"

"Detective, I'm not here to talk about the company."

"Sorry. I wasn't trying to pry. It was my awkward way of pointing out the common ground between us. You might say that you and me both are in the information business, right? I gather and organize information to do my job. You do the same."

"Can we get on with this, please?"

"Sure. What were you doing in Chicago?"

"That's confidential business information. And what difference does it make here?"

"None, I suppose. Lemme shift gears. I didn't notice any security cameras in the penthouse or on the terrace. Your daughter said she didn't know if there were any."

"The building has a security guard in the lobby twenty-four/seven. We have a dedicated private elevator that won't move unless it recognizes your retinal scan. If a credible threat arises, I post another security guard outside the door."

"So no cameras in the apartment?"

"No."

Kate went to the refrigerator for something to drink. It was empty. For a moment, she'd forgotten that no one actually lived there. She kept listening.

"Kind of odd," said the detective, "no security cameras. Seems a guy like you, CEO of a big tech company, would have cameras everywhere."

"I don't know what you're implying, but if it's that important, let me say for the record that it wasn't my decision. Elizabeth wouldn't allow them."

"Why not?"

"She drank a lot. Too much. When I mentioned security cameras, she thought I wanted them because I didn't trust her to stay out of the liquor cabinet. She didn't want me spying on her."

Kate's interest piqued. She'd never heard this before.

"Let's talk more about the drinking," said the detective. "Your daughter said Elizabeth had been sober for a long time."

There was a long pause. Longer than Kate could understand. Her father's voice lowered, but with a little more effort, she could hear.

"By any chance, was there a flower delivery to the apartment today?" she heard her father ask.

"Matter of fact, there was. Your security guard said it came this morning. Twenty-four calla lilies."

"Check the flowers," her father said.

"Check them for what?"

"Elizabeth had flowers delivered every morning. Not always calla lilies, but fresh-cut flowers. I used to wonder why the flowers were always dead the next day. Then I checked out one of her deliveries. The flowers never came in a vase. They came in a box, and each stem had one of those three-inch water vials attached to it. The idea is to keep the flowers fresh until you can put them in a vase. Except that Elizabeth had a special arrangement with her florist. Hers came with vodka."

Kate climbed down the chair and moved closer to the door, secretly hanging on her father's next words.

"Vodka?" asked the detective.

"Twenty-four vials for twenty-four stems. About twelve shots, I'd estimate. She thought she was fooling me into thinking she'd emptied the liquor cabinet into the sink. Apparently, she fooled Kate."

Kate's heart sank.

"I hope this doesn't sound like a stupid question," the detective said. "But why did your wife drink so much?"

"Because she was addicted."

"I understand the chemical dependency. But sometimes there's a reason."

"What are you getting at, Detective?"

"I understand there was a call to nine-one-one from the penthouse."

"Yes. Kate called when—when she realized what happened."

"Not that call. Department records show that there was a call two years ago. From your wife."

Kate knew all about that call. She couldn't imagine why the detective had brought it up.

"That was unfortunate," she heard her father say.

"I have a transcript of the call, if you'd like to refresh your—"

"I don't need to see a transcript. I know what she said."

"She said you threatened her."

"Which was a lie."

Kate could have corroborated the statement, but on the night of her mother's death, she didn't want any part of this discussion. Her father could handle himself.

"Why would she lie about something as serious as that?" asked the detective.

"Because she was drunk and angry."

"Angry about what?"

"The trash she'd read in the tabloids."

"About your extramarital affair?"

"There was no affair. That was something the tabloids made up to sensationalize the story about Sandra Levy."

"Sandra Levy was one of your closest confidantes at Buck Technologies, as I understand it."

"That was a mistake on my part."

"She was a spy, right? She was stealing corporate secrets and classified information."

"She's in prison, where she belongs. Look, Detective, what happened two years ago with Sandra Levy has absolutely nothing to do with the terrible thing that happened to my family tonight. And the Fairfax

County Police Department has no business reopen-
ing an espionage investigation after the Department
of Justice got the conviction it wanted and closed the
case."

"I'm not talking about espionage," said the detective. "I'm talking about domestic violence."

Kate could hardly believe her ears, shocked that, on
this night, the detective would dredge up allegations that
even her own mother had admitted were false.

"You're way out of line," her father told the detective.

"Sadly, a suicide is sometimes a sign we arrived
too late. But that doesn't mean there wasn't a crime
committed two days ago, two weeks ago, two months
ago—or when a call to nine-one-one was made two
years ago."

Kate heard the chair scrape the dining room floor,
her father rising. "I've had enough of this," he said.

"Just a few more questions."

"I'm asking you to leave," he said firmly.

The silence lingered, and even through the closed
door, Kate could feel the tension between the two men.
She'd had enough eavesdropping and needed to look
her father in the eye. She pushed open the swinging
service door to the dining room.

"Are you two almost finished?" she asked, as if she
hadn't been listening.

"The detective was just leaving," her father said.

"There's one more issue to address," the detective said. "The identification of the body."

"Is there any doubt as to that?" asked Gamble.

"There rarely ever is, unless the victim is a homeless person. Still, it's a formality I offer to the family. We can accommodate almost any request, mindful of the sensitivities. Some families only ask to see a tattoo or a birthmark. Some do it by photograph. Others don't do it at all. You don't have to decide now. You can think about it and call me in the morning."

"I don't need to think about it," her father said. "I don't want to do it."

"I do," said Kate.

Her father shot her a look of surprise. "Are you sure, Kate?"

Kate had no second thoughts about not looking over the balcony, no need to see her own mother's violent and senseless death on public display. But having one last moment in the same room with her mother, if only her body, felt like her most lucid decision of the evening.

"Yes. I'm sure."

Chapter 4

It was an hour-long Uber ride from Kate's apartment in DuPont Circle to the historic town of Manassas, site of the medical examiner's office for northern Virginia.

Kate's first visit to Manassas had been at age eleven. She'd told her parents she was ready to do a summer sleep-away camp for young theater actors. Her mother cried, but her father was so proud of his "big girl" that he'd immediately plopped down deposits on programs at Lincoln Center in New York, Steppenwolf in Chicago, and even the West End in London. On her own, Kate had found the Manassas ARTfactory—perfect not only because the old building was once a candy factory, but also because it was just thirty minutes from home.

Kate stopped her car on Battle Street, where her

parents had dropped her off, and the memories flooded back.

"If you change your mind and want to come home, honey, it's okay," her mother had said, to which her father had a predictable and firm response:

"She's staying."

Kate cut the trip down memory lane short and arrived only a few minutes late for her 2:00 p.m. appointment. The medical examiner's assistant led her down the hallway to the autopsy room.

"Are you ready, Ms. Gamble?" he asked.

"I think so."

The door opened, and Kate followed the assistant inside. Torrents of icy air gushed from the air-conditioning vents in the ceiling. Bright lights glistened off the white sterile walls and buffed tile floors. Kate said nothing as they continued across the room to the mound beneath a white sheet on a stainless-steel table. The assistant reached for the upper-right corner of the sheet, near a dissection table upon which the medical examiner's scalpel and other instruments were neatly arranged.

"I'm not here to rush you," he said, holding the sheet by the corner. "You tell me when."

"I only want to see her hand," said Kate.

The assistant nodded, as if to say, *Good decision.*

"The right hand is fractured, so—"

"The left is fine," said Kate.

He peeled back the sheet a few inches. Kate stared down at the familiar hand that had once held hers. She didn't gasp and collapse to her knees, the way television melodramas invariably portrayed the reaction of the next of kin. It was all a bit numbing.

"Where's her jewelry?" asked Kate. "Her engagement ring and wedding band?"

"Everything is secured in a locker until after the autopsy. Your father advised that someone from his security detail will pick it up."

Kate wondered what jewelry they would recover. Had she leapt to her death wearing her wedding ring? The Tiffany necklace Kate liked to borrow? Her favorite earrings? How does one decide such things?

Kate laid her hand atop her mother's. It was cool to the touch. Holding it there, even for a minute or more, didn't warm it. Nor did the chill of this final, brief physical connection even begin to answer the most basic of questions her mother had left unanswered.

Why?

Kate opened her purse, removed a bottle of nail polish, and unscrewed the top.

"What are you doing?" asked the assistant.

"When I was a little girl, my mother would let me

paint her nails. It was our thing. I wanted to do that for her today."

The assistant looked pained. "I don't mean to be insensitive, but you can't do that until after the autopsy. It's scheduled for later this afternoon."

Kate had observed an autopsy as part of her Law and Forensic Science practicum. She glanced at the cold, stainless-steel scale, where the medical examiner would weigh the brain, kidneys, heart, liver, and other organs upon removal; and then her gaze drifted toward the dissection table, where the scalpel would do its work. The procedure would be done with proper respect, she was certain, but the battered body was already in poor condition. An autopsy would leave only a hollowed-out husk.

"I don't think I want to come back after the autopsy," said Kate.

"I wish I could bend the rules. But I can't."

Kate felt cheated at first, then thought maybe the assistant was doing her a favor by keeping this short. She put the bottle of nail polish away. "I understand."

Kate rested her hand atop her mother's for a moment longer and said goodbye.

The assistant led her back to the lobby. "Do you have any questions I can answer for you?"

"How long will it take to get a toxicology report?" she asked.

"A few weeks."

"Will the media find out if my mother was intoxicated?"

"Virginia treats the records of the medical examiner like medical records. Without the consent of the next of kin, a toxicology report isn't typically public information in cases where there are no legal proceedings."

That was good news. Kate had felt due for some. She thanked the assistant and waited outside for a ride. She checked her Uber app to make sure her ride preferences were set to "no conversation." The last thing she needed was a chatty driver all the way back to the city. The first two drivers canceled on her; apparently, the morgue came up on their phones as a haunted house. Finally, she snagged a willing soul. An hour-long car ride was more than enough time to be alone with her thoughts, and by the time she reached DuPont Circle, it was a relief not to have to go up to her apartment for still more time alone. Earlier, Kate had agreed to meet an old friend for coffee, and despite her initial reluctance, she was actually glad to have company.

It had been almost two years since Kate had seen Noah Dunn. They'd met at Georgetown when he was in law school and Kate was an undergraduate. That morning, he'd been one of the first to call and tell her how sorry he was to hear the horrible news about her mother, which Kate appreciated. She wasn't sure which was the bigger surprise: that for some reason, she'd never removed him from her contacts, so that his name had popped up on her screen; or that they'd talked for another twenty minutes or so, without a moment of awkwardness. Until the end of the call, when things got a little strange. "I have something I want to give you," he'd said, "something important." The last time Noah had uttered words to that effect, Kate had assumed it was a ring and signed up for a semester-long study-abroad program. She really cared for Noah, but he moved fast—way too fast for Kate, who was well versed in the things a husband and wife should never say to one another.

She ordered a coffee at the counter and found him in a booth by the window.

"Good to see you," she said, as she slid into the bench seat across from him.

"Likewise. And sorry for being so secretive about this. I was afraid you wouldn't come if I told you what it was."

"Now you're freaking me out."

"I won't keep you in suspense." He opened his backpack and laid the script on the table.

Kate did a double take. "My play? How did you get that?"

"I'm a federal prosecutor. I specialize in retrieving important documents out of Dumpsters and trash cans."

Since their breakup, Noah had gone on to become the youngest "senior" prosecutor in the Cybercrimes Unit of the U.S. Attorney's Office for the District of Columbia. If cyberspace was the Wild West, Washington was Dodge City. Noah was right where he wanted to be, on the front line in the fight against cyber-enabled fraud, intrusions, hacks, scams, and anything else that the most brilliant criminal minds in the world could imagine.

"How did you even know I threw this away?" she asked. "Wait—did you follow me to Ford's Theatre?"

"Not exactly."

"Noah, this is getting weird."

"I saw the announcement in the Georgetown alumni magazine that you were one of the winners of Irving Bass's playwriting competition."

"Oh, God. My mother put that in there."

"The article said that the readings of all the winners were open to the public, so I went."

She froze. "Then you saw what happened?"

"Yes."

"Ouch."

"My plan was to say hello and congratulations on the award. But I saw how upset you were and thought it probably wasn't a great time to show my face and say, 'Hi, remember me? I'm the guy who used to tell you how great your script was.'"

She smiled sadly. Noah had been one of her precious few beta readers. Her biggest fan.

"You should have said something."

"I was torn. At first I thought, *No, leave her be.* Then I thought, *For Pete's sake, you came all the way over here, just say hello,* and I started after you. That's when I saw you pitch the script in the garbage. And I let you go."

"But you took the script."

He leaned closer, excitement in his eyes. "Kate, it's *fantastic.*"

"Irving Bass didn't think so."

"Irving Bass is a has-been and a—"

He stopped himself, but Kate knew what he was going to say. "A drunk. It's okay to say it. My mother didn't corner the market on alcoholism."

Noah pushed the manuscript closer. "Anyway, I just wanted to give this back and remind you of what you said when you applied to law school. You promised to keep writing."

"Writing was always just a dream. Not a goal."

"You have to stick with it."

"I did. On top of law school, it practically killed me. No regrets, but—"

"No buts. I loved your take on our own government's first taste of technology. The census of 1890 really was the dawn of the personal information crisis. I prosecute cybercrimes. I know what I'm talking about."

She flipped through the pages. The red ink made her smile. "It's bleeding."

"I made a few edits. Sorry. Couldn't help myself."

It was the way they used to work together. Kate would write all night, and Noah would edit in the morning as she slept. "Of course you couldn't," she said.

"So you'll promise me you won't put down the pen?"

Kate tucked the manuscript into her purse. "I promise not to throw it back in the trash. But I can't dive back into it now. I need to wait till I get past . . . all of this."

"*Wait?* Are you serious? Did Hemingway wait for the end of the war to write *A Farewell to Arms*?"

"About ten years."

"Okay, smarty-pants. But did Victor Hugo wait for the end of the French Revolution before writing *Les Misérables*?"

"The revolution ended before he was born. But I take your point."

"Yes. Because it's a good point. Only my examples suck."

"Irving Bass would shred you," she said, smiling as she slid out of the booth and rose. "This was really sweet of you. I needed it."

"No problem. And, hey, if you need an editor—or a friend—give me a call."

"Thank you. I will."

Kate headed for the door. Her cellphone rang as she stepped out onto the sidewalk. It was her father. She almost let it go to voicemail, not wanting to spoil the moment with Noah so soon by having to recount her visit to the morgue. But it wasn't fair to ignore him under these family circumstances. She answered on the fourth ring.

"Hi, Dad. What's up?"

There was a brief silence, and then he spoke in a very serious tone. "Your mother left a note."

Kate stopped in her tracks. "What?" she asked, but she knew exactly what he meant.

"Handwritten. Definitely her cursive."

Kate was almost afraid to ask. "What does it say?"

"I think you should read it for yourself."

She breathed in and out. "Right. I think so, too."

Chapter 5

Kate waited at the curb on Maryland Avenue. Her father had called from the back of his limousine and was just around the corner. Three minutes later, the car pulled up. The driver hopped out and opened the rear door for her. Kate slid into the backseat beside her father. As they pulled away, the glass partition rose, separating them from the driver so they could speak in private.

"Where are we going?" asked Kate.

"Fairfax Police Department. I'm delivering the note to them."

"Shouldn't they pick it up from where Mom left it?"

"Maybe. But I'm making sure this goes straight to the investigative file, not to some news outlet."

He opened the file beside him and removed a clear

plastic bag. The note was inside. On the outside, sealing the bag, was a tag bearing someone's initials, which confused Kate.

"How did the note get in an evidence bag if you haven't given it to the police yet?" she asked.

"Half my security detail is former FBI. They know how to handle evidence. I trust my security detail more than I trust that jackass who interrogated us."

Kate wasn't interested in arguing over the finer points of evidence collection. "Can I see the note?"

"You can't open the bag. You'll have to read it through the plastic."

"That's fine," she said, reaching for it.

He pulled it away. "First, I want to say something."

Kate suddenly realized why her father was sharing the note this way. She could have hung up on him over the phone. She could have run into the next room if he had come to her apartment. There was no escaping her father's explanation while in the backseat of a moving car. She had to hear him out.

"Contrary to what a lot of people think, alcohol is not a truth serum. Just because you say—or write—something when you're drunk, doesn't mean it's your true feelings."

"I know."

"Alcoholics can say horrible things. It's because they're sick."

"Dad, please stop. I don't need a public service announcement. I need to see her note."

He gave it to her. Kate stared through the plastic. It was written on watermark stationery, the kind her mother might have used to thank a friend for hosting a dinner party. Her mother had beautiful cursive, and her final note was no exception.

Dear Christian, it began, and the fact was not lost on Kate that her mother had left no note to her, just to her father. Kate read in silence. The body was just two lines, the first of which was two words:

I'm sorry.

Her gaze locked onto the second line, which was made all the more mind-boggling by the fact that the note was signed, *Love, Elizabeth.* Kate's hand trembled as she read:

I did it for Kate.

She read it a second time, and a third. The grayish-white blur of limestone government buildings in the car window reminded her that she was in a moving vehicle, but she felt more like she was underwater, her lungs filling with the cold dark ocean as she struggled to breathe, to comprehend.

"For *me?*" she asked aloud, her voice quaking.

"Honey, it's like I said—"

"What is that supposed to mean, she did it *for me?*"

"Your mother was not well."

"Well enough to leave a note. What is she saying here?"

"I have some thoughts on that."

"So do I. She's saying *I* wanted this. That I wanted her out of my life. So she did it. For me."

"It doesn't mean that at all."

"How else am I supposed to read it?"

Her father took the bagged note and put it back in the file. "Your mother did everything in her power to shake the beast. She lost. She relapsed, over and over again. This was the story of her life. Continuing on this way would bring nothing but heartache and disappointment to the person she loved most, and who loved her. So she ended it. For you."

Kate glanced out the window. Everything was still a blur, but her father had given her a moment of clear thinking. Again, her mind conjured up the black-and-white *Life* magazine photograph from her undergraduate class, the grotesque but captivating image of the young woman who had jumped from the Empire State Building. Kate had felt bad about digging into the life of a victim, but she was so intrigued that she'd gone behind the photograph and researched the young woman. Her mother had run off when she was young, leaving her father to raise nine children. She was twenty-three years old and soon to be married. She'd spent a weekend with her fiancé and seemed happy. And then she rode the elevator to the eighty-sixth floor, placed her neatly folded coat on the observation deck floor, and jumped over the railing. She, too, had left a note. She'd done it for the man who wanted to marry her. She could never be a good wife. "I have too many of my mother's tendencies," she'd written.

"Kate, are you okay?"

She glanced back at her father. "I will be, I think."

"There's something else I wanted to talk to you about."

Kate wasn't sure she had the "bandwidth," as her father liked to say, to talk about one more thing. "Is it important?"

"Yes. You don't have to answer right this minute. But I would like you to come work at Buck Technologies."

Kate's mouth opened, but the words were on a few seconds' delay. "This is not a good time for me to be considering job offers."

"You're graduating in December. What do you have lined up, other than becoming a playwright?"

"American University has the top master's program in arts management in the country."

"You're not thinking of another degree, are you?"

"No. The law school allows us to take three graduate-level classes toward our JD, so I did. I loved it. I probably should have enrolled in that program in the first place, but a law degree could land me the same job. This city is full of art centers, museums, and maybe even a few theaters that would hire me in their development or marketing departments."

"Actually, a friend of mine is on the board at the Kennedy Center. I could give her a call and—"

"Dad, *no*. This is why I can't tell you anything. You take over."

"Okay, I get it. If that's your dream, you should pursue it on your own terms. But hear me out. You can always leave the practice of law. It's almost impossible to pick it up once you take another path."

He was speaking from experience, a graduate of Stanford Law who'd never practiced.

"I'm pretty sure I don't want to be a lawyer."

"Give yourself options. Take an internship in Buck's legal department for your final semester. See if you like it. Then, maybe in January, you can start at the bottom like everyone else and come onboard as an associate general counsel."

"Dad, we've talked about this before."

"Not really. I brought it up when you started law school, and you dismissed it."

"That's because it was a bad idea."

"Things have changed."

"Nepotism is still nepotism. Mom's death doesn't change that."

"You won't be working for me. You'd work for the general counsel."

"Who works for you."

"I'm asking you to think about it. Let's work at this. Let's hold together what's left of this family."

Under the circumstances, it was hard to give a flat no to a plea for family strength. Kate glanced out the window, then back. "All right," she said. "I'll think about it."

Chapter 6

The phone call Kate had least expected came on her first day back at law school. It was from Irving Bass's assistant, the young man who had replenished the director's supply of vodka during Kate's reading.

"Can you hold for Mr. Bass, please?" he asked.

Kate was between classes, seated at a picnic table in the law school's courtyard. The semester was two weeks old, though she had missed everything through Labor Day, a few days for her mother's funeral, the rest for grieving and general inability to function.

"Sure," she answered. "I guess so."

"One moment, please."

Kate hadn't given her script much thought since reconnecting with Noah at the coffee shop. Even if she'd wanted to recycle it, so to speak, there'd been no time. Her father would have been content to create an algorithm—Medieval Scribes 2.0, perhaps—to generate "handwritten" responses to the boxes and boxes of expressions of sympathy he and Kate had received. Kate made it her job to give each the truly personal response it deserved.

Bass's assistant apparently had a long definition of "one moment." She was still on hold, seated on a bench, when she saw the dean of the law school walking across the courtyard.

"Congratulations on the internship, Kate," he said as he hurried past her.

It was the responsibility of all third-year law students to keep the placement office apprised of their employment status. Law schools loved to tout the fact that one hundred percent of their students had a job upon graduation. Kate had accepted the internship at Buck Technologies during her final semester, but the obvious assumption of the administration was that it would turn into a full-time position. Judging from the smile on his face, the dean was obviously delighted to have one less unemployed member of the December graduating class to worry about.

Kate was checking to see if the call had dropped when she heard that unmistakable voice of doom in her earbuds.

"This is Irving Bass."

Part of her wanted to say "whoop-de-doo," but she composed herself. "Hello, this is Kate."

"Kate, you've inspired me."

He definitely had her attention. "How so?"

"When I read your mother killed herself, I decided to check into rehab."

There was no "I'm sorry for your loss, Kate." Straight to the point, and it was all about him. Typical.

"I'm glad you were 'inspired,'" she said, using his word. "I hope it works out for you."

"But that's not why I'm calling. Your script inspired me."

"The one you said was—"

"Forget what I said. I was talking about the first ten pages, which were awful. My assistant forced me to read the rest. You're on to something."

"You really think so?"

"Kate, I'm a busy man, which means there are a limited number of questions I can take from playwrights. You've just wasted one of yours with a dumbass question like"—he shifted to his ditzy girl voice—"'You really think so?'"

Kate was certain she didn't sound anything like that, but she let it go. "Sorry. My bad."

"I'll be unreachable, in rehab, for thirty days. That should be enough time for you to do the first rewrite."

"A rewrite?"

"Damn it, Kate, you did it again. Knock off the dumb questions and meaningless jabber. If you talk that way, it will find its way into the dialogue of the characters you create. Yes, we are doing a rewrite. Many rewrites. I said you were on to something. I didn't say you *had* something."

"What are you looking for in the next draft?"

"Good, that was a much better question."

"Thank you."

"Don't thank me! I don't want your thanks. I want a script I can produce."

"You—you want to produce my script?"

"Kate! That's the third strike. I should be hanging up now."

"No, don't! Stop jerking me around and just tell me what you want me to do."

She worried he might hang up, but she was glad she'd said it.

"Okay. I can respect that. I want you to meet me between Fourteenth Street and the old Fifteenth Street across from the National Mall. One hundred Raoul Wallenberg Place."

"When?"

"Four o'clock."

"But—"

"That's the only slot I have. I have to check into rehab by six."

Kate would have to skip her favorite class, but a meeting with a Broadway director had to qualify as an excused absence for a course called the Law and Lawyers in Modern Literature.

"I'll be there. Should I bring my script?"

"No. I said rewrite, not revision. The old script will only hold you back. This is your first research trip on a brand-new act one, scene one, page one. You'll understand when you get there."

Oddly enough, Kate, too, was feeling inspired. And intimidated. "Okay," she said, but Bass had already hung up before she could add "Looking forward to it."

Kate put her cellphone away, and then took a minute to gather up the tangerine peelings, stray pieces of popcorn, empty water bottle, and other evidence of what passed for lunch in law school. She was trying to decide if her energy bar wrapper was trash or recycling when her phone rang again. Her first thought was that Bass had already changed his mind. She was wrong.

"Kate, hey, it's Noah. Sorry to bother, but I need to talk to you right away."

She returned to her seat at the table. "What about?"

"Buck Technologies."

"I think you have the wrong Gamble."

"I'm serious. This is important."

Kate could hear the tightness in his voice, which underscored his words. "Okay. I'm listening."

"I can't do this over the phone. Where are you now?"

She could only guess as to why it had to be in person, but when someone who prosecuted cybercrimes for a living told you not to talk on the phone, you followed his lead.

"I'm at the law school."

"Can you meet me outside the Judiciary Square station?"

She knew it well. It was near Georgetown University, where she and Noah had met, and even closer to the U.S. Attorney's Office, where he worked. "Sure. I've already blown off my afternoon class. I can be there in thirty minutes."

"Thanks. See you then."

"You're not even going to give me a hint as to what this is about?" she asked.

There was a moment's hesitation, and then his reply. "See you in thirty," he said, and the call ended.

Christian Gamble checked into the Mayflower Hotel and went straight to his suite. He'd been staying in hotels since Elizabeth's death, no plans to return to the penthouse at Tysons Tower. His selection of the Mayflower, however, was not without purpose. He was there for a wedding as a guest of the groom. Had it been anyone but David Walker, he would have sent his regrets.

Gamble had known David Walker nearly as long as Buck Technologies had existed. Like most tech companies, Buck could never have succeeded without the backing of a venture capital firm. Walker was the head of BJB Funding, the initials standing for "Bond, James Bond," the introduction made famous by Ian Fleming's iconic hero. The Bond connection was lighthearted but no accident. Following the terrorist attacks of September 11, 2001, the CIA was on a mission to fund elite tech companies, especially data-integration firms. A clever team of lawyers pointed out to the CIA's director that, under the United States Code, the agency's funds "may be expended without regard to the provisions of law and regulations relating to the expenditure of Government funds." In other words, while a typical venture capital fund raises money from passive investors such as pension funds, BJB could receive annual funding for investment purposes as part of the CIA's budget for the Directorate of Science and Technology. Some might consider it an odd use of taxpayer dollars, but that hadn't stopped Walker from steering millions from the CIA's very discretionary budget to Buck Technologies at a time when it was desperately needed.

No one regretted it more than Christian Gamble.

He walked to the credenza, which held a gift basket worthy of Martha Stewart. He glanced at the engraved invitation attached to the big white ribbon.

> *. . . the marriage of Imogene Miller to*
> *L. David Walker IV.*

It was a strange marriage, stranger than the marriage between the CIA and venture capital—and not just because the ceremony was on a Tuesday, which was the only open day on Walker's calendar for the next six months. Walker was fifty-seven, thirty years older than his bride. It may have worked for Gary Cooper and Audrey Hepburn in *Love in the Afternoon*, but Walker was no Gary Cooper, and, as Elizabeth had pointed out on one of their first dates while in line at Blockbuster Video, Cooper and Hepburn made kind of a creepy couple, even if the film was set in the 1950s.

There was a knock at the door. It was Walker. The

two men went to the sitting room, Walker on the couch and Gamble in the desk chair.

"I'm very sorry about Elizabeth," said Walker.

Gamble thanked him, though he knew there was a business purpose to the visit. There always was. Walker didn't take long to get down to it.

"I can't think of a delicate way to raise this, so I won't even try," he said.

"We have a history of being blunt," said Gamble.

Walker rose and checked out the gift basket. He seemed drawn to the bottle of 2007 Louis Roederer Cristal.

"Fairfax County Police are resurrecting the domestic violence accusations against you."

"That's already been proven false. Elizabeth recanted two years ago."

Walker checked the back label of the champagne bottle. "Not the first wife to come out and say, 'Never mind, it was all a misunderstanding.'"

"That's not what happened in my case, and you know it."

He placed the bottle back in the gift basket.

"Here's the problem, Christian. Plenty of people in Washington think it's a very bad idea for the CIA to have a venture capital arm investing taxpayer dollars in private companies."

"Critics have been saying that for years. It's not a new 'problem,' and I don't see how it has anything to do with Detective Anderson and these accusations against me."

Walker stepped away from the gift basket. "It's plain as day. If there's even a shred of truth behind these accusations of domestic violence, that means the CEO of Buck Technologies is vulnerable to extortion. If the CEO is vulnerable to extortion, the CIA can't do business with Buck. Our capital investment is worthless."

"Except that the accusations aren't true."

"I believe you. But the director of the CIA may not feel you're worth the risk."

Gamble gave him an assessing look. "What are you trying to tell me?"

Walker returned to the couch. "BJB has a seat on Buck's board."

"Yeah, you."

"Which effectively means that the CIA sits on your board. And from that seat, the CIA exercises enough influence over other board members to find a new CEO, if needed."

"This is bullshit. Buck is my company."

"And I never want to see that change."

"Then why are you threatening me?" Gamble asked, his voice rising.

"I'm just the messenger," said Walker.

"Yeah, a messenger named Brutus."

"I'm being your friend here, Christian. No one at the CIA is going to feel sorry for you because your wife jumped off a building. You need to be proactive."

"And do what?"

"Make Detective Anderson and these accusations go away. Before they make you go away." Walker showed himself to the door and stopped. "Glad you could come to the wedding, Christian. It means a lot to me."

Gamble watched as the gray-haired groom let himself out. The CEO held no illusion that Walker and the investors he represented were his "friends," but he was concerned about the extortion issue—more concerned than Walker and the CIA knew.

Gamble had yet to inform the board of directors, but the Department of Justice was pushing for a top-to-bottom cybersecurity audit of Buck. It wasn't up to the company to decide who at DOJ would lead it, but his attorney was already negotiating with the U.S. Attorney's Office about it, and Gamble suddenly had a very clear vision of who he wanted.

Gamble picked up his cellphone and dialed his attorney.

"Abigail, I have a name for you," he said, confident in his decision.

Chapter 7

Kate exited the Metro station to Judiciary Square, a neighborhood filled with more government employees than any other square block in America. It had always struck Kate as odd that neither the U.S. Supreme Court nor the U.S. Department of Justice was actually in Judiciary Square, but it was otherwise chock-full of federal and municipal courthouses and office buildings. Among those closest to the Metro station was the U.S. Attorney's Office for the District of Columbia, the largest of the nation's ninety-four U.S. Attorney's offices, employing more than three hundred assistant U.S. attorneys. Right outside the station, waiting on the sidewalk, was an AUSA named Noah.

"Walk with me," he said, and Kate went with him.

He led her away from his building, toward Holy Rosary Church. It was in this old Italian neighborhood near Georgetown Law School that Kate had first shared her secret about writing a play inspired by the tech industry. Eventually, after several edits by Noah, she would set the opening scene with the census enumerator in a Lower East Side tenement. But Kate's early drafts had featured this D Street neighborhood pre–wrecking ball, once the D.C. version of New York's Little Italy. Noah's offer to read her script had made her so happy, though it was an open question whether he was more interested in the playwright than in her play. "I can't wait to get inside your head," he'd told her, which made Kate feel naked, or at least like a little too much cleavage was showing.

"I've learned a lot about Sandra Levy lately," he said.

Not Kate's favorite subject. "I would have thought a prosecutor in the Cybercrimes section would already know all about her."

"She was indicted before I joined Cybercrimes. I was still doing local crimes."

The District of Columbia office was unique in that it served as both the local and the federal prosecutor for the nation's capital.

"What have you learned?" she asked.

"That she was an executive coach, which as best I can tell is a combination of a sports coach and a psychiatrist, someone who helps corporate leaders reach their full potential. Buck Technologies hired her to help identify who among current management should be groomed to be your father's heir apparent as CEO."

"Except she wasn't really an executive coach," said Kate.

"Actually, she was. A highly regarded one for almost fifteen years. What no one knew is that she was also a spy. Moscow planted her to tap into the deepest, darkest secrets of corporate America."

"I wasn't aware that the Russian connection was ever proved."

"It wasn't. The FBI arrested her too soon. It was a judgment call. If they'd waited for her to actually steal Buck's technology, the damage would have been irreversible. But by not waiting until they could catch her red-handed, that undercut our espionage case."

"Which is why she was never convicted of espionage."

"No. Convicted on multiple counts of lying to a federal investigator. But not espionage."

"You do realize you're not telling me anything I don't already know, right?" asked Kate.

He stopped walking. "How much do you know about

the consent decree that Buck Technologies entered into with the Department of Justice after the conviction of Sandra Levy?"

"I know the company never admitted any wrongdoing," she said. "In fact, the DOJ's cybersecurity audit found that Sandra Levy was working alone and that no national security interests were compromised. I hope you didn't call me here to tell me that's changed."

"No, it hasn't changed."

"Then what's up with this 'can't talk on the phone' walk around Judiciary Square?"

"The consent decree with Buck gives the federal government the right to do one follow-up audit within five years of Sandra Levy's conviction. Your father was notified this morning that we've decided to do it now."

"Why now?"

"I can't tell you that. The department doesn't comment on cyber audits of companies that have access to matters of national security."

"Then we probably shouldn't be having this conversation."

"Except for one very important thing that I *can* tell you, and that I wanted you to hear from me. I'm heading up the audit."

Kate took a moment, trying to comprehend. "Isn't that some kind of conflict of interest?"

"That's what I said when the section chief gave me the assignment. But a company can waive a conflict of interest like this."

"My father is okay with you leading a cyber audit of his company?"

"More than okay. You father is the reason I got the assignment. He specifically requested that I lead the audit."

"That's just wrong," said Kate, but she quickly softened it. "Not that I'm saying you would cut him any kind of break or anything like that."

"We both know that's literally not in my DNA."

"Well, maybe not *literally*, in a genetic sense. But I take your point."

"Seriously, it's genetic. Did I ever tell you about my fourth-grade teacher?"

"I don't think so."

"I had at least a B-plus in the class, possibly an A. She gave me a D. You know why?"

"Sounds like she didn't like you."

"She *loved* me. I was always my mother's favorite child."

"Your mother gave you a D when you deserved an A?"

"Mom didn't want anyone to think she was playing favorites. So she gave me a bad grade."

"That's harsh."

"Yes. And to be clear, I'm not saying I'll be harder on Buck than I should be with this audit. But I won't cut anyone any breaks."

"This whole arrangement is still awkward, Noah. Can't you tell your boss no?"

"I pushed back as much as I could. I flat-out asked him to pick someone else. He basically told me to put on my big-boy pants and act like a lawyer."

"Meaning what?"

"He said, 'What would you like me to do, Noah? Tell Mr. Gamble that, notwithstanding his request, you've decided that a relationship with his daughter that ended two years ago should stand between you and your ability to do your job?'"

"That is putting you in a tough spot."

"No kidding. How else was I supposed to respond to a question like that? It's been *two* years. It's not like I could say, 'Well, it's over between us, but it's not really over.'"

"No. You couldn't say that."

"Because it is over. Right?"

"Yes. Definitely. Over."

The silence seemed to hang in the space between them.

"Then there's no problem, I suppose," said Noah.

"No. No problem at all."

"So that's where it is."

"Yeah. That's where it is."

Noah looked away, then back. "I guess I'll head back to his office."

"Okay."

"You all right?"

"Yeah. Why would I not be all right?"

"No reason," he said. "Hey, I hope this doesn't mean you won't let me read your script anymore."

Kate laughed it off. "That's going nowhere fast. Sandra Levy will probably be out of prison by the time I turn in the next draft."

He seemed to know she was lying. "Glad we had this conversation," he said.

"Me, too," said Kate.

He turned and started down the sidewalk, the sound of his footfalls fading as he disappeared around the corner. Kate still had plenty of time before her meeting with Irving Bass. She headed in the opposite direction, sorting through old memories of the handsome law student who "couldn't wait" to get inside her head.

Chapter 8

The limo driver parked in the visitors' lot outside the Fairfax County Police Department. Gamble was in the backseat with his attorney.

Abigail Sloane was a former prosecutor and one of the most expensive criminal defense lawyers in northern Virginia. She'd become Gamble's go-to criminal defense lawyer the first time his wife was charged with drunk driving. The second time, Abigail had worked her magic to negotiate no jail time, but Elizabeth had to surrender her license. Six million Virginia drivers and their passengers were that much safer for it.

"It's still my advice that you let me do all the talking," said Abigail.

"It's my right to talk man to man to the detective

who's leading the investigation into Elizabeth's death. I won't let bogus allegations stop me from doing it."

"All right," she said begrudgingly. "But if I give you the signal, stop talking."

"What's the signal?"

"I'll look at you and say, 'Shut the fuck up.'"

"Got it."

They climbed out of the car and entered the building. The receptionist directed them to a conference room in the Major Crimes Division, where they seated themselves at the table. A minute later, Detective Anderson entered. A Sig Sauer P226 was holstered on his belt for a right-handed draw. An investigative file was tucked under his left arm. GAMBLE, the label read. Gamble introduced his lawyer, but her reputation had preceded her. Anderson shook her hand with all the warmth he could muster toward a criminal defense lawyer who'd skewered a long list of the detective's colleagues on the witness stand. It was like watching someone reach for the grimy doorknob at a gas station bathroom.

"What can I do for you folks?" asked Anderson, as he seated himself across from them at the table.

"I was notified this morning that the Department of Justice is launching a cybersecurity audit at Buck Technologies," said Gamble. "They wouldn't tell us why, but

I have reason to believe it was triggered in part by your investigation. Specifically, the domestic violence angle."

The detective nodded slowly, thinking, and it didn't take him long to connect the dots. "Extortion. I get it. They're worried that the only way the CEO has been able to hide the fact that he's an abuser is by handing over national security secrets to a blackmailer."

"Except there was no abuse, there was no extortion, and nobody handed over any secrets," said Gamble.

"Says you. Isn't that the point of an investigation? To verify facts?"

Abigail interjected. "Let me just stop you there, Detective. A cybersecurity audit pursuant to a consent decree between Buck Technologies and the federal government is not a criminal investigation. The only criminal investigation is the one you're conducting into the death of Elizabeth Gamble."

"Correct. And in the course of that investigation, I've learned that Mrs. Gamble called nine-one-one two years ago and said her husband was threatening her. Unfortunately, suicide is not an uncommon escape route from an abusive relationship, especially one that has been going on for years. So it's part of my investigation."

"Which is why we're here," said Gamble. "I want to set the record straight."

The detective settled back into his chair. "Feel free,"

he said, speaking over the steeple he'd formed with his hands.

Gamble took a breath. His lawyer appeared to be holding hers.

"Two years ago, at the low point of our marriage, my wife dialed nine-one-one and said I'd threatened her. That was a lie. It was a revenge call that she would never have made if she weren't an alcoholic."

"You told me that the night she died. It's in my notes."

"Right. I didn't come here to repeat myself. But there's something more I want to share with you. Something that only my daughter and I know."

The detective seemed intrigued, but said nothing.

"Elizabeth thought I was having an affair," said Gamble, and then he paused again before saying what he'd come to say. "She thought I was having an affair with Sandra Levy."

The detective smiled, not because Gamble had said something funny, but because of how delicious it all was. "You were sleeping with an 'executive coach' who was caught red-handed trying to steal top-secret technology for a foreign government?"

Gamble was getting beyond irritated, but he checked his anger. "I said my wife *thought* I was having an affair. I wasn't."

"And you want me to take your word for it."

"No. I want you to look at the evidence. When Sandra Levy was charged with espionage, the FBI examined every text message, every email, every communication of every kind between her and me. I would ask you to reach out and talk to them. They know I was not having an affair with her."

"Just because you weren't having an affair doesn't mean you didn't threaten your wife, like she said on the nine-one-one call."

Gamble's lawyer had made the same observation before the meeting.

"Not directly," he conceded. "But here's my point. My wife was drinking way too much when she made that nine-one-one call. She was imagining things that weren't happening. She was paranoid and making accusations that simply weren't true. There was no affair. There was no abuse."

The detective didn't respond right away, and Gamble was beginning to think that his plea had fallen on deaf ears. Finally, he spoke.

"I'm a reasonable man," said Anderson. "I'm not trying to ruin your life with accusations of spouse abuse. And I'm not trying to ruin your company with rumors that its CEO is vulnerable to extortion."

"I appreciate that," said Gamble.

"As I see it, part of my job is to keep you informed of important developments into the investigation of your wife's death. You came here in good faith and shared something I didn't know. Let me reciprocate."

Gamble glanced at his lawyer. She seemed surprised that her client was getting more than a simple "thank you for coming, and have a nice day."

"I checked with Mrs. Gamble's florist, like you told me to," said the detective.

"I assume he confirmed what I said."

"He did. Fresh-cut flowers delivered every morning, no vase. All the water vials were filled with vodka."

"I hate that son of a bitch," said Gamble, meaning the florist.

"Here's what's interesting," said the detective. "We checked the calla lilies that were delivered to the penthouse that morning. The vials were still on the stems. And the vodka was still in them."

"She didn't drink any of it?"

"No."

"I suppose it's possible she had another stash somewhere in the apartment."

The detective tightened his gaze from across the table. "Or maybe your wife was stone-cold sober when she went over the balcony rail."

Gamble glanced at his lawyer, then back at Anderson. "I guess we'll know for sure when the toxicology report comes back."

"True. But if she was sober, here's what troubles me. Mrs. Gamble knew her daughter was coming to see her, right?"

"Yes. Kate was one of the winners of a playwriting contest and was presenting her play. It was a big deal. She had dinner plans with her mother afterward."

"So ask yourself. Or better yet, ask your daughter. If Mrs. Gamble weren't drunk out of her mind, would a mother really do something like this knowing that her daughter was on her way over to see her?"

Gamble didn't rush his response, but he wanted to make sure he fully appreciated the implication. "Are you suggesting this wasn't a suicide?"

"It's more nuanced than that. Even if it was suicide, this isn't necessarily a case of someone getting drunk, hitting an unfortunate low point, and doing something stupid. We could be talking about a clearheaded woman who felt trapped and came to a tragic conclusion that there was no way out of a situation more terrible than you and I could ever imagine."

"Like an abusive marriage?" Gamble said, his voice taking on an edge. "We're back to that now? This is going full circle."

"I didn't say abuse," said the detective. "I said 'a situation more terrible than you and I could ever imagine.'"

Gamble didn't like the direction this was heading. "What does that mean?"

He felt his lawyer kick him in the ankle, and her admonition quickly followed.

"Christian, perhaps enough has been said here today."

Gamble didn't rebuff his lawyer lightly, but over his dead body would the meeting end on that note. "I want an answer to my question. I came here to shut down rumors of abuse and possible extortion. Now I'm hearing it could be even *worse* than that. What are you saying, Detective?"

"All I'm saying is this: If you want to know what's driving the decision to audit your company, you're talking to the wrong guy."

"So the audit is not driven by abuse and possible extortion."

"The audit could be routine. It could be driven by concerns over extortion. Or it could be driven by something else entirely. But—"

"That's not helpful at all."

"Let me finish," the detective said. "If the cyber audit

had anything to do with extortion arising from allegations of abuse, I would think the FBI would have already been here asking for my files."

Gamble considered the implications. "So it wasn't you who fed them this angle? You're not the one driving this bus?"

"Like I said, Mr. Gamble: You're talking to the wrong guy."

It was clear the detective had said all he was going to say, which was far more than Gamble had expected to hear. He thanked the detective for his time. He and his lawyer said nothing to one another until they were in the visitors' lot outside the building, walking past the rows of blue-and-silver patrol cars.

"Do you want me to set up a meeting with the U.S. Attorney's Office?" Abigail asked.

They stopped at the limo. "Not yet," said Gamble. "I have better ways to find out what this audit is really all about."

Chapter 9

Kate was across the street from the National Mall, standing exactly where Irving Bass had told her to meet him. At the nearby Washington Monument, the ring of American flags flapped in the afternoon breeze. Before her was the main entrance to the United States Holocaust Memorial Museum.

At least she'd thought it was the main entrance. As Kate approached, she discovered that the curved portico, with its squared arches, window grating, and cubed lights, was not an entrance at all. It was a graceful limestone curtain that opened to the sky, hiding the jarring architecture of skewed lines and rough surfaces of the real entrance behind it. Kate didn't know the architect's purpose, but the duplicity of the design reminded her of her own pilgrimage to Auschwitz and the sign at the entrance gate, the lie that all the victims saw upon entering the death camp: ARBEIT MACHT FREI; work will set you free.

"Right on time," said Bass. He was waiting, in Oz-like fashion, behind the limestone curtain. With his flowing silver hair and bushy white eyebrows, he could have been the wizard.

"So this is our research trip?"

"Have you been here before?"

"No."

"Pity. Follow me."

Bass had a pair of admission tickets in hand and led her inside.

"Anything in particular we're focused on?" asked Kate, as they crossed the lobby to the exhibit hall.

"Yes," he said, still walking.

"Are you going to tell me, or am I supposed to guess?"

"You'll know it when you see it."

Bass stopped, but only after Kate had already frozen in her tracks. His prediction had come true at the very first exhibit. Kate knew the moment she laid eyes on it.

"Is that a Hollerith machine?"

"Yes," said Bass. "Not the nineteenth-century version you described in your play. This one is vintage 1930s. The IBM Hollerith D11 card sorting machine."

Kate stepped closer for a better look in the museum's solemn lighting. She understood from her research how nineteenth-century Hollerith technology had made it easier for the U.S. Census Bureau to collect ever more information about its citizens. The fact that this gleaming black, beige, and silver electromechanical sorting machine was the very first exhibit in a Holocaust memorial museum only reinforced the premise of her play.

"'Reich to Take Census of Her 80 Millions,'" said Bass. He was reading aloud from a framed *New York Times* article hanging on the wall. Kate came up behind him and read over his shoulder. The dateline was Berlin, May 16, 1939:

> *The first census of the 80,000,000 inhabitants of Greater Germany will be held tomorrow. It will provide detailed information on the ancestry, religious faith and material possessions of all residents.*

"The Nazis used census data," said Kate.

"And processed it with state-of-the-art technology," said Bass.

"To find the Jews."

A flat, sad smile creased the director's lips. "Did you really think it was just neighbor informing on neighbor?"

"I read *The Diary of a Young Girl* by Anne Frank, like everyone else. Neighbors turned against neighbors."

"Sure. But what filled up the camps was people informing on themselves. And their families. Through the census."

"I guess that explains how people who didn't even know they were Jewish ended up in concentration camps," said Kate.

"Exactly," said Bass. "The order came from the top: 'The Führer wants the name and address of every man, woman, and child in greater Germany with a Jewish grandparent.' 'No problem,' said the engineers. 'Put it in the census questionnaire. Transfer the census data to Hollerith punch cards. Run the punch cards through the Hollerith machines.' Like this one."

Kate walked slowly around the machine, taking in all angles. "How many of these machines did they have?"

"Thousands. Including one at every death camp. Each machine processing twenty-five thousand cards per hour. A primitive rate by today's standards. But it was the technological gold standard for the world's first automation of mass genocide."

"So the very thing I warned about in my play about

the first use of technology in an American census—it actually happened fifty years later in Germany."

"Yeah. That's why I was so pissed off at you. Surely your research uncovered this."

"I—I don't know how I missed it."

"Kate, I can't work with a liar."

"Excuse me?"

"You didn't miss it. You steered clear of it. You didn't have the guts to write a play that might connect Big Data—your father's world—to the Holocaust."

The hum of an electrically powered wheelchair caught Kate's attention. A docent rolled up behind her, and the electric motor cut off. The old woman looked at least ninety.

"Are you familiar with the Hollerith machine?" she asked.

The sound of her voice suggested she was even older than Kate had first thought. She could have been a hundred.

"I am, actually," said Kate.

"I'm surprised. Most people your age understand computers perfectly. But they know nothing of the electromechanical punch-card sorting machines that gave birth to them."

Kate had struggled with that problem in her play.

She'd been toying with an explanation in her most recent draft, so she tried it out on the old woman.

"It's like the old player pianos," said Kate. "Inside the piano is a long scroll of paper punched with small holes. The holes are placed in exactly the right spot by a master piano player. Every hole is a note. Every note is a piece of information. The piano reads the holes and plays music. It's the same thing with the Hollerith machine."

The old woman looked at her quizzically. "How is that the same?"

"Every answer a census enumerator records is a piece of information. Every piece of information becomes a hole in a Hollerith card. One card for every person. Millions and millions of cards. All read by a machine, just like the piano that plays itself."

The old woman looked up from her wheelchair with dismay. "It's not like the piano at all," she said, her voice shaking.

Kate's heart sank, saddened that her explanation had fallen flat. "Why do you say that?"

"A piano makes *music*," she said. "The world needs all the music it can get. Why would anyone need so much . . . *information*?"

Kate was speechless, but the woman clearly wasn't expecting an answer.

A museum employee came up behind the wheelchair and said, "Time for your break, Mrs. B."

"I just had a break," she said.

"Doctor's orders," he said, as he wheeled her away, leaving Kate and Bass alone with the Hollerith machine.

"Who is that woman?" asked Kate.

"She's a volunteer," said Bass. "A survivor. And my aunt."

"Your aunt? But you didn't even say hello."

"She has no idea who I am anymore. But she remembers her time at Buchenwald like it was yesterday."

"I'm sorry," said Kate.

"Me, too. She'll be gone soon. They'll all be gone. No one to tell the stories."

"Those stories will live on."

"I'm afraid they won't. I see signs of it already. I call it Holocaust fatigue. We need storytellers who connect with people your age. A talented young playwright, perhaps."

"I'm young, I suppose. But one out of three is probably not what you're looking for."

"I do mean you, Kate. I want you to write a play about the world's first personal information catastrophe—the abuse of technology and the systematic identification of Jews for extermination."

"That's a totally different play from the one I wrote."

"Yes."

"You want me to pitch everything I wrote and create a new play?"

"Precisely. Aren't you flattered?"

"Thoroughly," she said, but with only half a heart. "But I'm also nervous."

"Don't be. You should feel nothing but liberated."

"But you said it yourself a minute ago. Maybe I was subconsciously steering clear of this story out of fear of my father's reaction."

"I didn't say subconsciously."

"I didn't *choose* to write the less compelling story."

"Yes, you did, Kate. And I'm asking you to reconsider. Because I don't think that's the playwright you want to be—doomed to writing small because you're afraid to think big. Or afraid of what others might think."

That was exactly how the drunk Irving Bass had made her feel at Ford's Theatre. He was still a jerk when sober, but it was harder to disagree with him.

"That's not how I see myself at all," she said.

"Good. Then let's make a deal. Three months from now, if you haven't driven yourself mad trying to get your arms around a story this big, and on the off chance that I can stand living with my sober self, let's have another meeting."

He was serious about this, Kate realized. Very serious. "You name the place. I'll be there."

Bass stepped closer to the 1939 newspaper on the wall, then smiled wryly. "I'm thinking of an air base in North Africa. The two of us taking a slow walk down a wet runway on a foggy night."

The allusion was lost on her at first, but not for long. He was channeling a scene from one of the most famous World War II motion pictures ever.

"You're thinking, '*This is the beginning of a beautiful friendship*'?" she asked, borrowing the famous last line of *Casablanca*.

He seemed momentarily pleased that she'd caught his cinematic drift, but he quickly shrugged off the sentiment. "I don't need friends. I need a script."

Chapter 10

Kate's first day of work was the last Monday of September. She arrived early to settle into her new office at Buck Technologies. It was a windowless rectangular box between the supply room and the mini kitchen. If ever she found herself running short of Post-its or fruit-flavored sparkling water from another continent, she was in the perfect spot. Someone had gone out of his or her way to send a message that there was no special treatment for the CEO's daughter.

As much as her father liked to boast that he had left Silicon Valley behind him, the Buck compound looked as though it had been lifted from California and dropped in Virginia. The campus was spread across nine acres, complete with a first-class health club, a dining hall that catered to any culinary craving, a nature walk that would have pleased Thoreau, childcare facilities, and other amenities that served the type of employee who never wanted to leave work, which was exactly the type of people Buck hired.

Just before 8:00 a.m., the director of Human Resources poked her head into Kate's office.

"Five minutes, Kate. Don't want to be late."

She was talking about the new employee orientation. Kate was one of about twenty new autumn arrivals.

"On my way."

The director continued down the hallway toward the A/V room. Kate followed. She was certain that none of the other attendees had received a personal reminder from Human Resources, which was awkward enough. It was even more disquieting to find that she was the last to arrive. The room was nearly full, and Kate tried not to step on any toes as she squeezed into the last open chair in the back row. The lights dimmed and the murmur of conversation silenced. A projection screen lowered from the ceiling, and it quickly brightened with the trademarked logo of Buck Technologies—a dog, specifically a St. Bernard mix.

"Welcome," said the HR director. "We have a special treat for you this morning."

Scooby snacks? Kate wondered.

A side door opened, and Kate's father entered. Kate's

heart sank. So much for conveying the message that she was like everyone else. The CEO never did new employee orientations.

Someone on the other side of the room started clapping. Others joined, as did Kate.

"Thank you," said the CEO. "But it is I who should be applauding you."

The orientation included everyone from a new deputy chief financial officer to the lowly intern in the legal department, aka Kate. Her father greeted them as a group and then singled out the key new hires, including the engineers they'd lured away from Google and Apple. Kate sank lower in her chair, trying to hide behind the large man in front of her. Thankfully, her father spared her the spotlight of nepotism and began the official welcome.

"People often ask why I called my company Buck Technologies," he said. "No, it's not because I started with just a dollar to my name—though that's true."

The group chuckled, as if on cue.

"The fact that our logo is a dog clears things up to some extent, at least to make it clear that our 'Buck' is not a deer."

A few more chuckles from the group, then silence. The image on the screen transformed from the company logo to an old book jacket. It was simple artwork, almost primitive, laid out in three horizontal storytelling bands that were strangely reminiscent of ancient drawings on the walls of Egyptian tombs, except that this landscape was anything but a desert: two men, eight dogs, and a sled set against the snowcapped mountains of the Klondike.

"Who here has read Jack London's *Call of the Wild*?" he asked.

A few hands rose, Kate's among them.

"It's my favorite book," he said, which Kate already knew. "And Buck is my favorite literary character. The story is set during the Klondike Gold Rush of the 1890s, when strong sled dogs were in high demand. Buck is a one-hundred-and-forty-pound mix of St. Bernard and Scottish shepherd that is stolen from his home in California and sold into service as a sled dog in Alaska.

"Like Buck, my company was born in California. The technology we create here in Virginia is *exactly* like Buck. Strong. Reliable. Dependable. Buck will never let you down, no matter who you are. Buck is neither good nor evil. Buck is pure. In the right hands, Buck can do wonderful things. Buck, however, is not always in the right hands."

He paused, giving his new hires a moment to absorb his meaning.

"We do not control the sled driver. This is a serious

problem. No one expects the people in this room to solve it. I *demand*, however, that you live up to the challenge it presents:

"Our creativity and inventiveness can never be stifled by the unfortunate reality that, in the wrong hands, Buck can be a force for evil. *Never.*"

Kate knew all about Buck the reliable sled dog, and her father had been telling her all her life to find a passion and follow it. Never before, however, had she heard this "fly in the face of evil" spin. If the applause was genuine, the message seemed to resonate more with the others than with Kate.

The CEO spoke for only ten minutes, and the orientation was over by nine o'clock. Kate returned to her office, sat behind her desk, and pulled up the day's calendar of events on her computer screen. Her door was open, and the soft voice of a visitor startled her.

"Knock, knock."

Kate looked up, not immediately recognizing the handsome young man standing in the doorway. His eyes, however, were unforgettable, those beautiful blue eyes that everyone said would lose their sparkle as he grew. The color never changed, and he still had that mop of blond hair that Kate used to call "Albert Einstein meets surfer boy."

"Baby Patrick?"

"Not so much 'baby' anymore," he said. "Except to my mom. Or if I decide to become a rapper."

Kate had been Patrick's babysitter when she was in high school. She went to him and gave him a huge hug. Then she took a step back.

"My goodness, let me look at you," she said, and did take a good look. It was as if each side of her brain had grabbed the remote control and was switching back and forth between stations, one side channeling the cute kid in braces and *Star Wars* T-shirts, the other marveling at the man he had become.

"How long have you worked here?" she asked.

"Almost two years."

"No way. Have you been out of college that long?"

"I graduated MIT early. Boring. You know me. I just wanted to build things."

Babysitting Patrick had never been a simple matter of turning on the Disney Channel and counting the hours until his parents came home. Every Lego set known to the universe had been built, taken apart, and rebuilt at least once by Kate and Patrick, with Patrick of course the lead builder. He refused to go to bed until the last brick was in place. Kate wasn't particularly a fan of his Minecraft phase, but she still cherished her time on Patrick's virtual tours of his creations, from aircraft hangars to space stations.

"Sit for a second," she said. He did, and Kate sat on the edge of her desk, facing him. "How the heck are you?"

"I'm great," he said, then seemed to catch himself. "Well, a little sad, actually."

Kate nodded in appreciation. "Thank you. We all are. My mother was crazy about you."

He hesitated, seemingly puzzled. "Oh, right. Your mom. Well, that, too." He removed his earbuds. "What I meant was that on the way over here I was just listening to the saddest song."

"A song?"

"Yeah. This poor girl really liked a boy at school, but all her friends convinced her that he wasn't good enough for her, so she refused to go out with him. Like two years later, she's sitting at home with a baby of her own and turns on MTV, and there he is, slamming on his guitar, and—"

"Okay, very funny," she said, laughing. He was referring to much-younger Kate, who used to listen incessantly to Avril Lavigne's "Sk8er Boi," which was about as "sad" as "Video Killed the Radio Star."

"It's just so sad," he said, wiping a nonexistent tear from a bone-dry eye. And then they both laughed. It pleased her to see that Patrick still had that quirky and irreverent sense of humor that could make her smile even when—in his own way—expressing his condolences for her mother's passing.

"How's your play doing?" asked Patrick.

"How did you know about my play?"

"Well, for starters, you've been writing plays since you were my babysitter."

"That's true."

"And your mom used to pop by and say hello whenever she came to the office. Last time I saw her, she told me you were going to be presenting at Ford's Theatre. She said she wanted to go, but she was afraid she'd make you nervous."

Kate wasn't sure what to make of that: afraid to make her daughter nervous, but not too afraid to throw herself off a building.

"I guess she thought I might want to watch," said Patrick. "But it didn't really interest me. No offense. I'm not much into live theater. But I did like the flying car in *Chitty Chitty Bang Bang*."

"Of course you did."

"So I'm guessing you got the idea from Project Naïveté, right?"

"The idea for what?"

"Your play. Project Naïveté is like the same—" He

stopped himself. "I thought for sure you cleared this with your dad. Are you saying your play was not inspired by—"

"Patrick, I think you should stop talking."

If there was one thing Kate knew about Buck, it was that projects with code names were not discussed freely among coworkers. Information was shared on a "need to know" basis only.

"Well, how about that," said Patrick. "I just got myself fired."

"No, you didn't."

"Maybe I got you fired, too."

"No. Patrick, listen to me. This conversation never happened."

The color slowly returned to his face. "Like the time we built a moat around the lifeguard stand so deep that the stand fell over?"

"Yes. Thankfully, the lifeguard was off duty."

He smiled, but then it faded. "I think I have to turn myself in. This is a huge breach of policy."

Another thing that hadn't changed. Once a scout, always a scout.

"Before you do anything, let me speak to my father."

"It was my mistake. I should own up to this myself."

"Patrick, please. Let me speak to my dad."

"Okay," he said, but it was more acquiescence than agreement. "Speak to your dad. But do it soon."

"Sure," said Kate, still a bit unsettled by the fact that her play bore any similarity to a Buck Technologies project. "I'll do it first thing."

Chapter 11

Christian Gamble stood to one side as his longtime business partner, Jeremy Peel, took his place at the podium before a bouquet of microphones on a warm afternoon in the nation's capital. More media than expected had shown up for the press conference, so they'd moved the gathering from the air-conditioned lobby to the courtyard outside Buck's office on New York Avenue, a stone's throw from Lafayette Square and within an easy walk to the north end of the White House.

The Department of Justice cybersecurity audit was officially underway. The local U.S. attorney had a policy of "no comment" on any pending investigation, which was nothing unusual. However, the fact that he'd extended this policy to something as routine as an audit—which was not, technically, an "investigation" into any wrongdoing—led to wild speculation that this particular audit was anything but "routine." A reassuring public statement from Buck management was needed if the company's stock was to avoid a serious hit on Wall Street. The board of directors decided that Peel, as chairman, should be the one to deliver it.

"Good afternoon, everyone," said Peel. He was flashing what Gamble referred to as his partner's "corporate smile," that toothy expression worn by business executives spinning unhappy news, also popular with politicians accused of adultery.

Politically speaking, both Gamble and Peel were independents, not wanting to ruffle red or blue feathers. While Buck's data-integration technology was flexible enough to serve both the public and private sectors, the fact that it was used by investment banks to guard against money laundering or by pharmaceutical companies to expedite development of new drugs didn't grab headlines. The hot stories usually had a Big Brother component, some nefarious link to government, like the *New York Times* revelation that while the Department of Health and Human Services had a perfectly legitimate $31 million contract to use Buck's software to analyze public health issues, the same software could also be used to access private health records. In short, the business of Big Data was hopelessly intertwined with politics. Of Buck's two founders, Peel was the more politically savvy. Gamble served as president and CEO, running the corporate campus in Virginia. Peel was the chairman of the board, keeping his office close to the Washington power elite.

"When Christian and I formed this company after the terrorist attacks of nine eleven, we had two overarching ambitions. The first was to make software that could help keep the country safe. The second was to prove that there was a technological solution to the challenge of balancing public safety and civil liberties—a 'Hegelian' aspiration, as my philosophical friend put it," he said, casting a smile in Gamble's direction. Then he turned serious. "But we both feared that personal privacy would be a casualty of the war on terrorism.

"So, today, we welcome the announcement that the U.S. Attorney's Office for the District of Columbia will be conducting a cybersecurity audit at Buck Technologies. The public deserves transparency, and we are happy to provide it. At the end of the day, this exercise will only confirm that Buck has held true to its mission. We make software that saves lives and also preserves privacy. Thank you, and I'm happy to take any questions."

Reporters immediately began shouting over one another, but the question that rose above the others was directed to the CEO.

"Sir, is there any connection between the security audit and the Fairfax County Police Department investigation into your late wife's domestic violence allegations?"

Gamble's business partner stepped to the side in graceful and almost unnoticeable fashion, as if not wanting to be within camera shot of the response to that question.

"There has never been any domestic violence in the Gamble household," said Gamble. "So I don't understand your question."

"Is there or isn't there a connection between the investigation into your wife's suicide and the cybersecurity audit?"

"I'm not aware of any such connection."

"Sir, can you categorically state that there is no domestic violence investigation?"

"I can only tell you that there has never been—"

"Mr. Gamble, you're unable to deny a connection between the domestic violence investigation and the cybersecurity audit. Isn't that correct?"

Gamble pulled out the most forceful denial he could muster. "I have no reason to believe that this is anything more than a routine cybersecurity audit. *Routine.* Thank you all very much."

The two executives came to silent agreement that it was time to shut down the press conference, but the cacophony that followed them from the podium was a sure sign that this issue wasn't going away anytime soon. The questions kept coming, and the flock of reporters followed them into the building. Peel led the way to the executive elevator. The two men entered, and Peel smiled until the doors closed on the media.

The CEO was not smiling.

"I can't believe the way these bastards have twisted the story of my wife's suicide," said Gamble, as the elevator started upward.

"It's not necessarily a bad thing," said Peel.

The elevator doors opened to the lobby of the executive suite. "That's not funny," said Gamble, as they exited.

Peel stopped. "Christian, you had a complicated marriage. That's none of my business. But if the media wants to go down a rabbit hole, following a bullshit story that this company is vulnerable to extortion because its CEO had a volatile marriage, then let it play out."

"Easy for you to say."

"Would you rather they speculate about what the cybersecurity audit is *really* about?"

Gamble turned and faced his partner. "Jeremy,

if there's something you know about this audit that I don't know, let's hear it now."

"You saw how the media reacted to your statement that the audit is 'routine.' They aren't buying that for a minute. They need some red meat. Spousal abuse with threats of extortion is red meat wrapped in bacon."

Gamble seethed inwardly. Peel wasn't acknowledging that *he* was the red meat. "You make it sound like it's some kind of strategy. This thing is out of control."

Peel laid a hand on the CEO's shoulder and looked him in the eye. It was a patronizing gesture that Peel sometimes pulled as chairman of the board, and Gamble hated it.

"That's where you're wrong, Christian. Nothing is out of control."

Gamble glared back at him as the pieces clicked into place. "You planted that question, didn't you? It was one of your media puppets who asked me about domestic violence."

Peel checked his cellphone, then shared the screen with his CEO. It was a stock market app. "Well, looky there. Buck Technologies is up two points. It seems the market isn't all that troubled by a CEO under fire for personal problems."

"Don't ever do that to me again," said Gamble.

"I didn't *do* anything to you. You did this to yourself

by staying married to an alcoholic who could be one very vindictive drunk."

"I have never allowed my personal life to hurt this company."

"Until now."

"Meaning what?"

"Both you and I know that the current administration wants the CIA out of the venture capital business. The DOJ won't stop until this audit turns up something to support the president's view that spying and private investment don't mix."

"The DOJ won't find anything."

"They may have already found it," said Peel. "A CEO who is vulnerable to extortion may be just enough to please everyone. The DOJ can claim its audit was a complete success because it led to the ouster of Buck's CEO. And once the tainted CEO is gone, the CIA will be happy because it can continue business as usual."

"Where does that leave me?"

"You've had a good long run, Christian. Twenty years."

"That's it, then? Buck just finds itself a new CEO?"

Peel didn't answer.

"Might that new CEO be you, Jeremy?"

"If I'm asked by the board, I'd consider it."

"So that's your angle? You want to be both CEO and chairman of the board? The boss and the boss's boss?"

"It's not unprecedented. Zuckerberg did it at Facebook. Gates did it for a time at Microsoft."

"Have you spoken to David Walker about this?"

"David Walker is a venture capitalist. He'll bless whatever is necessary to protect the CIA's investment in this company."

"You ungrateful prick. After all I've done for you."

"Oh, that's rich. We would have been out of business twenty years ago if I hadn't brought David Walker and BJB Funding onboard."

"BJB and the link to the CIA has been the bane of our existence. Foreign governments think we're the CIA's pawn."

"Yes, and who had to pull the strings behind the scenes to smooth things over? Me. Always *me*. But you were more than eager to step up and accept the National Medal of Technology and Innovation, the Stevie Award, the Bower Award, and all the other awards that put you on the cover of every publication in America."

"So that's what's going on here? Payback's a bitch, and this is all a long-overdue personal power play on your part?"

"No, Christian. What's going on here is called business. And yes, it is long overdue."

Peel walked away, leaving the CEO alone in the lobby.

Chapter 12

Kate's first day at Buck ended early, with assurances that Day 2 would be her "real" first day of work. Rather than head straight home, she redid her research trip for her play—this time with Patrick.

It was probably the old babysitter in her, but she was worried about Patrick, fearing he might walk over to HR and turn in his resignation for his slip of the tongue on Project Naïveté. She tried to remember the name of that video game he used to play, the one where his avatar looked like a blond GI Joe. Call of Duty: WW II? Or maybe Fall Out? Whatever it was, she knew the Nazis' use of technology would fascinate him. They spent two hours at the Hollerith machine exhibit, and knowing Patrick, he would be up all night researching it. By morning, Patrick the sponge would know more about Hollerith machines and the Holocaust than Kate could ever hope to learn.

"You're going to talk to your dad, right?" asked Patrick.

She'd taken his mind off his mess for a couple of hours, but not completely. "I promise I will. I'm meeting him for a drink in twenty minutes."

They said goodbye, and Patrick headed toward the Smithsonian Metro station. Kate walked south toward the river. To tourists, the Tidal Basin conjured up images of cherry blossoms and the National Mall. To Washingtonians, it also meant the revitalized Wharf District on the southwest waterfront. Kate met up with her proud father at the rooftop bar at the Mandarin Hotel. He was seated at a comfortable outdoor armchair near a flickering gas firepit.

"There's my future general counsel," he said, as he gave her a kiss on the cheek.

"Not so fast, Pops."

She was barely seated when the waiter brought two preordered glasses of champagne. Her father raised his in a toast.

"May you fall in love with the transactional side of the law," he said.

"Dang. Now what am I supposed to do with my 'Have You Been Injured?' billboard?"

"Burn it," he said, glancing at the flames. He drank, then shifted gears. "How do you like this neighborhood?"

Kate took in the view of the glowing Washington Monument in twilight. "What's not to like?"

"How'd you like to live here?"

"At the Mandarin?"

"Next door. I'm told it's the safest apartment building in the city."

"Who told you that?"

"I won't name drop. Let's just say there are several residents who are entitled to Secret Service protection, and I know one—actually I know all of them."

"I'm happy with my little place. It's closer to the law school."

"You're graduating in December. It's time to think ahead. I've already sold the unit I was holding for you at Tysons Tower."

Kate wasn't surprised. Her father had yet to set foot in the building since her mother's death. "Have you decided what to do with the penthouse?"

"The real estate broker advised me to hold it for a while. Sometimes it improves marketability to have a story attached to a property, but this is not that kind of story. We need to give it time. Then sell it."

"That's probably good advice."

"But let's not lose focus. What about the building next door?"

Kate glanced at the man dressed in a black suit two tables away, her father's bodyguard. "Can we slow down a little? It's going to take me some time to warm up to the idea of returning to a world where everything is about security. And secrets."

He seemed to pick up on the way she'd pivoted from security to secrets. "Did something happen today?"

"Patrick Battle came by my office today to say hello," she said, and then quickly got to the nub of it. "He slipped."

"Slipped how?"

"He said something he shouldn't have about a project he's working on."

"Very unlike him. He's one of our rising stars. Which project?"

"Project Naïveté."

Her father didn't appear angry, but he definitely looked concerned. She waited for him to say something, but he was silent.

"I told him I would speak to you about it."

Her father seemed caught off guard, at a loss for words. Then he burst out laughing.

"What's so funny?" asked Kate.

"My apologies to Patrick, but I can't keep up the

ruse any longer. He got you. That's the oldest joke in the company. Pretend that you spilled the recipe for the secret sauce and act like you're both going to get fired over it."

Kate's mouth fell open. "What?"

"There is no Project Naïveté. But I give the boy points for coming up with the perfect code name. Naïveté. He was seeing how naïve you are."

"That stinker. He said it was like my play."

He smiled, then turned serious. "You mean the play you've been hiding from me?"

Now Kate was caught off guard. "I wasn't hiding anything. It just never came up."

"You still haven't forgiven me, have you?"

The conversation was taking a turn, and it was making Kate nervous. "Forgiven you for what?"

"That play you wrote your senior year of high school. What was it called?"

"*With L.*"

"Right. The high school boy who had a crush on a classmate and sent her a Christmas card signed 'With L.' A dangerous thing in the 1940s in the Deep South, when the boy is Black and the girl is white."

"Willie James Howard. It was a true story."

"And still relevant. That play deserved an audience."

"It deserved to *find* an audience. It didn't deserve

to have one bought and paid for by the playwright's father."

"I'm sorry for that. I went a little overboard."

"A *little?* You rented a theater and hired a director and a team of actors. Thank God Mom stopped you."

"Is that why you've kept this new play a secret?"

"Partly."

"What's this one about?"

It didn't seem like the right moment to reveal her dramatic take on the dangers of Big Data. "It's about player pianos," she said.

"Well, then Patrick really pulled your leg. None of those around Buck."

Twilight was turning to darkness. An attendant brought blankets, but it wasn't nearly chilly enough to need them.

"Speaking of music to one's ears," her father said, though it took Kate a moment to connect the awkward segue from player pianos, "what did you think of my presentation to new employees this morning?"

"It made we want to run out and get a big dog."

"They allow pets next door."

"*Stop,*" she said with a roll of her eyes. She drank her champagne. "I did have a question that I didn't dare ask in front of the group."

"Ask it now."

"What did you mean when you said Buck can't control who's driving the sled? I've heard you say a thousand times that you don't do business with buyers unfriendly to the West."

"That's true."

"Then what was the point of your analogy? Sometimes you get duped? You might sell to a 'sled driver' who's actually just a front for the Chinese or Russian governments?"

"That would never happen."

"How can you be sure?"

"We have people who vet that for us. Very talented people."

"Like who?"

He smiled. "When you accept permanent employment in the Buck legal department, I'll be glad to tell you."

"Okay, that's fair. But if your vetting process is that good, what did you mean when you said you don't know who is driving the sled?"

He paused, then seemed to turn philosophical, almost professorial in his tone. "Even if you don't do business directly with the enemy, it's still a leap of faith as to how the technology will be used. There are bad apples everywhere. In every company. In every government. It's impossible to know what's in every customer's heart."

"That's unsettling," said Kate.

"Is it? You make a car, someone might drive drunk. You make a gun, someone might use it for something other than sport or self-defense. Technology is no different."

Kate drank her champagne, wondering if he really meant what he was saying.

"Can I buy you dinner, Kate? There's a great restaurant downstairs."

She accepted, and they started across the rooftop. He was walking slowly, controlling their pace, as if he needed to get something else off his chest before dinner. "I suppose by now you've seen today's press conference."

"I watched it live," she said.

He stopped. "I'm sorry, Kate. On top of the loss of your mother, now this nonsense has reared its ugly head again."

"Why do you think it's come up?"

"I don't know. But Jeremy Peel has already claimed dibs on my job. He wants to be both CEO and board chair, which would be a disaster. I need to get to the bottom of this—and quick."

"Is that why you asked the U.S. attorney to have Noah lead the cybersecurity audit?"

She'd genuinely caught him off guard. "How'd you hear that?"

"Noah told me. He wanted me to hear it from him. I would have liked to have heard it from you."

"I'm sorry. I don't want you in the middle of this."

Such a lame explanation from such a smart man was exasperating. "You asked the U.S. attorney to put Noah in charge of the audit. How is that *not* putting me in the middle?"

He was appropriately contrite. "Guilty as charged."

"Dad, what are you really thinking?"

"Here's the deal. You know and I know your mother got all worked up about something that never happened."

Kate didn't disagree, though in truth, she was only ninety-nine percent sure that "nothing had ever happened" between her father and Sandra Levy. "Mom admitted everything to me the next morning."

"What did she admit, exactly?"

"I've told you this before."

"I know, and I'm sorry to bring this up, but it's important."

"Mom had it in her mind that there was something going on between you and Sandra Levy. She got drunk and called nine-one-one to get even."

"You and Noah were dating when your mother made that revenge call."

"So?"

"By any chance did you tell him about the conversation you had with your mother?"

"No," she said firmly. "That was between Mom and me."

He glanced toward his bodyguard, as if to make sure that not even he was close enough to hear what he was about to ask. "Would you?"

"Would I what?"

"Tell Noah."

"Do you mean now?"

"Yes. It comes across as self-serving for me to explain it. Coming from you, it rings true."

Kate was getting annoyed. "So you want me to throw Mom's memory under the bus because this audit has you in a jam."

"That's not a fair statement, Kate. Your mother was very sorry for what she did. She would set the record straight herself, if she were still here and could see the ridiculous direction in which this audit is headed."

That was probably true. But the whole thing still felt manipulative. "Is this why you asked for Noah to lead the audit?"

"Someone has to lead it. I figured it might as well be someone I know."

"You mean someone you can influence?"

"Someone I can trust."

Kate looked at him quizzically. "What are you trying to accomplish, exactly?"

He took a half step closer, very serious. "Half of Buck's business is government contracts. This company can't afford to fail a cybersecurity audit. I want to know what's driving it."

"It could be routine, like you said at the press conference."

"That's wishful thinking," he said. "It's more likely that the Justice Department really is worried that I'm vulnerable to extortion. Or . . ."

"Or what?"

"Is something else entirely driving it?"

Kate felt the need to sit down, or at least put a little more space between her and her father. She found an open couch by another firepit and placed her near-empty champagne flute on the table.

"Dad, if you want to know what's driving the audit, you should ask Noah that question yourself."

He joined her on the couch. "He would never tell me," he said, the flickering flames of the firepit reflecting in his eyes. "But he might tell *you*."

It was exactly as Kate had feared. "Are you asking me to be your spy?"

"I wouldn't put it that way. I'm just saying that I

need to know, and it would appear that you're in the best position to find out."

"What makes you think Noah would tell me anything?"

"Come on, Kate. He obviously still cares what you think, or he wouldn't have rushed to tell you it was my idea that he be in charge of the audit. From what I remember, that boy would empty the ocean with a teaspoon if you asked him to."

"You still think I should have married him, don't you?"

"Not necessarily. But I do think it was a mistake to let the sad state of your parents' marriage foreclose the possibility."

Kate drew a breath. "I'm not really comfortable with this conversation."

"I understand. You don't have to give me an answer tonight. Let's put that question aside and just have a nice dinner."

"Good plan."

"But if, come the morning, you can see your way clear to helping your old man save his company from the financial ruin of a wrongheaded cybersecurity audit, then happy day."

He rose and started for the elevator, but Kate stopped him.

"Just so I understand, are you asking as my father or as my employer?"

He shrugged, as if he hadn't really considered it. "Both."

"Then my answer is no. And maybe."

She got up from the couch and started walking. Her father caught up. "Maybe, as to which?" he asked.

Kate stopped at the elevator and pressed the call button. "You'll figure it out."

Chapter 13

September ended. *Good riddance*, thought Kate.

Morning classes had kept her on the law school campus until nearly lunchtime, so it would be just a half-day at the office. She exited the train at the Tysons Corner Metro station, buttoned her coat, and started her ten-minute walk to Buck Technologies.

It was starting to feel like late January. Not the weather, but metaphorically speaking—specifically, the way friends and colleagues greeted Kate upon seeing her for the first time since her mother's death. During the immediate aftermath, without fail their first words had been "So sorry about your mother." By week three, the expressions of sympathy had dropped by about fifty percent. By week five, it was only occasional, like the oddball who wished you "Happy New

Year" in the last week of January. Life went on. But Kate still had her dark moments of grief, especially late at night, when she was alone and trying to write—rewrite—the script she'd promised Irving Bass. The words weren't coming, or at least they weren't finding their way onto the page. In a way, Kate had been witnessing her mother's suicide for years, powerless to stop her from drinking herself to death. Even that, however, hadn't prepared her for the choice her mother had finally made.

Kate was a block away from the Buck Technologies campus when her cellphone rang. It was Sean O'Hara, the young man who'd assisted Irving Bass at Ford's Theatre.

"First of all, let me say how sorry I am about your mother," said Sean.

Happy New Year to you, too, thought Kate. "Thank you, Sean. How's Irv doing?"

"Crankier than ever. He can't work while in rehab, so he asked me to make sure the play is moving forward on schedule. Can I see what you've written so far?"

Kate stopped at the red light, her pulse quickening. She had nothing shareable.

"Just the first ten pages is all I need," Sean added.

The WALK light flashed green, but Kate didn't move. "By when?"

"How about tomorrow?"

Panic set in. She needed a few days. Actually, she needed the full ninety days that Bass had given her. "How about Friday? They might still be a little rough."

"No worries," he said. "I promise I won't show them to anyone until they meet the 'Irv test' for the first ten pages."

"What's the 'Irv test'?"

"Do you want to get to page eleven?"

"Irv's a smart man."

Sean agreed, and the call ended.

Kate crossed the street, checked in with Buck security at the gated entrance to the company campus, and then caught a ride on the golf cart with the security guard to the athletic facility. In ten minutes she was dressed and on the squash court for a challenge match against the CEO.

"How long has it been since you've played?" her father asked.

"Since the last time I beat you."

"You mean the time I let you win."

Kate laughed. Her father had picked up the English-invented game as a philosophy student at Oxford. There, one by one, his classmates had discovered that this brilliant young American's philosophy was "win at any cost." He never let *anyone* win *anything*, going all the way back to Tic-Tac-Toe with his five-year-old daughter.

Kate served first, and her father answered with the crack of a kill shot. More followed. Game one was their most lopsided ever: Dad, eleven; Kate, one. Kate called for a water break. It was obvious to her father that she was not herself.

"You seem distracted," he said. "What's on your mind?"

"You don't really want to know."

After several volleys of "Yes-I-do"/"No-you-don't," Kate came clean and told him about the rewrite she was doing for Irving Bass.

Her father drank from his water bottle. "You're still working with that guy, huh?"

"What do you mean by 'that guy'?"

He laid his racquet aside and took a seat. "I thought you were done with him after the contest, so I kept my opinions to myself."

"That's probably a safe place to keep them."

"I hear he's a washed-up alcoholic who holds contests to capitalize on the hopes and dreams of aspiring writers."

A teenage Kate might have hit him with her racquet. But she'd come to understand how he operated, saying outrageous things that he may or may not believe just to make sure she had considered the worst-case scenario.

"Let's not go down this road."

"What road? I'm saying what you need to hear."

"*That* road. What *I* need to hear. It's one thing to tell an eleven-year-old girl that she has to keep her commitment and stay the full four weeks at Manassas theater camp, even if Mom says she can come home anytime she wants. That's tough love. But being nasty to me because you think you know better is not tough love. That's not any kind of love."

"I'm not making things up."

"Irving is abrasive. He's made enemies. You're repeating rumors started by people who don't like him."

"Sometimes rumors are true. How do you know he isn't just a charlatan who picks winners who have money and tells them he can get their play produced if they pay him?"

Her teenage anger was long behind her, but he was edging dangerously close to getting hit with a racquet. It was starting to sound like he actually believed what he was saying.

"First of all, I'm not paying him anything. And it sucks for you to say he picked my script because I have a rich father."

"Kate, it gives me no joy to tell you this. But there's

a forty-two-point-three-seven percent chance Mr. Bass is a fraud."

"Well, that's a relief. I had calculated it at forty-two-point-three-eight."

"Joke all you want, Kate. Millions of decisions are made every minute of every day using Buck's algorithms."

"That's what you said when you canceled my prom date. And when you got my freshman roommate assigned to another dormitory. You even made Mom change gynecologists. Now that I think of it, the only person who was ever good enough for your algorithms was Noah, which is no surprise, seeing how he had to pass an FBI background check to work at the U.S. Attorney's Office."

"They use our software."

"Naturally. But I don't want to live like that. A green light from Buck's algorithms is not going to be the standard I set for all future relationships—personal, professional, romantic, whatever."

"Take a look at Bass's report. Judge for yourself."

"I don't what to *judge* him."

"No accountability? Is that your philosophy?"

More of his "tough love." *Fuck off* might have been the deserved response, but Kate took the opportunity to tell him what *he* needed to hear.

"We are accountable for things we do. Not for things we're projected to do based on every 'friend' on social media, every Tweet we've ever liked, every website we've ever visited, every video we've ever watched, and whatever else goes into your predictive software."

"Welcome to the twenty-first century, Kate."

"You mean the twentieth century," she said, thinking of her play.

"Huh?"

"Nothing." She tossed him the hollow rubber ball as she led the way back inside the squash cubicle. "Your serve."

Gamble took a quick shower, still smiling at the way Kate had roared back to win the best of three after losing the first game 11–1. Saying there was a 42.37 percent chance that Bass was a fraud had pissed her off enough to bring out the real Kate. It was like the old joke that 54.8 percent of all statistics are made up on the spot, and it had worked like a charm. But he had to be careful. That kind of button pushing used to bring out the best in Kate's mother, too, until it brought out resentment—and worse.

He stopped at the self-serve refreshment bar to refill his water bottle and checked his cellphone. The text message from Detective Anderson grabbed his attention, terse as it was: pls call me. Gamble stepped outside, found a quiet place in the gazebo overlooking the pond, and got the detective on the line.

"Toxicology report is in," he said. "Your wife's blood-alcohol concentration was point-two-nine percent. For point of reference, a BAC of point-zero-eight is the legal limit for driving."

"But you said she didn't drink any of the vodka from the florist."

"Apparently, you were right. She had a stash."

Gamble took a seat on the white railing. "Exactly how drunk is point-two-nine?"

"Blackouts happen, so a person might have no memory of the things she did or the people she did them with. Last year, we had a college student who choked to death on his own vomit because his gag reflex was so impaired. Basically, we're in the territory where really bad things happen."

Like suicide, Gamble was about to say, but he went in a completely different direction. "Is it possible Elizabeth fell over the railing? She didn't jump?"

"People who accidentally fall off a balcony don't leave suicide notes."

"Not everyone who writes a suicide note intends to go through with it. Sometimes they want to be saved, right?"

"Sometimes."

"And sometimes they get drunk and take it too far, don't they?"

"Do you really believe that's what happened here?"

"I'm just trying to understand. Maybe she wanted Kate to walk into the apartment and see her leaning over the rail. Maybe she wanted to be saved. Maybe she wanted her daughter to save her."

"Mr. Gamble, this is a sad case, but the law requires us to put a label on it. I sympathize that it may be easier for a family to cope with an accident, but this was no accident. That whittles down the choices to suicide or homicide. I'm leaning suicide—unless there's something you're not telling me."

The detective's question had put him on the defensive. "Do you think there's something I'm not telling you?"

"Maybe. Or maybe it's something you're just not ready to admit to yourself. Either way, now's your chance to tell me."

The voice of Abigail Sloane was suddenly in the CEO's head, and while her delivery was more colorful— "*Shut the fuck up*"—it was the same advice he would have received from any good lawyer.

"There's nothing," he said. "Nothing I can think of."

The detective's response was slow in coming, and

even though they were on the phone, Gamble could almost feel his stare, the penetrating gaze of an inquisitive detective who could discern the truth better than any polygraph machine.

"All right, Mr. Gamble. We'll leave it at that. Have a good day, sir."

"You as well," he said, and the call ended.

Kate walked from the athletic facility to Building C, where Patrick worked.

Kate had texted him after dinner with her father and said she knew "Project Naïveté" was fake, that she could take a joke, and that all was cool between them. But he hadn't answered. She chose not to text him again. Creepy old babysitter texting the precocious little boy who'd grown up to be a twenty-two-year-old blond and blue-eyed Adonis was not cool. But she was curious to know why he hadn't answered her.

Kate went inside, and there was yet another security checkpoint in the lobby. The guard recognized her as the CEO's daughter and apologized for having to put her through the same routine they followed for all visitors.

"Rules are rules," he said.

Building C was a more modern design than the law department. The multitiered workspace was accessible by ramps instead of stairs, with shiny chrome railings, wide-planked floors of white oak, and perfect ambient lighting that made Kate feel as though she were entering MoMA. All interior offices had glass walls so that you could see all the way through from one exterior wall to the other. Patrick's office had his nameplate on the glass door, but Kate would have guessed it was his even without the nameplate. The assortment of junk food on the desk was classic Patrick. In all her years of babysitting, Kate had never seen him eat anything but McDonald's fries, pizza, the occasional pizza pocket for variety's sake, full-sugar sodas, and giant Icees. He'd obviously not outgrown his eating habits.

A coworker emerged from the neighboring glass box. He was wearing a colorful Hawaiian shirt, which seemed to be the unofficial uniform among Buck engineers. "Patrick's not here," he said.

"Do you know when he'll be back?"

"Not sure."

"Okay. I'll leave him a note."

"Well, he won't be back anytime soon," he said. "They sent him away."

"What do you mean, 'sent him away'?"

"It's like an outward-bound program. He's camping in the wild on some kind of survival exercise."

"Who sent him?"

"HR. It's a new program they just started for engineers. No cellphones, no technology of any kind. It's supposed to prevent burnout."

"How long will he be gone?"

"No idea."

Kate glanced toward his desk. It seemed odd that he'd leave food out if he was leaving for an extended period of time, though there were probably enough preservatives in that junk to last a millennium. "I just saw him last week. Weird he didn't mention he was leaving."

"I didn't know, either. Nobody did. Like I said, it's a brand-new program."

"Is Patrick the first?"

"Yep. Patrick's the guinea pig. Hopefully, he'll get bitten by a snake or something and they'll nix the whole program before I have to go. Life without tech. What's the point? Know what I mean?"

"Not yet," she said, glancing one more time at the empty desk chair. "But I'm learning."

Chapter 14

On Saturday morning, Kate received a text message from Bass's assistant. Meet me for tea, it read.

Kate texted back: Where?

Moments later, Sean's response: At the Reichstag.

Kate knew what was coming next, and she laughed as the bubble popped up on her screen: With Adolf Hitler.

Ordinarily, there was nothing funny about Hitler, unless you were a producer named Mel Brooks and it happened to be springtime in Germany. But Sean's text warmed her heart.

Kate had delivered more than the first ten pages by the Friday deadline. She'd fleshed out the entire first act with new material on the life and career of IBM's founder and CEO, Thomas J. Watson, Sr. In June 1937, Watson became president of the International Chamber of Commerce, urging "world peace through world trade." His inauguration was at the annual ICC banquet, held at Friedrich Wilhelm III's romantic eighteenth-century castle outside Berlin, organized by chief Nazi propagandist Joseph Goebbels in what would go down as the most elaborate party in the history of the Third Reich. That same evening, Watson became the first American to receive the Merit Cross of the German Eagle with Star, the highest honor the Reich had, up until that point, ever bestowed on a non-German, surpassed only by Hitler's subsequent decoration of Henry Ford, a known anti-Semite. At a separate, more intimate meeting, Watson took tea with Hitler at the Reichstag. No one knows for sure what they said to one another. They may have talked about the weather. Or, Watson might have mentioned his plan to double the output of his German subsidiary, increasing Hollerith card production to 74 million per month by the end of 1937, enough to accommodate the Führer's need to process an emerging mountain of census data and other personal information that would soon expand to include the populations of Austria, the Sudetenland, and Memelland.

Kate had worried how her dramatization of tea at

the Reichstag might be received. Sean's text was the reaction she'd hoped for.

Coffee at 11? she texted back, adding a link to her favorite spot. Sean quickly accepted.

When John Adams, second president of the United States and first resident of the White House, denounced tea as "impatriotic," it may not have been his intention, but he nonetheless established the nation's capital as a city of coffee lovers. Kate's go-to coffee bar was just a few blocks from the White House, Swing's Coffee Roasters, which had been serving Washingtonians for over a century. The mosaic-tiled floors were so beautiful that, on her first visit, Kate had almost felt guilty stepping on them. Her usual seat at the black quartz counter offered prime people watching, as the aroma of freshly ground coffee wafted from a pair of shiny, dependable espresso machines on the other side. That morning, however, Kate didn't go inside. The unexpected sight of the silver-haired gentleman seated at an outside table stopped her in her tracks.

"Irving? I thought I was meeting Sean here."

"He's doing what he does best. Fetching coffee."

Kate settled into the empty chair, not wanting to sound impertinent, but she had to ask. "Aren't you supposed to be in rehab?"

"Eh. Rehab, schmeehab."

Sean joined them with three coffees and put one in front of Kate. "Mesco Blend, one Splenda, a little cream," he said.

"How'd you know?"

"The barista told me. Apparently, you're quite the creature of habit."

Bass pulled a hard copy of Kate's script from his leather satchel. "Sean sent me your pages. I was up all night with them."

She glanced at Sean, who had promised not to show them to anyone, unless . . .

"You passed the first-ten-pages test," Sean explained.

"You work fast," said Bass. "I like that."

"But do you like what I've written?" she asked, sounding a tad needier than intended.

"First of all, it doesn't matter if I like it. It matters only if I love it. And if I love it, I'll tell you. But if you must know, as of now, your script is in the category of fixable."

"That's a compliment," Sean volunteered.

"I'm open to changes, of course," said Kate. She drank through the lid of her go-cup and braced herself for the director's feedback. An awkward minute of silence passed, then Bass seemed to digress.

"Do you know what I really hate?" he said. "I hate it when a waiter comes to my table, tries to memorize the order, and puts it in to the kitchen without ever writing it down. I just know it's going to come back wrong."

Kate took the hint, dug into her purse, and found a pen but no paper. Bass gave her the title page to write on.

"Now then," he continued. "You've made the right decision to tell this story through the CEO. The audience won't like Watson, but they're not supposed to like him."

"He's so complex. I think there's a lot to like about him."

"We'll get rid of all that."

"Oh," said Kate, making a note of major surgery number one.

"The key line is when Watson rationalizes his decision to ramp up production of his German subsidiary in 1937. Keep in mind that by the time he accepts the Merit Cross, the Nuremberg Laws have already been passed. Jews were no longer German citizens. They couldn't marry an Aryan or even fly the German flag. Jewish doctors couldn't practice in German hospitals. The same month Watson took tea with Hitler, another camp for political prisoners opened in Weimar. Buchenwald. And we know what became of that."

Kate was writing furiously, getting it all down. The guide at the National Holocaust Memorial Museum, if she recalled correctly, had lost her family at Buchenwald.

"With all this going on," said Bass, "Watson lands in Berlin touting world peace through world trade. 'Ford sells a car,' he says, 'and someone might drive drunk. Smith and Wesson makes a gun, and someone might use if for something other than self-defense.' That's a great line."

Kate didn't tell him that it was a direct quote from her father. "I'm glad you like it."

"I *love* it. But you need to expound on it to develop the real theme of the play: the evils of capitalism."

Kate stopped writing, her ballpoint frozen to the page. "I didn't see this as a play about capitalism. It's the story of the world's first personal information catastrophe."

"Caused by capitalist greed," said Irving. "Are those words a direct quote from Watson?"

"'World peace through world trade,' yes. The rest, no."

"That's fine. This isn't a documentary. Watson could have said them. And any man who *would* say them is the worst kind of capitalist. He's Fagin."

"*Oliver Twist*'s Fagin?"

"Yes. 'In this life, one thing counts / in the bank, large amounts.' That's what Watson is about."

Kate paused. The words were her father's, not Watson's, and she'd never viewed her father as Fagin. She'd always thought of him as one of those lucky guys whose creative passion and intellectual pursuit proved financially rewarding. Like Patrick.

"Point two," said Bass. "Too much humor. I want this play to be dense."

Kate bristled. "I've never thought of 'dense' as a literary aspiration."

"I mean dense in a good way. Dense like *Oslo.* Have you seen *Oslo*?"

"No."

"You need to."

"Where's it playing?"

"Nowhere," said Sean, jumping in. "It's too dense."

Bass shot him a look of disapproval, which suddenly devolved into an almost gruesome expression. His eyes closed. He placed his palms flat on the table and drew a deep breath.

"Irving, are you okay?" asked Kate.

He breathed out slowly. "Just a little indigestion."

It looked much worse than indigestion to Kate.

"Sean, can you share the rest of my notes with Kate and walk her back to the Metro? I'd like to sit alone for a minute."

"Are you sure you're okay?" asked Kate.

"I'm fine. Just go."

Kate gathered her purse and her coffee cup. Bass didn't rise to shake hands. She thanked him, which he ignored, still focused on breathing. Sean started down the sidewalk, and Kate walked with him.

"I'm worried about him," she said.

"Don't be," said Sean. "He gets overly dramatic every time he tries to stop drinking. It's as if he wants someone to tell him, 'Irv, stop suffering and pour yourself a drink—*please*.'"

Kate was suddenly thinking of her mother. "The problem is that he doesn't want *a* drink. He wants ten drinks."

They stopped at the Metro entrance. Sean buried his hands in his pockets, as if unsure of his next words. "I don't think I can find an active production of *Oslo*," he said. "But *The Little Foxes* is playing at Arena Stage. I was wondering if you'd like to see it."

"Love Lillian Hellman. I'll definitely check it out."

"I meant . . . see it with me."

"I know you did," she said, smiling. "Yes, that would be fun."

He smiled back. "Great. I'll check on tickets and shoot you a text."

"Perfect." Kate turned and started inside.

"Hey," said Sean, stopping her. "Your play still doesn't have a title. What are you going to call it?"

"Don't know yet. Hope to figure that out before the end of the next act."

"Looking forward to it," he said. "The next act, I mean."

"Me, too," she said, taking his double meaning, and then she continued into the station.

Kate went home to an apartment full of boxes. The movers were scheduled to arrive on Monday, and then she would be moving south of the National Mall, to the apartment her father had found in the Wharf District. Her decision had pleased him.

"You're going to love it there," he'd told her. "And you'll be very safe."

Kate had felt perfectly safe in DuPont Circle. She wished he would stop talking as though the family were suddenly under attack.

Packing had been a veritable walk down memory lane. Kate was not a hoarder, but it was amazing how much stuff a single person could accumulate in three years, even in a small one-bedroom apartment. In the middle of the living room were several overflowing boxes of things marked "undecided" on the keep-or-throw-away tick list. Her running shoes were as yet unpacked. She laced them up and headed out the door to clear her mind.

Kate's usual route was through Montrose Park, near Georgetown, an immediate escape from the city to life among chipmunks, squirrels, and an occasional white-tailed deer. When feeling strong, she'd continue through Whitehaven and Glover-Archbold parks on up to American University. Memories abounded here, too. The way to even lovelier Dumbarton Oaks Park was downhill along Lover's Lane, the place where Noah—corny as ever—had stopped in the middle of their run to say, "I love you." They'd known each other for about three weeks. Kate had thought he was joking and laughed. He'd said of course he was kidding and joined in the laughter. Only later did she learn how much her reaction had hurt him.

"Kate?"

She stopped and looked back. It was the runner she'd just passed on the trail. He, too, had stopped, and the two of them were standing in the shade of a chestnut tree.

It was Noah.

Each expressed the same sentiment—how weird it was to run into each other—though in truth it didn't shock Kate. Noah also lived in DuPont Circle, and technically this was *his* route, the one they used to follow. She'd found a new one after they'd stopped dating, but she'd decided to follow the old one, one last time for nostalgia's sake, before moving. She hadn't expected to see him. But maybe a part of her had hoped that she would. They talked with hands on hips, catching their breath, as they walked along the trail.

"How's the play?" asked Noah.

"I was up till three a.m. every night this week re-writing it."

"You always worked best that way. You happy with it?"

"I will be. If I can keep Irving Bass from turning it into a polemic against capitalism."

"Since when did you become such a capitalist?"

"I don't want my play to be a polemic against any-thing."

Kate left it at that, as running was her way of es-caping from her worries, not dwelling on them. She changed the subject and told him she was moving, managing to steer clear of Buck Technologies and the DOJ audit, until Noah brought it up.

"I hope you don't mind me talking a little shop."

"I'd rather we didn't. But truthfully, I'm totally walled off from your audit. I'd have nothing to say about it, even if I wanted to."

"I was going to ask you about Patrick Battle. I un-derstand he's a friend of your family."

"I used to babysit him when he was a boy. What do you want to know?"

A jogger passed with her chocolate Lab on a leash. Noah waited, then continued. "I gave the company a list of the first ten employees I wanted to interview. His name was on it."

Kate forced herself not to react. "Wow. Baby Patrick, on your A list. That's so amazing to me."

Noah brought their walk to a halt, his expression serious. "When I sent the list, he was coming and going to work every day like normal. Then my list of names landed on somebody's desk, and suddenly he's gone, out of the country, supposedly on some kind of corporate bonding adventure."

Kate didn't volunteer anything. "I'm sure he'll be back."

"It seems that no one can tell me when that might be."

"What would you like me to do?"

"This is not cool, Kate. Games like this inevitably make matters worse. Maybe you can mention it to your father."

Kate felt a knot in her stomach. First her father had asked her to talk to Noah, and now Noah was using her as the go-between with her father. She was starting to feel like the scarf knotted around the frozen rope in a proverbial tug-of-war.

"I'll see what I can do," she said, and then she checked her smartwatch. "Wow, it's later than I thought. I'm going to head back. Lots of packing still to be done."

"Good to see you," said Noah.

"Likewise," said Kate, and they headed off, Kate in her direction and Noah in his.

Chapter 15

Patrick woke to the patter of falling rain on a sagging canvas tarp. A proper tent was apparently too much to ask for on this corporate survival exercise. They'd been kind enough to provide hiking boots for the climb into the mountains, but beyond that, he had only the basics: a knife, a few lengths of rope, a pack of matches, a blanket to fend off the chill of the damp mountain air, and a tarp to lie upon on clear nights. Patrick had spent the previous two nights sleeping on the cold ground, each corner of his tarp tied to a banana tree for shelter from the misty rain.

Patrick still had no idea where he was. He'd flown commercial from Reagan National to Miami International Airport. An evening flight on a private jet, "window shades down," had landed him on what appeared to be a private runway in a valley, the surrounding mountaintops glowing in the moonlight. A boat took him upriver. The pilot and his mate spoke no English, and even though Patrick was somewhat conversant in Spanish, they had no interest in answering his questions. The boat stopped somewhere in the jungle at dawn. There, he met Javier, who'd introduced himself as Patrick's "safety net" and laid out the rules.

"I'll be nearby at all times. I may choose to bandage a blister on your foot. I might take your temperature, if I think you look ill. I may even give you extra food, if I think you've earned it. But I'm here mainly in case of an emergency. However, if you call on me—if you use your safety net—you fail. Any questions?"

Patrick had answered in Spanish, guessing from the length of the flights that he was somewhere in South America, perhaps the Andes. Morning brought confirmation that he'd guessed correctly.

"*Buenos días*, Patrick," said Javier. "You have company."

Patrick sat up and looked around. The rain had suddenly stopped, and streaks of sunlight shone through the thick canopy overhead. Beyond the giant elephant-ear-leaf plants in the middle distance, he counted four other tarps like his strung from tree trunks, makeshift tents. His gaze drifted toward a wisp of smoke rising from a smoldering campfire. Three men and a woman were seated on an enormous log, warming themselves, their blankets draped around their shoulders.

"Is this my team?" asked Patrick.

"No. Your competition."

Patrick almost smiled. He liked games, and as he walked over to the campfire to meet the other corporate superstars, he liked his chances against this group.

"I'm Patrick," he said, and the others introduced themselves. The accountant from New York was a fish out of water. Same for the insurance executive from Chicago. The engineer from British Columbia might offer some competition, but surely he'd underestimate someone like Patrick, the "tech kid" who everyone assumed was more comfortable in the virtual world. He wouldn't let on that he'd spent every summer of his boyhood camping and exploring the mountains of North Carolina, no video games allowed.

Javier brought them breakfast in a pot. Beans and rice.

"Same as last night's dinner," said the accountant.

"Which was left over from yesterday's breakfast," said Patrick.

Javier set the pot on a rock near the fire. "Better food to come. But only if you earn it."

Patrick took the bait. "How?"

Javier removed a knife from his pocket and whistled. Only then did Patrick realize that each of his competitors also had a guide, as two other men and a woman emerged from Javier's extralarge tent, all dressed in the same camouflage uniform. They stood in a group on the other side of the campfire, as if waiting for some form of entertainment to begin. Javier dropped to his knees and placed his left hand flat on the log, palm down, fingers spread.

"The challenge is on," he said, as he unsheathed the large hunting knife on his belt.

The other guides hooted and hollered, egging him on.

"What the heck are you doing?" asked Patrick.

Javier held the hunting knife vertically, grasping the handle like a ski pole and placing the tip between his outstretched thumb and index finger. Slowly, he raised it and brought it down between the index and middle finger. Up again, then down between the middle and ring finger. Up and down once more between the ring and pinkie finger. Then he started all over again between the thumb and index finger, a little faster this time, counting as he moved from one to the next.

"One, two, three, four," he said with each poke at the log.

The guides looked on with fascination, smiling and

talking among themselves in Spanish. Patrick and the others found it harder and harder to watch. All was silent, save for the tapping of the blade against the log and Javier's counting, the pace quickening.

"One, two, three, four." *Tap, tap, tap, tap.*

"You don't have to prove anything," said Patrick.

The shiny blade moved from one position to the next faster and faster still. The tapping became like machine gun fire, the counting like one long word. The accountant jumped to his feet and hurried away, muttering something about the insanity of this place. Javier's motion built to what seemed like controlled frenzy, if there was such a thing—back and forth, thumb to pinkie. The knife was a blur, the tapping nonstop, the rhythm ever escalating—until a deafening scream echoed in the mountains.

Patrick looked away, then back.

Javier emitted a second scream, even louder, as he thrust the unbloodied knife triumphantly into the air. It was his game, and Javier had won. His steady hand and coordination had prevailed. He took the knife by the blade and offered the handle to Patrick.

"Now you try."

"What?"

"You want better food, or don't you?"

"Not at the cost of my fingers."

Javier offered the knife to the others. "Any takers?"

Not a one spoke up.

Javier sheathed the knife on his belt. "Pussies. Pack up. All of you. We head out in fifteen minutes."

Patrick and the others left the campfire without saying a word, stunned and confused by what they'd just witnessed. Patrick's hands were shaking as he untied the tarp from the tree. He wasn't sure what to make of this corporate adventure and the "games" they were asked to play. But one thing was certain.

There was something not right about this guide named Javier who loved knives more than fingers.

Chapter 16

Kate dropped a box of wineglasses on the floor of her new kitchen.

"Shit!"

It was move-in day, and a few casualties were to be expected. Still, would the universe have been any less satisfied if she'd dropped a box of towels instead?

Sean entered from the hallway, having heard the crash. Kate had mentioned the move when he'd called to tell her that *The Little Foxes* was sold out for the coming weekend but he'd like to take her to the symphony instead. Perhaps his offer to help had been a token gesture, just being nice, but Kate had taken him up on it.

"Let me help you with that," he said, tiptoeing around the shards of glass.

"Thirty minutes in my apartment, and you already know where I keep the broom?"

"It was in the *broom* closet," he said dryly.

The shrill whine of a power drill came from the other side of the wall, the bedroom.

"Are you allowed to drill holes in the wall?" asked Sean, shouting over the drill.

"No!"

"I think you should tell the movers."

Kate hurried to the bedroom, where two men were mounting her television on the wall. She pulled the plug on the electric drill, literally.

"First of all, whose TV is that? And who told you to mount it on the wall?"

"It's in the work order," said the guy holding the drill.

"Whose order?"

A voice came from the other room. "Kate, are you here?"

Her father. Things were suddenly coming clear.

"Just leave the TV," she told the movers. "Let's get everything off the truck first."

The movers left, and Kate went to the living room. Her father was standing in the open doorway.

"There you are," he said, entering. He seemed confused to see Sean. Kate made the quick introduction.

"I've heard a lot about you," said Sean.

More than you realize, thought Kate, thinking of the Fagin-like line from her script that Irving Bass had loved so much.

Her father was suddenly too distracted to exchange pleasantries. He quickly crossed the empty living room, stopping abruptly at the glass doors to the balcony.

"What's this? I specifically asked for an apartment with no balcony," he said.

"I changed it," said Kate.

"Why would you do that?"

"Because it's my apartment, and I want a balcony."

He seemed utterly perplexed, then glanced at Sean. "Would you give us a minute, please?" he said, pointing to the open doorway.

Sean excused himself to the corridor and closed the apartment door behind him.

"Sweetheart, I'm not trying to run your life."

"Really?"

"I just thought that waking up every morning and looking at a balcony would be a painful reminder for you."

"Well, it isn't. At least it wasn't, until now."

He took a deep breath. "I'm sorry. I'm just trying to do the right thing. Maybe I'm trying too hard."

He seemed genuinely contrite, and Kate might have

felt sorry for him, except that all she could think was that this tender moment was a side of the evil capitalist that Irving Bass would cut from her play.

"It's okay, Dad. We're both struggling, trying to figure out what went wrong, what to do next."

He turned and faced the sliding glass doors, looking out over the balcony railing toward the river. Kate had yet to ask him about Patrick's sudden departure, as she'd promised Noah she would, but this didn't seem like the time.

"I spoke to Detective Anderson," he said.

"You told me. Mom was drunk."

"I asked if he thought it could have been an accident. If it was possible that she fell."

The possibility piqued her interest. Kate crossed the room and stood at his side, peering through the glass and out over the railing. "How high was the railing at the penthouse?"

"Forty-two inches," he said. "Not that I've ever measured it. I checked the building code. But don't let your mind go there. Your mother was only five foot two. Even if she was drunk and stumbled, she couldn't just fall over the railing."

"But what if she was so drunk that she got sick? If she was leaning over the railing, trying not to mess up her dress and—"

"Kate, we're grasping at straws. We have to deal with the facts. Your mother left a note."

"But the note said—"

"I know what it said. 'I did it for Kate.' I don't think we'll ever understand that."

She stepped closer, her voice taking on added urgency. "That's my point. Did *what* for Kate? The note says, 'I *did* it.' Past tense. After the fact. She didn't write this from the grave."

"Maybe—" he started to say, then stopped herself.

"Maybe what?"

Her father reluctantly finished his thought. "Maybe in her mind she was already dead."

Kate looked away. "Not where I thought you were going with this."

"Sorry if that sounded harsh. It was Detective Anderson who pointed out I was refusing to say things that needed to be said—things I wasn't willing to admit to myself."

"I suppose we'd both feel better if it was an accident, if we could look ourselves in the mirror and say we hadn't missed an opportunity to prevent this—that we hadn't let her down."

"*You* didn't let her down, Kate."

"I'm just saying that if there's any blame to go around, it goes equally."

"No. I'm her husband."

"Stop it," she said.

"Certain facts are undeniable," he said, smiling sadly. "Like the wise old man once said, 'Truth is like poetry. And everybody fucking hates poetry.'"

There was an abrupt knock at the door, it swung open, and the movers carried in a leather couch.

"Where does this go?" the crew chief asked.

"I'm glad we talked," her father said softly.

"We need to do more of it," said Kate, and she turned to direct the movers.

Chapter 17

"Just don't look down," said Patrick.

Olga, the only woman on Javier's team of guides, was behind him, clinging to the rocky face of a cliff, paralyzed with fear.

They'd walked for hours, mostly uphill along a narrow and sometimes overgrown jungle path. As they approached the gorge, Javier had made an announcement. "Olga," meaning the female guide, "is a virgin. This is her first trip with us. She will lead the way from here."

It was soon obvious to Patrick that Olga the rookie was not passing this test of acrophobia. The path was at its narrowest along the edge of a steep cliff. The rocks were slippery; the footing unsure. Each hiker was equipped with a Y-configured rope and two carabiners, a type of quick-release shackle used by mountain climbers. Pitons, steel spikes with eyelets, protruded from the cliff face, hammered into cracks in the rock by previous climbers. The technique was to have at least one carabiner clipped to an eyelet at all times, connecting, disconnecting, and reconnecting along the way. Still, it was an unsettling fact that, with one misstep, a cheap metal clip was all that stood between life and the certain death of a two-hundred-foot fall into the gorge below.

"I'd rather take the challenge of the dancing knife than do this," said Olga.

"Just a few more steps," he said.

Patrick chose his next step carefully, planted his foot, then moved to the next spot. Olga followed his exact foot placement. The final step was a bit of a reach. Patrick imagined himself at the top of the climbing wall he'd mastered as a teenager at camp, always the fastest to reach the top, never one of those kids who gave up and had to be lowered to the ground by harness. He stepped onto flat ground and pulled Olga toward him. She fell into his arms, which he rather enjoyed, and for the first time he saw her smile. It was a pretty one.

Javier approached. "All right, Romeo. Balcony scene's over. On to the hot tub."

Patrick thought he was joking about the hot tub, but

Javier's gaze directed them toward the pond ahead, a gaping hole in the jungle canopy where the sun made rainbows in the clouds of steam that wafted up from the surface. Patrick could feel the heat in the soles of his boots, and each step toward the water's edge brought the audible crunch of ancient volcanic cinders beneath the overgrowth of fallen jungle foliage, grass, and mosses that had gathered over the centuries.

Olga knew the area well enough to explain.

"It's an extinct volcano," she said.

A tiny geothermal paradise where nature warmed the waters to bath temperature. For Patrick, who hadn't showered since leaving Washington, this was heaven on earth.

"You have ten minutes," said Javier.

Patrick stripped down to his underwear, humility be damned, and jumped in. The others quickly followed.

"You too, Olga," said Javier. "You're one of them until you prove yourself guide-worthy."

Patrick looked away as she shed her clothes, but from the looks on the male guides' faces, they seemed to very much enjoy the view.

The waters warmed Patrick to his core, soothing the joints and muscles that ached from sleeping on the cold, damp ground. He'd done more than enough climbing in the last four hours, but he couldn't resist the boulder beside a towering stand of wax palm trees, the shortest of which had to be at least a hundred feet tall. He pulled himself up on the rock, shimmied up a few yards of the waxy tree trunk, and soaked Javier with a well-aimed cannonball. Then he swam toward Olga, who was talking to the other men about Javier's knife trick.

"I think he's crazy," said the guy from Chicago.

"No," said the accountant. "Everything here is choreographed. He didn't want anyone to accept his challenge. He wouldn't have *let* anyone accept it."

Olga agreed, careful not to discredit her boss. "It's just a mind game. Something to test your mental toughness."

The two men swam toward shore, leaving Patrick alone with Olga. She was treading water, the ripples on the surface making a blur of her body below, which made her even more alluring.

"By the way," she said, "don't let Javier's crack about Romeo bother you."

"It didn't. But I am surprised he knows Shakespeare."

She laughed. "I've watched the real movie at least ten times, but I'm sure Javier plucked that line from the martial arts version, *Romeo Must Die.*"

A bird sang from somewhere in the forest.

"Ah, 'tis the nightingale," said Olga, borrowing from the playwright.

Patrick smiled, liking her sense of humor. "No. 'Tis the lark."

"Are you saying it's time for you to go home?"

It was a clever question. Patrick's high school English teacher had made a point of explaining how Juliet tries to convince her lover that the bird outside their window is the nightingale, meaning it was still night, not the lark, which would mean it was morning and time for Romeo to leave. Olga had surely picked up Patrick's vibe that he wasn't long for this place.

"I could possibly be persuaded to stay a while," he said.

"Cool," she said, and even with all the hours he'd logged in the virtual world, Patrick knew that smile on her face was *actual* flirtation.

The ten-minute break was over, and Javier called them to shore. Putting on the same dirty clothes after bathing seemed to defeat the purpose, but such were the rules, whoever made them.

Javier laid out the afternoon agenda. "We have one more cliff to conquer, followed by two more hours of hiking. Then we make camp."

The newly restored color seemed to drain from Olga's face. The New York accountant and his insurance executive friend from Chicago were on the verge of mutiny.

"Unless Romeo wants to take the challenge," Javier said, looking at Patrick.

Patrick glanced at Olga, who smiled back.

"I'm listening," said Patrick.

"I lead the way down the next cliff. You follow. If you can keep up with me, the rest of the group walks the easy path on the other side of the mountain. From there, we all ride mules to the next campsite. No more hiking today."

"I thought you said this was a competition," said Patrick.

"It's pretty clear you're today's winner," said Javier.

"Do it," said the accountant.

Olga didn't say anything, but Patrick could see it in her eyes: she couldn't handle another cliff.

Patrick looked Javier in eye. "All right. We're on."

Javier led him up the side of the next hill, an even steeper climb through the jungle than before. The footing was unsure, and a misty rain made the rocks especially slippery. The warm waters of the pond had actually made Patrick's legs rubbery, and after a full morning of hiking followed by a traverse of the cliff, fatigue was taking a toll. Upward they continued, until the foliage thinned, the mist seemed to evaporate, and the air turned colder. They stopped at a rocky ledge. The view of the valley and winding river was breathtaking, like a scene out of *National Geographic*, as the fog crept through the lush green forest hundreds of feet below.

"We start here," said Javier.

"And go where?"

"Down," said Javier, glancing over the ledge. "Straight down to the valley floor."

"That's pretty far," said Patrick, more than aware of his own understatement.

"You want me to go back to the group and tell them you chickened out?"

Patrick didn't answer.

"Remember, this is not a race," said Javier. "All you have to do is keep pace with me. I didn't say you had to beat me."

Patrick considered his options. Going straight down might actually be easier than hiking back down the slippery, forty-degree grade they'd just climbed.

"Okay. I'm up for it."

Patrick attached his Y-configured climbing rope, connecting the base to his safety belt, and took hold of the carabiners, one at the top of each outstretched arm of the Y.

"There are two columns of pitons hammered into the cliff face. One column is mine. The other is yours. Start with both carabiners connected to the eyelets."

He connected Patrick's for him, then connected his own.

"Step down with your left foot," he said, doing so. "When you have firm footing, disconnect the left carabiner and reattach it to the eyelet below it."

Patrick followed his example.

"Now step down with the right foot, get your footing, disconnect the right carabiner, and reconnect to the eyelet below."

Javier went first, then Patrick.

"We do that all the way down. Got it?"

A gust of wind cut through the canyon. Patrick was glad to have both carabiners fastened.

"Got it," said Patrick.

They started slowly. Step down with the left foot, unclip, reclip. Step down with the right, unclip, reclip. Patrick was finding his rhythm, though his legs were painfully reminding him of how far they had to go—at least another four hundred feet.

Javier quickened the pace. Patrick kept up, step for step, clip for clip. With three hundred fifty feet to go, Javier bumped up the pace a notch. Patrick responded, but he was feeling rushed, not entirely comfortable. At three hundred feet, Javier had him working so furiously that he was breaking a sweat, despite the cold. Patrick wasn't sure he could sustain this pace, and he prayed it didn't get any quicker, though his mind flashed with the disturbing image of Javier and his knife back at camp, the *tap-tap-tap* between outstretched fingers that built to a wild frenzy all the way down.

Clip, clip, clip.

Patrick glanced over at Javier. He showed no sign of slowing down, but of greater concern was how shiny and new Javier's pitons were compared to Patrick's, which were discolored and much older. At two hundred fifty feet, Patrick was having difficulty clipping onto them, the eyelets were so rusted. The pace quickened. Patrick unclipped the left carabiner, and before he could reattach to the piton below it, the weight of his body snapped the rusty right piton from the rock. Patrick was exactly where no climber ever wanted to be, both carabiners disconnected at the top of the Y, hiking out from the cliff with nowhere to go but straight down.

"Javier!"

Javier grabbed him by the wrist. Patrick had just one foothold on the cliff, his left leg dangling, his body hanging off the sheer face of the mountain at a fifty-degree angle.

"Pull me in!"

Javier didn't. Not only that, but he seemed to resist Patrick's efforts to pull himself up.

"This isn't funny! Pull me in!"

Patrick worked from his core, as if trying to do a sit-up in midair. But Javier's elbow was locked in place, making it impossible for Patrick to save himself.

"Help me!"

Javier's arm only stiffened. Patrick tried to plant another foot on the cliff face, but he couldn't get traction. His left leg was shaking, weakening, as Patrick came to the terrifying realization that there were not two columns of pitons to allow side-by-side climbing; there was only one *usable* column of new pitons, which had replaced the old one. He locked eyes with Javier, and could see that no help was forthcoming. Javier said something in Spanish, but what Patrick thought he heard made no sense in the moment.

"Boss's orders."

Then he didn't just let go of Patrick's wrist. He pushed off, as if ejecting Patrick from his only foothold.

Patrick felt as though he were flying, but only for an instant. Gravity grabbed him, his body falling at incomprehensible speed, arms and legs flailing, as the jungle canopy below rushed toward him.

Chapter 18

Kate exited the law school's main lecture hall at 3:00 p.m., her final class of the day.

Cyber Law was the hottest course at American University, so high in demand that it was virtually impossible for all but third-year students to enroll. Most of her classmates dreamed of landing with the NSA or other government agency, or snagging a high-paying job in the cyber department of a Washington mega-firm. A few wanted to go straight to Silicon Valley, not necessarily to practice law, or to companies like Buck Technologies. Kate guessed that she was the only one writing a dramatic play.

Kate's cellphone rang as she was heading down the stairway to the student lounge. It was her father's assistant.

"Mr. Gamble requests that you stop by the house after class," she said. "It's very important."

Kate said she could "be there in twenty," grabbed a green iced tea from the café, and started the scenic walk across campus toward Georgetown.

Kate and her father were in agreement that his next residence should be nothing like the penthouse in Tysons Tower, and he'd settled on a classic Italianate-style house on Cooke's Row on Q Street. Georgetown architecture was often associated with Federal-style town houses, but the Italianate style prevailed from the 1840s to the 1880s, and the finest remaining examples evoked the romantic ideal of an Italian villa. It would be Kate's first visit to her father's new address, and she fully anticipated the most secure Italianate-style villa on the East Coast since Al Capone's dream villa in Miami Beach, and definitely the most tech-smart. True to form, there was no bell to ring outside the stone wall. Kate peered into the retinal scanner, and the iron gate swung open. She continued across the courtyard, between the north and south towers, to a grand set of entrance doors that, in classic Italianate style, formed an upside-down U. Kate entered and found her father in the first-floor study. He was on the telephone but quickly wrapped up the call upon seeing her.

Kate immediately saw the concern in his eyes.

"What's wrong?" she asked with trepidation.

"I don't have many details, so there's no reason to assume the worst. But this could make the news, and I wanted you to hear it from me first. Patrick Battle has gone missing."

Kate lowered herself into the armchair. "I was told he was on a corporate adventure. But I didn't hear where."

"Colombia. The mountains and the jungle make it pretty challenging, but everyone has their own guide. The report is that he told his guide he was quitting and walked off."

"Walked off to where?"

"That's the worrisome part. This territory used to be controlled by the FARC—Revolutionary Armed Forces of Colombia. They funded their operations by kidnapping ordinary Colombians and collecting ransom."

"You think Patrick may have been kidnapped?"

"No, that was in the past. The point is that FARC was so successful because the Colombian mountains and jungle are so impenetrable that a rescue mission was virtually impossible. It's easy to get lost. Not so easy to be found."

"Didn't Patrick have a tracking chip?"

"No," he said with a sigh. "That will be a bit of egg on our face in the media."

Kate rose and walked to the window. "So many things about this sound wrong to me."

"What does that mean?"

She turned to face him. "First of all, Patrick never quits anything. I took him to his first cross-country meet in middle school. He pulled a hamstring on the first hill. The race was over in about twenty minutes. Two hours later, Patrick crossed the finish line, practically hopping on one leg. Quitting is not in his DNA."

"We're talking about a twenty-two-year-old man, not a twelve-year-old boy."

"There's more." She told him about her conversation with Noah on the jogging trail—his suspicions about Patrick's sudden disappearance.

"What was Noah implying?" he asked. "That we sent Patrick away to undermine his security audit?"

"Noah put him on his list of employees to interview, and the company sent him on a survival venture in the Colombian jungle with no way to communicate with him. Are you saying that's a complete coincidence?"

"I had no idea Patrick was even gone. The first I heard of it was an hour ago, when I learned he was missing."

"Really?" she asked, not in an accusatory tone, but hoping it was true.

"Yes. Kate, do you have any idea how many employees there are at Buck Technologies? I'm the CEO, not the attendance taker. I don't keep track of everyone's comings and goings."

"Then who sent him?"

"I don't know."

"Can you find out?"

"Has Noah asked that I find out?"

"Not explicitly. But Noah was doing you a favor by reaching out to me, indirectly."

"How is that doing *me* a favor?"

"He was giving you a chance to produce Patrick for an interview before reporting back to the DOJ that Buck Technologies was playing games with witnesses. When he hears that Patrick has gone missing, that will only confirm his suspicions."

"In his mind," he said.

"In the minds of many," said Kate. "You need to get to the bottom of this, Dad. Not just for your own sake. For Patrick's."

He paused, seeming to consider it. "Sit down, Kate."

She did. Her father pulled up the matching armchair and seated himself on the edge of it, facing her. He was looking her in the eye but not in a penetrating manner. It was more on the level.

"Certain things at Buck Technologies are dark to me," he said.

The words took Kate by surprise. "Dark, meaning what?"

"There are projects for which I don't have security clearance."

"How can that be? You're the CEO."

He didn't respond.

"How much is dark to you?"

Again, no response.

"Who decides what's dark to you?"

Silence.

Kate stopped asking questions for a moment, collecting her thoughts, trying to figure out what her father was trying to convey—why he had chosen this occasion, Patrick's disappearance, to share his "darkness." Then it came to her.

"Project Naïveté is real, isn't it? It wasn't a joke."

"The questions you're asking all raise matters of national security."

She'd heard those words many times before—or, more precisely, overheard them—starting when she was a little girl witnessing an argument between her parents. It was usually in response to the question, "Where were you, Christian?" Kate didn't like his answer any more than her mother had.

"Is it really about national security?" she asked.

"Why else would a CEO allow certain silos of his own company to operate in the dark?"

Kate rose. "I can think of only one thing."

"What?"

"Willful blindness, Dad. It's a corporate disease. Sometimes fatal."

She started toward the door.

"That's a cruel thing to say, Kate."

She stopped in the foyer and looked back at him, drawing on his own simile about truth. "Or is it 'poetry,' as you call it."

He started after her. "Kate, don't leave like this. Where are you going?"

"To say a prayer for Patrick. It sounds like he could use one."

Kate let herself out without saying good night.

Chapter 19

Javier rode by mule toward the sunset. He knew these parts of the valley like his own backyard.

The five-thousand-mile Cordillera de los Andes runs the length of South America, then splits into three ranges in Colombia. Sandwiched between the peaks of the Cordillera Occidental, Cordillera Central, and Cordillera Oriental are two great valleys, Valle del Cauca and Valle del Río Magdalena, whose rivers run northward until they merge and flow into the Caribbean Sea. The valleys in western Colombia, the country's most mountainous region, were savanna, with a broad belt of trees about halfway up the mountain, then more savanna at the mountain crest. All of it was swampy, even the mountainside. Thick grass, clover, and mosses held rainfall like a sponge well into the higher elevations.

Javier's first trip through the valley had been as a teenager—a guerilla. He'd joined the FARC, Colombia's largest rebel group, at the age of fifteen. Armed with an AK-47, it had been his job to wait at the base of the mountain to receive the "catch of the day" from his fellow revolutionaries, specialized terrorists trained in urban abduction. Each night, they drove from Cali, past the endless fields of sugarcane to, quite literally, the end of the road. Javier never knew who or what he was going to get until the car stopped and the trunk popped open. At first, he'd found it surprising that the hostages were not the superrich. Most were businesspeople, middle- and upper-middle class, whose families were expected to liquidate their entire net worth to free a loved one. For these unfortunate souls, traveling on foot or by mule through the chest-high grasses of the savanna and on into the mountains with young guerrillas like Javier was the most dangerous part of the journey. Teenagers, drugs, and semiautomatic weapons were a deadly mix. Javier had always considered his hostages lucky; he never shot anyone just for the fun of it. Kidnapping was a business for the FARC, as many as three thousand per year at its peak. Javier saw no reason to deplete the inventory—unless it made business sense, which was sometimes the case. Not until he was sixteen did he execute his first hostage, the forty-three-year-old owner of a cabinet-making factory in Bogotá. Javier had guarded him for nearly eleven months, moving from one camp to another to stay one step ahead of the Colombian army. The businessman had begged for his life, even promising to pay double the ransom. Javier chose not to tell him that his wife had refused to pay a single peso. Instead, he'd taken him to the field, unchained him, and told him that freedom was just over the hill. A single bullet to the back dropped him to the ground like a fleeing gazelle. Javier considered it an act of mercy. He'd died a happy man.

Some FARC dissidents were still active, but Javier had been out since the dissolution of the military in 2017. He no longer believed in the cause. He wasn't sure he'd ever believed in it. Bottom line, whether it was kidnapping, murder for hire, or myriad lesser offenses, crime paid only if it put money in his *own* pocket. Business had been good for Javier. He'd never made a mistake. At least not until that morning on the face of the cliff.

Where the hell did that boy land?

The long shadows of twilight stretched across the grassland as Javier rode into the new camp. His search for the body had been without success. He'd already told the other guides that Patrick had quit and gone home, and they'd passed the news along to the others. He would just stick with his story.

"*Cómo andas*, Javier?" asked one of the guides, greeting him.

Javier could smell the whiskey. The war was over, and these young men were true adventure guides, not a revolutionary bone in their bodies. But the bottle passed quickly around a campfire, and some things never changed.

Javier dismounted, and the guide tied the reins to the nearest tree. His hand was bandaged, Javier noticed. The fool had tried to duplicate Javier's knife trick.

"*Idiota*," he said.

"Just a scratch," the guide said in Spanish.

Javier had honed his trick to perfection as a guerrilla, making it look easy. True enough, back in the day, it had often ended badly—but only for the hostage. Of course he hadn't expected Patrick to accept his challenge that morning. No hostage, however, had ever been given a choice in the matter. A severed finger, delivered to the family, was a common "proof of life" tactic—a dramatic confirmation that the hostage was still alive and, at the same time, a horrifying reminder that time was running out. The hostage, in effect, chose his own proof of life: the first digit nicked in Javier's unwinnable game.

"Twenty years ago, you would have lost that thumb," Javier replied in Spanish.

The other guide laughed, even though he didn't know what Javier was talking about. He invited Javier over to the campfire to share in the whiskey, but Javier declined. He removed the satellite phone from his satchel and walked deep into the grassy meadow, where reception would be uninterrupted by the forest. It was time to report back to the client.

"I can't find him."

Javier had told his client nothing about pushing Patrick off the mountain. He'd fed him the same lie he'd told the guides—that Patrick was a quitter and had headed off into the jungle to find his own way home.

His client was not the least bit understanding.

"He's still missing?"

"I'm afraid so."

"Damn it, Javier. All I asked was that you take him outside the subpoena power of the Department of Justice for a while. Now he's lost in the jungle."

"No worries. I'll search again in the morning."

"Find him. We have enough problems."

The call ended, and Javier was glad to have it over with. But the call to his "client" was the easier of the two calls he needed to make. He took a moment and dialed the boss—or, more precisely, the boss's representative. It was Javier's practice never to have direct communication with the person who actually ordered the hit.

"It's done," Javier said into the phone. "I think."

There was a pause on the line. "You *think*?"

"No one could have survived a fall from that height. But when I climbed down after him, I couldn't find the body."

"Then you didn't look hard enough."

"He must have hit the ground and just kept on rolling toward the river. Maybe a croc got him. They're around here. Big ones. A girl got dragged into the Sardinata River, same elevation, a few years ago."

"What if he just got up, dusted himself off, and walked away on his own power?"

"I don't see how that's possible."

"You're guessing."

"It's an educated guess."

"We don't pay you to guess. Call me back when you have an answer."

Javier switched off the telephone.

He could deal with an unhappy "client." It was rare, but shit did happen on corporate adventure challenges—snake bites, dengue fever, heart attacks— and all clients understood the risks. But the boss was the top of this pyramid. He expected perfection, and

Javier had promised "no screwups" in the dispensation of Patrick Battle.

He was cursing himself, muttering under his breath, as he started back toward the campsite. Then he heard a noise in the weeds. He stopped and saw Olga emerge from behind a scrub of bushes.

"What are you doing out here?" he asked.

"*El baño*," she said.

Mountain bathrooms. That was another thing that hadn't changed since the heyday of the FARC.

Javier stepped closer. The glow of twilight was fading, but with some effort, he could study her expression. "Did you hear the conversation I was just having?"

"No. But don't be alarmed. I'm told it's quite normal to talk to yourself. Only when you start answering is it time to worry."

He didn't appreciate the attempt at humor. "I was talking on the satellite phone."

"Oh. Cool. No. I didn't hear anything."

Javier tightened his gaze. If he had to guess, he would have said she was playing dumb.

We don't pay you to guess.

"I heard Patrick quit," she said.

It was the ruse Javier had shared with his team: Patrick quit. "Yeah. There's a quitter in every group."

"I was hoping you could change his mind. But he's not coming back, is he?"

Javier let her question hang in the air, and he watched closely to see how she dealt with the silence. He could still only guess as to her truthfulness, but one thing was certain: he would need to keep a close eye on this Olga.

"No," he said. "Patrick is not coming back."

Chapter 20

It was almost midnight, and Kate was still angry at her father.

She'd been typing furiously on her laptop since returning to her apartment, alone—out on the balcony. If she wanted a balcony, she'd have one. If she wanted to write a play about Big Data, she'd write one.

If she needed a new hero, she'd find one.

Kate had never told him, but the final assignment in her seventh-grade English class was to write an essay about a personal hero, which each student read aloud to the class. Most chose well-known figures: LeBron James, Jesus Christ, Ruth Bader Ginsburg, Dr. Martin Luther King, Jr., and so on. Kate was the only one to catch grief from her classmates. She'd chosen her father.

The problem with her essay was honesty. Her father *was* her hero, but she didn't feel comfortable standing before her classmates and telling them why. Her essay heralded his business success, his study of philosophy at Oxford, and other distinctions that belonged on a resumé. She couldn't tell a bunch of seventh graders that her mother was an alcoholic—that it was her father who assured her that "Mom didn't really mean it," that Kate really was smart and pretty and not a manipulative little "mean girl" who thought only of herself, and that she could be anything from an astronaut to a zookeeper when she grew up, as long as it made her happy. "Be true to yourself and follow your dreams," he'd told her, and she'd let herself believe that he lived his life by the same credo. Not for a moment did she think he was actually following the money.

"That just sucks," she said, deleting the last eight lines she'd just written. She'd been on a tear, working without so much as a bathroom break, but too much was landing on the proverbial cutting room floor.

Honesty. Like her seventh-grade essay, there just wasn't enough of it in her play. She wasn't being true to her own research. It was tempting to sensationalize the story and turn Watson into a corporate monster, to portray the founder and CEO of the world's first tech powerhouse as Hitler's strategic ally in genocidal warfare. Had she really wanted to go that route, there was plenty of low-hanging fruit to exploit—Willy Heidinger, in particular, the CEO of Watson's German subsidiary and member of the National Socialist Party. Kate uncovered a speech he'd delivered in 1939, urging Germans to follow the Führer in blind faith. "Our characteristics are deeply rooted in race," the German CEO had said. "We must cherish them like a holy shrine which we will—and must—keep pure." But Watson was no Heidinger. And he was definitely no anti-Semite. Other than family, the first person through the church door at Watson's funeral in 1956 was Charles Gimbel, co-owner of Gimbels department stores, a Jew.

Irving Bass was right. It was up to the world to judge whether or not he was evil, whether it made him any less culpable that he wasn't motivated by hate. Simply put, Thomas J. Watson, Sr., was a capitalist to his core.

And so, it seemed, was Kate's father.

She stepped away from her laptop and went to the balcony railing. She'd reached a pivotal point in the play. By the late 1930s, IBM's crown jewel in the world of electromechanical technology was the model 405 alphabetizer. The Germans didn't have them. Hitler demanded state-of-the-art technology for the 1939 Polish census. No one knows for certain how the decision was made. All Kate could do was follow Irving's guidance and write, in fairness, what could have been said. She returned to her laptop and started typing.

It was no accident that, as she imagined the words flowing from Watson's mouth, she heard her own father's voice.

"I read the *New York Times*," Watson said into the telephone. "I know the kind of questions that the Third Reich asked in the May census."

Watson was speaking on the telephone from his town house on the Upper East Side. Heidinger replied from his office in Berlin, speaking in a matter-of-fact tone:

"I presume you mean the requirement that all Germans state whether a grandparent was a full Jew by race."

"Exactly."

"You Americans are such hypocrites."

"What does this have to do with Americans?"

"The U.S. Census Bureau used Hollerith machines to ask about quadroons and octoroons. It's okay for the Americans to identify their Black bogeyman. But let the Germans ask who has Jewish blood, and it's an international crisis."

"I have no time to trade insults," said Watson. "Germany made my decision for me when they invaded

Poland. No 405 alphabetizers to the Third Reich."

"Germany is not at war with the United States," said Heidinger. "Have you asked your shareholders how they feel about your decision?"

"Making a decision like this is *my* job."

"No," said Heidinger. "When it comes to Germany, it's your job to bow your head as you receive the Merit Cross. It's your job to smile for the press as you trumpet your slogan as president of the ICC, 'World peace through world trade.' It's my job to know all the things *you* don't want to know."

"That's enough, Willy."

"You know I can't make these machines in Berlin. The 405 requires rationed metals that Dehomag cannot get."

"That's not my problem," said Watson.

"You're being a fool! In a week, all of Poland will fall. If we don't deliver these alphabetizers, you *will* lose your Polish sub."

"I understand the risk."

"Sacrificing your shareholders will not save the world! The Führer will get these new machines from someplace. Even if he has to steal the technology from Dehomag and make them in a government-run factory."

Watson hesitated, then asked the question that

was on the mind of every American CEO in 1939: "Is that what you believe is coming? Nationalization of U.S. companies by the Third Reich?"

"Let me be very clear on this. There is one way to make sure the Third Reich *will* nationalize Dehomag. And that is if *you* keep us from getting the 405 alphabetizers."

Watson did not reply.

"Watson, do you hear what I'm telling you?"

More silence.

"I need an answer," said Heidinger.

There was none, which only infuriated the German CEO.

"*Watson!*"

Finally, Watson spoke, trouble in his voice. "I'll have to call you back," he said.

Kate's cellphone rang, and she was suddenly back in the real world. It was Noah.

"Hey, sorry to call so late," he said.

"No problem. I was up."

"I have some disturbing news. Patrick Battle has gone missing."

"I know. I heard."

There was silence on the line, and Kate could tell he had something more to say.

"Go ahead," said Kate.

"Go ahead and what?" asked Noah

"Ask me what you really called to ask me."

Noah took a moment, as if summoning the nerve. "Have you ever heard of a Project Naïveté?"

Kate froze, but she managed not to convey any reaction over the line. "What if I have?"

"I want to know about it."

Kate took a breath. "I'm sorry, Noah. I can't help you."

"Actually, I want to help *you*."

"I don't understand."

"Then let me explain."

"Go right ahead."

"Not on the phone. Meet me tomorrow morning at eight a.m. Same place I not so accidentally ran into you on Sunday. No one will have to know about it."

He meant their "chance" encounter on the jogging trail.

"I can't do that," she said.

"I hope I'll see you there."

"Good night," she said, but Noah had already hung up.

Chapter 21

Patrick's eyes fluttered open to the strange equivalent of a seventh-story view. Surrounding him were enormous green leaves, tangled vines, skinny branches—and flowers. Brilliant white. Spotted purple. Bold magenta. Thousands of dew-covered orchids that clustered in the treetops and thrived in midair. The valley floor was about seventy-five feet below. Suddenly, the realization came to him.

He'd been swallowed by the jungle's canopy.

The last thing Patrick remembered was flying. Then darkness. Somewhere between flight and unconsciousness had come the fall, but he had no memory of that sensation. It had all happened too quickly.

Patrick shifted gently to his left, but even the slightest redistribution of his body weight caused a spindling branch to slide out from beneath his legs and catapult toward the sky. Patrick lay perfectly still, even forcing himself not to breathe too deeply. The loss of another supporting branch or vine could be the proverbial straw that broke the camel's back, sending him from this heaven-like field of orchids in the sky to a most unfortunate landing far below.

He took stock of his condition. The canopy had broken his fall, but the rips and tears in his shirt and pants were too numerous to count. Scratches covered his body. Most were minor, but a bloody wound to his forearm had left a large brown stain on his sleeve. He tried to move his wrist but couldn't. Slowly, biting through the pain, he rolled up the sleeve and, to his relief, saw no protruding bone. Just a sprain, hopefully.

Lucky to be alive, he reminded himself.

A pair of blue-and-yellow macaws landed on a branch above him to feast on berries, and then flew away. He envied their ability to fly but did not despair. He'd climbed countless trees as a kid, sometimes a bit too high for his mother's comfort, but he had always managed to make his way down, though a sprained wrist wasn't going to make this any easier. He took a firm grasp of the nearest vine with his right hand and then, slowly, drew his knees toward his chin. A second spindling catapulted upward, then another, and the chain reaction was unstoppable. In an instant, the supportive bed of vines and branches beneath him was gone, and gravity did its dirty work. Patrick dropped like a stone but held tight to the vine. His arm nearly ripped from his shoulder, as the fall became more of a swinging sensation. Flashes of Tarzan crossed his mind, though his landing was more city boy than king of the jungle. His chest slammed into the tree's massive trunk, but he managed to wrap his arms around a sturdy branch about twenty feet above the ground. From there, he lowered himself safely to the ground. He couldn't see the river, but the comforting sound of rushing water was coming from somewhere beyond the thick underbrush, which only made him thirstier. He followed the noise through the jungle and drank like a man who'd found rain in the desert.

A large rock near an eddy offered a dry and comfortable place to sit. The winding river cut an S of daylight through the jungle canopy, and as the breeze coursed through the treetops, Patrick caught a glimpse of the gray granite cliff that had nearly taken his life. Those final terrifying moments were still a blur, but his recollection was that Javier had done nothing to help him. It was hard to fathom, and the details still eluded him, but Javier, it seemed, had actually been worse than no help.

Patrick considered his options. He could stay put and wait for someone to find him. But if Javier had let him fall—or had even *made* him fall—waiting for rescue was no option at all. He climbed down from the rock and started walking downriver. If he could just keep walking, putting one foot in front of the other, he was certain that eventually he'd find a camp, a farm, a town—maybe even a Starbucks. He walked nonstop for thirty minutes, he guessed, though he had no reliable way to measure the passage of time. He saw plenty of wildlife, but no sign of civilization. Hunger was becoming an issue. His last meal had been beans and rice at camp. He wondered if they were looking for him.

He wondered if Javier had tried to push any of the others off the mountain.

The jungle was thinning. Another hour or so into the journey, the terrain became more agricultural. He pulled a plant from the ground. It was an onion, which he quickly devoured. Before him lay an entire field of onions, intercropped with a magnificent, blackish-purple plant with bright scarlet flowers. He recognized the blossoms only because he'd binge-watched *Narcos* on Netflix, the story of drug lord Pablo Escobar. It occurred to him that he was one of very few Americans ever to see firsthand the raw materials for heroin.

Patrick kept walking downriver, but there was no

192 · JAMES GRIPPANDO

sound of rushing water in these flatter stretches of land. The world was so quiet at this altitude, which triggered thoughts of the proverbial tree that falls in a forest. The weather changed quickly, too, and it was suddenly raining, lightly at first, but then a downpour. He headed away from the river and into the forest for cover. The rain pattered on the leaves above him. Several yards into the jungle, completely unnoticeable from the river, he found a cottage on stilts. It was constructed of roughly hewn logs and had a thatched roof. Several smaller huts were nearby, but the place was overgrown with foliage, and he saw no sign of another human being. Perhaps it was seasonal housing for the *campesinos* who worked the onion harvest, whenever that might be.

"*Hola!*" he called out, but there was no response.

Patrick continued deeper into the forest and soon discovered that the camp was much bigger than he'd thought. He found benches and tables configured like an outdoor mess hall. He passed another cottage and a latrine, beyond which was another cluster of small huts. Some of the huts had doors. Others didn't. He stopped and looked inside one of them. It was empty, except for the chains on the ground, and the ceiling was too low for any grown person to stand upright.

He felt chills, realizing that this was not seasonal

housing for farm workers. The chains were shackles, and the quick history lesson that Olga, the trainee, had given him about the FARC came back to him. The place may have been abandoned, but enough evidence of human suffering remained to mark it as one of the many remote locations where the FARC kidnappers had kept their hostages, this godforsaken mountain outpost in the middle of nowhere, next to the fields of poppy. It pained Patrick to consider how many months or even years of a person's life had been wasted in this hut, chained to a post. Who could do that to another human being?

Who could push someone off a mountain?

On his knees, staring into the empty hut, that crucial moment on the cliff came flooding back to him. Once again, he could see the coldness in Javier's eyes. He could see Javier's lips moving, and he struggled to recall what was said. As the image came clearer in his mind's eye, the words, or at least Patrick's understanding of the words, remained a fog.

Boss's orders.

The sound of Javier's voice was in his head, but Patrick wasn't sure if he was remembering or imagining it. Had he actually uttered those words before pushing Patrick away? He could have. But did Javier mean *he* was the boss? Was it Javier's boss who had given the order?

Or was it Patrick's boss?

Patrick suddenly sensed the presence of someone or something directly behind him, but before he could turn around, he felt the pressure of a gun barrel on the back of his neck.

"*Manos arribas!*" the gunman said.

Patrick obeyed, raising his hands slowly, not sure what to make of this abandoned guerrilla stronghold that wasn't exactly abandoned.

Chapter 22

Kate went for a run on Tuesday morning and stopped long before she was tired. It was 8:00 a.m., and she was just a few steps from the start of Lover's Lane, the pathway to Dumbarton Oaks Park, exactly where she'd connected with Noah the previous weekend. She'd arrived by way of the tree-shaded ropewalk, a stretch of redbrick walkway in Montrose Park that was once used for laying out hemp to be turned into long ropes for the shipping trade. It brought to mind the old saying about "giving a fool enough rope," and she wondered if it was indeed professional suicide to be secretly meeting with Noah about Project Naïveté.

Or maybe it was a strategic act of self-sabotage, calculated to propel her in the direction she really wanted to go—out of the law, away from Buck Technologies, and into a career in arts management, where her dream of being a playwright had some chance of survival.

"Wasn't sure you'd show up," said Noah, as he approached.

Kate silenced the music from her smartwatch and removed her earbuds. "Me neither," she said.

Noah, too, was wearing running clothes. The fanny pack around his waist was a new addition. He kept walking, and Kate went with him.

"Does your father know you're here?" he asked.

"Does your mother know you're here?" she asked.

"Not exactly the same thing," he said.

"I came to listen, Noah. Not to answer any questions."

"Fair enough. Let me tell you what I know. If you want to fill in any blanks, feel free."

Kate kept walking, no reply.

Noah continued. "Patrick Battle's name was near the top of my list of Buck employees I wanted to interview. Buck immediately sent him on a corporate adventure. No one could tell me where he was, but just yesterday I heard from the State Department that he is missing somewhere in Colombia."

"Which has me very worried," said Kate.

"With good reason," said Noah. "It took over fifty years of fighting to get the FARC to lay down its arms, but there are still pockets of dissidents in the mountains. For them, the Marxist-Leninist war against imperialism goes on."

"I know. I read just enough online last night to scare the crap out of myself. So let me just say this much. If this meeting is about helping Patrick, I'm all in. But if this is about me becoming a spy on my father's own company to help you find out about Project Naïveté, you've got the wrong girl. I don't know anything about it."

"Then why did Patrick come to your office on your first day of work? And why did you go to his office in Building C the following Monday?"

"How do you know that?"

"I'm doing a cybersecurity audit. Entry logs for all Buck's buildings are clearly within my domain."

"Those were personal visits," said Kate.

"You two had no discussions whatsoever about Project Naïveté? Is that what you're telling me?"

"Patrick was already gone by the time I went to see him."

"What about your first day? Did you and Patrick talk about Project Naïveté?"

Patrick had mentioned the project in his visit, and technically she'd gone to tell Patrick that her father had blown the cover on his ruse. She wasn't so sure it was a ruse anymore.

Noah seemed to sense her hesitation.

"Kate, as of right now, my job is to conduct a cyber-security audit. If necessary, I will recommend to my supervisor that we should convert the audit to an investigation, which means that I would have the power to subpoena witnesses. Based on what I know so far, I'd have to subpoena you. You would have to answer, and I know you wouldn't lie under oath. So you might as well tell me now."

Kate stopped. She knew Noah was just doing his job, but she still didn't like it. "You and my father are even more alike than I thought."

"How do you mean?"

"He asked me to try to get you to tell me what your audit is really about—what's really driving it. Now, you're asking me to spy on my father's own company. Does anyone give a damn how I feel about all of this?"

"I'm sorry," said Noah. "I understand this is awkward in a lot of ways."

"Let me ask *you* a question," said Kate. "What do *you* think Project Naïveté is about?"

Noah unzipped the jogger's hip pack that was fastened around his waist. Inside was a thick roll of manuscript pages. Kate recalled the comparison Patrick had drawn between her play and Project Naïveté.

"Is that my play?" she asked.

"It's an opinion from the United States Supreme Court, written by Chief Justice John Roberts in 2019. It's almost two hundred pages long."

"You didn't have to kill so many trees. You could have emailed me a link."

"Going forward, I don't want any electronic messages between us. No email, no texts, no voicemail. Phone calls should be brief and nothing of substance."

He handed her the printed opinion, and Kate skipped to the last page. He wasn't kidding: one hundred ninety-two pages.

"Be sure to read *every single word*," he said.

"Then what?" she asked.

"Meet me again tomorrow, eight a.m. Right here."

"What if I can't?"

"You'll come. If you read every word."

His continued emphasis on every single word was curious.

"Oh, one other thing," he said. "Take shorter strides when you run downhill. Your back will thank you." He turned and continued his run through the woods.

"I'll keep that in mind," she said.

Kate found a picnic table just around the bend, took a seat in the shade, and laid the printed court opinion on the tabletop before her. The case caption was on page one: DEPARTMENT OF COMMERCE V. NEW YORK.

Noah had piqued her interest, and it was her intention to sit down and read as much of an overstuffed Supreme Court opinion as she could stomach in one sitting. Almost two hundred pages of legalese was no jog in the park, so to speak. She'd read hundreds of cases in law school, but the only one of this length was the *Dred Scott* decision, required reading for first-year law students, in which the chief justice of the U.S. Supreme Court, a former slave owner, and his associate justices had taken over two hundred pages to decide that people of African descent, whether enslaved or free, were not citizens of the United States under the Constitution. She hoped for better from Chief Justice Roberts.

From the first sentence, she was gripped, the chief justice's words unleashing a cascade of possible parallels to the play she was writing: "The Secretary of Commerce decided to reinstate a question about citizenship on the 2020 census questionnaire."

Kate raced through the first paragraph, and she was still on page one when a call came up on her smartwatch. It was Sean's number, but it was Irving Bass on the line.

"Did you steal Sean's phone?" she asked, kidding.

"He's driving. I want you to meet us at the theater."

"When?"

"As soon as you can get there."

"I'm all sweaty and in my running clothes."

"I don't care if you're covered in baby oil and wrapped in a bedsheet. Get down to the theater before I change my mind. I'm going to produce your play sooner than I thought."

The pages in Kate's hands fluttered in the breeze. "I'll be there by nine," she said, walking fast, talking even faster, and reading faster still as she started on her way.

Chapter 23

Patrick's eyes were finally adjusting to the darkness. He was staring at the thatched roof overhead, grateful for the pinhole of daylight that connected him to the outside world.

His hunch about the huts had proved correct. It had been years since the FARC's surrender, but their former camps and strongholds stood like ghost towns in Colombia's mountains. Patrick had stumbled on an eerie reminder of a kidnap-and-ransom industry that had funded decades of war and terrorism. Like so many others held captive before him, a tiny hut with a dirt floor was his cell, and he was at the mercy of a band of well-armed guerrillas. He could hear them talking right outside his hut.

"*El Rubio es muy peligroso,*" said one of them,

which made the others laugh. Translated: "The Blond is very dangerous."

The name fit Patrick, but he also got the joke. Patrick was a gamer, so he knew that "El Rubio" was also the world's most notorious narco trafficker in a popular Grand Theft Auto video game called the Cayo Perico Heist. If only he could have gotten his hands on the Perico Pistol, El Rubio's weapon of choice, a distinctive handgun that was a cross between a real-life P08 Luger and James Bond's golden gun.

Patrick's leg was cramping. He tried to stretch it out, but the hut was too small for him to stand up straight or lie flat. He sat with his back against the door, extended his legs, and leaned forward to touch his toes. The chain that tethered him to the post wasn't long enough to allow him to reach forward and touch his toes. He wondered how long he could stand this. He wondered how many days, weeks, or months the hostages before him had been forced to live this way.

He wondered what those two yellow dots in the darkness were.

They seemed to be staring at him from the corner of the tiny hut, a pair of fixed, beady eyes. It was too dark to see any facial features, the shape of the head, or the body. But if the frozen eyes were any indication, the entire creature was locked in an unshakable pose. Stiffened with fright, maybe. Or poised for an attack. The piercing eyes glowed brighter, and finally they blinked. A chill ran down Patrick's spine, and one question came to mind:

Do snakes have eyelids?

He was pretty sure they did not. But the jungle was filled with strange predators, all of them hungry. This one seemed to sense Patrick's fear. Slowly, the eyes were creeping closer, and Patrick had to make a decision. Calling out for help was not an option. That would only startle the creature, and he could end up dead from a venomous bite. If he broke down the door, he could be shot by his captors. He feared the bite more than the bullet. On the mental count of three, he drew his knees up to his chest, braced his feet against the center post, and pushed with every ounce of his leg strength.

The door flew open, and Patrick burst from darkness into the daylight. A screeching noise followed him out, which only propelled him faster. His wrists were still shackled, and as the chain pulled taut, all but his hands had made it outside the hut.

"Don't shoot!" he shouted.

The guards were laughing hysterically. Patrick counted five of them, each dressed in combat fatigues and toting a semiautomatic rifle. They'd obviously put the creature in the hut, another good joke at El Rubio's expense. Patrick watched the animal scamper into the forest. It was a strangle jungle species unknown to him, perhaps harmless. Perhaps not. Either way, Patrick was relieved to be rid of his yellow-eyed cellmate.

"*Bien hecho, Carlos!*" one of the men said. Patrick assumed it meant something along the lines of "that was a real knee slapper, Carlos."

Carlos unchained the prisoner, still laughing. Then his smile faded, and he directed Patrick with the point of his rifle.

"Walk," he said in English. "That way."

As Patrick recalled, "that way" was out of the thick forest and toward the river. He rose and started walking. Carlos was right behind him, and four other guerrillas were behind Carlos, still sharing a laugh over El Rubio and his four-legged cellmate. Patrick guessed it was the oldest trick in the FARC joke book, locking the hostage in a hut with some nocturnal creature, and these goons never got tired of it.

The vegetation thinned as the walk continued, and Patrick caught sight of the river across the savanna. The flowering poppy field that Patrick had crossed on his way to the camp was farther downriver, and the guerrillas had him marching along a path that took them in the opposite direction. The cramp in Patrick's leg worked itself out, and he was walking without a limp as they reached the dirt road near the river.

"*Hacer alto,*" said Carlos, and Patrick stopped on his command.

One of the guerrillas came up behind him and blind-folded him with a scratchy black rag. The first thought that came to Patrick's mind was that this place, in the middle of nowhere, was the one his captors had chosen for his execution. He expected that, any moment, one of the men would press a lit cigarette between his lips, followed by Carlos yelling, "Fire!" He waited, but no cigarette came. Then a gun went off, and Patrick dropped to the ground.

The guerrillas burst into laughter once again. Patrick couldn't see them, but it was an even bigger belly laugh than the one triggered by the yellow-eyed creature in the hut. Carlos had fired his weapon into the sky and made the hostage shit his pants. What a riot.

In the distance, as the guerrillas' laughter subsided, Patrick heard the distinctive sound of tires on a dirt road, a vehicle approaching. Carlos ordered him to stand up, and he did. Patrick could hear the engine running, the brakes squeak as the vehicle came to a stop, and then silence.

"*Vaya,*" said Carlos, and he nudged Patrick forward with the barrel of his gun.

Patrick took small steps, the blindfold making it impossible to see where he was going, but he assumed they were heading to the vehicle, which was better than the firing squad. Carlos ordered him to stop and grabbed him by the shoulder to make sure he did. Patrick heard a car door open. Someone shoved him inside—the backseat, he presumed. Patrick hadn't realized how foul-smelling these guerrillas were until one of them slid into the backseat to his right, and another to his left, sandwiching him between his captors. The engine started, but then suddenly Carlos was shouting in Spanish at the driver. He was speaking too fast and with too much urgency for Patrick to translate, but something was afoot. The guerrilla to Patrick's right flung open his door, grabbed Patrick, and dragged him out of the vehicle. Patrick heard the trunk pop open, and two men picked him up like a duffel bag and threw him inside. He landed with a thud up against the spare tire, and the lid slammed shut.

Patrick heard the car doors opening and closing as the guerrillas piled into the vehicle. The driver found first gear, and they pulled away slowly. Patrick was on his left side, his back to the spare tire. He shifted his weight to get more comfortable. His head was near the wheel well, and he could hear the tires kicking up dirt and loose stones as they continued down the road.

They'd gone less than a mile, he estimated, when the vehicle stopped.

It was dark, hot, and hard to breathe in the trunk, but Patrick was focused on only one thing: listening. He heard another vehicle approaching. It stopped right alongside them. Then he heard Carlos from inside the car, telling the others to let him do the talking. This was no ordinary *campesino* they were encountering along the road. Patrick suddenly realized why the hostage had been moved from the backseat to the trunk.

He pressed his ear to the quarter panel so that he could hear the conversation.

"Buenos días," the man said, and Patrick knew the voice immediately. Carlos engaged him in idle chitchat, and the more they talked, the more certain Patrick became: it was Javier.

Patrick listened as carefully as he could, translating the conversation as best he could.

"Have any of your men seen a blond young man?" asked Javier. "An American?"

"No. No Americans out here," said Carlos.

"Well, if you do happen to see him, do me a favor, will you?"

"Of course. What?"

"Kill him," said Javier. "I'll make it well worth your while."

"*Con mucho gusto*," said Carlos. With much pleasure. Javier's Jeep pulled away.

The vehicle jerked forward, causing Patrick to roll to the back of the trunk and slam his head on a metal box. A tool box, Patrick guessed. Filled with tools, some of which might make excellent weapons.

Gotta get out, he told himself. *Gotta save yourself.*

Chapter 24

Kate stopped at her apartment for a quick shower and change of clothes. She made it to the theater before nine. Sean told her to take a seat in the main auditorium and that Irving would be ready for her "in a minute." Thirty minutes later, she was still alone in the auditorium. But it wasn't a waste of time. She had Justice Roberts with her, or at least his opinion.

Sean returned, took the seat beside her, and glanced at the single-spaced text with way too many footnotes. "Now, *that* looks boring."

Kate could have dropped it there. But her meeting with Noah had left her mind awhirl with questions. Sean probably didn't have any answers, but it might clear her head just to hear herself talk.

"It's a Supreme Court decision from 2019. It relates to my play, in a way."

"What's it about?"

"The Court said the Commerce Department couldn't add a citizenship question to the 2020 census."

"I have a vague recollection of that from the news," said Sean. "What does that have to do with Nazis using Hollerith machines?"

"Here's an interesting fact. In the early days, sometimes the U.S. census included the citizenship question and sometimes it didn't. But starting in 1890 and going all the way to 1950—seven times in a row—the full-count census asked every U.S. resident if he or she was a citizen."

"So?"

"I said, 'starting in *1890*.' That's where my play starts: the first time the U.S. Census Bureau used technology to process census data."

"Interesting coincidence."

"It's not a *coincidence*. It's the slippery slope of Big Data meets Big Government. Who's a citizen? Who has a great-grandparent of African descent? Who has a Jewish grandparent? This is exactly what my play is about."

"Actually, it's not. Irving is more firm than ever that it's about capitalism."

"Irving can go to hell."

"Irving will be there soon enough," said the director himself, coming down the aisle behind them.

Kate shrank in her orchestra seat. "I didn't know you were there."

"Obviously. Now, if you're done cursing me out, come with me. And leave behind whatever that is you're reading. I need your complete focus. No clutter."

"I'll be in Irving's office," said Sean, taking Kate's bag and the papers with him.

Kate stepped into the center aisle and walked with Irving toward the main stage.

"Kate, what you are about to experience will probably make you nauseous," he said.

"What is it?"

"A table reading for the next play I'm supposed to open. It's called *Trillary*."

"Trilogy?"

"No. *Trillary*. It's a dark comedy about the next presidential election. Trump runs against Hillary Clinton all over again. It's too close to call. Both candidates are up all night, and finally the media makes the announcement: it's a tie. Two hundred sixty-eight electoral college votes for each."

"What do they do?" asked Kate, as they climbed the stairs at stage right.

"Trump still has his key to the front door. Bill Clinton still has his. So . . ."

"They race to the White House, literally," said Kate.

"Exactly. It's four in the morning, and we have not one, but two presidents-elect barging into the East Wing in their pajamas trying to lay claim to the master bedroom. *Trillary*."

"It sounds kind of funny."

"Think *War of the Roses* meets Washington."

"What's *War of the Roses*?"

"An old Michael Douglas and Kathleen Turner movie. They play a married couple in a bitter divorce, but neither one will leave the house. So they draw a line down the middle of every room—this half's yours, this half's mine. Of course, they end up killing each other. Which, in the case of *Trillary*, I see as a happy ending."

Bass parted the curtain, and they joined the cast onstage. Two men and a woman were seated around a table, each with a script in hand. Irving set the scene for Kate.

"We're in the presidential bedroom suite. There's a bright red line that runs right down the middle of the bed and continues across the room. Hillary slides under the covers on her side. Donald slides under the covers on his. And there's this tense silence between them."

Bass waited a beat, then rapped on the table, a door knock: "Enter Bill."

214 • JAMES GRIPPANDO

Donald read his line. "Beat it, doughboy. This bed is for the presidents-elect."

"Cool," said Bill. "Does this mean I get to sleep with Melania?"

"No!" shouted Trillary—Hillary and Donald in unison.

"Cut," said Irving. He excused himself from the actors and led Kate back outside the curtain. "You see, Kate? The script is terrible. And the playwright won't let me change a word. If I do, he'll sic the Dramatist Guild on my ass."

"Well, it *is* his copyright."

"That's what I was afraid you'd say. I can't work under those rules. Not with him and not with you."

Kate's antennae were up. "It sounds like you want total control of my script."

"I need control. For starters, the play needs a narrator."

"I don't want a narrator."

"Tom Watson, Sr., is the perfect narrator."

"Why does my play need any narrator?"

"Because there's so much good material. The only way to keep all of it in the play is by compressing it through a narrator."

"How much compression?"

"Get it down to one act. No intermission. Ninety minutes."

"That's impossible."

"It's not only possible; it's imperative. My plays start at eight p.m., and eighty percent of my audience are boomers who want to be in bed by ten."

"I'd rather cut scenes."

"We can't. Not with the additions I have."

"What additions?"

"Charles Lindbergh. He received the Nazi Merit Cross a year after Watson did. Watson must have met him at some point."

"He did. His son wanted to be a pilot, so Watson took him to meet Lindbergh."

"Perfect! Work that into the narrative. And we need another minute or two of Watson meeting Joseph Kennedy and Father Coughlin."

"Father who?"

"Father Charles Coughlin, the radio priest. He had thirty million listeners. The Roosevelt administration finally forced the cancellation of his show when his message turned anti-Semitic and pro-Hitler."

"Are you sure Watson actually had a meeting with Father Coughlin and Joseph Kennedy?"

"I'm sure he didn't. But he could have."

"Except that he didn't."

"I'm asking you to take artistic license. Coughlin was an anti-Semite, no doubt about it. The verdict is out on Joe Kennedy, but he made some pretty questionable remarks when he was FDR's ambassador to Great Britain."

"I thought we were in agreement that Watson was not an anti-Semite."

"It's up to the audience to decide."

"It's up to us not to lie to them. I can't portray Watson as an anti-Semite based on meetings that never happened with men who may or may not have been anti-Semitic."

"Fine. Cut Joseph Kennedy."

"And Father Coughlin."

"Oh, all right," he said, grumbling. "But Watson as narrator is non-negotiable."

Kate hesitated. "I'm not sure I'm the right playwright to pull this off. Watson is a sixty-something-year-old man. I'm a twenty-seven-year-old woman."

"No. You're a writer. You have the tits of Aphrodite and a dick so hard you could cut diamonds with it. You have whatever your director wants and everything your director would give himself, if only he had the talent to write. Give me a play, Kate."

Irving was such a contradiction to Kate. He could be the crudest, biggest ass on the planet and, in the same instant, he could lift her up like no one else, as if there were nothing she couldn't do.

"I'll give it a shot," she said with a sigh.

"Attagirl. Then it's all set. I'm pulling the plug on *Trillary*. Your play opens January fifteenth. I'll need a finished script by Thanksgiving at the latest."

Kate's mouth fell open. "But you're essentially asking me to start over."

"Do you want the slot, or don't you?"

It had been Kate's dream since middle school. Crazy as it was, the answer was obvious: "I want it."

"I'll let the actors know. The men can fight it out for the role of Watson. Hillary is perfect to play Watson's wife. You get with Sean and set up a timetable for the next draft."

Irving disappeared behind the curtain. Kate stood numb for a moment, then suddenly found herself struggling to contain the urge to leap into the air and scream with delight. She hurried down the stairs and took the side exit toward Irving's office, where Sean had said he'd be waiting. She knocked eagerly and entered on his invitation.

"Are we on for January?" he asked, seated in Irving's battle-scarred leather chair.

"Yes!" she said, louder than intended.

He came around the desk, and it seemed as though they might embrace, but it turned into an awkward retreat into professionalism, a combination of a handshake and a high-five.

"I can't wait to get started," he said.

"Me, too," she said.

He returned to Irving's chair. The Supreme Court's opinion was on the desktop. Kate noticed that Sean had moved well beyond the last page she'd read.

"By the way, I love the way this guy writes," said Sean.

"You read Justice Roberts' opinion?"

"To be honest, I skipped to the end. Spoiler alert: the whole two hundred pages come down to whether the Commerce Department stated a valid reason when it ordered the Census Bureau to include the citizenship question in the census questionnaire."

"Right. The department said it was for the benefit of minority voters."

"And here's what Justice Roberts wrote," Sean said, picking up the opinion. "Accepting this explanation would require the Supreme Court to have 'a naïveté from which ordinary citizens are free.' Isn't that a great line?" he asked, then saying it again like a chief justice: "'A naïveté from which ordinary citizens are free.'"

Kate froze. Naïveté. As in Project Naïveté. Noah's voice was suddenly in her head—his insistence that she "read the whole opinion," that she "read *every word*."

"Yeah," said Kate. "That is one great line."

Chapter 25

Kate found her father in his office. He was on the phone or, more precisely, speaking into his hands-free headset while pacing from end to end of a museum-quality Sarouk rug that stretched the length of his enormous corner office. He motioned for Kate to take a seat, and she did.

"Be with you in one sec," he told her, and then he resumed his conversation on the headset.

Kate could wait "one sec," or perhaps even a minute. Beyond that, she wasn't sure. Technically, her visit wasn't urgent. Noah had given her until 8:00 a.m. to decide whether to meet with him again about Project Naïveté. She wasn't sure she would go back to see Noah. The only thing for certain was that she needed to talk to her father.

He stopped, looked in Kate's direction, and said, "Maybe you should come back in five."

Kate leveled her gaze and slowly shook her head, which seemed to catch her father off guard. He wrapped up the call, removed the headset, and took a seat in the armchair facing her.

"I didn't realize it was important. What's up?"

"Project Naïveté. I know it's real, so don't lie to me again."

He paused, absorbing the blow. "I'm sorry I was less than truthful. But—"

"Please don't say it was for my own good."

He started again. "I was going to say: but I hope you didn't figure this out by going beyond your security clearance."

"Is that really your response? You're turning it around, as if *I* was the one who did something wrong."

"I'm very sorry I misled you. But as CEO of Buck, I need to know if you breached."

"I didn't breach anything. I heard it from the United States of America."

He didn't immediately take her meaning. "You mean Noah? He told you about Project Naïveté?"

"He told me it's real. I know nothing about the details, other than what I can infer from the Supreme Court opinion he told me to read," she said.

"'A naïveté from which ordinary citizens are free,'" he said, quoting the chief justice—and confirming that Noah wasn't wrong. "I can see why it would be part of his cybersecurity audit," he added.

"You can?"

"Absolutely. Under Buck's security protocols, project names must be random. It's against every rule in the book to choose a name that could give an outsider any clue as to what the project is about," he replied.

"Who came up with the name Naïveté?"

"I didn't know at the time. I've since been told it was Patrick."

"You mean since he's gone missing?"

The point of reference seemed to make him uncomfortable. "Yes. Since then."

"So Patrick was being truthful when he said my play was like the project. Or I should say my play before Irving Bass told me to change a few things, like the beginning, the middle, and the end. They both dealt with the U.S. census."

"You said your play was about player pianos, so I can't speak to that. But Project Naïveté isn't about the census, per se."

"I get it that I don't have clearance. But there must be something more you can tell me."

"I can give you the thirty-thousand-foot view. I

won't pass judgment as to why the Commerce Department wanted to include the citizenship question in the last census or why the Supreme Court shot it down. But the whole exercise revealed two important things. One, the census isn't the best way to find out who is and who isn't a U.S. citizen."

"People lie," said Kate.

"Or they just don't respond. Number two, the U.S. government already has massive amounts of administrative data on citizenship, like Social Security records."

"Which are probably more reliable than census responses."

"But here's the thing. Even all that data is only eighty percent accurate."

Kate could see where this was leading. "So they came to Buck."

"Yes. And there's nothing illegal or immoral about the federal government trying to get a more accurate assessment of how many people living within its borders are citizens and how many aren't."

"What does the federal government plan to do with Buck's 'more accurate assessment'?"

"I can't tell you that."

"Because I don't have clearance?"

"Because the next time you see Noah, I want you to

be free to tell him everything I've ever told you about Project Naïveté."

The mention of a "next time" seemed presumptive on his part.

"What makes you think I'll talk to Noah again?"

"Because I *need* you to keep the dialogue going."

"I wish you wouldn't put me in this position."

"I'm not. Noah is. And I'm fine with it. This conversation has been very helpful to me and to the company."

"But my stomach has been in knots all day."

"Stop worrying, Kate. I swear, sometimes you're so much like your mother."

He rarely drew the comparison, and this was the first time since her passing, which made for an awkward moment. As always, it rang false to Kate. It was something he would say once or twice a year, usually when Kate's self-doubt edged toward self-destruction, or when he could tell she was tipsy, and he felt the need to remind her that children of alcoholics were twice as likely to develop a use disorder. Funny thing was, Kate didn't see herself as being "like" either parent, and if she went back far enough in time, she remembered only wanting to be like her father, not her mother. Just being in his office triggered memories of her father bringing in Kate to sit at Daddy's desk and play CEO, overseeing a "staff" of American Girl dolls. Samantha, the most responsible, was her star employee and had a chair right beside her. So long ago, so much mischief. The fish in the saltwater aquarium she used to chase with the little net. The screensavers on Daddy's computer she used to tinker with. Her father favored words over images, and he liked to post something philosophical or inspirational, a line from a book he was reading or a takeaway from a TED talk he'd attended. When he wasn't looking, Kate would replace it with the latest words of wisdom from Mary-Kate and Ashley Olsen.

Her gaze landed on the present message, which scrolled across the screen, but she was too far away to read it.

"I'm drained, and I have a ton of reading to do in my Securities Reg class," she said. "I'm going to head home."

"You go right ahead," he said.

She rose, and as she headed for the door, she passed close enough to the computer to read the scrolling message on the screen. This one was from Sophocles: NOTHING VAST EVER ENTERED THE LIFE OF MAN WITHOUT A CURSE.

She stopped at the door and looked back at her

father. "Do you think Sophocles was right?" she asked, pointing at the message with a jerk of her head.

Her father shrugged it off, offering a weak smile. "I don't know. But I do believe we all need to keep our sense of humor in this business."

Kate left, feeling nothing in her funny bone.

Chapter 26

P atrick was sure he was alive, but only because he could feel himself sweating.

It was so hot inside the trunk of the car that he'd faded in and out of consciousness over the course of a journey that seemed to have no end. A noisy gravel road had long since given way to the monotonous hum of tires on paved highway. Minutes seemed like hours, and there was no doubt they'd been on the road all day. The rusted-out hole in the quarter panel through which he'd watched Javier negotiate with his new captors had gone black with night. The heat had actually gotten more unbearable since sunset, which told Patrick that they were at a lower elevation, no longer in Colombia's mountains.

Finally, the car stopped. An amber glow appeared in

the rusted-out hole, which moments later turned red. It confused Patrick at first, and then he almost laughed at the realization: even ex-FARC bandits slowed for yellow and stopped for red to avoid getting pulled over by police when they had a valuable hostage in the trunk.

Red turned to green, and the car lurched forward. Patrick was regaining his bearings. He heard the sound of other vehicles around him, the blast of a car horn in the distance, the rumble of a passing motorcycle. They were in a city. Based on the brief lesson in Colombian geography that Olga, the trainee, had given him in the mountains, he made his best guess:

Medellín, if they'd taken him north. Cali, if they'd gone south.

Patrick heard the car doors open and slam shut. He prepared himself for the opening of the trunk lid. He'd run through the options in his head a dozen times. If he heard no voices and had reason to believe the man popping the trunk was alone, he would attack. If there was talking—clearly more than one of them—he'd obey and take his shot later.

He heard the men talking in Spanish. There were at least three of them.

Patrick stuffed his "weapon" inside his pants. Rifling through the tool box in the pitch darkness hadn't been easy, but he'd found a suitable tool. It was made of iron and had a claw on one end for removing nails, but it wasn't a hammer, and it was too small to be a crowbar. It was a whatchamacallit.

The trunk popped open, and the laser-like glare of a flashlight immediately blinded him. His Plan A—attack—would have failed miserably.

"Out," one of the men said in English.

Patrick complied, trying not to bang the metal whatchamacallit on the bumper as he climbed out of the trunk. One of the men slipped a blindfold over his eyes and tied it tightly behind his head. Another man grabbed him by the elbow and led him forward.

"Where are we going?" asked Patrick.

"Hostage Hotel," said the man who spoke English, and he quickly translated for the amusement of his friends. They laughed, as if terrorizing the gringo was one big joke.

Patrick put one foot in front of the other, keeping pace with his captors. His blindfold was so tight that it had risen up on the ridge of his nose, giving him a narrow line of sight beneath the hem. As best he could tell, they were in an alley, which accounted for the lingering odor, a foul combination of raw sewage and uncollected garbage. The Hostage Hotel may have been a joke, but not entirely. They were at the rear entrance to an apartment building of some sort; it could well have been an old hotel. Patrick let his head roll back slightly, not too much, but just enough to peer up from beneath the blindfold and see all the way up to the third-story floor. The hotel had windows, but they were boarded over with graffiti-covered plywood.

One of the men shoved Patrick's head forward, forcing his chin to his chest. A sudden glow from somewhere revealed that they were standing outside a metal door. The light was from a cellphone, and Patrick overheard and understood enough to know what the phone conversation was about.

Delivery.

"Delivery of what?" Patrick asked in decent Spanish.

"Shut up, gringo. This is where we find out if you are worth more alive or dead."

The metal door opened, and someone from behind shoved Patrick inside. He stumbled over the threshold but caught his balance. He heard more Spanish—too many conversations at once for him to discern what was being said, but he'd already heard enough to realize the danger he was in. His value "dead" had been vaguely established by Javier's roadside offer that morning: *Kill him. I'll make it well worth your while.* His value alive would surely be measured in ransom.

"I can pay," said Patrick, though truthfully he had no idea how much money was in his bank account.

"*Silencio!*"

That voice didn't belong to any of the men who'd brought him from the mountains. The "hotel" manager, Patrick presumed, or maybe just the bellboy.

They led him to the end of the hallway, opened the door to the last room on the left, and forced him into a chair. One of the men cuffed his hands to the back of the chair and then, from the footfalls on the floor, it sounded like several people left the room. But he was not alone.

"Don't move," he was told, and the voice was a woman's.

She tugged at his blindfold and removed it. Patrick blinked a few times, and things came into focus. She was wearing a blue baseball cap that read *Los Dodgers*, which covered everything above her eyes, and a hospital mask that hid everything below, the combined effect of which was to keep the hostage from being able to identify her.

"Hold still and look straight at the wall," she said.

With a handheld camera, she scanned his face up and down, left to right, right to left.

"Turn your head to the left," she said, and she scanned his profile, first the right side and then, with another turn of his head, the left. She laid the camera aside, and her fingers danced across the keyboard.

Patrick couldn't contain his fascination with the sophistication of this group of mountain bandits and their Hostage Hotel. He had expected an interrogation—name, employer, relatives—but he had no identification on him, and he could have told her his name was Mickey Mouse. His captors had a workaround for lying hostages.

"Are you using Façade?" he asked, meaning the face-recognition software.

She ignored him, hit ENTER, and waited. Patrick couldn't see the LCD screen from where he was sitting, but his captor and her computer software had converted his face into the technological equivalent of a Google search on steroids. She typed in a few key words to narrow the results, and in short order the internet delivered the kind of personal information that the FARC kidnappers of old could only beat out of their hostages.

"You work for Buck Technologies in Virginia?" she asked, though it wasn't really a question.

"No, that's actually Lucas Hedges. My movie-star good looks must have thrown off your software."

"Bad jokes can get a person killed here, Mr. Patrick Battle."

He took her point, but his disavowal of any connection to Buck was anything but a joke. It was his employer who'd sent him on this adventure in the Andes in the first place, and it still wasn't clear to him who was giving orders to Javier, the knife-wielding, cliff-hanging psychopath.

She switched off the LCD screen. Her work was apparently finished, which made Patrick's heart race. Her job, after all, was to decide whether he was worth more alive or dead.

"What's the verdict?" asked Patrick.

"I'm sure a company like Buck Technologies will pay *mucho dinero* for your return."

"So there's room for me here?"

"*Sí.* There's room."

He was tempted to request a pool view, but he'd already been warned once. "What now?"

She went to the door, opened it, and called down the hallway for the bellboy or whoever it was who'd delivered Patrick to her. Patrick kept an eye on the doorway as she crossed the room, collected his blindfold, and refolded it afresh. She was doing a better job than the punks who'd blindfolded him outside, and he held little hope that she would leave any openings. Patrick cut one last glance toward the doorway, and he did a double take.

"Don't move," she said, annoyed.

His reflex-like reaction had made her drop the blind-fold. As she refolded it, he peered more deeply into the dimly lit hallway. His eyes had not deceived him.

It was Olga.

Patrick's eyes widened and, before he could show any further reaction, Olga raised her index finger to her lips, shushing him, as if to tell him that she wasn't really one of them and that he was going to get them both killed if he didn't play it cool.

The cloth slipped over his eyes and all went dark, not a slit of light above or below the blindfold made perfect.

Chapter 27

Wednesday was Kate's Groundhog Day, a repeat of Tuesday morning. At 8:00 a.m. she was at Lover's Lane, the pathway to Dumbarton Oaks Park, just as Noah had predicted.

"I see you read every word of Justice Roberts' opinion," said Noah.

At the sound of his voice she turned and said, "The operative wording being 'naïveté.'"

"Walk with me," he said.

They continued down the path, toward a stand of towering sycamore trees as old as the republic. It was possible that one or two leaves had taken on a hint more fall color overnight, but it was not enough to counter the sense of déjà vu. Kate picked up where they'd left off the day before.

"I'm sure it would get me nowhere to ask what the U.S. attorney sees as the connection between Justice Roberts' opinion and Project Naïveté."

"A total nonstarter," said Noah.

A squirrel scurried across the path in front of them. Another chased after it, screeching, as if the faster one were making off with the last nut in the forest. Noah kept talking.

"Let me guess what you did after we spoke yesterday. You got yourself a Mesco Blend—one Splenda, a little cream—sat down with your pink highlighter, and started reading."

Kate didn't see the need to bring in Sean and her meeting with Irving Bass. "Pretty close. But I haven't used pink since I was an undergraduate."

"Somewhere around the penultimate page of the opinion, you started cursing me again for killing trees, thinking this has absolutely nothing to do with Buck Technologies. There's an interesting historical triangle involving your play, the opinion, and the first use of technology by the Census Bureau. But not a damn thing to do with your father's company."

Kate didn't answer, still choosing to leave Sean out of it.

"Then you got to the last page," said Noah, "and Justice Roberts' turn of a phrase."

"Justice Roberts was actually quoting forty-year-old language from Judge Friendly, who, by the way, has one of my favorite names ever for a judge, second only to Justice Story."

"Let's keep our eye on the ball here, all right?"

"Sorry," said Kate.

He was smiling, but it faded. "Then you went to see you father."

"You get zero points for that guess. Of course I went to him."

"And he told you there's nothing illegal about mining and collecting data on citizenship."

He knew her father well—perhaps even better than she'd thought. "I'm not going to tell you what my father said."

"No need. The truth is, Kate, the government already has ways to collect citizenship data. Much better ways than a census."

She held firm on her position, offering him nothing her father had told her about the efficacy of existing data.

"But let me cut to the quick of it," said Noah. "Do you think Patrick Battle went missing over the collection of citizenship data?"

She stopped. "I wasn't aware he went missing *over* *anything*. All I know is that he's missing."

"Forget I said that."

"Forget, hell. Patrick is like a little brother to me. You can't make a statement like that and expect me to skip over it. Are you saying he ran away? Or are you saying somebody"—she swallowed hard, not even wanting to think it, let alone say it—"that somebody made him disappear?"

"I'm not saying either of those things. Not yet. But here's the way I see it. The problem for guys like Patrick is that this project has morphed into something very different since the company named it Project Naïveté."

"Why is that a problem for Patrick? Why is that a problem for *anyone*? Some of the best inventions in the world are the result of scrapping the original concept and going back to square one."

"Kate, you're asking me questions I can't answer. The bottom line is that it's really important that I talk to someone knowledgeable about Project Naïveté."

"I wasn't lying to you yesterday," she said. "If you're looking for information about Project Naïveté, I'm not your source."

"I know you're not. Patrick Battle is. That's why he was so high on my list of people I wanted to interview."

"I have no idea where Patrick is, if that's what you're asking me. None."

"My question is a little different: If you were in my shoes and couldn't talk to Patrick, who would you talk to?"

"Honestly, I have no idea."

"Your answer doesn't surprise me. There's a pretty thick emotional barrier between you and the obvious answer."

"You mean my father?"

"Nope."

"Then who?"

He looked away, then back. "Sandra Levy."

The name took Kate's breath away. "If you're talking to me to get to her, you're really barking up the wrong tree."

"I think you're the only shot I've got."

"Sandra Levy hasn't said a word to anyone since the FBI arrested her and took her out of the building in handcuffs. I've *never* spoken to her."

"At the very least, she owed your mother an apology. Your mother is gone. Now she owes it to you. With a full explanation."

"An explanation *of what?*"

He was clearly struggling, and it was Kate's sense that he wished he could say more. But she was no mind reader.

"Kate, if this conversation is going to continue, I need a firm commitment from you up front."

"What kind of commitment?"

"That you will speak to Sandra Levy. I can't lay my cards on the table only to have you say you'll think about it or you need to check with your father. I have to know now: Are you in or out?"

Kate drew a deep breath. "I can't believe you're going to make me visit that woman in prison."

"Is that a yes?"

Those two crazy squirrels were back on the jogging path, their chase resuming but the roles reversed, the pursuer having become the pursued.

"Noah, I'm saying yes because you've led me to believe that Patrick is in serious danger and this will help him. If it turns out you're playing me—if you're stringing me along just to get something the U.S. attorney needs from Sandra Levy—I will never speak to you again. Do we understand each other?"

Their eyes locked, and Kate was determined not to be the first to blink. Finally, Noah nodded. He started walking slowly down the path. Kate went with him.

For the next ten minutes, Noah did all the talking. Kate just listened.

Chapter 28

At noon Christian Gamble and his bodyguard climbed out of the limousine near Ford's Theatre. Across the street was Lincoln's Waffle Shop, not far from Abe's Café and Gifts, which was around the block from Petersen House, where the sixteenth president expired from his gunshot wound. A busload of tourists, oblivious to the irony, were eagerly picking over the colorful "I DC" T-shirts on sale—"Two-4-One"—on the sidewalk racks outside the historic house. To the west, in Abe's day, would have been a clear view down a muddy trail all the way to the White House grounds. Gamble walked east, toward the FBI headquarters, which he hadn't visited since the Sandra Levy investigation. Right around the corner, he entered the restaurant he'd chosen for his lunch meeting with Irving Bass.

"Have a seat at the bar," he told his bodyguard, and the maître d' led Gamble to the only open table, where the director was waiting for him.

Gamble had patronized fine restaurants all over the world, but Succotash on F Street was the only place to get soulful Southern dishes reinvented by a Korean American chef. His first visit had been with Kate, years earlier, when he'd taken her to see *A Raisin in the Sun* at Ford's Theatre. She couldn't stop talking about the play, and while he would have sooner seen her as president of the United States than a playwright, there he was, having lunch with her director.

"Another bourbon on the rocks," said Bass the moment Gamble was seated.

The maître d' took his empty glass. "I'll let your waiter know."

The alcohol confused Gamble. "Kate said you were in rehab. You're drinking again?"

"Oh, I don't drink. I just want to smell it."

"Yeah? How did that last one smell?"

Bass smiled in a way that said, "Touché."

The waiter brought menus, told them about the fried chicken and waffles special, and left them alone. Bass seemed eager for the smell of his second bourbon.

"Thank you for meeting on short notice," said Gamble.

"No problem. I'm giving your daughter the opportunity of a lifetime, so I guess I'm entitled to a free lunch."

It was probably a joke, but Gamble couldn't tell for sure.

"Kate has no clue about this meeting. I'd like to keep it that way."

A server set up Bass's glass of bourbon and disappeared. "Sure. As long as she hears nothing of how I enjoy certain olfactory pleasures with my Southern cuisine."

Bass opened his menu. Gamble left his on the table.

"What's your story, Mr. Bass?"

"Excuse me?"

Gamble had said some unflattering things about the director on the squash court with Kate. Those were hunches, not facts. But if he was lying to Kate about his drinking, it was a hunch worth testing.

"What if someone were to say that you're stringing Kate along, and that it won't be long before you come calling on her father to write a check in order to present her play? How would you respond?"

Bass laid his menu aside. "How cynical of you."

"Is it?"

"Your daughter is writing a very important play. To

be clear, the idea was completely mine, not hers. Do you even know what it's about?"

"I understand it has something to do with the census."

"It's the story of Thomas J. Watson, Sr., and the Nazis' use of the old IBM punch-card technology for the systematic extermination of Jews."

"You mean *misuse*. I hardly think the founder of what was then the most powerful tech company in the world was knowingly supporting genocide."

"What do you know about Mr. Watson?"

"I'm an admirer of his son, who took over the company after his father died. Talk about the greatest generation. Tom Junior's autobiography is probably one of the most honest books ever written by a tech executive. Until the last fifty pages or so, when he goes on and on about all he did for the Carter administration, which is about as exciting as—well, the Carter administration."

"Does the book mention that his father was one of the very few Americans to receive the Nazi Merit Cross?"

"As a matter of fact, it does. And to his credit, Watson Senior was the only one who ever gave it back."

"But why?" asked Bass, putting the question with a touch of melodrama. "Was it because human rights organizations were protesting right outside his office on Madison Avenue? Or was it just a smart business decision?"

"You seem to be excluding the possibility that it was genuinely an act of courage and conscience."

Bass chuckled. "Mr. Gamble, we're talking about the CEO of a tech giant."

The waiter returned to take their order. Bass ordered the special, but Gamble had already wasted enough precious time. He opened his wallet and placed two hundred-dollar bills on the table.

"Something's come up," he told the waiter. "Cut him off at three bourbons and keep the change."

The waiter thanked him, tucked the menus under his arm, and left with the cash.

"That's quite the thin skin you've got there," Bass said.

"Is this your idea of fun?" said Gamble. "Commissioning the daughter of a tech CEO to write an indictment of the world's first tech CEO?"

"You're being very unfair."

"You're using my daughter."

"I'm allowing your daughter to come to terms with where she is in life and emerge as a playwright."

"What kind of literary 'human condition' bullshit is that?"

"Kate has yet to accept what the play is really about.

It will take a few more rewrites. She's very fast, so I'm confident she will get there soon enough."

"Get where?"

"At bottom, Watson was a narcissist. His employees sucked up to the CEO by writing silly songs about him, and he made the entire workforce sing them over the intercom during morning announcements."

"Why would Kate even want to write about that?"

"Because writers should write what they know. Ultimately, this play is about Tom Junior. He's the conscience his father lacks. He alone had the courage to speak truth to power."

"And that's obviously how you see me."

"It's not about *you*. It's about the only hope we have in the world of Big Data. Watson Senior gave back the Merit Cross in 1940. His son was born in 1914. That would have made Tom Junior roughly—"

"Kate's age," said Gamble, totally getting it.

Bass raised his glass. "To daughters and sons. And to opening night."

"Fuck you," said Gamble, and he walked out of the restaurant.

Chapter 29

Kate took a commuter plane that evening to Greenbrier Valley Airport. The lucky ones on her flight were headed to the famous Greenbrier Resort to enjoy the brilliant colors of autumn at the foot of the Allegheny Mountains. Kate rented a car and spent the night at an airport motel. Soon after she finally fell asleep, her alarm went off. Six a.m. It was time to get up and drive to the women's federal prison in Alderson, West Virginia.

FCP Alderson is a 159-acre minimum-security prison camp nestled in the scenic hills near Greenbrier State Forest, on the bank of the Greenbrier River. Built in 1928 as the first federal prison for women, Alderson uses a reformatory model where each "cottage" houses up to sixty women and each inmate has only one roommate. The nearest barbed-wire fences are on privately owned farms along the river, and inmates are free to wander the grounds until 4:00 p.m. when not doing chores or participating in a vocational or educational class. Jazz singer Billie Holiday learned to sew at Alderson while serving time for drug possession in the 1940s. Manson cult member Lynette "Squeaky" Fromme saw opportunity in the openness and escaped for two days while paying her debt to society for the attempted assassination of President Gerald R. Ford. In what Kate found to be an interesting coincidence, former inmate Martha Stewart was convicted of the same crime that had landed Sandra Levy at FCP Alderson: lying to federal investigators in violation of Chapter 18 of the United States Code.

"I'm here to visit an inmate," Kate announced at the gate, and she gave the name.

The guard checked Kate's identification and radioed ahead for clearance. Kate had submitted her visitation request online, and she attributed the quick turnaround to Noah's hand in the matter. The fact that her request was approved by the warden didn't necessarily mean that Sandra would show up—inmates could not be forced to see visitors—but Kate took it as a positive sign that the guard didn't turn her away.

"They're doing the morning count," he said. "You can wait inside with the other visitors."

Kate thanked him and continued past the stone pillars and tree-lined driveway that looked more like the entrance to a college campus than a prison. She parked in the visitors' lot. Handbags and cellphones were not allowed inside, so Kate locked hers in the rental car and followed the sidewalk into the visitation center.

Kate and Noah had agreed on a very narrow purpose for her visit. Neither one expected that, after two years of silence, Sandra would break down and confess all to Kate. Just as the government had failed to prove its securities fraud case against Martha Stewart, the espionage case against Sandra Levy had fizzled. Stewart served only five months for her lies to federal agents. Sandra would serve longer, but not nearly as long as she might if she opened up to Kate, only to be convicted on the substantive charges against her. Noah, of course, had coached Kate on what to ask and how to handle herself.

Kate very much had her own agenda.

She entered the visitation center and signed the visitors' log. The sign on the wall advised that visitors were subject to search, but in Kate's case it was cursory, and the visitation officer led her directly to the visitation room. Kate was aware that Alderson was minimum security, but still she was surprised.

"It's so . . . un-prison-like."

"This ain't *Orange Is the New Black*, honey," the guard said.

FCP Alderson was designed for open visitation, so there was no security glass to separate inmates from visitors, no talking by closed-circuit telephone while law enforcement monitored every word. Tables and chairs were set up in a room as big and open as a gymnasium, with appropriate spacing between them. A designated play area accommodated mothers with young children. It struck Kate that, even with guards patrolling the visitation area, conversations in this minimum-security prison were probably more private than the average cellphone conversation in the "free" world.

Kate was seated at a table opposite an empty chair. She and a hundred or so other visitors waited at their assigned spot for the end of the morning count, after which the guards would bring in the inmates.

A woman at the next table looked over and said, "Haven't seen you here before. You new?"

"My first time," said Kate. "But I'm seeing someone who's been here a while."

The woman nodded knowingly, as if to say that she understood Kate's situation perfectly. "Your mom?"

"What?"

"I asked, are you here to see your mom? 'Cause I get it. Took me a while to put aside the anger and come visit mine."

"No, it's not my mom." *Far from it*, thought Kate.

Happy voices from across the room caught Kate's attention, the sound of inmates and visitors reuniting. A kiss and a hug were allowed at the beginning and end of each visit, and lonely people made the most of it. Kate watched from afar, trying not to let her gaze intrude on private moments on public display. Mothers hugged their children in the play area. Wives and girlfriends clung to husbands, partners, and significant others. The woman at the next table embraced her mother, which for some reason made Kate feel good, even though she knew almost nothing about them.

Twenty minutes passed. Still no Sandra Levy.

Kate had seen her only once before in person. An attractive woman. More than attractive, actually, though not the classic beauty her mother was. She was a brunette, and Kate wondered what that gorgeous long hair would look like with no gold highlights inside prison walls.

A guard approached the couple at the table catty-corner from Kate. They were definitely taking liberties with the "one kiss, one embrace" rule.

"And no sitting on each other," the guard told them,

as he stepped away. Then he came toward Kate and glanced at the empty chair.

"How long do you want to wait, miss?"

Kate hadn't considered it. "As long as it takes, I guess."

Patrick was locked inside a windowless room about the size of a closet. In fact, he was pretty sure that it was once a janitor's closet, as it still smelled like cleaning fluids. He ate there, slept there, and tried not to drive himself crazy marking the passage of time. He'd been fed three times so far, which could mean one day in captivity. But was he getting three meals a day? No way to know when the kitchen closed at the Hostage Hotel. Bathroom breaks were completely sporadic. They took him down the hall and let him do his business when it was convenient for them, not based on the hostage's needs.

Patrick heard the jingle of keys outside the door. "Stand in the corner, facing the wall," the guard said.

Patrick did as he was told. The guard opened the door and tied the prisoner's hands behind his back. Some guards were careful to tie the blindfold tightly, but this one wasn't. Either way, Patrick was getting good at using his facial muscles to shift the blindfold just enough to get some line of sight. As the guard led him down the hallway, another guard said something, and Patrick caught a waist-down glimpse of another prisoner. Women's shoes, he noted, and it made him shudder to think what the Hostage Hotel was like for the opposite sex.

The guard untied his hands, removed the blindfold, and opened the bathroom door. The stench had nauseated Patrick the first time, but he was getting used to it.

"Two minutes," the guard said.

Patrick entered. The guard left the door open a crack, for some modicum of privacy. Patrick took all of his two minutes, if only because the small window in the bathroom was his only view of daylight.

"Time," he heard from the hallway. But it wasn't the same guard. The voice was a woman's, and it sounded familiar.

Olga?

The door swung open and Olga entered. She closed the door, and with her back braced against it, she spoke in a hushed but urgent tone.

"You are in a lot of danger."

"No shit," he said, barely above a whisper.

"Some of these kidnappers are ex-FARC but most aren't. They're just thugs, and money is their only ideology."

"Are you one of them?"

"Sort of. Not really. I do certain jobs for them on a contract basis. My particular skill set makes me welcome in most any operation of this type."

"Who *are* you?"

She didn't seem eager to tell him, but time was short. "I was hired to make sure you didn't bail out of the corporate adventure and go home. It was my job to make sure you were a happy boy and in no hurry to go back to the United States."

Only by looking into her eyes did he fully understand what she was saying. "You're . . . a prostitute?"

She looked away, then back. "I can leave, if you've got a problem with that."

He saw his one glimmer of hope receding and rushed to stop her.

"No, don't leave! Who hired you?"

"Javier runs the show in Colombia. But you're missing the point. Javier hired me because someone hired *him* to keep you out of the United States for a few weeks—maybe a month or two. Someone *else* hired Javier to make sure you never came back. Get it?"

He did, having survived the attempted murder-by-freefall. But even more chilling was the way Javier's words—what he'd actually said—finally came clear to him.

"*El jefe del jefe.*"

"What?"

"I was confused about what Javier said before shoving me off the mountain. He was talking in Spanish, and I thought he said he was taking orders from 'the boss.' But it was '*el jefe del jefe*.'"

"The boss of the boss," she said.

"Which is still only one person. But you're saying there are two people giving Javier orders. How do you know that?"

"I heard Javier talking on his satellite phone."

"Are you still working with him?"

"No! Why would I be telling you all this if I was still working with Javier?"

"Why *are* you telling me all this?"

"Because I'm going to get you out of here."

"But *why*?"

In her eyes, he thought he saw the answer, and he was suddenly reminded of the lark and nightingale. But his question drew resentment.

"Why would a girl like me do the right thing if there's nothing in it for me? Is that what you're asking?"

"No. That's not at all what I was getting at."

"I thought you were different, Patrick. Thought you'd see me as a real person."

"I do. I'm sorry."

She breathed out some of her anger. "Fine. If it puts

you at ease, I swear, I expect nothing in return. Javier hired me to keep you happy and make you want to stay. But I never signed up to get you or anyone else killed. Do you want me to help you, or don't you?"

"I do," he said, no more questions asked.

Olga opened the door and slipped away, leaving the door open a crack, just as Patrick's guard had left it. Patrick heard the pounding of the guard's boots in the hallway as he returned.

"I *really* do," he said softly.

Chapter 30

The clock on the wall said 11:00 a.m., and Kate was still alone at the visitation table. Her cellphone was locked in the rental car, per prison rules, which left her with nothing to do but obsess over her predicament or observe the real-life boredom of prison life. A remark from her father, which at the time she'd dismissed as irrelevant, now seemed sage. "Once upon a time, Kate, in a world you'll never know, people stood in line at grocery stores, stuck behind a shopper arguing with the cashier over a three-inch stack of expired coupons, and all we could do was read the *TV Guide* or the tabloid headlines. No texting. No emails. Nothing to 'like' on social media. Technology is good."

"Okay, I'm here."

The woman's voice from behind startled Kate, and

she sprang from her chair. Standing before her, dressed in the standard prison uniform of khaki button-up shirt with khaki pants, was Sandra Levy.

"I didn't think you were coming," said Kate.

"That makes two of us. May I sit?"

"Please."

Sandra walked around to the other side of the table, and the women settled into chairs opposite one another. The steady buzz of conversations continued all around them, but Kate was suddenly less aware of it.

"Where to begin," said Kate, breathing out.

"That's up to you. You came to see me."

"That I did," said Kate. "I guess I'm wondering if there's anything you've ever wanted to say to me."

Sandra arched an eyebrow. "Are you here for an apology?"

"Do you think you owe me one?"

"For what?"

The list began to form in Kate's mind. *Stealing secrets from my father's company? Making my mother so jealous she called 911 on my father in revenge?*

"It wouldn't be much of an apology if I had to answer that question," said Kate.

"Okay. I'm sorry."

Kate let out a mirthless chuckle. "Seems we're going around in circles here. You're sorry for what?"

She was looking Kate straight in the eyes, arms folded. "I'm sorry your mother died thinking that I was sleeping with your father."

"I see."

"Not the apology you were expecting?" asked Sandra.

"I don't know what I was expecting."

Sandra sat forward in her chair, leaning into the table. "Do you think your father and I were having an affair?"

"He says he wasn't."

"I didn't ask you what he says."

Kate felt that pang she felt whenever she questioned her father, or whenever she questioned the man she thought he was. "I've wondered. Sometimes."

"Because of something your mother told you?"

"Mom said some things, yes."

"You realize your mother was paranoid, right?"

"I'm well aware that she had a drinking problem."

"She was an alcoholic. But she was also clinically paranoid."

"And that is, what? Your professional opinion as an executive coach?"

"I was a practicing psychiatrist for ten years before I burned myself out talking to teenage girls," she said. "Yes, I was hired to help Buck Technologies identify your father's successor as CEO. But I was much more than that to Christian."

Kate heard no anger in the use of her father's first name—quite the opposite. "'More' in what way?" asked Kate.

"Being married to an alcoholic is a terrible burden. Your father needed help dealing with it. But he was in a tough spot. People like to think society is getting better at understanding mental health issues in this country. But how do you think the CIA, as the company's largest shareholder, would feel about the CEO of Buck Technologies seeing a psychiatrist?"

Kate took her point, but she was one of those people who liked to think attitudes toward mental health were changing. "I guess it would depend."

"No, it doesn't *depend*. We're talking about the CIA. If your father had started seeing a psychiatrist, it would have been professional suicide."

They paused, the word "suicide" seeming to have an awkward place in their conversation.

"What are you telling me?" asked Kate.

"The relationship between your father and me was not sexual. I was, in effect, your father's psychiatrist. He told me everything. Is that intimacy? I suppose. Is that a betrayal? Your mother thought so."

"I don't think you can presume to know what my

mother thought based solely on what my father told you."

"It's based more on what your mother told me."

Kate came to a hard stop. "When did you speak to my mother?"

"A few weeks before she died."

"She came to see you *here*?"

"You didn't know?"

"No," said Kate, and then another thought came to her. "Has my father been here?"

Sandra shook her head, almost laughing at the ridiculousness of the question. "Your father's not stupid. We've had zero communication since my arrest."

Kate leveled her gaze and saw nothing that made her think Sandra was lying.

"Maybe that should tell you something," Sandra added.

"Like what?"

"It's probably best for everyone that this conversation end," said Sandra, rising. "But before I go, I want to clear up one thing. When I said your father told me 'everything,' I don't mean company secrets. I mean his personal secrets."

Kate reminded herself that this visit was at Noah's request, and she phrased her next question accordingly. "Are you denying you accessed company secrets?"

"I admit I broke the law when I lied to the FBI," she said, her eyes narrowing.

"That doesn't really answer my question."

"That's the best answer you're going to get," said Sandra. She started away from the table and then stopped. "Strange. You never asked why I did it."

"Lied to the FBI?"

"Whatever it is you think we're talking about."

"Okay. I'll ask: Why?"

Her expression turned very serious. "I did it for Megan."

"Who's Megan?"

"My daughter."

Kate felt chills. She did "it" for her daughter.

I did it for Kate.

Kate watched her walk away. Sandra never looked back as she crossed the room, passing one table after another on her way to the exit. The corrections officer opened the door, and the inmate was gone.

Kate was back where she'd started, alone at the table, her mind awhirl with questions.

Chapter 31

Kate skipped the weekly law-school happy hour. She had a date with Sean.

It was their first date—possibly their second, if helping her move into a new apartment was "a date," or maybe even their third, if you counted "tea at the Reichstag." A third date, of course, would have implied certain rules, but Kate had just one for the evening:

"The rule is we can't talk about Irving or my play," said Kate.

Sean agreed, and for the first half of the date, it was easy to stick to the rule. They were in the Kennedy Center Concert Hall enjoying the National Symphony Orchestra perform Tchaikovsky's Symphony No. 5. At intermission they got a glass of wine, red for Kate and white for Sean. They waited in the grand foyer, near the thirteen-foot-high, three-thousand-pound bronze bust of John F. Kennedy that almost seemed to be eavesdropping on their conversation.

"Just one thing about your play," he said.

"Breaking the rule already?"

"Sorry. We have to cut the scene where Watson's wife jumps down his throat for writing that letter to Adolf Hitler."

"That letter is real."

Sean drank his wine. "But it sounds made-up."

"I've seen a copy of the letter. It's real. November 1938. Right after Kristallnacht. Over seven thousand Jewish homes and businesses were vandalized. They burned synagogues to the ground. Dozens of people were killed. And what does Watson do? He fires off what he thinks is a strongly worded letter to Hitler saying, 'I respectfully appeal to you to give consideration to applying the Golden Rule in dealing with these minorities.'"

"Do they even have the Golden Rule in Germany?"

"Yes," said Kate, resisting the urge to add, *you moron*.

"Maybe you should double-check."

"Trust me, they had the Golden Rule. What they didn't have was IBM's latest technology. Unless Watson was willing to sell it to them. That's why this scene has to stay."

"Claude says it has to go."

"Who's Claude?"

Sean hemmed and hawed, then answered, "A screen-writer. He's in Hollywood."

Kate froze. "Irving Bass is shopping my play to Hollywood without telling me?"

"Actually, Irving knows nothing about this."

"So *you're* shopping it behind Irving's back *and* mine?"

"I wouldn't call it 'shopping.'"

"But you admit you went behind our backs."

"Look, Kate. Irving is delusional about this play. It was his idea, so he's trying to shoehorn it onto the stage. But it's too big for live theater. This story is screaming to be a five-part series."

"But I'm not writing a TV series."

"That's why I connected with Claude."

"You have no right to show Clyde my script."

"Claude, not Clyde."

"Whatever the fuck his name is."

An elderly woman within earshot gave Kate a reproving look. Sean moved closer and said, "Calm down, Kate."

"Don't tell me to calm down. This is *my* story."

"Technically, it's a true story."

"As imagined by *me*, which you are feeding to Claude, through *my* script."

"No. This story is based on actual historical figures and events, which Claude is reimagining through *his* script."

Technically, he was right—the law doesn't prevent multiple dramatic interpretations of the Kennedy assassination—but that didn't make it okay for another writer to use her script as a blueprint, and it didn't lessen Kate's feeling of betrayal.

The chime sounded, calling all patrons to return to the concert hall. The crowd migration began, but Kate didn't move.

"I'm leaving," she said.

"Come on, Kate. Don't be like this."

"You are a fucking snake."

Kate placed her wineglass on the table, but Sean stopped her before she could step away.

"Kate, I'm sure they did have the Golden Rule in Germany. But in this business, we live by the Crypto Rule. The sooner you learn that, the better."

"I have no idea what you're talking about."

"Ask your old man. He'll know."

Sean returned to the concert hall. Kate headed for the exit.

A stiff autumn breeze met her outside the door, and by the time she reached the taxi stand, her hair was a hopeless mess. She climbed into the backseat, gave the driver the address to her father's house in Georgetown, and did her best to brush out the windblown look on the ride there.

The point of her visit had nothing to do with Sean. Kate had been avoiding her father's calls, worried about how he might react to her having visited Sandra Levy without telling him. His relationship with Sandra was still confusing to her, and Kate wasn't convinced that sharing secrets, if not a bed, wasn't some form of infidelity. Maybe all that was none of a daughter's business. But she had every right to understand her own mother's suicide note. A straight talk with her father was overdue.

The taxi dropped her at the curb, the guard let her inside, and Kate found her father in his study. Work was what he did every Friday night for as long as Kate could remember. He took one night off a week, Saturday, if he had a free night at all.

"Wow, don't you look pretty," he said. "Date night?"

"Disaster night."

"What happened?"

"That's not what I came to talk about. This is important."

"Okay," he said, leading her to the club chairs, where they each took a seat. "What's up?"

"Did you know Mom went to see Sandra Levy in prison?"

The question seemed to catch him off guard, but he didn't dodge it. "Yes. Did your mother tell you about it?"

"No. Sandra did. I went to see her yesterday."

His face went ashen. "Why on earth would you do that?"

For Patrick, she reminded herself. But all that, coupled with her conversation with Noah, was way too much to explain.

"Let's put a pin in the 'why' question for now. I want to talk about the things she told me."

He seemed curious, perhaps in the way that anyone would be curious to know what his de facto psychiatrist had to say about him. Perhaps it was more than that.

"All right," he said. "I'm not at all happy you did this without telling me, but let's hear what Sandra had to say for herself."

Kate skimmed over most of it and went straight to her final exchange with Sandra—the words that had been playing over and over in her head.

"Her daughter's name is Megan," Kate said.

"I know. She's in high school," Christian replied.

"She said she did it for Megan."

Her father was silent. Kate pressed him.

"It's like Mom's note. 'I did it for Kate.' Sandra told me she did it—"

"I get it," he said abruptly.

Kate couldn't understand his reaction. "Don't you think that's important? They both did '*it*' for their daughters. It raises the same question I asked the day you helped me move into my apartment. What does '*it*' mean?"

Her father rose, walked to the bar, and poured himself a brandy. "I would frame the question differently. Brandy?" he asked.

"No, thanks. What do you mean? How would you frame the question?"

He swirled the brandy in his snifter and returned to the club chair. "To me, it's an 'either/or' question. And I'll let you answer it for yourself.

"Either Sandra Levy is your new best friend, and she's trying to tell you something important."

"Or?"

"Or she found out what your mother's suicide note said, and she's messing with your head—to get back at me."

That would have been an incredibly mean-spirited thing for Sandra to do, and it almost made Kate afraid to ask what kind of anger and resentment could possibly have prompted it.

"To get back at you for what, exactly?" she asked.

Kate watched her father swallow his brandy.

"Sandra's a very complex person," he said.

Kate waited, but it was clear he'd said all that he cared to say on the subject. He rose and grabbed the television remote from the coffee table.

"Since your date is over, want to sit and watch a movie with me?" he asked, clearly wanting to turn the proverbial page.

She wasn't going to let him off the hook that easily, but she could bide her time and circle back to Sandra's "complexity" later. "Sure," she said.

He switched on the TV and started scrolling through the menu, which reminded her of her talk with Sean.

"Dad, have you ever heard of the Crypto Rule?"

He was focused on the menu, not really listening. "Crypto is short for cryptography, which is all about codes, which is the world I live in."

"I know what the word 'crypto' means. I asked what's the Crypto Rule, as distinguished from the Golden Rule. Do you know?"

"I've heard people use the expression before, mostly Silicon Valley types."

"What is it?"

He took a seat and handed her the remote. "Do unto others . . . before they do unto you."

It made Kate wonder if she'd been too kind in calling Sean a snake. "How nice," she said.

"Pick a movie, kiddo. What are you in the mood for?"

"Anything but a film stolen from a playwright," Kate said.

Chapter 32

They found his whatchamacallit.

Patrick was in the slow, disorienting transition from unconsciousness to the dark reality of life behind a blindfold. He remembered the guard shoving him against the wall, knocking loose the tool he'd found in the trunk of the car. It had slipped down the inside of his pant leg and fallen to the concrete floor with a clang. The guard had started yelling in Spanish, and the last thing Patrick remembered was the crushing blow of the whatchamacallit against the side of his head.

"Damn," he said, feeling the lump behind his ear. He smelled something strange, and for a moment he thought it was his own blood. But his wound was dry to the touch. He breathed in through his nose, sniffing out the odor. It was rum. Patrick wasn't much of drinker, having seen what it had done to Mrs. Gamble, but one semester of college was more than enough "education" to make the distinctive smell of a Cuba libre immediately recognizable.

A screech pierced the darkness, the sharp scraping of a chair pulling away from a table on a concrete floor. He heard footsteps, and it finally registered that he was no longer in the janitor's closet. He had no memory of being moved to another room—or was it an entirely different building? He wondered how long he'd been out cold from the blow to his head.

As the footsteps drew closer, Patrick instinctively raised his hands for protection. Chains rattled. The slack quickly disappeared, and metal handcuffs pinched his wrists. His hands were in front of his body, rather than the more restrictive behind-the-back method. Still, he had little range of motion with such a short chain tethering him to a pipe of some sort that protruded from the wall, perhaps a radiator.

"*Buenos días.*" The slurred Spanish was like bad Castilian—*Buenoth diath*—which oddly reminded Patrick of his own mother, who'd learned to speak Spanish while living in Spain. He wondered if he would ever see her again.

Patrick felt a swift kick to the belly, followed by more

slurred Spanish, something to the effect that Patrick was a rude *Americano* who couldn't even say "good morning." The voice was definitely the guy who'd brought him to the Hostage Hotel, but the inescapable breath was Bacardí.

"*Buenoth diath*," said Patrick, and another swift kick followed for having mocked his captor. It took a minute, but finally Patrick had enough wind to speak.

"Did you move me someplace new?"

"Can't tell you."

"How long was I asleep?"

"A while."

"How long do I have to wear this blindfold?"

"As long as I say."

As stupid as he was, this guy could handle questions with the skill of a Washington politician. "Just take it off," said Patrick. "I saw your face in the jungle. It's not like I forgot what you look like."

"That's not good for you."

"Dang. And I was on such a lucky streak." He'd said the last sentence in English, and the fact that he didn't get another kick to the stomach told him that the sarcasm was lost on his captor.

A pair of thick fingers fiddled with the knot behind Patrick's ears, and the blindfold slipped away. His eyelids fluttered in the sudden burst of light. The room was dimly lit, and the adjustment from total darkness came slowly. He wasn't chained to a radiator, as had been his guess. He was on the floor, tethered to a metal bed frame. The small room had no other furniture and no window. The walls were filthy, paint peeling away, graffiti everywhere. The concrete floor was a patchwork of stains, several the color of dried blood. The only source of light was a yellow bulb hanging by a wire from the ceiling. His gaze drifted toward his captor and settled on the hideous gang-style tattoo that crept from his shoulder, up his neck, and covered the entire left side of his face. It did a fair job of camouflaging a ghastly scar that started at the corner of his mouth, curled back across the cheek, and then up and over the ear. It looked as though someone had tried to remove the skin from his skull with dull scissors. The name Scarface came to mind, the old Al Pacino film, but that moniker was too cool for this talking turd. Patrick named him "Inkface."

"What are you looking at, El Rubio?"

Patrick averted his eyes, unaware that his staring had been so obvious. "Nothing. Takes a little getting used to the light, that's all."

A noisy commotion came from the hallway right outside the door. It was two men arguing, which made Patrick nervous, as he was certain that Inkface wasn't the only drunk piece of shit in the building who was packing a loaded pistol and a knife big enough to behead a rhinoceros. The tip of the blade was suddenly an inch from Patrick's nose.

"Make a peep, and you die—slowly. Understand?"

Patrick nodded. Inkface withdrew the knife and, as he crossed the room, yanked the string dangling from the ceiling to kill the light. The door opened, and Patrick caught a glimpse of one of the men arguing in the hallway.

It was Javier.

The door closed, but the argument continued—so loud that Patrick could overhear. Javier was looking for Olga. Patrick hadn't seen or heard from her since she'd surprised him in the bathroom of the Hostage Hotel and vowed to get him out.

"I know she's here!" Javier shouted.

"No, no," said Inkface. "Not here."

"You've seen her. Don't deny it!"

"No. Nobody seen Olga."

Inkface was lying, and Patrick didn't know why, and it only escalated the conflict. Someone tried the doorknob, which made Patrick start, but thankfully the door was locked.

"Who are you hiding in there?" Javier shouted.

"A hostage," said Inkface.

"Show me."

"Blow me."

"You're protecting Olga!"

The shouting came to an abrupt halt, but the tension was palpable even on the other side of the door. In his mind's eye, Patrick could see the staredown between the two drunk and overheated men. Finally, Javier spoke, saying something that Patrick couldn't quite hear, but he presumed it was on the order of "This is far from over."

Javier's boots pounded the floor, and as the sound faded at the end of the hallway, one thought consumed Patrick. Javier clearly didn't know her whereabouts. Inkface had lied about not seeing her.

Where the hell was Olga?

Chapter 33

Kate walked to the National Mall and called Noah on a burner phone.

Buying a "burner" had been Noah's final instruction at their meeting in Dumbarton Oaks Park. As any drug dealer would attest, the only thing safer than talking face-to-face was a conversation—no texting—on a prepaid cell purchased for cash with no long-term carrier contract. Prosecutors were of the same opinion.

"Meet me at the Fun House," said Kate.

"Be there in five," said Noah.

The call lasted all of five seconds, and Kate switched off the power. Even though Kate had disabled Wi-Fi and Bluetooth on the burner, she powered it on only when away from home or other locations that could link her to the phone via GPS tracking, and it remained on only when in use.

The Fun House exhibit was inside the National Building Museum, located in the historic Pension Building, one of the most spectacular interior spaces in the city. The soaring Great Hall, adorned with eight colossal Corinthian columns, was home to Grover Cleveland's Inaugural Ball before the building was even finished, and many others followed. Kate entered from Judiciary Square and took a seat on the large bench shaped like the letter F. It was part of a popular temporary exhibit, and seven other benches completed Kate and Noah's code name: FUN HOUSE.

Noah sat on the letter U, facing her.

"I'm feeling manipulated," said Kate.

A five-year-old girl was doing a handstand on the H. A frantic mother rushed over and turned her right-side-up.

"Manipulated by *me*?" asked Noah.

"Yes. You told me Project Naïveté morphed into something bigger than personal data on citizenship. You led me to believe that's the reason Patrick is in danger."

"All that's true."

"But you didn't even begin to tell me what I needed to know going into my meeting with Sandra Levy."

"Exactly what do you think I'm holding back?"

"I want to know: Did she steal secrets from Buck Technologies, or didn't she?"

The little gymnast was back, using her body as a bridge between letters, her hands on the N of the word "fun" and her outstretched toes on the H of "house." Kate wanted to sign up for her planking class.

"We have proof she did," said Noah.

"Then why wasn't she charged and convicted with espionage?"

"The FBI moved in and arrested her too soon. My section chief thinks they would have caught her red-handed if they'd waited. The bottom line is we don't have proof of guilt beyond a reasonable doubt."

"What did she steal—or what do you think she stole?"

"I can't tell you. That technology isn't just proprietary to Buck. It's classified as a matter of national security."

"Throw me a bone, Noah."

"All I can tell you is that the technology Buck developed for Project Naïveté is a dangerous tool in the wrong hands."

"But you're not going to tell me what it is, are you?"

"No. And my advice to you is that you don't ask your father, because if he tells you, he could go to jail. You don't have clearance."

Kate could see only one way around the wall he was hiding behind. "How do I get clearance?"

"Are you asking me to get it for you?"

"Yes. I'm tired of being a pawn in a game of chess where I can't even see the board."

Noah stared back at her, silent. Kate couldn't tell if the accusation had wounded him more on the professional or personal level.

"I'll make a deal with you," he said. "Bring me something. Something big. If you do, I'll see if I can get you clearance to tell you what Sandra stole."

"What do you mean by 'something big'?"

"I want to know who Sandra was stealing for."

"She wouldn't even give me a straight answer when I asked if she accessed company secrets. How am I supposed to find out *who* she was stealing for?"

"Help us find a motive. If we can find her motive, we can figure out who she was working for."

"So, you're asking me to meet with Sandra again?"

"Yes. Obviously, you can't just come right out and ask her, but I want the focus of your visit to be on one thing—why she did it."

I did it for Megan. The words replayed so loudly in Kate's mind that she feared Noah might hear them.

"Can you do that, Kate?" he asked.

One option was to tell Noah that she did it for her

daughter. But Kate was an outsider to Noah's investigation, and putting that information in his hands might only make it harder to find an answer to the question that really mattered: what had her mother meant by "I did it for Kate."

"I'll have to think about it," said Kate.

Chapter 34

Patrick heard noises coming from the party room.

He was blindfolded and handcuffed to a bed frame, but the routine trips down the hallway to the bathroom had allowed Patrick to orient himself. The smell of food wafted from one end of the hallway, opposite the bathroom. Halfway between his room and the bathroom was the "*fiesta* room," as he called it. The guards gathered there at night, drinking and laughing over the fear they instilled in their prisoners.

The door creaked open, footfalls crossed the room, and Patrick felt the barrel of a gun pressing up under his chin.

"Be still," he said, and the voice belonged to Inkface.

Patrick felt a moment of comfort as Inkface unchained his wrist from the bed frame, but it was short lived. With a rope, Inkface bound his wrists behind his back. He did a poor job of it, Patrick noted. Much more slack than usual. Definitely drunk.

"Up," said Inkface.

Patrick obeyed and immediately felt the barrel of the gun against the back of his head. With hands behind his back and a drunken Inkface breathing down his neck, Patrick walked down the hallway, as directed. He figured either this was the end or he was the night's entertainment in the *fiesta* room. He wasn't sure which would be worse.

They stopped halfway down the hallway, and it sounded like a sports bar on the other side of the door—music blasting as men laughed at their own jokes and competed to be the loudest voice in the room. Patrick was beginning to think this was not an "either-or" situation—clearly he was the night's entertainment—but maybe this was the end, too.

Patrick heard the door open. Inkface shoved him, and Patrick fell into the room. The men inside cheered the arrival of the guest hostage of honor. Inkface horse-collared him, pulled him up onto his knees, and yanked off the blindfold.

"Look what you did!" Inkface shouted.

It took a moment for his eyes to adjust. He was

surrounded by drunk men laughing like hyenas. They were sharing rum straight from the bottle, one man taking a swig and then passing it to the next. One of them was on the floor, passed out and completely naked. A mattress was on the floor beside him, no bed frame. A woman, naked from the waist up, was kneeling on the mattress, her face bruised and swollen from slapping—or worse. The look of terror in her eyes cut right through Patrick. Pangs of guilt rose up so powerfully inside that he was almost nauseous.

It was Olga.

Patrick didn't know how Inkface had figured out she was there to help him. Most likely, someone had overheard them talking in the bathroom, where Olga had tried to keep the conversation short, and Patrick had gone on and on, questioning her motives and struggling to get his head around the fact that she was a prostitute. He'd turned a ten-second encounter into a five-minute meeting between co-conspirators. He'd blown her cover. This was Patrick's fault.

"I'm so sorry," he said, though it was impossible to be heard over the loud music and the shouting.

Inkface muted the stereo. The room was far from quiet, and only then did Patrick hear the retching sound of the guy in the corner puking his guts out.

"El Rubio, how do you like what you see?" asked Inkface.

Patrick glared, saying nothing.

Inkface seemed to enjoy his anger. "Ah, see?" he said to his men. "I told you. El Rubio's got a girlfriend!"

The men laughed, and it was bizarre in so many ways to Patrick, this collective scum who reveled in middle-school jokes for murderers.

"We know Olga likes to suck all night, right, boys?"

They howled like cat-calling construction workers on steroids. Inkface leaned closer to Patrick and spoke in a voice that feigned concern. "But poor El Rubio. You want it to stop, no?"

Patrick did. And then he wanted to kill Inkface.

"Only *you* can stop this," said Inkface. "Do you want to stop it?"

Patrick didn't give him the satisfaction of a reply, but Inkface grabbed him by the throat.

"Answer me! Do you want to stop it?"

Patrick glared into those cold black eyes. There was no doubt that Inkface would strangle him for the slightest reason, or for no reason at all—just for the fun of it, if he so desired. Patrick nodded. Inkface released his grip, and Patrick could breathe again.

"Negotiations are not going well," said Inkface. "We

286 · JAMES GRIPPANDO

know you work at a rich American company. They know we have you. But you must be a pain in the ass to your boss. Nobody gives a shit if you come back alive or not."

A *"pain in the ass"* was an understatement, and Buck's refusal to pay only underscored Patrick's fears that his trip to Colombia was designed to deal with an employee seen as dangerous, a plan with a darker corporate purpose that he'd been pondering since Javier threw him off the cliff at the order of *el jefe del jefe.* But he kept his poker face.

"That can't be," said Patrick.

Inkface grabbed Patrick by the jaw and jerked his gaze upward, forcing him to look into his captor's eyes, those two burning embers. "Are you calling me a liar, El Rubio?"

Patrick shook his head.

"I'm giving you one last chance," said Inkface. "I'm going to untie your hands and give you a phone. You get one phone call. You call the one person in this world who will pay a ransom. A *big* ransom. If you do that for me, you live. And your whore of a girlfriend gets the rest of the night off."

Inkface let go of Patrick's jaw, untied his wrists, and offered the phone for Patrick's taking.

"Your move," said Inkface.

Patrick stared at the phone before his eyes. The thought of paying a ransom to this band of thieves, rapists, and murderers was enough to make him sick. Had he been alone in the room, he would never have taken it. But he glanced in Olga's direction, and for the first time in his life he cared less about living than about stopping someone else's suffering.

Patrick's mind was a trap for numbers of any sort, and he recalled the ten important digits from the text messages she'd sent him.

He took the phone from Inkface's hand. And he dialed Kate's number.

Chapter 35

Kate was at a Mexican restaurant, having dinner with a couple of friends from law school, when her cell rang. Her real cell, not her burner. The display read UNKNOWN CALLER, which was reason to ignore it, but with Patrick missing, any phone call could be important. She picked up. The voice on the line was not a woman's. It was a boy's, or rather, the voice of the man she still thought of as a boy.

"Kate, it's Patrick."

"Patrick!" she shouted, and the exclamation drew immediate reaction from her girlfriends.

"Who's Patrick?"

"Can I meet him?"

Kate shushed them and pressed the phone to her ear.

"I need your help," said Patrick.

Trumpets blasted from two tables away. The five-piece mariachi band was starting up again. Kate jumped up from her chair and ran to the restroom, where she could hear.

"Patrick, where are you?"

"Patrick is in deep shit." The reply was in English, but the accent was Hispanic.

"Who is this? Where's Patrick?"

"You've heard enough from Patrick. Now you know he's alive. The question for you is, do you want to keep him alive?"

Kate's conversation with Noah was proving prophetic. The Colombian government's crumbling peace treaty with Marxist guerrillas was no longer an abstraction, the revival of kidnappings for ransom no longer theoretical.

"What do you want?"

"Two million dollars."

Kate hesitated, but only because she didn't know how the game was played. She wondered if she was expected to negotiate.

"It's not negotiable," the man said, as if reading her mind.

"I'll need time," said Kate. She wasn't sure where those words had come from. Probably a movie or a TV drama she'd watched. Kate had no idea what to say or do, no conception of how much time she needed. It was almost incomprehensible, the fact that she was in a restaurant bathroom, talking on her cellphone to a Colombian kidnapper, trying to ransom the boy who used to haggle with her over eating his vegetables, as a Mexican mariachi band played on the other side of the door.

"You have forty-eight hours," the man said. "I will call you. And if you want to see Patrick again, the only acceptable answer is that you have the money. Is that clear?"

"Yes."

"And don't bother calling the Colombian police, the American police, the U.S. embassy, the FBI, or anyone else you might be thinking of calling. That is the quickest and surest way to end up with the dead hostage. This is a private transaction. Understand?"

"Yes," she said, and the line went dead.

Kate fell back against the wall, emotionally spent. Her legs wobbled, no longer able to support her weight. Her cashmere sweater against a tiled wall was like butter on a griddle, and she slid all the way down, slowly, until she was sitting on the floor. Tears were about to flow, but Kate fought them off. Her first instinct was to call Noah, her best law enforcement connection, but the kidnapper's clear warning—"This is a private transaction"—was not to be ignored.

She gathered herself and dialed her father's cell.

Patrick looked on with contempt, still on his knees, as his captors hooted, hollered, and slapped each other on the back as if they were all heroes.

"*Dos millónes!*" Inkface shouted. "Kiss my ass, Javier. El Rubio is ours!"

"Olga, too!" said another.

Patrick's gaze swept the room. They were all smiles and laughter, except for the naked pig on the floor, who was still out cold, and the youngest one in the group— probably still a teenager—who was throwing up in the corner. Another, who looked like the teenager's older brother, was so drunk he couldn't even slap a high-five without staggering to the floor. He was down on one knee and unable to stand, which struck him as hysterically funny. Two others, the least drunk in the group, had left before the phone call to deal with the other hostages. That left just Inkface, a shirtless muscleman, and a third guy with gold teeth to guard Patrick and Olga. They weren't totally incapacitated like the others, but the rum had robbed them of the alertness needed to guard hostages. It seemed they'd forgotten that Patrick's hands were still free, Inkface having untied them for the phone call. Patrick kept them behind his back to keep the illusion alive and discreetly looked in Olga's direction. She cut her eyes toward the chair beside the bed, where the naked blob of blubber on the floor had left his clothes. Patrick spotted the pistol beside the fat man's dirty underwear, and at that moment he and Olga reached their silent agreement to escape.

Inkface stepped toward the mattress.

"You think you're better than us, don't you, Olga?"

She didn't answer.

"Javier made you his high-class whore for his American clients. That doesn't make you high-class. That makes you a whore."

The muscleman laughed and cranked up the stereo. Inkface cracked open another liter of rum.

"Take those pants off, Olga. Let's have a look at the jewels that fetch Javier such a high price."

"Leave her alone," said Patrick.

Inkface chuckled. "Stupid boy. Did you think I meant it when I said your girlfriend could have the night off?"

Patrick couldn't say if this was the end of the line for Olga, but it was debatable whether death would have been worse than what Inkface had in store for her. It was time to act, and Patrick had to seize the first opening.

Inkface raised the bottle to his lips and belted back more rum. As he swallowed his third gulp, Patrick leapt to action. In a blur, he sprang from the floor, grabbed the bottle, and smashed it against the tattooed side of his head. Patrick was acting on instinct, not according to any well-conceived plan, and the neck of the broken bottle became his weapon. He lunged toward Inkface and burrowed the jagged glass into his neck, pushing down hard, twisting and turning the razor-sharp edges, gouging directly at the carotid artery, until his hand was covered in gushing crimson. Inkface fell to the floor, screaming as blood spouted from his neck like a fountain.

Olga dived toward the chair, grabbed the pistol, and started squeezing off one round after another. The muscleman by the stereo went down first, followed by the guy with the gold teeth—definitely a kill shot, the second slug taking out those golden chiclets before exiting through the back of his skull.

"The blood, stop the blood!" shouted Inkface. He was rolling on the floor and grabbing his throat. But the bleeding was unstoppable, and Olga didn't waste a bullet by putting him out of his misery. She let him writhe and, instead, delivered a swift kick to the nuts of the naked pig on the floor, which roused him from his unconscious state just long enough to see her deliver a bullet between his eyes—and told Patrick all he needed to know about what had happened in this room before Fat Boy had passed out.

Inkface groaned, and one last gurgle emerged from the hole in his throat before his body was suddenly still.

Party music was still blaring from the stereo, but Patrick had counted six shots, which was far too many to have gone unnoticed by the other kidnappers down the hall or in the next room. Olga took aim at the sick guy in the corner, but the sicker he got, the more boyish he looked to Patrick.

"Enough," said Patrick, turning Olga's gun away.

She didn't resist, but she went from body to body, rifled through pockets, and grabbed ammunition and cash. She handed the dead muscleman's Glock to Patrick.

"Do you know how to use a gun?" she asked, as she pulled on her shirt.

"My dad used to take me to the shooting range with him. But to be honest, I'm much better at paintball."

"This is a nine millimeter. Semiautomatic. Fifteen rounds in the magazine and one in the pipe. Make your dad proud."

"Got it."

"The only way out of this building is to shoot our way out. Can you handle that?"

"Do I have a choice?"

No answer was required. "Follow me," said Olga, and she started toward the door.

Patrick said a quick prayer, his quickest one ever, and was right on Olga's heels as she flung open the door. She grabbed Patrick's hand, leading with her pistol as they burst into the hallway, greeted by the *pop pop pop* of return gunfire.

"Olga!" Patrick shouted.

She hit the floor, never letting go of his hand, taking Patrick down with her.

Chapter 36

Christian Gamble waited alone at a table in the prison visitation center. It was his first trip to FCP Alderson, and it would be his first communication with Sandra Levy since the day of her arrest. His lawyer would have killed or at least maimed him had she known he was there.

"Inmate's on her way," the corrections officer said.

Gamble thanked him, still finding it bizarre that Sandra was an "inmate." Even stranger was the fact that he was third on the list of Gamble family visitors, after his wife and daughter.

"Was that your Super Puma that touched down on the helipad?" the officer asked in a West Virginia accent.

Gamble had flown up from Virginia on the company

helicopter, a Eurocopter EC225 Super Puma. Kate had called twice during his flight, which he'd ignored, not wanting to have to explain where he was going. It was another trait Kate had inherited from her mother, the innate ability to know exactly when he was stepping out of line.

"Yeah, that was me," said Gamble.

The guard whistled and said, "That's one sexy bird."

"Was that a compliment or a come-on?" asked Sandra, as she emerged from around the corner.

The guard started to explain, but Gamble told him to drop it. He stepped away, leaving the inmate and visitor alone at the table. Sandra crossed one khaki pant leg over the other, interlaced her fingers, and sat with her hands folded in her lap.

"You look good, Christian," she said.

"Is that a compliment or a come-on?" he asked.

Sandra smiled. "Let's not rewrite history. You were the one who had the crush on me. Not the other way around."

"It was a safe crush. I knew nothing would come of it."

"How did you know that?"

"A psychiatrist can lose her license for having a relationship with her patient."

"You weren't technically my patient."

"Look, Sandra. I know you think I led you on. But I

was starving for . . . just for someone to *talk* to. Before we were married, Elizabeth once said to me, 'There's only two kinds of people who can be totally honest with each other, lovers and strangers. Everyone else is just negotiating.'"

"I like that."

"It's especially true when you're CEO of a company like mine. Elizabeth and I used to have that kind of honesty. We lost it when her 'lover' became vodka."

He wasn't looking for sympathy, but he saw a glimmer of it in her eyes.

"But you would never leave her."

"How could I? You said it yourself. Alcoholism is a disease."

"So?"

"If my wife got cancer, would I leave her? If she developed dementia, would I find someone new?"

"That's not the same thing," she said, any sympathy supplanted by pure frustration. "Cancer and dementia don't come in a bottle."

"Either it's a disease or it isn't, Doctor. 'In sickness and in health,'" he added, referencing the traditional vows.

"I suppose some people would find that admirable."

"You don't?"

"It doesn't matter. Not as long as I'm in this place."

"You won't be in prison forever," he said.

"I will if I succumb to the father-daughter tag team you and Kate are playing, trying to get me to admit to something I didn't do."

"That's not what this is about."

"Then why did you come here?" she asked.

His gaze tightened. "I want to hear how you knew about the note."

"The note?"

"The note Elizabeth left me. 'I did it for Kate.'"

Sandra looked away, then back, and Gamble knew her well enough to see that she was going to dodge the question.

"Your wife came to see me," said Sandra. "She was jealous of me."

"No kidding. She made that nine-one-one revenge call just to spite me."

"This was a different kind of jealousy. It had nothing to do with what she thought had happened between us. She was jealous because she'd had a front-row seat for all I'd gone through with you, your company, the FBI, the Justice Department. And now prison. It boggled her mind that I never cracked. I was so strong, and she felt so weak."

"What did you tell her?"

"I told her never to compare your inside to someone else's outside."

The words hung in the air between them. It was one of the reasons he'd found it so easy to talk to Sandra. She was more than just a good listener. She'd helped him simplify things, without all the psychobabble. It reminded him of the way things had once been with Elizabeth.

"You still haven't answered my question," he said. "How did you know what was in the note?"

"Detective Anderson from Fairfax Police visited me."

The answer didn't surprise him. "When?"

"More than a month ago. He wanted to know if you were abusive to Elizabeth and if that was why she killed herself."

"What did you tell him?"

"The truth. I said he couldn't be farther off track with that theory. Then he told me about the note and asked me what I thought it meant."

"What did you tell him?"

"Far less than I could have," she said.

"I'm not sure what that's supposed to mean."

She sat forward and leaned into the table, looking him straight in the eye. "I knew immediately it was *not* a suicide note."

The room suddenly felt ten degrees colder. "You 'knew' because you're a psychiatrist, or—"

"I *knew*."

He studied her expression, staring right back at her. "Are you messing with me?"

"Not in the least."

"You need to give me more."

"Why should I?" she asked, her tone turning sarcastic. "Because I owe you so much for the way you courageously rallied to my defense?"

"There was nothing I could say in your defense. You used my credentials to access classified areas of the Buck campus. The FBI all but caught you walking out the door with top-secret code."

"It's like I told *your* daughter: I did it for *my* daughter."

"I'd love for you to tell me exactly what 'it' is?"

"Not gonna happen."

"Why not?"

"If I told you, it would take all the urgency out of bringing Patrick Battle home, safe and sound."

"Meaning what?"

"Meaning, now that your wife is dead, Patrick is the only person other than me who can tell you what *'it'* is."

She rose and started away from the table. Gamble started after her, but a guard stopped him and said, "Sir, you can't leave the table."

"Sandra!"

She stopped and turned to face him.

"You're definitely messing with me," he said.

Her eyes narrowed. "I'm dead serious, Christian."

He could see that she was. She turned and headed for the inmate exit, nothing more to say.

Chapter 37

Kate's hair whipped in the swirling wind as she watched her father's helicopter touch down in northern Virginia.

She was still angry at him. She'd texted, emailed, and left at least a half dozen voicemail messages, and still it had taken him over an hour to get back to her. His excuse—"I was busy"—rang hollow. To his credit, not a moment was lost after hearing about her call from Patrick and the kidnapper's ransom demand. They were in his limo two minutes after touchdown, heading to one of the most expensive homes in Fairfax County.

Kate's father didn't exactly hide his wealth, but his business partner put his on display like no one else. According to a *Haute Living* feature story Kate had read some years earlier, Jeremy Peel's Tudor-style mansion was on a thirty-acre estate that spanned three towns and had five addresses, putting his annual property tax bill somewhere north of $300,000—all worth it, no doubt, if you and your third wife needed nine bedrooms, twelve bathrooms, two swimming pools, a clay tennis court, a putting green modeled after the famous twelfth hole at Augusta, a collection of bee-hives, and three large paddocks. Throw in a river running through the wooded backyard and a trout-stocked private lake, and life had to be good. Most of the time.

The Peels' butler took Kate and her father to the study. Peel was standing at the credenza between a pair of Tiffany lamps. David Walker, head of BJB Funding, the CIA's venture capital arm, was seated in a tufted leather armchair. With her father seated beside her on the camelback couch, Kate had the entire holy trinity of Buck Technologies in one room to discuss the fate of Patrick Battle.

"We can't pay," said Peel.

Before Kate could reply, her father said exactly what she was thinking.

"Jeremy, we're talking two million dollars. Not two *hundred* million."

"It's not the amount. It's about precedent. If we pay a ransom to these hoodlums, Buck Technologies will be known as an easy mark. Our wives, our children, our employees will be targets all over the world."

"That's why we have bodyguards and kidnap-and-ransom insurance," said Gamble.

Kate was both surprised and encouraged by what she'd just heard. "Buck has insurance for kidnappings?"

"Yes," her father said. "It covers the ransom and pays for a private negotiator. But the policy is void if you tell anyone you have it. So that information does not leave this room."

"Is Patrick covered?" she asked.

"Unfortunately, no," he said. "Obviously I would have told you, if it did."

"Why isn't he covered?" asked Kate.

"We don't buy it for every employee in the company. It's very expensive."

Kate assumed she was covered, as the daughter of the CEO. Before she could decide if there was any need to confirm, the venture capitalist jumped in.

"Jeremy is right," said Walker. "Buck can't pay a ransom. And there's no room for debate on this matter."

"I don't understand," said Kate.

Walker and Peel exchanged glances, and they seemed to come to agreement that the CIA should do the talking. "This company's biggest investor is the CIA. The CIA doesn't pay ransom to terrorists."

"How do you know Patrick was kidnapped by a terrorist organization?" asked Kate.

"The Revolutionary Armed Forces of Colombia has been on the State Department's list of foreign terrorist organizations since the Clinton administration. Technically, the FARC laid down their arms under a peace treaty, but they're still on the list."

"I never said anything about the FARC," said Kate.

"Let's deal in facts, please. Thousands of FARC dissidents have lost faith in the peace process and rearmed. Kidnapping for ransom is their chief source of revenue. The CIA isn't going to contribute to their war chest."

Kate glanced at Peel, then back at Walker, and they were clearly aligned against her father, two against one. She refused to be the irrelevant fourth voice.

"I can't just sit here and have you tell me there's nothing we can do for Patrick because the CIA might end up with egg on its face if Buck pays a ransom. I can't and I won't let that happen."

"It's not debatable," said Walker. "Buck can't pay a ransom in any amount."

"Then I'll pay it," said Gamble.

"Christian, I'm not trying to be difficult," said Walker, even though he was. "But when it comes to the kidnapping of a Buck employee, there's no distinction between Buck paying a ransom to terrorists and its CEO paying it. If this were a kidnapping of someone in your family, it might be different."

"Then I'll give two million dollars to Kate, and she can do whatever she damn well pleases with it. Can the CIA live with that?"

"The CIA is going to have to live with it," said Kate. "Dad, I accept your gift. Thank you."

"My head of security is former FBI. I've already spoken to him. He said I should coordinate with the Hostage Recovery Fusion Cell."

Walker immediately shook his head. "Not a good idea."

"What's the Hostage Recovery Fusion Cell?" asked Kate.

Her father answered. "It specializes in international kidnappings of U.S. citizens. The teams operate out of FBI headquarters, but they pull talent and resources from the Department of Defense and the State Department."

"But the CIA is part of the State Department, and Mr. Walker just said the CIA won't pay a ransom."

"Your daughter is right," said Walker. "The money invested by the CIA in Buck Technologies is taxpayer money. That's the problem here."

"It's *my daughter's* money. I just gave it to her. The

fusion cell will help if Kate wants to use her own money to pay Patrick's ransom. It just won't pay a ransom using taxpayer money." He looked at Walker, and then at his business partner. "Why are the two of you being such pricks about this?"

Kate wanted to side with her father, but she couldn't. "There's another problem, Dad. The kidnapper said not to contact the FBI, the State Department, or anything of the sort. That's the quickest way to get Patrick killed."

Her father paused to consider the wrinkle. "All right. Plenty of families use private security firms and never report it to law enforcement. We can work that out. Unless the CIA has a problem with that, too."

He was clearly fed up with the two obstructionists in the room, as was Kate. There was no response from Peel or Walker—just an icy silence.

Kate's cell rang, and she checked the screen. It was the same number Patrick had used to call her.

"It's them," she said, her voice like a reflex.

"Put it on speaker," said Walker.

It was a split-second decision, but her gut instinct wouldn't let her trust a man who clearly cared more about the CIA than about Patrick.

"Fuck off," she said, as she hurried out of the study. She continued down the grand hallway toward the foyer, answering on the fourth ring.

"Patrick?" she said into the phone, hoping to hear his voice.

"No, but it is the next best thing," his kidnapper said.

Kate opened the front door and stepped out onto the porch. "I have your money."

"That's good news."

The voice on the line sounded different, less of an accent than on the first call. Kate figured he wasn't the first kidnapper to try and disguise his voice. "When do I get Patrick?"

"There's been a new development."

Kate froze, fearing the worst. "You'd better not have hurt him."

"He's fine. But I changed my mind about the two million."

Kate could have kicked herself. She shouldn't have been so quick to tell him that she'd already raised the money. Not a good negotiating tactic.

"You can't keep asking for more money," she said, and then she found the fortitude to talk tough. "I have my limits."

"This deal is not about money anymore," he said.

"Kidnapping is always about money."

"Not this one. Keep your money."

"What do you want?"

"Code."

"What kind of code?"

"Buck Technologies code."

"You're asking for something I can't deliver."

"Don't lie to me, Kate. I know who your father is."

Kate stepped a little farther away from the front door. "You asked for money, and I got it. That was the deal."

"*Was* the deal. The deal's changed. If you want to see Patrick alive, you're going to deliver exactly what I want."

"You can't just say you want code. What code are you talking about?"

"I think you've got enough to chew on for now, Kate. Keep your phone on. Answer when I call."

The voice on the line was definitely different. The deal was different. Too much was changing, and it was making Kate's heart pound. "Who are you?" she asked.

"Silly question."

"You don't sound like the man who called me before. I want to talk to Patrick. I need to know he's there."

"Soon," the man said. "We'll talk very soon."

The line went silent.

Kate stood alone on the porch, still holding her phone, wondering what to tell her father.

Chapter 38

The open Jeep was speeding toward the coast, and Javier smelled seafood. Not the rich aroma of *cazuela de mariscos* or some other tasty Colombian dish, but the pervasive stench of the seafood industry at Colombia's main Pacific port of call.

Buenaventura—literally, "good fortune"—has evolved into a twenty-first-century hub of trade and commerce, blessed by proximity to Chile and Mexico and direct access to trade routes with the Asian markets. It hadn't always lived up to its name. Javier was a product of the old port of Buenaventura, one of the deadliest places in Colombia, where "good fortune" meant living to see another day in the never-ending cocaine wars for control of the port.

"Stop here," said Javier.

His driver slammed on the brakes, overreacting to the command, which nearly sent Javier flying through the windshield.

"*Comemierda*," Javier said, as he slapped the "dumbass" with the back of his hand. "Don't you know how to drive?"

"Not really," he said, cowering.

Javier reminded himself that he was just a kid, which was probably the reason Patrick Battle had let him live after killing the others. Javier had found the kid cowering in the corner, clutching the cellphone he'd used to call Javier—the same cell Javier had then used to call Kate.

"She knows it was a different caller this time," said Javier, as he stuffed Inkface's cellphone into his pocket. "She said my voice sounded different."

"You don't sound at all like my brother," he said, meaning the dead negotiator.

Javier pulled his pistol from his belt and pressed the business end of the barrel to the kid's temple. "You told me everything that was said, right?"

"Yes! Everything!"

"You didn't leave anything out?"

"No!" he said, his voice quaking. "Manuel let the hostage talk first, and then he got on the line. He said two million, no police. I told you every word I heard."

"And what about Olga?"

"What about her?"

"You didn't join in the fun with the other slobs?"

"No! I got sick on rum."

Javier pressed the barrel of the pistol harder against his head. "So you *would have*, if you could have."

"No. I swear! I know Olga is yours. I would never disrespect you like that."

The teen closed his eyes tightly, bracing for execution Buenaventura style. Javier considered squeezing the trigger, and he definitely would have, had he thought the boy was lying about not defiling Olga, his prize possession. Mercy would have been in order had he called Javier and ratted out his fellow kidnappers at the Hostage Hotel *before* they'd all ended up dead on the floor. But he'd done right by calling soon enough for Javier to reach out to his contacts at the port. *Anyone* seeking to escape Buenaventura would head to the port, and it had taken all of ten minutes for a call to come in with the first sighting of the six-foot-plus American with the mop of blond hair on his head and the gorgeous brunette at his side.

"Please, don't kill me," the teen said, sniveling.

Javier had heard many such pleas. But the smell in the air, the stench of the port, was triggering memories of his own. It had happened at a place like this one, alongside a chain-link fence topped with razor wire, where towering cranes worked around the clock to unload mountains of metal containers from Chinese freighters loaded with electronics and other goods. Javier and his older brother, two of the FARC's newest foot soldiers, had gone there to collect payment for a shipment of California-bound cocaine. The delivery wasn't up to the buyer's standards, an infraction for which the sentence was death. His brother got a bullet to the forehead that had literally blown off the top of his skull. For some reason, the buyer had decided to let Javier live.

Javier put the pistol away. "Congratulations. You, too, are now a survivor of Buenaventura."

The kid could breathe again, but he seemed unable to move, frozen by a trauma-filled night.

"Go!" shouted Javier.

The teen snapped into action, hopped out of the Jeep, and was off like a sprinter out of the blocks.

Javier dialed his cell and called the boss—*el jefe del jefe*—for an update.

"I'm on them," he said into his phone. "They boarded a freighter about half an hour ago. MV *Ali Bey*. Panamanian flag."

The reply was all business. "That should make your work easy. How did the call go?"

"She wants to know what code we want."

"The kid can tell you. If you make him."

"Just to be clear. The hit is off?"

"No. It's postponed. Until I get the code I paid for."

"Consider it done."

Javier hung up, checked his ammunition, and climbed out of the Jeep. He didn't know the details of the code or the transaction, but he was all too familiar with the consequences of delivering less than promised.

He took a long look down the dimly lit street. The kid was still running, guard dogs barking from the other side of the long chain-link fence as he flew past them. Javier had no regrets about letting him go. But it would be his last show of mercy.

He tucked his pistol away and started walking toward the berth for the MV *Ali Bey*.

Chapter 39

For the first time since their dating days, Kate found herself at Noah's front door on a Saturday night. He probably guessed she wasn't there to see if he wanted to walk down to DuPont Circle and catch a movie.

"Can I come in?" she asked.

He was standing in the open doorway and glanced back over his shoulder. "I actually have company."

If it weren't clear enough what "company" meant, she came up from behind and put her arms around him. "Oh, is our pizza here already?"

"We didn't order pizza," said Noah.

Kate rolled her eyes. For such a smart man, Noah could be so dumb sometimes.

"I got a call from Colombia," she said, cutting to the chase. "It's not good."

Noah unwrapped himself from his date and grabbed his coat from the hook on the wall. Kate started slowly down the sidewalk, giving Noah a moment to explain the situation to Pizza Girl. She was halfway to the corner when he caught up.

"Patrick's been kidnapped," she said.

Noah stopped and reached for his cellphone. "I can help. The Hostage Recovery Fusion Cell operates twenty-four/seven. They are literally five blocks from here."

"No," she said, and she told him why.

"Kidnappers always say no law enforcement," said Noah. "I think you're making a mistake."

"It's not your decision," said Kate.

"Kate, listen to me. Not a day goes by without an American being kidnapped somewhere in the world. The fusion center and its cell are the best of the best. They know more than any private security firm. Use their expertise."

"Put your phone away. That's not what I came here for."

Noah tucked it into his coat pocket. He seemed to grasp quickly that this was going to be no small request. "Okay. Talk to me."

"I want clearance to know everything there is to know about the code you think Sandra Levy stole from Buck Technologies."

"I promised you that I'd work on that, and you promised to help us figure out who Sandra Levy was working for. That's the arrangement."

"I need clearance now."

"That wasn't our deal."

"Patrick's kidnappers changed the deal on me, so I'm changing ours."

Noah glanced toward the busy traffic circle down the street, then back at her. "I understand Patrick's kidnapping changes everything for you. But I can't just go back to Justice and say the kid Kate used to baby-sit got kidnapped, so we need to give her clearance on Project Naïveté. Work with me. What's changed?"

Kate wanted *someone* to trust, and she'd once trusted Noah more than anyone. Still, the man standing in the glow of the streetlamp, hands in his pockets, ready to call the Hostage Recovery Fusion Cell, wasn't the old Noah. She was negotiating with an assistant U.S. attorney whose loyalty was to the Department of Justice and whose new girlfriend was waiting for him back at the apartment that, for all practical purposes, Kate had once treated as her own.

She took the indirect approach. "Let me ask you something—hypothetically. What if Patrick's kidnappers wanted something other than money?"

"It's pretty common to demand ransom payments in Bitcoin. Is that what you mean?"

"No. Let's say they don't want dollars, euros, crypto-currency, gold, frankincense, myrrh, doubloons—nothing like that. What if they want—"

She stopped herself. Noah waited. Kate didn't want to say too much, but she couldn't effectively negoti-ate with Patrick's kidnappers without first negotiating with Noah.

"If they wanted *what?*" asked Noah.

"Code," she said.

"You mean code from Buck Technologies."

"Yes. Hypothetically."

Noah seemed to catch his breath. "You need to be very careful here, Kate."

"I'm trying to be careful."

"It doesn't matter how good your intentions are. Even if you think it's the only way to save Patrick's life, you can't just hand over code from Buck Technologies."

"I didn't say I was handing over anything."

"I hope you're not even thinking about it, hypothet-ically or otherwise. If you give Patrick's kidnappers code that isn't classified, that's corporate espionage. One to five years. If you deliver code that *is* classified, that's ten years. And it gets worse, depending on who the kidnappers are. If they're a terrorist organization, tack on violations of the Patriot Act. If they're a foreign government, you could be talking treason—the death penalty."

"Wait. Who said anything about a foreign government?"

He didn't respond, but Kate wasn't about to let it go.

"I've been thinking a lot about this, Noah, so don't go silent on me. You and the whole Department of Justice are so sure Sandra Levy stole code from Buck Technologies. But you said it yourself: the FBI moved in and arrested her too soon for prosecutors to have the evidence they needed to prove at trial that she actually stole anything. Right?"

He seemed reluctant to answer, not because he hadn't told her, but perhaps because he regretted having told her too much.

"*Right*, Noah?"

"Yes. That's right."

"What if she didn't actually steal anything? Isn't it at least possible that Patrick's kidnappers are demanding Buck code as ransom in order to get their hands on the very thing they *didn't* get from Sandra Levy?"

Noah paused, and even in the dim glow of residential streetlights at night, Kate could see that her words had him thinking.

"It would depend on what code they're asking for," he said.

"They haven't said. But that'll change soon. If I'm going to negotiate for code, I need to know what code I'm talking about. I need clearance."

"Even if you get clearance, you're not going to be able to hand over classified code in order to save Patrick."

"I'm not asking for permission to hand it over. I know I'm in an impossible situation here. But I need the ability to talk a good bluff. And I need you to help me."

Noah took a deep breath, but he seemed to be coming around a little, perhaps enough to at least try and help her. "This is a really big request, Kate."

"I know."

"No, I mean this is *really* big."

"I understand. But if you come through for me, I'll bring you a pizza. I'll bet what's-her-name doesn't even know you actually *like* anchovies."

He forced a little smile, but it didn't hide the nervousness. "I'll see what I can do."

Chapter 40

In a port lined with countless ocean freighters, some of them longer than soccer fields, the MV *Ali Bey* was a 100,000-ton rust bucket. And it appeared to be deserted.

Cargo of every description floats into Buenaventura from China and elsewhere, much of it in twenty- and forty-foot containers stacked like giant Lego blocks, eight to ten units high, on the main deck. Patrick guessed the MV *Ali Bey* carried thousands of units when fully loaded. From the looks of things, however, this old ship hadn't carried anything in ages. Vessels at nearby berths showed signs of life—lights on inside the bridge, glowing orange dots from the lit cigarettes of bored crew members on deck, and the white-hot spark and flare of welders doing repair work late into the night. The MV *Ali Bey* was completely dark, no sign of a crew. Weeds had sprouted from crevices on the main deck, which was littered with debris. Patrick and Olga minded their step in the glow of a full moon, as they walked along the ship's portside rail.

"It's like a ghost ship," said Olga.

Their escape plan—hopping a freighter at the port—had been hatched on the run from the Hostage Hotel. Olga had put the odds at fifty-fifty that going to the police would put them in the hands of a corrupt cop friendly to the kidnappers. They had no passports or identification, so the airport was no option. All they had was the cash Olga had plied from the dead men's pockets, which could buy them a spot on a freighter out of Colombia. The destination didn't matter.

A breeze was blowing across the harbor, and a slight shift in direction brought a hint of smoke from the ship's stern. Patrick and Olga both noticed it.

"Smells like charcoal," he said.

It was coming from the other side of the navigational bridge. In a seafaring phase of his virtual building career, Patrick had designed the world's largest cargo ship, big enough to haul the equivalent of a freight train forty-four miles long, so he recognized the multistory structure rising from the main deck as crew accommodations. They started cautiously in that direction.

"Maybe we should hop a different freighter," said Olga.

Patrick looked around the harbor. The nearest alternatives were in various states of loading or unloading. Massive cargo cranes were designed to move one container unit at a time. It might be days before the nearest ship was ready to leave port.

"This could be a good place to hide until we figure things out," said Patrick. "If we're alone."

Olga pulled the pistol from inside her belt. "Yeah. If."

They continued toward the stern and climbed a set of stairs to the poop deck, where they discovered that the ship was not quite as dark or deserted as first thought. A long yellow extension cord ran from somewhere inside the superstructure to a mechanic's trouble light that hung from the poop deck's covering. Across the deck, at the starboard-side rail, a man was warming his hands over a smoldering can of burning charcoal. Olga called to him in Spanish, asking if it was okay to approach. Olga translated his response for Patrick.

"He says we can come if we have his money."

"Tell him we might be able to get it for him, if he can help us."

She did, he waved them forward, and they started toward him, taking cautious steps.

"This guy could be expecting a suitcase full of

hundred-dollar bills," Olga said quietly, so only Patrick could hear. "How are we going to pay him his money?"

"I'll figure that out," he said, thinking of Kate. "As long as he can get us out of here."

The smell of burning charcoal intensified as they approached. They were ten feet away when the man told them to stop. Even Patrick could tell that Spanish wasn't his first language, but he was able to make himself understood to Olga.

"He says he's from Indonesia," she said, translating. "He's not leaving the ship until he's paid the wages he's owed. Fourteen months' worth."

"Ask him why he wasn't paid."

She did, and she translated. "The ship is old, and the company decided it's not worth fixing. They scrapped it and left it here. None of the crew was paid. The others left, but he has nowhere to go without his money."

"Tell him we'll pay him his wages and more if we can use his cellphone."

She did, and the man laughed through his reply.

"He doesn't have a cellphone," said Olga. "He says all he has is rice. That's it. Nine bags of rice left to eat. He's been eating rice for the last three months."

The man stepped away from the smoldering can, opened the door to the nearest cabin, and invited them inside to see for themselves. Patrick didn't need the proof of rice, but the man apparently had another deal in mind.

"No cellphone," he said, as he started toward the counter. "Radio."

Patrick's hopes soared, thinking he meant a ham radio. He didn't. He switched on a portable AM/FM radio resting on the countertop. Salsa music filled the cabin.

"*Baile, jóvenes amantes,*" the man said with a smile.

"He wants the young lovers to dance," said Olga.

"Tell him we'll dance all the way to the United States, if we can find a way out of this place."

Olga stepped closer. "Dance with me."

Patrick thought she was joking, but the look in her eyes was serious.

"I don't feel like dancing."

"No better reason to dance."

He realized it was her way of saying that they'd had enough stress for one night, that his constant intensity wasn't helping, and that it wouldn't kill them to relax for thirty seconds.

"Maybe later," he said.

"Come on. It's been so long since I danced *with* someone."

She was immediately embarrassed by her own words,

and Patrick didn't let on that he'd caught her implicit juxtaposition of dancing *for* someone—some creep who found pleasure in forcing a sex-trafficking victim to do much worse than dance against her will. If he could make her smile for a minute, if only by tripping over his own feet for her amusement, it was the least Patrick could do for this Shakespeare-quoting enigma from the dark side who'd risked her life to save him and asked for nothing in return—so far, at least.

"All right. I'll try my best."

She started to move her hips and took his hand. "I will teach you to dance like a Colombian."

She pressed the palm of her right hand against the palm of his left, then took his other hand and placed it on her hip. Patrick felt the warmth of her skin through her jeans, but he was equally taken by the sheer mechanics of movement, all between her thighs and narrow waist.

"How do you do that without even moving your feet?"

"Listen for the counter rhythm."

"What's a counter rhythm?"

"You'd be pathetic if you weren't so cute. Follow my lead."

She moved left, Patrick went the other way. He apologized, and they started again. The old man turned up the music on the radio, and this time Olga counted the steps for him aloud.

"You got it," she said, as she pressed his hand more firmly into her hip, as if to help him feel the music.

The old man started singing. They were face-to-face, hips swinging, as Olga led him back and forth across the small cabin. Patrick crushed her foot only once, but she smiled and kept counting. The old man was clapping to the music, which replaced Olga's counting, and soon Patrick was leading.

"You're dancing," she said.

"Like a Colombian?"

"Hmmm. Close enough."

The music stopped. The old man grabbed the radio and shook it, trying to make it work again. It was dead, but Patrick and Olga remained in their dance pose, choosing not to pull apart, her right hand in his left. Slowly, her left hand slid from his hip, gently, all the way up to his shoulder blade. Her shirt had a long opening in back that followed her spine, and his fingers traveled from the gentle curve of her hip to the small of her back. Their bodies drew closer, so close that the space between them was almost gone. Patrick tingled with the imagined feeling of her breasts pressed against him. Her breathing caressed his neck as she looked up at him with those dark brown eyes. His hand slipped inside the opening of her shirt, and he duplicated the light swirling motion across her back, skin so warm and smooth. So smooth. Until it wasn't. The tips of his fingers found an inch-long ridge, then another, and another. Her body stiffened in his arms.

"Scars," she said.

"From what?"

"Not important."

Patrick didn't pursue it, but it saddened him to know that this fallen angel in his arms lived in a world where getting stabbed in the back, literally, was an occupational hazard.

"They're nothing," she whispered.

The cabin door suddenly burst open. Olga dove to the floor and took Patrick with her. The old man shouted, but he was quickly silenced by a single gunshot. It resounded like cannon fire, sandwiched between the metal floor and ceiling.

"Don't move!" the gunman shouted, and Patrick knew that voice.

Javier had found them.

Patrick and Olga lay side-by-side on the floor. Until then, Patrick hadn't noticed that the old ship was listing, but it was evident from the port-to-starboard flow of blood on the floor from the crewman's mortal chest wound.

Javier stood over his hostages, pointing his gun first at Olga and then at Patrick.

"Nice move, El Rubio. You boarded the one ship in the harbor that isn't going anywhere."

Chapter 41

It was a cloudy Sunday morning in the District, and Kate reached the theater on two hours of sleep and three cups of coffee. She had hardly thought about her play since the blow-up with Sean the Snake. But Irving Bass was still committed to a January opening, and Kate couldn't miss the first table reading, even if it was the last thing she felt like doing. If nothing else, she needed to confront Irving about shopping her script.

"Places, please," said Sean, as he and Bass entered.

Kate and three actors took seats at the round table in the center of the stage, each with a printed copy of Kate's script. To Kate's right were two men in their sixties, one cast in the lead role as Watson and the other as his secretary. The actor across the table from Kate was about her age, a Brit who, to Kate's continued amazement, played

Thomas J. Watson, Jr., with absolutely no British accent. Bass and his assistant joined them at the table, no chitchat.

"Act three, scene one," said Bass.

It was the newest material, and it was Kate's favorite scene in the play. The setting was Watson's corner office at IBM headquarters on Madison Avenue. Watson was with his son, some years before Tom Watson, Jr., would succeed his father as CEO. It was October 1946, at the conclusion of the world's first war crimes trials.

Even though it was just a table reading, the actors brought it to life. Kate was so exhausted that it unfolded like a dream for her. She could hear and see it the way she'd imagined it, as Watson's most trusted secretary— all of his secretaries were men—burst into the office to deliver the news.

"Verdicts are in at Nuremberg," said Burns.

"And?" asked Watson.

"I see a very busy month in the hangman's future. Twelve death sentences."

"They all deserve it," said Tom Junior.

"What about Hjalmar Schacht?"

"There were just three acquittals. Schacht was one of them. Which is remarkable, considering that his successor as head of the Reichsbank got life in prison."

Watson glanced at the wall, where his Merit Cross—draped around his neck by Hjalmar Schacht in Berlin—used to hang.

"Mr. Schacht is one very lucky man."

"His luck doesn't make what you did any less stupid," said Tom Junior.

"Burns, would you excuse us for a moment?" asked Watson, and his secretary exited quietly. The father glowered at his son. "Don't you *ever* speak that way to me in front of Burns."

"Did you expect me to just sit there and listen to you wax on about Schacht's luck, as if he'd just won the pot at church bingo? The man who draped Hitler's medal around your neck stood trial at Nuremberg for conspiracy to commit war crimes and crimes against humanity."

"And he was acquitted."

"Imagine that: the businessman gets off, scot-free. Just as *you* did when the Justice Department indicted you for criminal violations of the antitrust laws."

"Don't you dare compare me to a Nazi!"

"You should have never accepted the award!"

"I accepted it only because it was given in recognition of my efforts for world peace through world trade."

"Yeah? How did that peace thing work out?"

Tom went to the door and called to his father's secretary, asking for Sunday's edition of the *Times*, missing not a beat in the showdown with his father.

"You should be glad I speak up," Tom continued. "Don't you realize people laugh at you for having the longest entry in the history of *Who's Who in America*? Sixteen and a half inches! Seriously: it's a record. What self-respecting businessman goes on and on about himself for three columns of fine print in *Who's Who*? I thought Burns was pulling my leg when he told me you belonged to the Honorable Order of Kentucky Colonels. But then I checked the *Who's Who* and, lo and behold, there it was. You're so full of yourself, you couldn't even turn down an award from Adolf Hitler!"

"I gave the medal back."

"Only after the Brits were literally running for their lives at Dunkirk. Why you kept that thing so long I'll never understand."

"You don't even *try* to understand."

"*No one* understands it!"

Burns entered with the newspaper, as requested, and Tom flipped angrily through the pages.

"What are you doing?" asked Watson.

"Showing you how blind you were," he said, as he

laid the paper flat on Watson's desktop before him. "Here. Yesterday's *Times* summarized the key evidence against each of the Nuremberg defendants."

"I know, I read it."

Tom read aloud, making his point. "'Hjalmar Schacht. Reich minister of Economics and president of the German Reichsbank. May 1937: attended secret "War Economy" games at Godesberg. July 8, 1937: issued written report to General Werner von Blomberg, commander in chief of the German Armed Forces, laying out "measures for the preparation of the conduct of war."'"

He stopped reading, looking his father in the eye. "When did Schacht give you Hitler's medal for world peace?"

Watson didn't answer.

"*When*, Father?"

"At that time, how was I to know what was coming?"

"What *day* was the award?"

Watson was silent, but his secretary replied, as if it were a day he would never forget. "July third, 1937."

Tom slapped the desktop. "Five days," he said in quiet but angry disbelief. And then his voice erupted. "*Five days* before Schacht's written report to the commander in chief of the German Armed Forces, you let him double-kiss your face and decorate you with the Nazi Merit Cross."

"You're linking events that have no connection. No fair-minded person is going to tie this together the way you are."

"Most fair-minded people don't work for you, sing silly songs in your honor every morning, and worship the ground you walk on."

"You have no idea what it means to be a CEO, do you, son?"

"Stop it! Stop that tap dance right now! You are not going to make this about *me*!"

"Do you think it just happened by accident that IBM never lost a single company to the Nazis? Entire countries fell. German custodians took over our factories. Still, hardly any IBM employees lost their jobs overseas. And now that the war is over, there's a good chance our lawyers can unfreeze profits tied up in Nazi bank accounts. And you know who benefits the most from this? My shareholders. Many of whom are Jewish."

"So, it's *their* fault? Your shareholders?"

"It's not about *fault*. It's *business*. And sometimes business is a matter of survival. When you finally come to terms with that basic fact, you'll be ready to step up and lead my company. Because then you'll know there's a world of difference between a CEO who is trying to protect the interests of American shareholders in a foreign country that has lost its bloody mind, and a traitor to his own country who wants to help the Nazis."

Tom turned sharply and headed for the door.

"Tom!"

He stopped, but his back remained to his father.

Watson checked his anger and spoke in an even tone. "You know something, son? Charles Lindbergh *never* returned his Merit Cross. Not even after we entered the war."

Tom turned slowly, facing him, and breathed out his response.

"Charles Lindbergh is not my father."

"Hold, please!" shouted Sean.

His words stirred Kate from her creative zone, and then she held her breath. Whenever a director's assistant shouted "hold, please!" at a table reading, it meant the director had changes.

"Cut page thirty-four, line one, to page forty-one, line eight," said Bass.

The actors marked their scripts in red ink. Kate checked her copy to see how much damage Bass had done, and her blood was about to boil. "That's the entire scene we just read."

"It's out," said Bass.

"That's a critical scene. Clearly, Tom Junior loves his father, but Watson measures his worth not by the love of his son, but by how he compares in the public arena to people like Charles Lindbergh."

"That's not the story we're telling," said Bass.

"That *is* the story."

"No, the story is about capitalism and exploitation of personal information."

"It's about the people who have to live with the decisions they make and how they justify their actions."

Bass groaned. "Listen, Katie."

"Kate."

"Fine. Kate. I don't know what kind of screwed-up, love-hate relationship you have with your father, and I don't care. Maybe it's therapeutic for you to sit at your computer late at night and write scenes about Tom Junior confronting his father the way you wish you could confront yours. But I'm a director, not a psychiatrist, and this shit is not finding its way into my play."

"*Your* play? *I'm* the playwright."

Sean raised his index finger, interjecting. "Actually, I've been meaning to raise this with Irving. The billing credit for the play should be a single line: 'Developed and directed by Irving Bass.'"

"No," she said. "It's a play *by Kate Gamble.*"

"You'll receive an appropriate acknowledgment as an independent contractor for a work made for hire."

Any law student who'd taken a course on copyright law understood that a "work made for hire" was the lowest form of credit. Worse, it gave the writer no ownership rights. The sneaky assistant who was shopping her script to Hollywood behind her back was now claiming ownership of the copyright.

"Irving, are you in agreement with Sean?"

Irving made a face. "Sean, what the hell are you talking about? Kate never agreed to give up her copyright."

"She has to give them up, or she'll kill the film deal!" said Sean.

Irving glared with the intensity of burning lasers. "Have you been shopping the film rights without telling me?"

Sean stood silent, but Kate answered for him. "He has an agent."

Irving pointed at the door, his hand shaking. "Get out."

"You can't fire me," said Sean. "You can barely stand up, let alone direct a play."

"Get out!" he shouted, his voice booming, but he

was suddenly pale. The grimace on his face twisted into the same gruesome expression Kate had seen that morning at Swing's Coffee Roasters. Just as he'd done there, Bass closed his eyes, placed his palms flat on the table, and drew a deep breath.

Then he passed out and fell to the floor.

"Irving!" one of the actors shouted.

Bass lay in a heap on the floor, motionless. Sean hurried to him, knelt at his side, and checked his vitals.

"He's not breathing! Now look what you did, Kate!" Sean yelled.

Kate grabbed her phone and dialed 911.

Chapter 42

Kate caught a ride to the hospital with "Watson" behind the wheel. Fueled by fear of the show closing before it opened, he tailed the speeding ambulance all the way to the emergency room entrance. Kate and the entire cast watched from the sidewalk as paramedics whisked the gurney toward the ER. It was a relief to see that Bass was fully conscious. More than just conscious. He was practically himself again.

"Get lost!" he said, wagging his finger, his silver hair flowing in the rush of wind as the pneumatic entrance doors parted. "I don't want any of you here! All I want—"

"Is a script," said Kate, finishing for him.

Watson offered her a ride home, but she caught a ride with one of the other cast members who was headed her way—toward Jeremy Peel's country estate. Kate phoned ahead and told him it was imperative that they speak in person. One of Peel's staff met her at the gate in an all-terrain vehicle. They drove along the creek and then over a set of rolling hills to the grassy meadow, where they found Peel at the skeet-shooting range.

"Pull!"

A pair of clay pigeons took to the air simultaneously, one from each tower. Two quick shots followed, obliterating each target in rapid succession.

"Well done, sir," the driver said. He motored away, leaving Kate alone with Peel and whoever was inside the towers launching the clay pigeons.

Peel switched on the safety and opened his break-action shotgun, releasing the spent cartridges. He left the chamber open, muzzle pointed at the ground, as he walked toward Kate.

"Sorry to interrupt your shoot, Mr. Peel."

"Please, I think it's time you started to call me Jeremy."

That wasn't going to be easy. It was like shaking the "Baby Patrick" habit. "All right, Jeremy."

"Since this was too important for you to discuss on the phone, I'm guessing it has to do with the kidnapping."

"I'll get to that. First I wanted to ask you about Sandra Levy."

He fished a couple of fresh cartridges from his ammunition pouch. "Not my favorite subject. What do you want to know?"

It was a perfect setup for the question she'd come to see him answer, face-to-face, so she could gauge his reaction—the question that had been burning since her visit to FCP Alderson.

"Why do you think Sandra did it?"

Peel's gaze drifted off toward the woods, and then he looked back at Kate. "The only way to know *why* she did it is to pinpoint exactly *when* she made the decision to do it."

Kate had hoped her question would lead to a discussion of what "it" was—what Sandra meant by her remark that she did "it" for her daughter. But Peel's response had thrown her.

"I'm not sure I follow you," said Kate.

"It's simple. Did Sandra decide to steal code and then sleep with your father toward that end? Or did she sleep with your father, see an opportunity, and then decide to steal code?"

"And what if the premise baked into your questions is false?"

"You're a good daughter, Kate. But you're kidding

yourself if you think your father wasn't sleeping with Sandra Levy."

"How can you be so sure?"

His expression turned very serious. "Your mother told me."

The predictable response would have been that her mother was an alcoholic and said a lot of things that weren't true. But she hadn't journeyed all the way out to this country estate to replow old ground. "Is it something *she* told *you*? Or that *you* told *her*?"

"Are you asking if I called your mother and ratted out your father?"

"'Ratted him out' isn't exactly what I was suggesting. I was thinking more along the lines of putting ideas in my mother's head."

"The idea was already firmly in your mother's head when she called me."

"And you confirmed her worst fears, without any proof."

"You make it sound like I went out of my way to hurt your old man. Why would I do that?"

A gust of wind whipped between the towers, and Kate felt the chill. "The same reason you overruled my father on paying Patrick Battle's ransom."

"Buck shouldn't pay a ransom. The reasons I gave are all valid."

"They sounded like BS to me."

"Fortunately, you don't run the company."

"And neither does my father. Wasn't that the point you and Mr. Walker were making when you put on the dog and pony show for me?"

"Excuse me?"

Kate had never spoken this way to her father's business partner, and she wasn't sure what was driving it. Maybe it was Irving Bass's crack about her screwed-up relationship with her father—her need to prove, if only to herself, that it was more love than hate.

"Buck could have found a way to pay Patrick's ransom. The reason you said no has nothing to do with the CIA. The point was to humiliate my father in front of his daughter, so I could see with my own eyes that Jeremy Peel has the power to outvote him, even when he's right. Even when it's a matter of life and death."

"Interesting," he said, as he loaded two more shells in the chambers. "And I was under the impression that Sandra Levy was the only quack psychiatrist who had your father's back."

"It doesn't take a psychiatrist to see how jealous you are of him."

"Now you're way out of line, young lady."

She probably was, but that didn't stop her. "It was

always my father who got the glory, the awards, the cover of *Time* magazine."

"None of those things were important to me."

"I believe you. I truly do. The issue isn't that you never got those things. What bothers you is the fact that *my father* did."

"And what bothers your father is that he reports to me. The CEO is boss, but the chairman of the board is the boss of the boss."

"Dad told me what happened after your press conference. How you're angling to be both chairman and CEO."

"I never wanted his job. But for the good of the company, I would take the position."

"*Take*," she said, seizing on it. "That's the key word. For a man like you, who literally has everything he wants, there comes a point in life when there's no joy in getting more stuff. Unless you can take it from someone else."

He closed the break on the loaded shotgun, ready for action. "Whatever 'it' means."

"Could be just about anything. Money. Power. Life, liberty, the pursuit of happiness. Whatever it hurts the other guy most to lose. After all, if there's no loser, what's the point?"

He raised his shotgun, aimed, and looked ready to yell "pull."

"Live!" he shouted.

Two live doves flew from opposite towers. Peel waited for them to cross in the middle and brought them both down with a single blast of birdshot. He broke open his shotgun and looked at Kate.

"Exactly," he said, shooting a quick glance toward the dead birds on the ground. "What's the point?"

The house was too far away for Kate to walk, but she suddenly couldn't stand being in the same zip code as him. She held her ground for a minute longer, glowering.

"Let me ask you, Mr. Peel. Did it make you feel like a bigger winner when you lied and told my mother her husband was cheating on her? Or when you heard my mother killed herself?"

Peel hand-signaled to the driver of the all-terrain vehicle, who started motoring toward them.

"I think it's time this conversation ended," he said.

"It was long overdue," Kate said, as she started walking toward the dirt road.

Chapter 43

A hint of dawn colored the dark cabin's only porthole. Patrick and Olga were alone, seated back-
to-back on the floor, their wrists behind their waists
and bound to the upright metal pole between them. It
had been two hours since they'd seen Javier, when he'd
dragged the crewman's body out to the poop deck and
pitched it over the ship's rail. Patrick wondered how
many bodies the harbor at Buenaventura had swallowed. He wondered if his or Olga's would be next.

"Olga, you awake?" he whispered.

She didn't answer. Dozing off under these conditions
was the very definition of exhaustion. Patrick pressed
his elbows into her back, nudging her awake.

"Olga, I think I hear footsteps."

They listened. The door was closed, and all was

quiet, save for a faint shuffling in the distance. It sounded like footfalls on the deck.

"Could be Javier coming back," said Olga.

"Could be someone who saw the body go over the rail," said Patrick.

It was reason for hope. Olga screamed for help. Patrick stomped his feet, as if running in place from a sitting position. The cabin door opened.

"I'm *ba-ack*," said Javier.

They fell silent. How foolish it had been to think rescue was possible. The crewman had waited months for his wages, and no one cared what might become of him.

"You two look thirsty," said Javier. He placed his knapsack on the counter, removed two bottles of water, and opened one.

"Something to drink, El Rubio?"

"No," said Patrick.

"Don't be stupid," said Olga. "You need water."

She was right, and with Javier holding the bottle to his lips, Patrick drank almost half a liter. Then Javier went to Olga.

"How about you?" he said, as he held the bottle for her. "Or do you need something stronger to wash last night's taste out of your mouth?"

Olga ignored him and drank, but Patrick wanted to

grab that bottle and smash it against Javier's skull, the way he'd done to Inkface.

Javier stepped away and placed the near-empty bottle on the counter. "I'm guessing you could use a bathroom break. But first, let me explain how you get out of here alive. Sound good?"

Patrick didn't answer.

"Yes," said Olga.

Javier smiled insincerely. "Smart girl, Olga. El Rubio, you have some learning to do. If I ask a question, I expect an answer. If you don't answer, that shows disrespect. If you disrespect me, there are serious consequences."

He punctuated the sentence with a boot to Patrick's belly, which left him gasping for air.

"Do we understand each other?"

Patrick managed to find enough breath to say, "Yes."

"Good. Now, back to how you get out alive. I spoke to your friend Kate Gamble. I know exactly who she is. Or, should I say, I know who her father is. I told her this is no longer about money. There's a new ransom demand."

Patrick had a sick feeling as to where this monologue was likely heading.

"I give you one guess, El Rubio. What's the new ransom?"

He didn't answer. Javier delivered another swift kick, but this time it was to Olga's ribs.

"Consequences," said Javier. "Disrespect always has consequences. One more time, El Rubio: What's the new ransom?"

"I don't know," said Patrick.

"But you do know," Javier said, pacing like a professor as he spoke. "In fact, you are one of a very few people actually in a position to know. The new ransom is code. Not just any code. I'm talking about the code that you and Sandra Levy came within a whisker of stealing from Buck Technologies."

He stopped and leaned toward Patrick, putting his face right in front of him. "That's a name you didn't expect to hear from me, isn't it, Patrick? And for Olga's sake, you'd better answer me."

"It was unexpected."

"So now you know I'm the real deal. And you know what you're up against."

"Who are you?" asked Patrick.

"Just a hardworking man who always keeps his customers happy. Whatever they want, I get it for them. Right, Olga?"

Patrick could almost feel her reluctance to answer.

"Right," she said in a weak voice.

"At the moment, I have a very unhappy customer. But we're going to fix that. Right, Olga?"

"Whatever you say," she said.

"Exactly. Whatever *I* say. So listen to me, El Rubio. Listen good. I know you and this Sandra Levy tried to steal some kind of computer code from Buck Technologies."

"That's not true."

Javier grabbed him by the throat. "Are you calling my customer a liar? Because a hostage is in no position to call anyone names. Got it?"

"Yes."

He released his grip. "It's the hostage *taker* who does the name-calling. Do you know what you are?"

The guy who is going to kill you the first chance he gets, was Patrick's first thought. But he kept it to himself.

"You, El Rubio, are a computer geek. Which is a good thing. Because I am not a computer geek."

Javier seemed to be waiting for a response of some sort, but Patrick didn't want to say the wrong thing—something that would get him or Olga hurt. "Okay," he said tentatively. "But I'm not sure what you're getting at."

"Then you're the stupidest computer geek ever. Let me spell it out. You are being held for ransom. The ransom is code. To be honest, I can't even begin to understand that code, much less explain it or describe it to Kate Gamble when I make my ransom demand. That's a problem, right?"

"It could be," said Patrick.

"Good answer, El Rubio. It could be. But it's not. Because you *can* describe it. And you will."

"I have no idea what you're talking about."

Javier took a step back, his eyes narrowing with anger. "Seriously? That's your answer? I make a simple request. I want the code that you and Sandra Levy tried to steal from Buck Technologies. And you're telling me you have no idea what I'm talking about. Is that really where we are?"

"I didn't try to steal anything. And I don't know what code Sandra Levy was trying to steal."

"We'll see about that," said Javier. He walked to the counter, pulled a hunting knife from his knapsack, and returned to the hostages. With a flick of the blade, the cord that bound Olga's wrists to the pole was severed.

"On your belly," he told her.

Olga complied, but it didn't suit Javier.

"Over there," he said, "so El Rubio can see."

She slid on hands and knees to the other side of the pole and then lay flat on her stomach, just beyond the reach of Patrick's feet.

Javier knelt beside her, away from Patrick, so that Olga lay between the two men. Then he placed his left hand flat on her back, palm down and fingers outstretched. The knife was in his right hand.

"Remember this, El Rubio?"

Patrick swallowed hard. Of course he remembered Javier's insane display of machismo on Day 1 in the mountains—his hand on the stump and the rapid *tap-tap-tap* of the tip of the blade between his fingers.

"I told you: I don't know the code," said Patrick.

"If I do this just right, it should feel like a pinprick," Javier said. He placed the tip between his thumb and index finger.

Olga flinched, as if jabbed by a needle.

"Perfect." He moved the tip to the space between the index and middle finger, then between the middle and ring finger. Up and down once more between the ring and pinkie finger.

Crimson dots appeared on Olga's shirt.

"Patrick, tell him nothing," she said through clenched teeth.

Javier started again, a jab between the thumb and index finger, the blade moving with increasing speed over his knuckles to the next open space. "One, two, three, four," he said with each precise poke at her back.

Watching was painful, but Patrick couldn't tear his eyes away. The tiny dots, too numerous to count, were merging into one crimson stain. Tears rolled down Olga's face.

"One, two, three, four." Jab, jab, jab, jab.

"Enough!" said Patrick.

The shiny blade moved from one position to the next, faster and faster.

"Tell me the code," said Javier.

"Tell him nothing," said Olga.

Up and down the blade moved, from one gap to the next, with the speed and precision of a sewing machine. The knife was a blur, the sharp tip a veritable death by a thousand cuts on steroids—until Olga's scream filled the cabin.

Blood bubbled up through the slit in her shirt, as Javier pulled the red tip of the knife from the flesh wound. The scars Patrick had felt across her back while dancing with Olga were no longer a mystery.

"That one was just a scratch," said Javier, and then he raised the knife high above Olga's spine. "On the count of three, the tip of this blade goes through the spine and touches the floor."

"Don't tell him!" said Olga.

Javier began his countdown. "One."

"I swear, I don't know the code!" said Patrick.

"Two."

"He'll stab me anyway!" said Olga.

"And—"

"Okay!" shouted Patrick.

"Okay what?" asked Javier.

Patrick looked at Olga, who was speaking only with her eyes, begging him not to do it. The fact that he might be breaking the law by revealing Buck's secrets was the furthest thing from his mind. Javier had left him no choice.

"I'll tell you what to ask for! You'll get the code!"

Javier lowered his knife. "Wise decision," he said.

Chapter 44

Kate spent Sunday evening at home. A quiet evening on the roof of her apartment building by the firepit, glass of wine in hand, the moonlight glistening on the river in the distance, would have been nice. Instead, it was her, Noah, and Special Agent Corey Lang of the Hostage Recovery Fusion Cell seated around her dining room table. Kate was in training.

"Rule number one is to be an active listener," said Lang. "The kidnapper can't see you. For all he knows, you're checking text messages while he's talking. An active listener uses verbal cues to let the caller know she's listening."

There were more rules, and Kate listened carefully, though at times she wondered if she was talking to an expert in hostage negotiation or a marriage counselor.

By rule number four, she decided it was time to pivot away from how to negotiate with a kidnapper and focus on closing the deal on her arrangement with Noah.

"Where do we stand on getting me the clearance I need?" asked Kate.

Noah and the special agent exchanged glances, as if they'd been hoping that Kate would get so caught up in Hostage Recovery 101 that she wouldn't raise the subject.

"You'll have limited clearance," said Noah.

"Limited," said Kate, repeating the word, not so subtly demonstrating her newly acquired "active listening" skills. "Like limited visibility. Limited bandwidth. Limited warranties. Never a good thing."

"There's no need for you to have full clearance to the most sensitive program in the history of Buck Technologies," said Noah.

"I can't negotiate with the kidnapper if I have no idea what code he's talking about."

"Actually, you can," said Noah.

"How?"

Noah pitched it back to the special agent.

"You won't ever be on the phone with the kidnapper without me also on the line," said Lang.

"That will get Patrick killed. The kidnapper said no law enforcement."

"He won't know there's an FBI agent on the line. You'll do the talking. But when we get into the nitty-gritty of the code, I'll feed you the lines in real time."

"So you want me to pretend like I know what I'm talking about. Is that it?"

"When it comes to Buck's code, you say exactly what I tell you to say. Nothing more, nothing less."

"What if you're not on the call?"

"I'll be on the call. If not me, my stand-in will. Your phone will be monitored twenty-four/seven. Answer on the fourth ring. That's all the time we need."

"How will you feed me the lines?"

Lang opened her laptop. "If we're in the same room, like we are now, I'll type them for you in real time."

"What if there's no set time for the kidnapper's call? My phone might ring at three o'clock in the morning."

"Good question. Typing won't work if we're not in the same place at the same time. You'll have a new set of earbuds. In the right ear you'll hear the kidnapper. In the left, you'll hear me. I'll be like the producer talking into the earpiece of the morning show host. We'll need to practice, but you'll get it."

"What if I don't hear you? Or if you and the kidnapper are talking at the same time? Or if I just don't understand what you're saying?"

"I'm going to give you three or four stall lines you

can say to the kidnapper. When I hear one of those lines, that will be my clue that you need me to repeat."

"This seems cumbersome," said Kate. "Wouldn't it just be easier to give me full clearance?"

The agent looked at Noah, then back. "Don't take this the wrong way, Kate. But I'm starting to wonder what's more important to you: getting the hostage released, or getting clearance to Buck's technology?"

"Is there a *right* way for me to take that?" asked Kate.

Kate's cellphone vibrated on the dining room table. "It's him," she said.

The tech crew had already linked Kate's phone to the FBI. Lang positioned the laptop so that Kate could read her screen.

On the fourth ring, she typed. She could have said it aloud, but she was conditioning Kate to watch the screen. Kate took a breath, let it out, and then answered.

"This is Kate."

"Who's with you?" the caller asked. It was the same voice.

"No one," said Kate, before the real negotiator needed to type it.

"Why should I believe you?"

"Because I'm a truthful person," she said, a bit too

quickly to suit the FBI. Agent Lang signaled her to slow down the pace.

"Then tell me the truth, Kate: Am I negotiating with the right person?"

The question was a bit open-ended, but Kate sensed where he was going with it. Agent Lang was typing furiously, and a quick glance at her computer screen confirmed Kate's hunch:

Don't let him use you to get to your father.

Kate rolled with it. "I can tell you this much. I will do the best I can to get you whatever it is you want."

There was silence on the line, and then his reply. "That's not good enough."

Kate knew she was in a delicate situation, and she didn't want to say the wrong thing. She glanced again at Agent Lang's screen, and the prompt worked for her.

"Then let's fix it," she said.

"There's only one way to fix it."

Kate had dealt with the "my way or the highway" mindset before, but it felt different coming from someone who considered violence a solution.

"Maybe if you tell me the problem, we can find a way to fix it together."

It wasn't a scripted line, but Agent Lang seemed to approve. The caller, however, was losing patience.

"Look, I know what I want, and I've played this

game enough to know if the person on the other end of the line is capable of delivering what I want."

"Try me."

"I'm not going to start talking code with you so that the FBI can feed you bullshit answers and stall for time while their tech team tries to figure out where I'm calling from."

Busted. Kate's skepticism over the line-feeding strategy was borne out. Even her unscripted lines were sounding scripted.

"That's not going to happen," said Kate.

"You're right. It's not. Because the next time I call, you are going to have someone on the line who will know what I'm talking about and who has the authority to deliver it."

Agent Lang was typing a response, but Kate used her own words. "I can't make any promises. But if you agree to put Patrick on the line right now, I'll agree to talk to my father."

He chuckled over the line. "Your *father*? No. I want Jeremy Peel."

His demand threw her, and Kate borrowed Agent Lang's response on the screen. "I want to be straight with you. I won't promise things I can't deliver."

"Then don't make promises. Just make it happen."

"I want to speak to Patrick."

"He's not here. I don't negotiate in front of my hostages. What kind of amateur do you think you're dealing with? Just get me Jeremy Peel."

"That's a big request."

"It's not a request. It's a demand. If you ever want to see Patrick alive, have Jeremy Peel on the next call with you."

"I'll need time," said Kate.

"I'll call you in the morning."

"That's too soon. You have to give me time to persuade him."

"Here's all the persuasion you need, Kate. Tell Jeremy that hearing his voice would mean the world to me. And to Olga."

Kate wanted to ask who Olga was, but he didn't give her the chance.

"No FBI on the next call," he said. "Just you and Jeremy. Or someone is going to get seriously hurt."

The call ended. Instantly, the screen on Agent Lang's computer switched to video conference, and a tech agent's voice came over the speaker.

"Triangulating now," he said.

Lang's LCD was a split screen. On the left was a satellite map showing the location of cellphone transmission towers in Colombia. On the right was a stream of numbers and other figures, which Kate could only assume were mathematical calculations. It was the key to triangulation, the process of collecting and interpreting the electronic pulse that a cellphone in power-on mode transmitted to surrounding cell towers.

"Got it," he said.

The split screen vanished, leaving only the map. The target area was shaded.

"What are we looking at?" asked Kate.

"The city of Buenaventura, on the Pacific coast of Colombia. That's where the call originated."

"That's the best you can do?" asked Kate. "Narrow it down to a city of how many people?"

"About half a million," said Noah.

"I was hoping for better," said the tech agent.

So was Kate. The FBI's Cellular Analysis Survey Team was the best in the world. "Did I do something wrong?" asked Kate.

"You had nothing to do with it," said Noah.

The tech agent explained. "A cellphone sends out a pulse in forty-five miles in all directions. If there are three towers within that radius, we can triangulate and calculate a fairly precise location of the phone. If we have two towers, we can at least narrow it down to a few hundred acres. Unfortunately, this call originated from a place where there was only one cell tower within forty-five miles, which is not unusual in this part of the world. So the call could have come from anywhere within forty-five miles in any direction of that tower."

"So a circle of ninety miles in diameter. Basically, anywhere in the city."

"I'm afraid so. Sorry. Anything else I can help with?"

"No," said Agent Lang.

"Only if you can tell me who Olga is," said Kate.

There was silence, both from the computer and in the room.

Kate looked at Noah. "How about you? Can you or anyone else in the DOJ tell me who Olga is?"

Noah didn't answer. Neither did Agent Lang. Kate's read was that it had nothing to do with keeping her in the dark. They had no clue.

"Sounds like I need to ask Jeremy Peel," said Kate.

Chapter 45

Kate grabbed her coat and was out the door before Noah could even push away from her dining table. As she hurried down the hallway, she heard him call from behind to "hold the elevator." She pushed the DOOR CLOSE button and rode down alone. She was outside the building and on her way down the street to the Metro station when Noah caught up with her.

"Talking to Jeremy Peel is not a good idea," he said.

"You lied to me, Noah."

Kate continued through the crosswalk toward the National Mall. They were three blocks from the Smithsonian station.

"I've never lied to you," he said.

"You just lied again."

"Can you give me at least some idea of what you're talking about?"

Kate stopped on the sidewalk and faced him. The night had turned cold, but there was virtually no wind, and their words collided in puffs of conversation in the glow of city lights.

"You led me to believe my father shipped Patrick off to Colombia so you wouldn't be able to interview him. But you knew all along it was Jeremy Peel."

He looked away, but there was no denial. "In fairness, I didn't know if it was Peel, your father, or the CIA."

"You mean Walker? The venture capital arm of the CIA?"

"I can't get into details."

"Of course you can't," she said with sarcasm. "It's only Patrick's life hanging in the balance. Why would you share any details?"

He drew a breath, then let it out slowly in a steam cloud of capitulation that vaporized in the frosty night air. "All right. I'll level with you. There was interagency distrust. Some folks in the CIA thought the purpose of the DOJ's audit was to prove what a bad idea it is for the CIA to invest taxpayer dollars in private tech companies."

"But that's not what you're trying to prove?"

"No."

"Then what's the audit really about? Stop playing games with me."

"Are you pretending not to know? Or do you really need me to tell you?"

"Are you trying to piss me off? Or does it just come naturally to you?"

"Don't get mad."

"I'm beyond *mad*. First, you asked me to spy on my father's company, but you wouldn't tell me what Project Naïveté was. Then you asked me to be your informant and get Sandra Levy to tell me why she was willing to commit espionage, but you wouldn't give me credentials to understand what code she was trying to steal. Now I've agreed to partner with the FBI to negotiate for Patrick's release, and I still can't get credentials to understand the code the kidnappers have demanded as ransom. Meanwhile, all these secrets could get Patrick killed!"

"I've done everything by the book."

"It's time for me to close this book."

Kate turned and started up the sidewalk. Noah followed.

"Where are you going?"

"None of your business."

He kept pace, walking at her side, talking fast

to match her pace. "You know something, Kate? I thought Agent Lang was out of line when she asked what was more important to you, getting clearance or getting Patrick home safe. But maybe she had a point."

"Nothing is more important to me than getting Patrick home."

"Maybe. But something else isn't far behind."

"Kiss off, Noah."

Her tone silenced him, and it surprised her as well. Kate wondered if she was directing too much of her anger toward him. Patrick was unquestionably the priority, but she wished she could tell him exactly what that "something else" was. But he'd surely think her a desperate fool—or worse—for hoping any of this might explain her mother's bizarre suicide note.

I did it for Kate.

"What if I told you that Sandra Levy did it for her daughter?"

Noah seemed puzzled. "What do you mean by '*it*'?"

The question was more pertinent than he could have possibly imagined.

"Not sure. But the more I learn, the less '*it*' looks like stealing code from Buck Technologies."

"Are you suggesting Sandra Levy is innocent?"

Her thoughts were spinning with confusion. "I'm

not ready to have this conversation with you, Noah. If anything, I need more distance."

"What does that mean?"

"Putting you and the FBI in charge of my negotiations with Patrick's kidnapper was a mistake. He's even more at risk."

Noah clearly didn't like the change of direction. "Kate, don't do this."

"I'm sorry. You're out. I'm going private."

She turned and started toward the Metro station.

"Kate!"

"Call me when I have clearance."

She continued up the sidewalk, alone.

Chapter 46

It was springtime south of the equator, where October showers bring November flowers. The steady patter of raindrops on the poop deck woke Patrick just after dawn.

"Olga, you up?"

She was on her stomach, still lying at Patrick's feet, where Javier had left her. At least he'd bandaged the knife wounds on her back before binding her wrists. The crimson dots on the floor had turned brown overnight.

"I never fell asleep," she said.

"How do you feel?"

"Like a human pincushion."

It almost came across as a bad joke, but Patrick realized it was her way of conveying in English that it still hurt.

She tried another position to get comfortable, still on her stomach but with her chin resting on her hands, using them like a pillow on the floor. "So who is this Kate on the phone?" she asked, looking up at Patrick. "Your girlfriend?"

"She's actually my old babysitter."

Olga started to laugh, but she was quickly reminded of her knife wounds. "Ow! Don't make me laugh."

"Sorry. But it's true. She used to call me Baby Patrick."

Olga couldn't hold it in. "Ow, ow, *owww!* Stop it!"

"I'm not messing with you, I swear. But don't worry. Kate really can help us. Her father runs the tech company I work for in Virginia. Buck Technologies."

"Her father is Jeremy Peel?"

"No. But wait. You've heard of Jeremy Peel?"

"I have," she said, blinking slowly. "I was a virgin when I met him."

Patrick had no idea what to say. He hadn't expected to find a reason to hate Peel more than he already did, but there it was.

"I'm sorry," he said.

"Not your fault."

"It is, sort of. I work for the man. One of his whiz kids. I build the toys that make him feel invincible, like he can have anything he wants. *Anyone* he wants."

"We're all responsible for our own actions."

He wasn't sure if she was talking about him, Peel, or herself. Maybe all of the above, in which case, she was being way too hard on the victim.

"Do you mind if I ask how you met him?"

"Same way I met you. Javier."

He had more questions, but he sensed she'd rather not talk about it. "Peel will get what's coming to him," he said.

"You think so?"

"I know so."

"He's not a nice man," said Olga, the understatement of the year.

"Not at all," said Patrick.

The sound of gentle rainfall soothed the silence between them, but it was suddenly interrupted by squeaky footfalls right outside their cabin. The door opened, and a soaking wet Javier entered. He removed his coat, shook off the rain, and hung it from a peg on the wall.

"Hey, El Rubio. Does this rain make it harder for me to call Kate?"

"Any atmospheric water vapor can scatter radio waves. Rain, snow, fog, clouds. All of it."

Javier laid his cellphone on the countertop and took a seat on the barstool. "It'll stop, eventually. No rush."

"Babysitters don't mind waiting," Olga whispered, teasing Patrick.

"What's that, *chica*?"

"I said we don't mind waiting."

"I don't give a shit what you mind," said Javier. "Just listen up. I got some rules to cover. Normally, I never negotiate with hostages in the same room, so these rules are going to be simple and strictly enforced. Number one. Olga, you say nothing. Not a word. Got it?"

"Yes."

"El Rubio, when I put the phone up to your face, you get fifteen seconds on the line. You don't say hello. You don't answer any questions. You sure as hell don't say where you are. You say exactly what you said last night to keep the knife out of Olga's back. Understand?"

"Yes."

"I don't speak geek. You do. So talk real pretty, and make your own ransom demand. Tell them the code I want. We clear?"

"Crystal," said Patrick.

Javier climbed down from the barstool, went to the porthole, and checked the weather. "I give it half an hour," he said. "Rain or shine, the call is on."

Chapter 47

Monday morning marked Kate's second visit to Jeremy Peel in twenty-four hours, this time at his office in the District. She hadn't expected a warm welcome, and it wasn't. He'd refused to answer her phone call, and she probably wouldn't have made it past the receptionist if she hadn't instructed the young woman to pass along the magic words:

"Tell him I want to talk about Olga."

Peel's assistant entered the lobby and escorted Kate to the sitting room adjacent to Peel's office, where it was just Kate and the chairman of the board. She declined coffee. Peel drank a cup while Kate recounted her phone conversation with Patrick's kidnapper. Then she turned to her decision to take the negotiations private.

"I know why the kidnapper wants you on the next call," she said.

He placed his cup in the saucer. "Yes, you just told me. He said he needs someone with authority to deliver the code he wants."

"That's not the real reason. Or at least it's not the *only* reason."

"I have zero interest in guessing games. If you have something to say, say it."

"The kidnapper knows that if you're on the line, the FBI won't be. You won't allow it. Or should I say, you can't risk it. You can't take the chance that he'll say more about this Olga with law enforcement on the line."

He didn't answer. Instead, he dialed on his cell and put the call on speaker, which came across to Kate as a man trying a bit too hard to prove he had nothing to hide.

"Christian Gamble's daughter needs to beat a possible Title III wiretap on her cellphone," he said. "I want all calls to her cell forwarded to a single encrypted line accessible by two phones, one for me and one for her."

"How soon?" the man on the line answered.

"Now."

"You got it."

Peel ended the call.

Kate picked up right where they'd left off. "I'm right, aren't I? You can't risk having law enforcement on the line when you're talking to the kidnapper."

He drummed his fingers on the arm of his chair. "My, aren't you clever. Fine. I sent Patrick away on a corporate adventure. There's nothing illegal about that. A company has no obligation to make it easy for the Justice Department to stick its nose in places it doesn't belong."

"So who's Olga?"

"It was her job to make Patrick want to stay there as long as possible."

She knew exactly what he meant, but this Olga and her Baby Patrick didn't quite compute. "You hired a prostitute?"

"Indirectly. But that's not important. The point is, I did *not* get him kidnapped. I don't want to hurt that kid in any way. He's this company's golden boy—we need him alive."

"How does the kidnapper know about Olga?"

"No clue. You'll have to ask him."

Kate wasn't convinced that he was telling her everything, but she got more than she'd expected.

There was a knock on the door, and Peel's tech guy entered. He asked for Kate's phone, which she gave to him. He poked at it with an unfolded paper clip, which didn't strike Kate as very high-tech, but apparently that was the way even the best and brightest at Buck Technologies removed the SIM card from an iPhone.

"Do you want all your calls forwarded away from the wiretap, or just calls from certain numbers?"

"I'm not even sure there is a wiretap," said Kate.

"It's safe to assume there will be," said Peel. "The FBI can't be happy about your taking the negotiations private."

"Can you fix it so we forward only calls from numbers not in my contact list? I don't need all my calls sent to the new encrypted line. Just the ones from—"

"Your bookie," said Peel. Apparently he wasn't comfortable with the word "kidnapper" in front of his tech guy, no matter how trusted he was.

"Right. My bookie," said Kate.

"Done." The techie handed Kate her phone, then gave her and Peel each a new encrypted phone that would receive the forwarded calls from Patrick's kidnapper. "No more wiretap worries," he said. "At least not on the forwarded calls."

Peel dismissed him and, when he left the room, addressed Kate. "Keep the encrypted phone with you at all times. As will I. When the call comes, we'll both be on. The FBI won't be."

It was exactly the result Kate had orchestrated, but

a partnership of any sort with Peel, especially one of necessity, made her uneasy. "Just to be clear on the rules, my father gave me the name of a private security consultant. It's my choice whether I use him or not, and to what extent I use him. You have no say on that."

"Fine by me. And I'll choose my own advisor."

"If you're planning to get your own, you need to move fast. The kidnapper said the next call would come this morning."

As if on cue, Kate's cell rang. So did the pair of encrypted phones. She checked the caller ID.

"It's him," said Kate. "I have to take it."

"I'm not talking," said Peel.

"You have to talk. He needs to know you're on the line."

The phone rang a second time.

"I'm not talking, unless you promise not to say a word about our arrangement to your father."

"Don't pull this crap on me."

Peel folded his arms and said, "I'm not talking."

The third ring. Kate was in a jam, but she couldn't let it go to voicemail. Kate answered, using the encrypted phone.

"This is Kate."

"Good morning, Kate. Is Mr. Peel on the line?"

"I can get him."

"Be quick about it."

"I need thirty seconds."

"Fifteen," he said.

Kate hit MUTE and looked at Peel. "I need you on the line *now*."

"Not a word about this to your father."

"Fine."

"I want a signed nondisclosure agreement."

"What?"

"You heard me."

Time was ticking. "Okay. You'll get your NDA."

"Of course the NDA needs teeth."

"I'll agree to a liquidated damages clause."

"Not money. I mean real teeth that will make you feel real pain. If you breach, here's the penalty: You assign to me the copyright of that play you're doing with Irving Bass."

Kate wasn't sure how he knew about the play, but she was so fed up with Irving Bass, she didn't even care about the rights.

"Fine. I'll sign."

Peel smiled with satisfaction and picked up his phone. "This is Jeremy Peel."

"I need proof it's you."

"I don't know how to prove that to you."

"Answer this question for me: What was Olga wearing the first time you laid eyes on her?"

Kate showed no reaction, but clearly her instinct had been right: Peel had told her less than everything about Olga.

"A white string bikini," Peel said with a begrudging look on his face.

A chuckle came over the line. "I'll bet she didn't wear it for long, did she?"

"Is that what this call is about?" asked Peel. "Embarrassing me in front of my partner's daughter?"

"No. This is all about the code you're going to direct Buck Technologies to deliver to me."

Kate reestablished herself as negotiator. "We're listening," she said. "Go ahead."

"I'm not even going to try," he said. "There's only one person on this end of the line who can put this demand into words that leave no room for misunderstanding."

Kate assumed he meant Patrick, but she wanted more than just his technical description of the ransom, which for all she knew was a recording. She needed confirmation that he was alive as of that very moment.

"One thing before we get into tech speak. You asked Mr. Peel a question to make sure it was him. I need to do the same with Patrick."

"Fair enough. Ask away. I'll get the answer."

Kate would have preferred to hear it straight from Patrick's mouth, but this would suffice.

"Ask him what his favorite breed of dog is."

A good guess would have been a St. Bernard or Scottish shepherd, given that the company logo was based on the mixed breed in Jack London's novel. But guessing would have been futile. Only Patrick could answer this question. Kate waited, and the kidnapper was back on the line.

"The Shiba Inu," he said.

It made Kate's heart sing. The Shiba Inu was the breed behind the meme that spawned the cryptocurrency Dogecoin. Patrick, of course, had gotten in on the ground floor as a teenager, turning a seventy-five-dollar investment into God only knew how much money.

"Satisfied?" he asked.

"Yes. Definitely."

"That's your one and only question. I'm putting Patrick on the line now. He will tell you exactly what you are to deliver as ransom, and he will say no more. Don't encourage him to talk, or it will be at the expense of his health and well-being. Understood?"

"Yes."

A few seconds of silence followed. Kate waited with anticipation. Then Patrick's voice was on the line.

"I could go on and on," he said. "But let me keep this simple and put it in terms you can understand. He wants Code Six. Got it, Kate? Code Six. That's the whole enchilada."

The kidnapper was back on the line. "Well, if the smart-ass had just told me it could be described in two words, I would have done it myself. But there you have it, and you know he's alive. Next call is in twenty-four hours. Be in Cali by then. Have the code on a flash drive."

"I can't go to Cali."

"You can. And you will—if you want El Rubio back. This exchange is not going to take place in your back-yard. It will be in mine."

The call ended. Kate put the phone away, her thoughts racing. The words Patrick had chosen, and the way he'd spoken to her by name, were not lost on her.

"What the hell is Patrick talking about?" asked Peel. "I have no idea what Code Six is."

For once, Kate had no reason to doubt him. "I know you don't," she said.

Kate grabbed her phones—old and new—and started toward the door.

"Hey," said Peel, stopping her. "You're not going anywhere until you sign that NDA. This is all our secret."

"I don't sign anything under duress, Mr. Peel. And Patrick just changed the whole ball game with Code Six."

"Do you know what Code Six is?"

She smiled thinly. "I know this much. Patrick Battle is the most courageous young man I've ever met."

Kate turned and hurried out of the room.

Chapter 48

Patrick couldn't breathe. He was seated on the cabin floor, knees to his chest, his spine firmly against the pole, his hands bound behind his back. Javier's grip was like a clamp around his throat, his mouth inches from Patrick's nose.

"Don't you *ever* make me look stupid on the phone!"

Patrick had expected him to be angry over Code 6, but he hadn't figured on a volcanic eruption. The tirade continued.

"You spent thirty minutes explaining the code to me in words I could never remember. Then I put you on the line, and you describe it in two words! *Why?*"

Patrick needed air. Javier wouldn't allow it, not even to get an answer to his question.

"Let him breathe!" said Olga. "He's turning blue!"

She was chained to the other side of the pole, also on the floor. Javier snarled at her but released his grip. Patrick gasped, thankful to be alive and breathing.

"Explain yourself," said Javier.

Patrick was still struggling for air. He took a moment, then answered. "I didn't think Mr. Peel would actually be on the line."

"What does that have to do with it?"

He took another breath. "Kate would have no idea what Code Six is. The shorthand reference could only make sense to Peel. I gave you the long version so you could tell Kate exactly what you want, and there would be no mistake about the ransom."

Lying didn't come naturally to Patrick. But he would do what needed to be done.

Javier stared into Patrick's eyes, a penetrating gaze, as if he were conducting some sort of telepathic lie detector test. "Code Six better be real," he said.

"It's the most real thing the tech industry has ever seen."

Javier seemed to accept it—at least for the moment. "I guess we'll find out."

"I need to use the bathroom," said Olga. "It's been hours."

Patrick appreciated the well-timed change of subject. "My bladder is calling, too."

Javier seemed annoyed, but acquiesced. "Hookers first," he said, and he unchained Olga from the pole. Her back cracked as she straightened and stood up. He left Patrick on the floor, his wrists bound to the pole. At gunpoint, he led Olga to the door.

"Don't get all Houdini on me and try to slip out of those chains," he said to Patrick.

"I don't think you need to worry about that."

"I'm not worried. If you're not here when we get back, it's Olga who pays."

It was a pointless warning, as there was no escaping, but Javier never missed an opportunity to intimidate Olga. The door closed, and their footfalls faded as they crossed the deck to the bathroom. Outside, the rain had stopped, and the remaining drops on the porthole glistened in the morning sun. Patrick focused on one drop, in particular, as it slowly made its way down the glass. He wondered if it would trickle all the way to the bottom, or if it would evaporate first, like a river run dry. Passing the time in solitary confinement made for small thoughts. He felt lucky to have Olga to talk to most of the day, though "lucky" probably wasn't the right word.

The click at the door caught Patrick's attention. The handle had dropped to the open position, no longer parallel to the floor. Slowly, the door opened, but only halfway. It was too soon for Olga's return from the bathroom. And Patrick didn't believe in ghosts. At least he didn't think he did.

"Is someone there?"

The possibility of rescue crossed his mind, but so did the memory of his last encounter with strangers, which had ended in kidnapping. He stared at the half-open door, waiting for a response. None came, but he could almost feel the presence of a visitor.

He tried in Spanish: *"Quien está?"*

The door opened a little more, and suddenly a man entered. He put a finger to his lips, shushing Patrick, as he quickly but quietly closed the door.

He looked Asian, though Patrick figured it was hardly unusual to see Chinese, Japanese, and countless other non-Hispanics in Colombia's Pacific ports. His dark, piercing eyes glimmered in the low, natural light, and he wore a tight black turtleneck that complemented his lean, muscular physique. His hair was hidden beneath a black knit beanie.

"Who are—"

Again, he shushed Patrick before he could finish the question, moving across the cabin with catlike quickness. It was feeling less and less like a rescue to Patrick. The man seemed to be looking for something. Or someone.

"I won't leave here without my friend," said Patrick, meaning Olga.

The man stopped. "Shut—your—mouth," he said, giving each word emphasis, speaking quietly but so firmly that it still gave Patrick chills.

The clap of footfalls on the poop deck followed. Olga and Javier were returning from the bathroom break. The man shot Patrick a look that said, *Not another word from you.* Then he stepped behind the counter and hid from view. The door handle turned, and the door swung open. Olga entered first, followed by Javier, who closed the door behind them.

"Back to the pole," said Javier.

Olga went to her spot on the floor, and Javier chained her hands behind her back.

Patrick didn't know what to do. The intentions of the man behind the counter surely were not good, but there was no way to warn Olga without tipping off Javier, too.

"All right, El Rubio. Your turn."

Patrick had almost forgotten that he'd joined Olga's request for a bathroom break. But he had no intention of leaving Olga in the cabin alone—or, rather, in the cabin with a stranger who might be worse than the devil they knew.

"I don't need to go anymore," said Patrick.

"Last chance," said Javier. "I'm leaving and won't be back until dark."

"You're not going anywhere, Javier," said the man behind the counter, no longer hiding.

All heads turned. He was standing in the marksman's tactical pose: forward leaning, arms straight out, and shoulders square to his target. The sights were at eye level, and the black pistol was aimed directly at Javier. Patrick noted the silencer affixed to the muzzle, as he felt Olga's fingernails digging into his forearm. They were back-to-back, so he couldn't see her, but he could feel her fear.

And then it suddenly occurred to Patrick that the intruder had addressed "Javier," even though Patrick had never identified his kidnapper.

"Relax, Olga. You're going to be just fine."

Patrick was even more confused. He hadn't mentioned Olga's name, either.

"Put the gun away," said Javier, but his voice betrayed him, cracking with fear.

The gunman smiled a little, and with that little flash of personality, he reminded Patrick of Simu Liu. It surely wasn't him—though, at least in Patrick's mind, it wasn't completely outside the realm of possibility that a Chinese-born Canadian actor who played the son of Korean immigrants on TV and a new avenger in a

Marvel Cinematic Universe film would have a secret life as a hit man in Colombia.

"I hear you've been talking directly to Jeremy Peel."

Peel—another name Patrick had never mentioned to the Simu Liu lookalike. Things just kept getting weirder.

"Is that true?" the man asked.

Javier was crumbling before Patrick's eyes. It was a side of his captor he'd never seen before.

"I can explain," said Javier.

"I asked a simple question. Are you negotiating with Jeremy Peel?"

"I—"

"Yes or no?"

There was silence. Javier looked too terrified to answer.

"I asked a question!" the man shouted. "Are you negotiating with Peel?"

"Please, I was just—"

"Answer me!"

Javier swallowed the lump in his throat. "Yes."

The gunman's expression relaxed a bit, but he seemed no less determined to finish the job.

"Well done, Javier. I already knew the answer. But for being truthful, you shall be rewarded. Olga? Should he live or die?"

Patrick felt her arms stiffen, her elbows burrowing into his back in reflex-like reaction to a question no person should be forced to answer, even if it was the worthless life of a sex trafficker hanging in the balance.

"Ah, never mind," the man said. "There's no option here. I'm afraid this is not going to end well for you, Javier. But truth telling has its virtues. So I'll make this quick."

Patrick heard the distinctive discharge of a silenced projectile, saw the slight recoil in the shooter's hands, and gasped at the sight of Javier's head snapping back, blood and gray matter splattering against the wall behind him as Javier's lifeless body fell to the cabin floor.

Olga screamed. Patrick didn't know what was coming next. But this was definitely no "rescue."

"Be quiet, Olga," he said, as he relaxed from his stance and lowered his pistol.

Her screams dissolved into muffled sobbing.

The man came out from behind the counter and stood over Javier's body, admiring his work. Then he looked at Patrick.

"Just another day in *lo-co-lombia*," he said, his Spanish-language wordplay on "crazy Colombia" not nearly as clever as he seemed to think.

Chapter 49

The Uber driver dropped Kate at her father's house in Georgetown. He was on a Zoom video conference when she arrived. Kate didn't technically interrupt, but she waited right outside the French doors to his study, making herself visible, repeatedly checking her watch, and all but tapping her foot to get him to wrap things up. Whatever his conference was about, it couldn't have been more important than the reason for her visit. She gave him five minutes and then opened the door, stuck her head into the room, and said, "Dad, I'm going to Cali."

He stopped in midsentence and looked at her as if she'd just announced a trip to the moon.

"Guys, I need to call you back," he said to his virtual guests, and the rectangles of talking heads vanished from his screen like popping bath bubbles. At his invitation, which sounded more like an order, Kate took a seat on the couch.

"I assume this is about Patrick," he said.

"And Jeremy Peel."

In five minutes she told him all that he needed to know—or, at least, as much as Kate thought he needed to know. He considered it for a minute, then spoke.

"No surprise that it was Jeremy who shipped him off to the Andes and put him out of the DOJ's reach. I swear, sometimes he thinks that because we're part-owned by the CIA, we can act like the CIA."

"What about the kidnapping?"

"What about it?"

"Do you believe he had nothing to do with it?"

"The man has been my business partner for twenty years, Kate. He's a lot of things—chief among them, a royal pain in the ass. But he's not a kidnapper."

"Why do you defend him? He hates you."

"He doesn't *hate* me."

"Dad, I see it in the way he looks at you. I hear it in his voice."

"There's resentment, no question about it. But not hatred."

"Call it what you want. It's irrational. It borders on sociopathic."

"Let's not get carried away."

"He knows things at Buck Technologies that are dark to you. And yet, *he* resents *you*. That's a sociopath. Even Patrick's kidnapper knows that, to get the code he wants, he needs to talk to Jeremy Peel."

Her words were more hurtful than intended, but before Kate could apologize, her father naturally got defensive—which, for the likes of Christian Gamble, meant going on the offensive.

"How do you know I can't deliver what they want?"

"I didn't mean that the way it sounded."

"Try me," he said, digging in for the sake of his own dignity. "Exactly what is the kidnapper demanding from Buck?"

"Code."

"What code?"

"All I know is what Patrick told me on the phone."

"Patrick's super smart, but there's no way he recited code from memory."

"No. I mean the words he used to describe it."

"Project Naïveté?"

"No. Code Six."

His expression went blank. "I guess you made

your point. Never heard of it. But that doesn't dilute my point. The thing that really drives Jeremy nuts is that people *think* we have the same security clearance. Which, of course, makes certain people think that if they want to bring down me and my company, all they have to do is steal my credentials."

Kate was pretty sure who he meant by "people."

"You mean Sandra Levy?"

"No," he said, pausing for an instant, as if not sure he should continue. "I mean your mother."

Kate's mouth was agape. "Mom stole your credentials?"

"No. But she tried."

"Why?"

"I call it the sequel to her call to nine-one-one."

"She just wanted to hurt you?"

He sighed at the size of the question. "Kate, in any marriage, there are two sides to every story. I don't see a malicious woman who was just trying to hurt me. I see an alcoholic—someone with a diseased mind— expressing herself in the most desperate way possible and saying, 'Hey, remember me? I'm your wife.'"

"What happened with her breach of security?"

"We handled it internally. That's all I can tell you. But I can assure you that she got nowhere near this Code Six, whatever it is."

"If it makes you feel any better, Mr. Peel has never heard of Code Six, either."

"Or he simply won't admit to it."

"I'm fairly certain he's not feigning ignorance."

Her father shook his head. "With his security credentials? Don't kid yourself. He's telling you that because, whatever Code Six is, he can't deliver it as Patrick's ransom."

"That's why *I* have to be the one to go to Cali."

"To do what?"

"Make the exchange."

"What exchange? I understand you want them to hand over Patrick. But you have nothing to give them."

"I'll have something. *Patrick* and I will have something."

Her father looked at her soulfully, searchingly. He seemed to understand that she was asking for his trust, not his blessing, and that she was going to Cali with or without the latter.

"You and I," he said in a halting voice. "All the family we have left is each other."

"I know. I'll be careful."

"There's a member of my security team," he said. "Enrique. Former special ops. Speaks perfect Spanish. Take him with you."

She reached out and took her father's hand. "Thank you," was all she said.

He smiled sadly. "You know, honey, this is 'above and beyond the call of duty' for a former babysitter."

Kate shared his smile for a moment, then turned serious. "There's so much more to it, Dad."

Chapter 50

Patrick was on cleanup duty, wiping, swiping, and wringing a bloody rag into a bucket of red-tinted water.

Javier's body was on the floor, covered by a canvas tarp. His killer had stepped out after the shooting and returned with the tarp, cleaning supplies, and a duffel bug. He left Olga chained to the pole but put Patrick to work, watching over him like an armed prison guard. It occurred to Patrick that thousands of people made an honest living this way, day after day, cleaning walls and floors, wiping up blood and body fluids at crime scenes all over the world. All things considered, Patrick would have much rather swabbed the poop deck. Or even walked the plank.

"Don't think about what you're doing," Olga said under her breath, trying to help him through it.

Patrick was dealing with a particularly nasty stain on the white wall. The blast had literally removed the top of Javier's head.

"Finished," said Patrick.

"You missed a spot," said Liu.

Patrick wiped away a clump of hair and rinsed his rag in the bucket.

"Nice work," said Liu. He was technically still nameless, but the movie-star moniker had stuck, at least in Patrick's mind.

"Can I wash my hands, please?"

He tossed Patrick a clean rag. "Later."

Patrick wiped away as much of the mess as possible and returned to his place on the floor. Liu chained him to the pole and went to the duffel bag on the counter. It had sat there, unopened, since Liu's return with the cleaning supplies, as if he were inviting his hostages to guess what might be inside. Body parts? Weapons? Instruments of torture?

"No shortage of supplies on this ship," said Liu, as he removed an empty paint can and a gasoline can from his bag. He placed the paint can on the countertop and poured in some gasoline. Next from his bag were chunks of a Styrofoam cooler, which he broke into even smaller pieces before mixing with the gasoline.

"What are you going to do with that?" Olga asked with trepidation.

"Amateur pyromaniacs stop as soon as the Styrofoam dissolves in the gasoline, which basically gives you a sticky gel that burns. But I'm no amateur. So I'm going to add the key ingredient. Not everyone can get their hands on it, but if you know where to look, you can find it on just about any ship.

"Benzene," he said, stirring the liquid into the can. "With this, I get essentially the same 'super napalm' used by the U.S. military in Vietnam."

He stepped toward Olga and removed the stick from the can. A big glob of gel clung to it. "This burns at about a thousand degrees centigrade," he said.

"Keep it away from me," she said.

"I will. As long as your boyfriend tells me everything I need to know. If not," he said, letting the glob of goo drop onto her thigh, "I'm going to ignite this hot mess and burn a hole right through your leg."

Patrick spoke up. "There's no need to hurt anyone."

"You're absolutely right. Let's you and I talk. About Code Six."

"Obviously, you've been listening to Javier's phone conversations," said Patrick.

"For quite some time. Started long before you mentioned Code Six."

"What do you want to know about it?"

"I want to know if Code Six is what you left out the first time."

"I have no idea what you're talking about. What 'first time'?"

Liu walked around to the other side of the pole, spooned another glob of goo from the can, and let it fall on Patrick's leg. It stung, even unlit.

"Keep playing dumb," said Liu, "and this will end badly for both of you."

Patrick wasn't playing, but Liu's perception of reality was the only reality that mattered. The sting on his leg intensified, and Olga was actually blowing on her thigh to cool the gel.

"Can you get that stuff off her, please?" asked Patrick.

"I'm okay," she said, but she clearly wasn't.

Liu didn't care, his laser-like gaze locking onto Patrick. "Algorithms grow and evolve over time. We can agree on that much, right?"

"Sure," said Patrick.

"In fact, an algorithm can make so many adaptations over time that the person who created it in the first place might eventually find his creation unrecognizable."

Liu was touching on a complicated and controversial subject. Buck was on the cutting edge of the algorithmic process of evolution, a virtual Darwinism of sorts, in which existing code improves every generation with little human interaction, effectively training itself based solely on experience with vast amounts of data.

"It's possible," said Patrick.

"By the same token, an algorithm that fails to adapt, that stays completely the same as the virtual world changes around it, could eventually become worthless."

"In some situations."

"So, even if I paid ridiculous sums of money, the code would be worthless if someone at Buck Technologies tweaked the virtual DNA, so to speak, and robbed it of any ability to self-improve."

"If you're suggesting that I altered code that is proprietary to Buck, you've got the wrong hostage."

"I don't care if it was *you* who altered it," said Liu. "I want to know if Code Six is what was missing from the code I bought the first time."

Liu's question only raised more questions in Patrick's mind. *Bought from whom? What "first time"?* But the sting of homemade napalm was making it hard for Patrick to think. Olga was in obvious pain, taking short, halting breaths.

"Are you okay?" he asked.

"Don't worry about me," she said, gritting it out.

Liu kicked back the tarp just enough to expose Javier's arm, and another glob of gel fell from his stick. It landed on the lifeless forearm. "Ever seen the photo of the napalm girl from Vietnam?" asked Liu.

Patrick had. It was haunting—so horrific that when the *New York Times* printed the chilling image of nine-year-old Phan Thi Kim Phúc screaming and running from a napalm attack, it was a turning point of public opinion against the war.

Liu put the can on the counter and pulled a pack of matches from his pocket. "Not a pretty sight, that napalm girl. Clothes burned off, running down the road naked, her burned flesh ready to fall from her body. This gel sticks to your skin, and you can't get it off. It just keeps burning and burning, hotter and hotter."

He struck a match, lighting it.

"Only your government is stupid enough to use it on entire villages for the whole world to see," said Liu. "I'm more selective. Or 'discreet,' shall we say?"

He dropped the match on Javier's body. A foot-long flare shot up from the gel, which quickly reduced itself to a glowing, white-hot circle that burned with the intensity of a nuclear meltdown. The sickening smell of burning flesh filled the cabin.

"If you force me to strike another match, I promise you'll hear screams like you've never heard before."

Patrick could only guess at who this man was, why he'd paid someone so much money for Buck's code, and how, apparently, he'd been swindled. But circumstances compelled only one answer to his question.

"Yes," said Patrick. "Code Six is all you need."

Liu put the pack of matches back in his pocket, took a rag, and wiped the gel from the hostages' legs, first Olga, and then Patrick. He rolled the rag into a ball and held it under Patrick's nose so that he could smell the concoction.

"Javier was smart. He spoke the truth and got the bullet. If you're lying to me, you're going to wish you'd never been born."

Patrick stared back at him, trying to remain strong, but it was impossible to hide his fear. Liu seemed to enjoy the smell of burning flesh, and he seemed genuinely disappointed that Javier was already dead—that there were no screams to go with the sickening stench. Patrick would have never dreamed it possible, but there was no denying how he felt at that moment.

He wished Javier were still in control.

Liu grabbed his pistol and took aim at Patrick's

forehead. "I'm going to unchain you now, take you to the latrine, and let you wash your hands. Then we are going to prepare for your next call with Kate Gamble."

"*My* next call?"

"You're going to do all the talking."

"What am I supposed to say about Javier?"

"Nothing. Not a single, solitary word about him. Or about me."

"So you want them to think Javier is still alive?"

"Meet the new kidnapper," he said, a smile creasing his lips. "Same as the old kidnapper."

Chapter 51

Kate took a direct flight from Dulles and landed in Cali that evening. Enrique Salazar, her father's most trusted bodyguard, was at her side. A driver met them at the airport. He greeted Enrique like an old friend and he offered much more than a ride to their hotel.

"For the pretty lady, I have the Glock 27 concealed-carry pistol. Ten rounds of forty-caliber ammunition readily accessible in your pocket or purse. For Señor Enrique, the Glock 19 with shoulder harness for concealment. There are two extra magazines, nine-millimeter cartridges, fifteen rounds each."

Kate opened her purse, but Enrique stopped her before she could tuck the pistol away.

"What did I tell you to do when someone hands you a gun?"

Enrique was a former Green Beret with three tours of duty in Afghanistan. He was fearless but not reckless. They'd spent two hours at a firing range before their flight, including a crash course in gun safety.

"Check the chamber," she said, doing so, "and make sure the safety is on."

"Captain Salazar never changes," said Diego.

"Sounds like you two go way back," said Kate, and she quickly got the story. Diego had served with Enrique in Afghanistan before joining the DEA. He was now an expat living in Cali doing private security.

Kate's hotel was in the San Antonio neighborhood, a twenty-minute ride from the airport. It was a misty night, typical of the September–November rainy season in Cali. Rainbow-like rings surrounded the glowing streetlamps. The *whump-whump* of the windshield wipers punctuated the silence.

"Can we talk about the elephant in the backseat of the car?" asked Enrique.

Kate knew the expression, usually expressed in connection with "the room," but she wasn't sure what he meant. He filled in the blank.

"Is there a Code Six?"

"There was."

"It doesn't exist anymore?"

"No. Thank God."

"Then what are you going to deliver to Patrick's kidnappers to make the exchange?"

"That's not my problem. That's Jeremy Peel's problem."

"How is it his problem?"

"You'll see. I have a plan."

Enrique looked confused. "Does Mr. Peel know what Code Six is? Or was?"

"He has no clue."

Enrique seemed even more puzzled. "But Patrick Battle knows?"

"Yes. Patrick knows."

"How?"

The mist was turning to rain. The *whump-whump* of the wipers quickened. Kate decided that if Enrique was willing to risk his life to protect her, he deserved to see at least part of the bigger picture.

"I wrote a play."

"Your father told me. He's very proud of you."

It warmed Kate's heart to hear that. She wouldn't have guessed it.

"What's the play about?" asked Enrique.

She gave him the short version.

"What's it called?"

"It doesn't have a title. But I think I'm going to call it *Code Six*. It was Patrick's idea."

"He read your play?"

"No. Right before Patrick disappeared, the director took me on a research trip to the Holocaust Memorial. They have a Hollerith machine on display there. I
thought Patrick would find it fascinating, so I went back
a second time and brought him with me."

"Why is there a Hollerith machine at the Holocaust
Memorial?"

"Because virtually every aspect of the Holocaust
was automated. It was the old punch-card technology,
but it was technology, nonetheless."

"And Code Six was part of that technology?"

"Yes."

"So, when Patrick told you to deliver Code Six as his
ransom, he was—"

"He was effectively saying, 'Don't give my kidnappers shit.'"

"Why would he do that? I mean, it's nice to see an
employee who is loyal to his company. But company
loyalty has its limits."

"Patrick has the highest level of clearance at Buck
Technologies. Higher than my father's. My guess is
that the technology these people *really* want is a matter
of national security."

Enrique's eyes brightened. His chest swelled like a
proud veteran. From where Kate was sitting, this man

who'd put his own life on the line in service to his country was having a "lightbulb" moment.

"He's risking his life to protect technology that is of vital interest to the nation," he said.

"That's about the size of it."

"The kid's a fucking patriot."

"In my eyes, he is," said Kate.

Enrique's expression turned deadly serious. Kate had never served, but she recognized that special "no soldier left behind" resolve when it was right in front of her.

"We're going to get that boy out of here," he said like a man on a mission. "I guarantee it, Kate."

Chapter 52

A package arrived for Christian Gamble at his home that evening. It was from Kate.

He was worried about her, as any parent would be. He trusted Enrique with his own life—literally—but entrusting anyone with the life of your daughter was another level entirely. He went to the study, slit open the large envelope, and peered inside. Papers. It was perhaps a sign that he was more worried than he would have liked to admit, but his first thought was that she'd left a Last Will and Testament.

Calm down, he told himself.

He took a seat on the couch and slid the pages from the envelope. A cover letter was on top, and it occurred to him that he could count on one hand the number of handwritten letters he'd received from his daughter in his lifetime. Actual *letters*, not store-bought Father's Day cards with a signature and hand-drawn heart. His mother, he'd learned after her death, had kept every letter he'd ever written to her. Technology was good. But not all good.

Dear Dad, it began, and he hoped this letter would be from Kate's heart, something he'd have reason to cherish, unlike the envelopes of information he'd sent to his mother, *classes are good, I got a new car, it's been snowing a lot*. None of the things he wished he'd said were in those letters, but somehow his mother had divined his intentions and kept a shoe box full of letters not worth keeping. Maybe Kate, in similar fashion, had finally come to understand and even appreciate the "tough love" that, in anger, she'd described as "no love at all." His hand shook as he read on, but only because Kate's first sentence was completely untrue:

I know you think it's a waste of my time to write a play.

Was *that* the *only* message he'd been sending? He couldn't have been more proud of her, and he'd been trying to convey that in his own way, but he wanted her to have options and make good choices. How could there have been such a disconnect between what she heard and what his heart was saying?

"I'm not a heart reader or a mind reader," Elizabeth

had once said to him. "I suppose you never stopped loving me, but it would have been nice to hear it."

He continued reading. The pages were from Kate's play, but she wasn't sharing them for his approval or comment.

I just want you to understand that Patrick and I have no intention of revealing vital company secrets. I want you to know what we mean by "Code 6."

The letter explained how she and Patrick had learned about the world's first personal information catastrophe. How technology drove the Nazi concentration camps. And how the last thing a Jew wanted to be was "Code 6."

After the war, there were trials. At Nuremberg, the world witnessed a complete absence of remorse. The verdict was just. The death sentences were carried out. But Nuremberg was the exception, not the rule. In some places, there were no courtrooms. There was no trial. Sometimes men just . . . disappeared. One of those men was Herman Rottke. He was the general manager of IBM's subsidiary in Berlin. Rottke knew what Code 6 was. This is my imagin-

ing of things, but here's everything I can tell you about Code 6.

He put the letter aside and picked up his daughter's script. Actually, she'd sent only a portion of it. Act two, scene three. He read, and he saw, exactly as Kate had imagined: Mr. Rottke's last moments on earth, as he sat with his head down and hands bound, bathed in the hot light of an interrogation lamp, facing a Red Army interrogator somewhere in the Soviet-occupied sector of Berlin in 1946.

"Do you mourn for your friends who hanged today?"

Rottke was silent, his gaze fixed on the floor. The Russian interrogator leaned forward, forcing the prisoner to look him in the eye.

"You knew these men, didn't you?"

"Some of them."

The officer resumed pacing. "Wilhelm Frick. Minister of the Interior. Author of the Nuremberg Race Laws. You knew him?"

"I met him."

"Ernst Kaltenbrunner. SS leader. Head of Secret State Police. Commander of *Einsatzgruppen*. Hans Frank. Governor-general of Nazi-occupied Poland.

Your company did business in Poland during the war, did you not?"

Silence from Rottke. The interrogator removed a short stack of Hollerith punch cards from a folder and fanned them out like a poker hand before Rottke's eyes.

"My men sacked the Nazi Labor Service Office in Warsaw. We found thousands of Hollerith punch cards like these. Tell me, Mr. Rottke. Why would the Labor Service Office need so many Hollerith cards?"

Rottke looked up with disdain. "I have no understanding of how they were used."

The interrogator held a Hollerith card up to the light, allowing light to pass through the punched holes. "These little rectangular holes: they're not positioned randomly, are they?"

"Punch-hole placement is by design," he said smugly, as if pleased to show off his superior knowledge. "It delivers information."

"About people?"

"It's possible."

"Let's say the Nazis wanted to identify every person with a Jewish grandparent. They could search millions and millions of paper records. Months of work. Correct?"

"Years."

CODE 6 • 417

"Or . . . they could transfer census data to punch cards like these, and let Hollerith machines sort the cards at—how many per hour?"

"Twenty-five thousand," said Rottke, too proud of his company's accomplishments to deny it.

"And if the Nazis wanted to know the street address of every man, woman, and child with Jewish blood, Hollerith cards could tell them."

"A very basic design for a German engineer."

"If the Nazis wanted a complete inventory of property taken from Jews, Hollerith cards could make such a list, no?"

The head of the "German engineers" had no answer.

"If the Nazis needed slave labor to build a wall around the Warsaw Ghetto, Hollerith cards could find Jewish masons. Right?"

Rottke offered only an angry glare.

"If the Nazis wanted every train to Auschwitz completely full and running on time, Hollerith cards could do that?"

"Hollerith cards are used by railways all over the world," said Rottke, speaking with even more contempt.

"But for people stuffed in boxcars like cattle, their fate was in these cards, no?"

"I don't understand what you are asking me."

The Russian selected one of the Hollerith cards from the stack. "This card. Female. Twenty years of age. Student at university."

"So?"

"This is what interests me about the cards we found. The coding might be different for age, sex, nationality, and such. But they all had one thing the same."

He held the card so Rottke could see the punch hole, then continued. "Column thirty-four: Reason for Departure. All punched in same place: Code Six."

The interrogator leaned closer, getting right in the prisoner's face. "I want to know: What is Code Six?"

"I have no idea."

"I want *you* to tell me!" he shouted.

Rottke tightened his jaw, refusing to answer.

The Russian grabbed him by the throat. "Tell me what is Code Six!"

Rottke groaned, his throat still in the interrogator's grip.

"Louder!"

The Russian released his stranglehold. Rottke gasped for air and tried to speak.

"Special . . . ," he started to say, but his voice dropped.

"In a voice as loud as mine," the interrogator shouted, "special *what?*"

"Special handling!"

Rottke's chest heaved with each breath. The interrogator stepped back, as if satisfied for the moment. Then he moved closer, tightening his glare.

"And what is 'special handling'?"

Rottke summoned his last show of defiance and spat directly into his interrogator's face. The Russian cocked his arm, ready to bludgeon his prisoner.

"Blackout?" said Gamble, reading the stage direction aloud. He put the pages aside, his heart pounding.

It was evident that his daughter could write, but that wasn't Kate's point in sharing these particular pages. Nor was it merely a history lesson—unless the lesson was that history repeats itself. Code 6 was a Nazi abomination of state-of-the-art technology. Good made evil. Gamble had given his speech a thousand times about the disconnect between technology on the one hand and forces of "good and evil" on the other. It was all packaged in his story about the famous fictional sled dog that was his company's namesake.

"Buck is neither good nor evil. Buck is pure. In the right hands, Buck can do wonderful things. Buck, however, is not always in the right hands. We do not control the sled driver. Our creativity and inventiveness can never be stifled by the unfortunate reality that, in the wrong hands, Buck can be a force for evil. *Never.*"

He wondered if Kate's play was her rejoinder. A strange memory popped into his mind, and he was suddenly at the kitchen table with a sixteen-year-old Kate, drilling her on SAT questions and those confounding analogies. He could almost hear her voice in his head, articulating the message behind her play in that sing-song pattern: "Code Six is to IBM as Patrick's ransom demand is to Buck Technologies."

It was a chilling thought, made all the more disturbing by the fact that he didn't have clearance to know exactly what code the kidnappers wanted. Patrick did, but he was unreachable. Jeremy Peel surely did, but he was unlikely to share any secrets, even if he could have done so without breaking the law. There was only one person he could think to ask.

He picked up his phone and dialed the women's federal prison in Alderson, West Virginia.

"I'd like to schedule a visitation with Sandra Levy," he told the operator. "As soon as possible."

Chapter 53

Patrick and Olga rode in the back of a box truck. Liu hadn't told them where they were headed, but Patrick assumed it was Cali, the city Javier had chosen for the exchange. Obviously, Liu was doing all he could to keep Kate under the impression that nothing had changed.

"He's going to kill me," said Olga.

The truck was loaded with twenty-pound bags of rice, which Liu had rearranged to make room for his hostages to sit inside the double cargo doors, toes touching and facing each other. The floor-to-ceiling crack between the locked doors provided just enough ventilation for them to breathe and enough daylight to see.

"Don't say that," said Patrick. "We're going to get out of this alive."

"You might. Not me."

"I won't let that happen."

"It's not up to you."

"We have to keep hope."

"We have to be realistic. Tell me this. Why would Liu keep me alive?"

The white noise of truck tires on pavement filled the silence between them. Patrick wanted to be positive, but it was hard to find convincing words of encouragement with Liu in control.

"See," she said. "You don't have an answer. Javier was different. With him, there was hope."

"Sorry, but I never saw Javier as a beacon of hope."

"Javier had reasons to keep me alive. This venture into the business of kidnapping was a sideshow. His bread and butter was sex trafficking. I was his product. You don't kill your product. This man has no reason to keep me alive, except to torture me and get you to do whatever he wants you to do. When it's over, he'll kill me."

Intellectually, it was hard to argue with her logic.

"Then we need to find a reason for him to keep you alive," said Patrick.

"Yeah, well, I guess we know the only thing I'm good for."

"Don't talk like that."

"It's the truth," she replied.

"That's not the truth. That's the lie they want you to believe."

"And who are 'they'?"

"The people who want to control the way you think. What you think. How you should think," Patrick said.

"People like Javier, you mean?"

"No. People like Jeremy Peel."

"The johns?"

Patrick had almost forgotten—or rather, almost put out of his mind—that Peel had been the first to violate Olga in her white string bikini.

"No. I'm talking about people who *really* run companies like Buck Technologies."

Even in the dim lighting, Patrick could see the confusion on her face.

"I don't follow you," said Olga.

"Let me put it this way. Remember when you used to unlock your cellphone with your fingerprint?"

"Yeah. Before there was face recognition."

"Exactly. And where do you think the fingerprints, the facial recognition, the retinal scanning, the voice recognition, and all the other stuff goes?"

"I don't know."

"Of course you don't. You just give it up, no questions asked. And Big Data just keeps taking, as long as you keep giving. I guess elbow scans and heartbeat recognition are next. Hell, by the time our kids are on social media, they'll be down to belly button scans and fart recognition. How scary is that?"

She laughed. "Very. I like you, Patrick, but I'm not sure I'm ready to have kids with you."

"Huh?" he said, and then his words "our kids" came back to him. "No, I didn't mean *our* kids. I meant—"

"I know what you meant. Just yanking your chain."

Patrick looked away, embarrassed, then back. He wasn't necessarily trying to change the subject, but there was something that needed to be said.

"Olga?"

"Yes?"

"What if I told you there is no Code Six?"

She paused before answering. "Then I'd say I was only half right when I said he's going to kill me when we get to Cali. He's going to kill *both* of us."

"He can't kill us. I came up with a phony name, but I know exactly what he wants. That gives me the upper hand. He can't even begin to describe the code he needs from Buck. All he knows is that the part of the code he already has is worthless without the piece I called Code Six."

"Okay. Then I take back what I just said. He does need to keep you alive. But not me."

"We can fix that."

"How?"

"I could tell you what I know."

She chuckled. "Sound great. Just put it on flash drive, stick it in my ear, and the top-secret code from Buck Technologies will just download into my brain."

"If I wanted to, I could put this in terms even Javier could have understood."

"Do you think it's important for me to know?" she asked.

"I do," he replied.

"Okay. Then I'll listen. But only if you do me a favor."

"What?"

"I'm freezing over here. Will you sit next to me?"

Their hands were bound behind their backs, but Liu had left their feet unchained. "Sure," he said.

Patrick pushed himself up, fighting to keep his balance in the moving truck as he crossed to Olga's side. He fell against the stacked bags of rice and, with his back to the wall, slid down to settle in beside her.

"How's that?" he asked.

She moved a little closer. "Better."

It was better, and Patrick would have liked to put his arm around her, but for the bindings on his wrist.

"So," he said, "let me tell you how something called Project Naïveté evolved into the worst thing in technology since the *real* Code Six."

Chapter 54

Kate took her morning coffee on the balcony to her room at the InterContinental Cali. The rain had stopped overnight, and she had a clear view of the Andes.

Cali is surrounded in natural beauty, nestled in the Cauca Valley between the mighty Farallones de Cali mountain range and the Cauca River. Rough terrain challenged rock climbers and mountain bikers from across the globe. Miles of hiking trails and riverbanks offered an up-close glimpse of more species of flora and birds than most people would see in a lifetime. For more than half a century, however, it was akin to the biblical "valley of the shadow of death," a stronghold for leftist guerrillas, drug dealers, and right-wing para-military groups. Kate wondered how many families, over the decades, had taken a room in Cali, a suitcase full of money on the bed, counting the hours until some criminal who claimed to have a worthy cause would bring a loved one down from the mountains for the most dangerous part of any kidnapping: the ever-problematic "exchange."

"You sleep okay?" asked Enrique. He'd spent the night in the adjoining room.

"Not really," she said.

Enrique pulled up the other patio chair and sat facing the aluminum railing, sharing Kate's mountain view.

"I've been thinking about the exchange," he said.

"I have a plan."

"I'd love to hear it."

"You will. When I'm ready," she said.

He rested his muscular forearms on his thighs, leaning forward so that he could catch more than a sideways glance of Kate.

"Your father chose me for a reason," he said. "I have experience in these things. I negotiated with terrorists for the release of my own interpreter in Kabul."

"And it worked out okay?" she asked, hopeful.

He looked away in silence.

"I'm sorry," said Kate. "I wasn't asking to be mean."

"It's all right. I have some success stories, as well.

Interpreters were a different thing altogether. They were seen as the worst kind of traitors."

"Like a tech engineer who gives up company secrets?"

"Except that Patrick isn't giving up any secrets."

"Not willingly," said Kate. "But everybody has a breaking point. I'm very afraid of what they might do to him if they figure out Code Six is a ruse."

"If? Or when?"

Kate's cell rang. It was the encrypted line that she shared with Jeremy Peel. Adjusting for the time change between Virginia and Cali, exactly twenty-four hours had passed since the last call, just as Javier had promised. Kate answered on speaker, expecting to hear Javier's voice in reply, but it wasn't.

"Kate, this is Patrick."

A rush of relief came over her. "It's so good to hear your voice."

"I wish I could say more, but I have a script. By now, you should have Code Six on a flash drive. I'm going to tell you exactly how the exchange is going to be made. So please listen carefully."

"No," she said.

Enrique did a double take, and even Kate was surprised by her own words.

"What do you mean, no?" asked Patrick.

She had no doubt he trusted her, but in his voice she heard more than a hint of hope that she knew what the heck she was doing.

"Tell Javier to listen carefully," said Kate. "We are going to do this my way. I'm here for one reason. That's to get you. Jeremy Peel will deliver Code Six. We'll talk again in six hours."

Kate hung up.

Enrique's eyes were the size of saucers. "What the hell was that?"

"That," said Kate, collecting her breath, "is step one of my plan."

"What's step two?"

"We wait for the shit to hit the fan," she said. "Three, two, one."

The phone rang. She didn't even have to check the caller ID to know who it was.

"Hello, Mr. Peel."

"What kind of stunt are you trying to pull?" he shouted. "I told you I don't know what Code Six is!"

"I accept that. But whatever it is that Javier really wants, only you can give it to him."

"I can't give it to him! We're talking national security. I'd be in violation of the Espionage Act."

It was a setup question, and Peel had fallen for it,

effectively admitting that he knew what Javier really wanted—just as Kate had suspected.

"That's your problem, Mr. Peel. Not mine."

"You've got it backwards," he said. "If there's no ransom, you don't get Patrick."

"If there's no ransom, the Department of Justice will be on the next call."

There was silence on the line.

"I thought that would get your attention," said Kate. "Here's what I think, Mr. Peel. I think you're more worried about the Justice Department hearing these negotiations than Javier is."

"That's preposterous."

"Is it?" she asked, and then she played the ace in the hole she'd just dealt herself. "Then how is it that you *know* what Javier really wants, and that giving it to him would violate the Espionage Act, when all he's asked for is Code Six—which doesn't even exist?"

More silence.

"Fine," said Kate. "If you don't want to do your part to get Patrick home, I'm going to dial in Noah right now and tell him to join us on the next call."

"No!" he said, and then Kate heard him take a breath, as if he recognized his own overreaction.

"Do we understand each other now?" asked Kate.

"What are you proposing?"

"I'm not on a mission to make a citizen's arrest. I don't care what you're hiding. All I care about is getting Patrick out of here. I'm not saying you should hand over the secret formula to Coca-Cola. Just give them the recipe for Coke Zero. If it comes directly from you, not me, they'll accept it. By the time they can tell the difference, Patrick and I will be back in the United States."

Kate waited, and finally he answered.

"Okay."

"Okay what?"

"I'll come up with something to deliver as ransom. Enough to get Patrick released."

"That's all I ask," said Kate. "I'll call you in one hour."

Kate hung up.

Enrique looked at her with amazement. "Has anyone ever told you that you have bigger balls than your father?"

Kate knew it was meant as a compliment, and in that light his question prompted a twenty-year-old memory of her father's warning that if she didn't clean up her room before he returned from work, everything out of place would land in the garbage. He came home to find her room in impeccable condition—and about half the things in his messy home office in the garbage. Kate's mother would tell the story for years to come, which usually ended with her using the same anatomical metaphor to describe their daughter.

"Only one person I can think of," said Kate.

Chapter 55

G amble took the Super Puma to West Virginia. Technically speaking, he wasn't traveling on Buck Technologies business, but he had bigger things to worry about than shareholder complaints about the use of the company helicopter for personal reasons. He reached FCP Alderson early enough to be among the first visitors of the day.

"I'm here to see Sandra Levy," he told the corrections officer at reception.

The guard checked his ID against the list of approved visitors, and Gamble held his breath. He had an appointment, but it was Sandra's prerogative to refuse to see him up until the last minute.

"Follow the guard into the visitation center," he said, which Gamble took as a good sign.

The guard led him to the same table as the last visit, which had Gamble guessing how long it had been since then. Two days? Three? He suddenly wasn't even sure what day it was. So much had happened in the interim. His need to know had grown exponentially. He wasn't sure how he would increase Sandra's willingness to talk.

She pulled up the chair opposite him and rested her hands on the table. "I wasn't expecting to see you again."

"So soon, you mean?"

"Ever."

He wasn't sure where to go from there.

"That's a handsome suit you're wearing, Christian. Like my outfit? Same one I wear every day. Khaki on khaki. They do let me wear a jacket when it gets cold. Sorry I can't model it for you. They're afraid we might use it to hide contraband, so I can't wear it here."

There was a bitterness about her that she'd managed to hide, for the most part, on the previous visit. Inmates had bad days and worse days, he supposed. Getting her to help him would be an even bigger mountain to climb than he'd anticipated.

"You got a raw deal, Sandra. I get it."

"That's an understatement."

"Not as raw as Patrick Battle's."

His words landed with the desired impact. Some of her resentment peeled away. "What do you want from me, Christian?"

"Patrick's kidnappers made a ransom demand."

"How much is that going to set you back?"

"They don't want money. They want code."

"What code?"

"That's the problem. I don't know. Kate doesn't know. They put Patrick on the phone to make the demand. Jeremy Peel and Kate were on. Patrick called it Code Six."

"Never heard of it."

"It doesn't exist," he said.

She smiled a little.

"What's so funny?"

"That's so Patrick. Mess with his kidnappers and make something up on the fly."

He didn't see the need to discuss his daughter's play. "Just because Patrick came up with a bogus name doesn't mean the code the kidnappers really want isn't real."

Her smile faded. "And you think I can help with that. Is that it?"

He checked left, then right, making sure no one was within earshot. "I have a theory. Do you want to hear it?"

"I have a feeling I'm about to."

"My theory is this: the code these kidnappers want is the same code you tried to steal."

Her expression went stone cold. "I told you before, Christian: I didn't steal any code."

"Cut the bullshit, Sandra. This is life or death for Patrick, and now my daughter's down in Colombia, trying to get him home."

"You're asking me to confess to a crime."

"I'm asking you to help save two lives that shouldn't be lost."

"I'm slated for release in less than two years. If I confess to espionage, I could be stuck here, or more likely someplace much worse, for another ten to twenty."

"Do you really think I came here wearing a wire, Sandra?"

"I don't know. Maybe."

He looked at her from across the table, and the way their eyes locked reminded him of how much he'd once trusted her. Apparently, she'd gotten the same reminder.

"No," she said, in a much softer voice. "I don't think that."

"That's good. Because I came here to have an honest conversation."

Sandra took a breath, and then began.

"The deal I cut was pretty favorable. Plead guilty

to three counts of lying to an FBI agent. Minimal jail time."

"You were fortunate. Some people thought the Justice Department was too lenient."

"That's an understatement. Even the Justice Department thought my deal was too lenient. Lucky for me, my deal was with the CIA."

"Federal prosecutors work for the Justice Department, not the CIA. Why were you cutting a deal with the CIA?"

"Three reasons. I uncovered the next phase of Project Naïveté. More important, I knew the CIA was behind it. Most important, I agreed to keep my mouth shut."

"Agreed to keep your mouth shut about the code? Or about the fact that the CIA was behind it?"

"It all boiled down to the same thing. The CIA is Buck's biggest investor. If I decided to be the next Edward Snowden and reveal what Naïveté Two could do, the blowback to the CIA would be astronomical."

"What kind of blowback?"

"The kind of blowback that comes when the public learns that the CIA invested tax dollars in a private tech company to develop technology to use against its own people."

He took a moment to wrap his mind around her

words. "You were a management coach. How did you uncover all this?"

"I slept with the founder of Buck Technologies and used his credentials," she said, completely matter-of-fact in her delivery, neither proud nor embarrassed.

"First of all, we never slept together," said Gamble. "And even if we had, the CIA has always kept me dark to its most sensitive projects, so my credentials wouldn't have suited your purpose."

"I didn't mean you," she said. "I meant Jeremy Peel."

A lower level of clearance was something Gamble had been forced to accept, given Peel's connection to Walker and the CIA. But hearing about Sandra with Peel, after living with rumors that had all but destroyed his marriage, was enough to make his head explode.

"You and Jeremy? How could you?"

"He was such an easy mark. I'm only five years younger than him, so I'm obviously way too old for his tastes. But all I had to do was suggest that I was sleeping with you, and of course he bit. If it means taking something from you, Jeremy is all over it."

Gamble was in a state of disbelief. "Are you saying you really *are* a—"

She cut him off before he could say the word "spy."

"It's not what you're thinking. But put that aside.

Does everything really need a label? The most important thing here is that I acted with good intentions."

"Meaning what?"

"Like I told you. I did it for my daughter."

She'd said the same thing in their last visit, and again it stirred up the confusion he and Kate shared over the suicide note.

"Did *what* for your daughter?" he asked, speaking in a hushed but urgent voice. "What does this Naïveté Two do?"

"How much time do you have?"

"As long as it takes."

Sandra was about to begin, but the corrections offered appeared at their table, and her voice halted.

"Time's up," he said.

"We were just getting started," said Gamble.

"Sorry," said the guard. "This inmate is limited to just one thirty-minute visit per week."

"Since when?" asked Sandra.

"Since the warden announced your punishment this morning."

Gamble looked at Sandra. "Punishment for what?"

"I smuggled in cigarettes," said Sandra, a bit like a schoolgirl caught smoking in the bathroom.

"Look, Officer," said Gamble. "I've traveled a long way. Can we have a few more minutes, please?"

"Sorry, sir. Rules are rules. Come back next week, and the two of you can have another thirty minutes."

Sandra rose. "Hope this can wait a week, Christian."

"I hope so, too," he said, watching as the guard escorted her away.

Chapter 56

Patrick watched and waited as his kidnapper laid Javier's cellphone aside. He and Olga were chained to an exposed metal stud in the wall, seated on a concrete floor.

They were in a warehouse, presumably in Cali. The box truck had pulled up sometime that morning. Patrick had heard the steel garage door open and close before the rear doors of the cargo box swung open, and Liu had ordered them out at gunpoint. Theirs was the only truck in the warehouse, but there were about a dozen cars and SUVs in various states of disassembly. Shelves lined the walls, twenty feet high, and they were loaded with harvested automobile parts. It reminded Patrick of the chop shops he'd seen in the Grant Theft Auto video game he'd played as a kid. Liu had his own desk, though the nameplate read LOPEZ, which Patrick assumed was the name of the actual warehouse manager. The hostages were to his right, near a closet-sized room marked EL BAÑO. Patrick thought the sign should have read "desperate," as no one in his right mind would have used it if he weren't.

"Your friend Kate is trouble," said Liu.

He spoke with none of the screams of anger they would have heard from Javier. His was a wholly different temperament, but it made Patrick even more fearful. He had the eyes of a killing machine, like the soulless black eyes of the great white shark before it tears off your arm.

"If she pulls another stunt like that on the next call, we'll have to demonstrate the virtue of a healthy fear of burning alive."

He was looking at Olga.

"It wasn't a stunt," said Patrick. "I know Kate. She's not a loose cannon. She'd take control like this only if there was no other way to make sure you get what you want."

Liu checked the clock on the wall. "Sounds like you're willing to bet your life on it, which is good. In six hours, either we have an exchange or we have a dead hostage."

He took a seat in the desk chair, put his feet up, and

escaped into some form of electronic entertainment on his cellphone.

"I told you he was going to kill me," Olga whispered.

"I'm not sure he meant you," said Patrick.

"He can't kill you. You're the goose that lays the golden egg."

"I can still lay eggs as long as Kate *thinks* I'm alive."

"He needs you to make an exchange."

"I don't think the actual delivery of a live hostage is part of his plan."

"Why do you say that?" she asked.

"Remember those two phone calls you told me about? It was the day I disappeared in the mountains, and you overheard Javier talking on his satellite phone."

"Yes. It was like Javier had two bosses."

"One was Jeremy Peel, who sounded concerned that I disappeared."

"Yes. Apparently, Mr. Peel just wanted to keep you happy enough to stay in Colombia for a good long while. Not lose you somewhere in the jungle."

"But the other caller had a different agenda."

"Totally. It sounded to me like he wanted you dead," said Olga.

Patrick's gaze drifted toward the kidnapper. "I think that other caller was Liu. He hired Javier to push me off the mountain. Javier screwed up the hit, and Liu had to come all the way to Colombia to finish the job himself. And take care of Javier."

"It's like the good book says," said Olga. "No man can serve two masters."

"For he shall hate the one, and be shot in the head by the other," said Patrick, putting his own spin on Matthew 6:24. It was his best attempt at humor under the circumstances, but he had a serious follow-up. "I didn't figure you for someone who knew her Bible."

"Religious education five days a week and Mass every Sunday. Until I was fifteen," she added, and her voice trailed off. "Until Javier took me."

It made Patrick glad that scumbag was dead. It made him hate men like Jeremy Peel even more.

Liu rose from the chair and walked around the desk to the hostages. He stared at Patrick with those shark-like eyes and held the phone up before him.

"On the count of three, I'm going to hit the RECORD button. I want you to say the following: 'Kate, it's me, Patrick. I'm fine. Do exactly as the man says.'"

The kidnapper counted to three and hit RECORD. Patrick repeated the message exactly as instructed.

"Well done," said Liu, and he walked back to his desk.

Patrick and Olga exchanged a nervous glance, and

no words were needed. Each could see it in the other's eyes:

Escape is our only hope.

A phone rang on the desk. It was Javier's cell, sitting right where Liu had left it. Liu checked the incoming number and answered in a voice loud enough for Patrick to hear.

"Hello, Jeremy."

Peel held the satellite phone a little closer to his ear. He'd placed the call at an altitude of 39,000 feet from Buck's corporate jet. Perhaps the reception was bad, or maybe the roar of the jet engine was making it hard to hear, but the voice on the line didn't sound at all like Javier.

"Who is this?"

"You know who this is."

Peel did. And he didn't dare hang up. "Where's Javier?"

"Javier can't come to the phone. Ever."

The news wasn't shocking, but it chilled him nonetheless. "I want you to know that I had nothing to do with the stunt Kate Gamble pulled in the last call."

"I believe you. You don't have the stones to deliver the code yourself. Never in a million years would you agree to that plan."

"But you're not expecting me to show up with a flash drive and—"

"That's exactly what I'm expecting, Jeremy. I like Kate's idea. Don't you?"

Peel didn't like it in the least, but he knew his preferences were irrelevant. "We'll do it the way you want."

"Good. How soon can you be in Cali?"

"I'm in the air now on my private jet, but we can't possibly land in time for the six-hour deadline Kate put on the next call."

"Call her from the plane and let her know you're on your way. Tell her you talked to Javier and agreed the next call will be tonight at eight p.m. Cali time. Don't mention me. Don't you *dare* mention me."

The call ended. Peel collapsed in his chair, emotionally spent, dreading the coming night in Cali. Then he dialed Kate's encrypted phone.

The call from Jeremy Peel lasted two minutes. Kate agreed to make herself ready for a phone call with the kidnapper at the new time of 8:00 p.m. Beyond that, it was like a game of liar's poker.

"Do you have the ransom?" asked Kate.

"I'd prefer not to have this conversation by phone, even if it is encrypted."

"I need an answer from you before the eight p.m. call."

"Let's meet at your hotel and talk."

"That's impossible. There's not another person on the planet who knows where I'm staying, and I'm certainly not going to tell you. Nothing personal."

They agreed to meet in the lobby of a boutique hotel in one of Cali's wealthiest neighborhoods, Ciudad Jardín. Kate hung up. She looked at Enrique, who was sitting in the armchair in her hotel room.

"I'm worried," said Kate.

"Stay cool," he said. "You took control in this morning's call. Kidnappers hate it when negotiators do that. So it's no surprise that Javier would try to reestablish control by pushing off the next meeting to eight p.m.—to a time selected by him, not you."

"I agree with all that," said Kate.

"Then what worries you?"

"From the previous calls, my impression of Javier is that he's impulsive and quick to react. I would have expected him to call me right back, immediately after I hung up, and retake control. He didn't. Instead, he waited two hours, called Jeremy Peel on a line that I'm not even privy to, and asked him to pass along a message to me. Doesn't that strike you as odd?"

"I hear what you're saying, Kate. You think he hurt Patrick."

"I can't live with myself if my plan backfires."

It was a cumulative effect: Patrick's disappearance, meeting Sandra Levy, her negotiations with Noah, the calls from the kidnappers, standing up to Jeremy Peel—all in the wake of her mother's suicide. Kate needed a tissue.

"Hey, it's okay," said Enrique, handing her a whole box of them.

"I'm so sorry," she said.

"Not a problem. If it means anything, I cried like a baby when I lost my interpreter."

Kate gathered herself and said, "I'm really glad you're here."

"Me, too," he said.

Chapter 57

C hristian Gamble arrived at the Washington office of BJB Funding before noon. He was there to see David Walker.

The CIA headquarters is in Virginia, but the agency fastidiously guards against any claims of overlap between its national security operations and its venture capital arm, so BJB operated out of a nongovernmental building on the other side of the Potomac River. The George Bush Center for Intelligence is too far north to be seen from the District, but Walker seemed to have gone the extra mile to assert his independence from the agency by choosing a corner office facing the National Mall to the south, his back squarely to the CIA while seated behind his desk.

Gamble hadn't spoken to Walker since the meeting

at Peel's house, where Kate had told the chairman of the board and the CIA to fuck off and announced that she was "going private" to negotiate for Patrick's release. Gamble had phoned ahead from the helicopter on the flight back from FCP Alderson to set up what he described as "a critical follow-up meeting," just the two of them in Walker's office.

"I went to visit Sandra Levy," said Gamble.

"I know," said Walker.

Smug remarks like that one, the air of omniscience that Walker conveyed, made Gamble question the actual degree of separation between the agency and its venture capital arm.

"Then am I correct that the prison guard's sudden decision to cut my visit short was no coincidence?"

"It was my understanding that her visitation privileges have been restricted due to a rule infraction."

"I'm sure. The fact that you know so much about it tells me that's bullshit."

"Christian, if you've come here to give me a tongue lashing, I have far more important things to deal with."

"Then allow me to readjust your priorities. My conversation with Sandra Levy gave me serious cybersecurity concerns. The DOJ's security audit is ongoing. I came to you because I wanted to discuss my concerns with you first. But if you don't have time," he said, rising, "that's unfortunate."

"Sit down, Christian. Before you embarrass yourself by going to the DOJ, what do you know about Sandra Levy?"

Gamble settled back into his chair. He didn't want to divulge too much of his conversation with Sandra, but it was simply a good negotiating tactic to show Walker that he wasn't there on a fishing expedition—that he had some critical level of knowledge.

"I know that the CIA played a key role in structuring what appears to be a very favorable sentence for her."

"Yes, that's true. You do realize Sandra Levy *works* for the CIA."

"What?"

"She was a plant, Christian. The CIA was concerned about a possible leak at Buck Technologies, and to protect its investment in the company, the agency sent in Sandra to find it. 'Management coach' was her cover. We wanted her close to you."

Gamble did a double take. "Wait. Are you saying *I* was the suspected leak?"

"Your wife, to be more precise. Using credentials she stole from you."

There was no use in denying that Elizabeth had

compromised his credentials. "She never actually used them to access anything."

"Your wife was an alcoholic who dialed nine-one-one and falsely accuse you of abuse. Who really *knows* what her intentions were?"

"She wasn't a criminal. Sandra's investigation must have confirmed that, right? If Elizabeth was actually using my credentials to steal company secrets, this wouldn't be the first time I'm hearing about this."

"Yes. Sandra Levy concluded that neither you nor your wife were the problem. And then she went badly astray."

"In what way?"

"She shifted her focus to Jeremy Peel without authorization. To make matters worse, she violated some cardinal rules about methods of extracting information from a target. I will spare you the lurid details."

Gamble had already heard it from Sandra, but hearing it from Walker put it in a new light. "Is that why she's in prison?"

"Very astute observation, Christian. She pled guilty to three counts of lying to investigators. Most people think those lies relate to espionage. In actuality, she had sex with Jeremy Peel in violation of CIA rules, and she lied about it. The CIA did her a favor by not making that public."

"All that aside, Sandra must have had a reason to target Jeremy. Has anyone ever followed up on that?"

"I can't discuss the status of an investigation with you."

"Forget the status of the investigation. Here's all I really want to know: What would make a person throw away her career like this? What was driving her?"

"I'm not at liberty to discuss her motivations."

"Well, fuck your liberty. Sandra discussed them with Kate. She said, 'I did it for Megan'—her daughter. Call me crazy, but that sounds an awful lot like the suicide note my wife left: 'I did it for Kate.' So I'd like to know what the hell is going on here!"

"Could be a coincidence."

"I'm not asking what it could be. What do you know?"

"I wish I could say more. I really do."

"Damn it, David! Your firm is the largest shareholder in Buck Technologies. My daughter's in Colombia right now negotiating with kidnappers to get one of Buck's key employees released. If you won't say it for my benefit, say it for hers. What does this all mean?"

"I have no idea what was in your wife's head."

"Fine. What was driving Sandra Levy? What did she mean when she said she did it for her daughter?"

Walker glanced out the window. It seemed that

Gamble's plea was getting through to him. Finally, he spoke.

"I'll say this much. Whatever she thought Jeremy was up to, Sandra saw it as particularly dangerous for girls and young women."

Gamble froze. It was as if he'd been in a dark room for months, with the answer sitting right beside him, and someone had finally switched on the light.

"I'm sorry, Christian. I can't tell you more than that."

"I got it," said Gamble. "You don't have to say another word."

Gamble showed himself out, rode the elevator to the lobby. A black SUV was waiting outside the building. He dialed Kate's number as he climbed inside, but she didn't answer. He thought carefully before making the next call, but decided it was the right thing to do.

"Noah, it's Christian Gamble," he said into the phone, leaving the prosecutor a voicemail message. "Call me back immediately. It's important."

Chapter 58

Diego picked up Kate and Enrique at the Hotel InterContinental to take them to the planning meeting with Jeremy Peel in Ciudad Jardín.

"Safety on?" asked Enrique. He was talking about the gun in her purse, and it was the third time he'd reminded her since leaving the hotel room.

"On," she said.

South Cali had some sketchy areas, but Ciudad Jardín was not one of them. Caleños called it a "city within a city" or, perhaps more accurately, a city apart from the city. Mansions lined the lush green avenues. The best high schools and universities were nearby, and an array of fancy restaurants and upscale bars made this wealthy neighborhood a pleasant and safe place to live. On the downside, Ciudad Jardín was a long way from the livelier and equally safe areas along the river to the west and north, where Kate was staying, and it was closer to the massive hillside neighborhood known as Siloé. Diego pointed it out on the ride south.

"Never go there," he said, pointing from the driver's seat. "If you get into trouble, even the police are afraid to go there."

The rule of thumb in Cali was to avoid the east, but gangs also controlled Siloé and other pockets of turf to the south.

They reached the hotel in plenty of time to talk strategy before the 8:00 p.m. call. Diego waited with the car. Peel's bodyguard was in the lobby and took them to a suite on the third floor so they could speak in private. It was Kate and Enrique on one side of the rectangular table, with Peel and his bodyguard on the other. The encrypted phone on which Kate received the kidnapper's calls was resting beside the centerpiece of white and purple orchids.

"Did you bring the flash drive?" asked Kate.

Peel laid it on the table. "Coke Zero," he said, confirming that he wasn't giving up the "secret formula," as Kate had called it.

"In terms of communications," said Kate, "I don't like you having separate phone calls with Javier. I need to be part of all negotiations going forward."

"I didn't initiate the last call. He called me. After you hung up."

"I was asserting control."

"You may have watched one too many *Die Hard* movies."

Kate had been second-guessing herself all day, so she couldn't push back too hard. "What's done is done. Going forward, we should speak with one voice, and that voice should be mine."

Kate's encrypted phone vibrated on the table. It was not yet time for the 8:00 p.m. call, but it wasn't a call anyway. It was a text that contained no message, just a voice recording. Kate played the voice message on speaker. It was Patrick.

"Kate, it's me, Patrick. I'm fine. Do exactly as the man says."

Kate looked at Enrique, who seemed equally bemused. "That's our proof of life? A voice recording? How do we know that's not from a week ago?"

Her phone vibrated again. This time, the text bubble contained a message:

Negotiations are over. No more voice calls. My orders to follow.

Kate stared at the message bubble, then looked at Peel. "This doesn't sound like Javier."

Peel didn't answer, but Kate didn't drop the matter.

"Who did you actually speak to on the phone earlier, Mr. Peel?"

"I told you it was Javier."

"I know what you told me. But I want the truth. Who did you talk to?" she asked, her voice rising. "I need to know who has Patrick!"

The phone vibrated. Another text message:

Mr. Peel: Take the flash drive to Café de Mariscos on Calle Obispo at 9 p.m. A table is reserved in your name. Sit and wait. One bodyguard is allowed. No one else.

Enrique googled the location. "He chose a public place in a good neighborhood to make you feel safe. That's a constructive first step."

"But what about Patrick?" asked Kate. "This has to be a simultaneous exchange."

The telltale moving ellipses appeared below the previous bubble message on Kate's phone, indicating another text was on the way.

"There's more," said Kate, and the message appeared.

If I'm convinced you were not followed, I will join you. The girl will be with me. I take the flash drive. You keep the girl.

"By 'the girl,' I assume he means Olga," said Enrique. "The one you told me about?"

"Yes," said Kate, shooting dagger eyes in Peel's direction. "The girl in the white string bikini."

Another text bubble quickly followed.

As soon as I verify that the code is genuine, I will release Patrick.

"Looks like he's not settling for Coke Zero," said Enrique.

"Shit," said Kate. She grabbed the phone and fired back a quick text.

Not acceptable. Simultaneous exchange only. Both Patrick and Olga.

It took more than a minute for a response to come. It was a phone call this time. Kate answered on speaker, so all could hear, but she didn't even get the chance to speak.

The sound of Patrick's scream filled the hotel suite.

Silence followed. The call was over, short but with the desired impact, as it had made Kate's skin crawl. A text bubble followed.

Final warning. Don't fuck with me.

Kate buried her face in her hands. Enrique laid a comforting hand on her shoulder. "We can work within his rules," he said.

"What choice do we have?" she said, her voice quaking.

Chapter 59

Patrick breathed deeply, in and out, trying to quell the pain in his left biceps.

Liu the pyromaniac had apparently left his napalm science experiment back at the ship, but he'd managed to improvise. A welding machine was standard equipment in any chop shop. He'd spared Patrick the direct and potentially lethal flame of the welding blowtorch—possibly an act of mercy, but more likely he was just too lazy to carry the entire machine from one side of the warehouse to the other. Instead, he'd selected a steel welding rod—one-sixteenth of an inch in diameter, by Patrick's estimate—and held it to the flame until the tip glowed like a sparkler on the Fourth of July.

"This is really going to hurt," he'd said, whereupon

the white-hot tip had burrowed into Patrick's arm like a lit cigarette, but so much hotter.

The pain was utterly disproportionate to the freckle-sized mark left behind. He worried where his scream into the cellphone must have led Kate's imagination.

"It's showtime," said Liu. "Olga, you're coming with me."

The hostages were chained to the same post but with separate padlocks. Liu unlocked Olga with the key, removed the chains, and pulled her to her feet. The gun to her head served to remind them who was in charge.

"Patrick, your life is in Olga's hands. If she obeys me, all will be fine. If she doesn't, then here's something you should know. That welding rod I jabbed into your arm was probably five hundred degrees Celsius. A welding arc is about fifteen *thousand* degrees. Tell Olga you don't want to go there."

Patrick noticed that the rod was still resting on the hood of the car nearest to the hostages, where Liu had left it to cool.

"Tell her she needs to be a good girl," said Liu.

"You're an animal," said Olga.

"You have to do as he says," said Patrick.

"How 'bout that, you're both right," said Liu. He led Olga away at gunpoint, wending between vehicles toward the side door to the warehouse. Patrick kept one eye on them and the other on the welding rod that Liu had left on the car hood. A foot-long rod of stainless steel was just a few feet away from him. He was padlocked to a pole, making it impossible to reach it, making it all the more imperative that he find a way to get it.

The rod was about the same thickness as a bicycle spoke, and the fact that Patrick's mind drew that comparison was no coincidence. Once, as a kid, he'd biked to the beach and, when it came time to pedal home, discovered that he'd lost the key to his bike lock while building a giant sandcastle complete with a moat, drawbridge, and three-foot-tall turrets. He had thirty minutes to get home or be grounded. For Patrick, it was just another episode in the long-running series *Internet to the Rescue.* His smartphone pulled up a YouTube video on how to pick a padlock with a reshaped paper clip. As it turned out, a 1.8-millimeter bicycle spoke worked even better.

With a stainless-steel welding rod, this job would be a piece of cake.

The side door opened and closed. A car engine started outside the building, and Patrick could hear the vehicle pull away. Olga and Liu were gone. He was alone in the warehouse. It was time for action.

Patrick would call this episode, "Harry Potter and the Quest for the Rod of Steel."

One end of the chain was fastened to a post. The other end coiled around his wrists and was secured behind his back with a padlock. His most comfortable position was seated with his back to the post, but the chain was long enough for him to lie flat on his back, if he could put up with the pain of a padlock pressed between his lower back and the floor. He concentrated on making his spine as long as possible, taking up every millimeter of slack in the chain. With his body fully extended, he finally managed to brace the crown of his head against the post and plant his feet squarely on the front bumper of the nearest vehicle—the car on which the metal rod rested.

Patrick pushed with his legs and released. It was like doing leg presses at the Buck fitness center. *Push. Release.* He built a rhythm, and before long, the car was rocking like a baby carriage.

He heard the steel rod move. Liu had left it near the windshield. It had rolled forward, halfway down the hood, following the sloped design toward the front bumper. Patrick pushed harder, legs pumping and heart pounding. The worst-case scenario was that the rod would turn sideways and get caught in the slit between the hood and side panel. He couldn't let that happen. He dug deep inside himself and pushed with all his leg strength. The rocking sensation built to a lurch, and Patrick heard the sweet *ping* of a steel rod hitting a concrete floor.

He stopped pumping, exhausted. The car was motionless. Patrick trapped the rod beneath the sole of his shoe and dragged it toward him. It required some contortion-like finagling, but he worked the prized rod all the way up along his leg and into his hands. He was almost giddy with excitement, until he realized that the hard part was still ahead of him.

Hard. But not impossible.

It had taken twenty minutes for a twelve-year-old Patrick to pick a lock with his bicycle spoke. Following the instructional video, he'd broken it into two pieces, one bent into the shape of an Allen wrench to apply tension to the wide base of the keyhole, like the flat edge of the key; the other bent at a forty-five-degree angle to "rake" the pins, like the jagged edge of the key.

This job would be no different, though it was his first attempt with his hands behind his back.

First time for everything.

Patrick snapped the rod in half and got to work.

Chapter 60

Christian Gamble spent the entire day on the Buck campus, exploring the depths of his own darkness.

The fact that certain Buck projects were dark to the CEO was not something Gamble talked about openly. The investment agreement with BJB Funding actually prohibited him from saying so publicly. But a twenty-year-old contract with the CIA's venture capital arm was not the sole, or even most important, reason to keep quiet about the limitations on his security clearance. It was beyond embarrassing. His own daughter had found it shocking.

Willful blindness, Dad. It's a corporate disease. Sometimes fatal.

His phone conversation with Noah had been short and to the point. "I need to know what I don't know," Gamble had told him. Noah balked and said he'd check with his supervisor. Gamble tired of waiting for a response. He showed up at the U.S. Attorney's Office in Judiciary Square to talk face-to-face, behind closed doors, just the two of them in Noah's office.

"I'm sorry," said Noah. "I can't share any preliminary conclusions of my cybersecurity audit with you or anyone else outside the department."

"I don't want your 'conclusions.' I want to verify some facts with you. That's your job, as auditor, correct? To base your decision on facts?"

"Of course."

"Then stop squirming like the spineless wimp my daughter dumped and answer my questions."

"You don't have to make this personal."

"My employee was kidnapped for ransom, and my daughter is risking her life, as we speak, to get him home. How is that not personal?"

"I don't see what that has to do with my audit."

"Can we just verify a few facts? *Please?*"

The "dumping" remark was harsh, but Gamble was in no mood to apologize. To his credit, Noah seemed willing to put it aside.

"Okay. I'm listening."

"Buck has a project called Naïveté Two. It grew out of Project Naïveté."

"I can't talk to you about Naïveté Two. You don't have clearance."

"But I do have clearance to numerous operations that feed in to Naïveté Two."

"How would you know what feeds in to Naïveté Two?"

"Process of elimination."

"I don't understand," Noah said.

"I know Jeremy Peel heads Naïveté Two. After twenty-five years, I know Jeremy's vision. I know which company assets he would draw upon to actualize that vision. I made a list. I spent all day pushing the limits of my clearance in each of those silos until I hit a brick wall."

Noah nodded, seeming to get it. "And you want me to tell you if that brick wall is Naïveté Two."

"No. Don't *tell* me anything. I'm simply going to read you my list of silos that I think feed in to Naïveté Two. If I'm wrong, there's nothing more to do. If I'm right, I would imagine you would want to shoot off an immediate email to your supervisor advising that it is highly possible that the kidnapping of Patrick Battle has compromised the security of Naïveté Two."

The two men locked eyes. Gamble pulled up his list on his smartphone.

"I'll spare you the obvious," said Gamble. "We all know that screen-related sentiment data is part of virtually everything Big Data does. Browsing history, social media connections, online purchases, likes, emojis, emoticons, LOLs and other sentiment-related acronyms, preferred slang, how often you type in all caps, how many fractions of a second you let your cursor linger over the image of a puppy as opposed to the image of a Kardashian.

"My list puts a finer point on the project. It focuses on non-screen data that tells Big Data how you think and feel. Ready?"

No answer from Noah, but he was clearly listening.

"One: smart speakers. By this I mean all the data collected from everything that operates on voice command. Your phone, your car, your house, your microwave oven—everything.

"Two: all those telephone conversations that are recorded with the caller's consent 'for training purposes,' which Big Data buys up so our algorithms can measure what your voice or syntax reveals about your emotions, sentiments, and personality—essentially, 'hear' what you say and how you say it when you're angry or trying to get a stranger to help you, so that you can be coded as 'logical and responsible,' 'creative and playful,' or 'tense and aggressive.'

"Three: personal health monitors, which can be linked to the GPS coordinates on your phone, so we know how fast your heart beats while you're watching the next James Bond film.

"Four: surveillance and security camera images, in case we also want to see the expression on your face when Mr. Bond removes his shirt, or when you run the red light on the drive home from the theater.

"Five, digitally captured internet videoconferencing, which never dies and, unlike General MacArthur and other old soldiers, doesn't just fade away. Six—"

Gamble paused and looked up from his list. "You get the idea. I believe Naïveté Two combines every non-screen data silo at Buck's disposal with traditional screen-sourced data to create a digital profile on every man, woman, and child in America. I'm talking about a massive collection of personal, psychological, and emotional dossiers that would make J. Edgar Hoover ejaculate in his grave."

He waited. Noah showed no reaction, verbal or non-verbal. Thirty seconds passed in silence. Finally, Noah turned in his swivel chair to face his computer monitor.

"Excuse me," he said. "I need to send an email to my supervisor."

He placed his hands on the keyboard and began typing.

Gamble rose and exited the office, Noah having "told" him nothing.

Kate's phone rang. It was her father. Calling to talk her out of danger, no doubt. She decided she should answer. Then changed her mind. Then changed it back.

"Dad, I can't talk now."

"It's a scraping tool," he said.

"What?"

"Code Six, or whatever you want to call Patrick's ransom demand. It's a scraping tool."

Kate was in the backseat of the car, and Enrique's friend Diego was driving. It was a safe neighborhood where people walked to bars and restaurants at night, so Kate and Diego circled the neighborhood while Enrique blended in with the crowd on foot, casing the restaurant where Peel was to make the exchange. The kidnapper had said "no followers" and only "one bodyguard," but it hadn't taken much in the way of persuasion for Peel to see the benefit of having Enrique nearby in case something went wrong.

"I don't even know what that means—a 'scraping tool.'"

"It could be a browser extension. It could be a lot of things. The bottom line is that it's a tool for outsiders to harvest data from platforms like TikTok, Facebook, Instagram, and all the other places where users give up way more than they should."

"And the platforms allow this?"

"No! That's the point. Facebook sends out cease and desist letters all the time. They even threatened the NYU Observatory for scraping data on political ads for academic research."

"So if scraping tools aren't allowed, why is Buck's so valuable?"

"Because no one knows it's there. It's the *stealth bomber* of scraping tools. We can scrape anything from any platform, and no one will know it. Do you understand how powerful that is?"

She did. "Are you sure about this?"

"Jeremy has talked about this for years. Today I pushed my credentials as far as possible in every data silo. Each time, I eventually hit a brick wall. On my side of the wall is the data we collected with proper consent. On the dark side of the wall, I believe, is the data we scraped."

"Illegally," said Kate.

"Without consent. It's a gray area. I wouldn't say illegally."

"Immorally," said Kate.

"We can debate that with Sir Thomas More in the next life. But here's the important thing."

The car stopped, and the passenger-side door suddenly opened, which sent Kate's heart into her throat. Enrique jumped in the backseat.

"Hold on, Dad," she said, relieved to see it was her bodyguard and not a carjacking.

"Peel is moving," said Enrique. "Kidnapper changed the drop site."

"To where?"

"Peel's bodyguard texted and said he'll send me a pin when they get there."

"What do you think happened?"

"Nothing," said Enrique. "I'm sure the kidnapper is just watching to see if anyone follows Peel to the new location."

"Like the police?"

"No, like us," said Diego, offering the insight of a local. "The kidnapper already knows we didn't involve the police. You can't call the police in Cali without the kidnapper getting tipped off."

Kate returned to her call. "Dad, I have to go."

"Wait. There's more."

"Dad, we're about to make the exchange!"

"Kate, I need to know: Is there any chance you're handing over the tool. The *real* tool?"

"No."

"Because this tool is dangerous in the wrong hands."

"This tool is dangerous in the *right* hands. But no, Dad, you don't have to worry. I'll call you when it's over."

Kate hung up. The car started forward. "Where we headed?" asked Kate.

"Club Siloé," said Enrique.

"Siloé? Diego, isn't that the place you told us never to go?"

From the driver's seat, Diego made eye contact in the rearview mirror. "The club's not technically in Barrio Siloé. But it's close."

"How close?"

"It's perfectly safe once you get inside," said Diego. "The fact that it's literally on the edge of danger is what makes it the cool spot in Cali. So you don't want to walk the area."

"We don't have to go, if you don't want," Enrique told her.

Kate hadn't come all this way to hang out with tourists and expats at her hotel while the exchange went down without her. On the other hand, there was a reason her father's kidnap and ransom insurance policy covered immediate family members.

"Just don't park the car," she said. "Circle the block. That's the plan."

"That's a good plan," said Diego, with a little more local insight.

Chapter 61

Peel's driver stopped outside the entrance to Club Siloé. His bodyguard, Jaime, was beside him in the backseat.

"I don't like this," said Peel.

"We want a public place, so he doesn't pull anything. But a five-star restaurant in Ciudad Jardín was a safer choice."

Peel had the kidnapper's number from their phone call on the jet. He dialed, was somewhat surprised to get an answer, and stated his position firmly.

"This location is not acceptable."

"I can see you. Go inside."

He'd assumed he was being watched, but until that moment, Peel hadn't felt it. "I'm not going in."

"Do I have to call Mr. Walker at the CIA?"

Technically, Walker wasn't "at the CIA," but that didn't diminish the threat. "You wouldn't do that," said Peel.

"I definitely will. And he'd be very upset to learn what bullshit it is that Buck Technologies only does business with Western allies. Unless you think he considers China a friend."

It could have been a bluff, as it wasn't in the interest of the Chinese government to "out" someone like Peel, a secret source of data on foreigners. But Peel couldn't take that risk. He had no choice but to fold.

"Ten minutes. In and out," said Peel.

"Your table is under the name Cruz. Wait for me there."

Not very imaginative of him to use the Spanish version of Smith, but Peel didn't quibble. The call ended, and with a quick nod to his team signaling "go," the driver opened Peel's door and his bodyguard whisked him inside.

Peel was no stranger to clubs of this sort, where naked young women worked on drunk businessmen, and the old song about a fool and his money was perpetually at the top of the charts. But it was his first time with only one bodyguard. It was risky behavior on his part, but it fed his macabre sense of curiosity to test the limits of what beautiful young women would do for money. Even more fun was to wager on it. "I'll bet you fifty thousand dollars the blonde will drink the redhead's urine for five hundred dollars." Not that he would ever have sex with one of these dancers. For that, men like Javier hooked him up with women like Olga.

Javier, you should have stuck to business as usual.

"Table for Cruz," he told the hostess.

"This way," the young woman said.

It turned out that the pole-dancing lounge was a small part of the action. Peel and his bodyguard followed the hostess through a set of chrome-clad double doors that led to the heart and soul of Club Siloé.

A salsa band was playing onstage, and a parquet dance floor was packed with couples making it clear that Shakira wasn't the only Colombian who could dance. Above the stage, stretching wall to wall, was an enormous rectangular meme of Leonardo da Vinci's *The Last Supper*, with whiskey replacing wine, and popular salsa musicians and their groupies replacing Jesus and His apostles. It was beloved by patrons, no doubt, but to Peel, this was art on the order of dogs playing poker. The hostess led them to a booth away from the band, a somewhat quieter section of the club where it was possible to have a conversation without shouting. She laid two menus on the table, and Peel checked the list of drinks. *Cervezas* were on the left; *tragos fuertes* on the right. The words in bold across the top of the menu made him curious.

"*Viva la vida, mira que se va y no vuelve,*" he read aloud in bad Spanish. "What does that mean, gorgeous?"

The hostess smiled. "No can say *en inglés.* Your waitress comes soon."

She left, and Peel put his bodyguard's Spanish to the test. "Do you know what it means?"

"The literal translation loses it. Basically: 'Live it up, 'cause, hey, life goes away and doesn't come back.'"

Peel laid the menu aside, and his gaze drifted toward the empty seats for their guests. "Good advice," he said.

Kate was on her second turn around the block. The plan was for Enrique to go inside the club and monitor the exchange while Kate and Diego circled Club Siloé. As the car stopped outside the club entrance, the voice of Peel's bodyguard came through in real time over the car's sound system, which was linked by Bluetooth to Diego's cellphone.

"Basically: 'Live it up, 'cause, hey, life goes away and doesn't come back.'"

"That's actually a decent translation," said Diego.

Enrique had the cellphone number for Peel's body-guard, and Diego had used it to hack the phone's micro-phone so that they could eavesdrop on Peel's conversation with the kidnapper. Technologically, it wasn't difficult to do, especially for a former DEA agent. Diego had busted many a drug dealer who didn't realize that his phone simply had to be powered on, not in use, for hackers to use the microphone as a listening device.

"A lot of background noise," said Kate.

"It's a nightclub. I can't help that," said Diego.

"That's why we still need eyes on the table," said Enrique. "I'll text you with updates."

"Good luck," said Kate.

Enrique got out, and the car pulled away. Diego hung a left at the traffic light, and they continued east, toward the luminous moon above the hilltop.

"That's Siloé," he said, indicating.

Glittering lights dotted the habitable portion of hill-side, from street level to an elevation of about one thou-sand feet. At the very top, jagged granite edges bathed in the moonlight.

"It's actually beautiful at night."

"*Sí*, at night."

Kate noticed a strange glowing dot in the distance. It moved slowly up the hill, like a meteor light-years away from earth, seeming to divide Siloé in half.

"What's that moving dot?" asked Kate.

"That's the new gondola public transportation system," he said, and then he hung a right. "The idea is that if people have transportation, they can get a job and build a better life. That's the station right ahead."

The car slowed, and Kate looked out the window as they passed the station at street level. About two dozen commuters were in line.

"They're all women," said Kate.

"Yeah, mostly housekeepers. The 'have nots' who serve the 'haves.' They work a twelve-hour shift, seven days a week, in Ciudad Jardín and other nice parts of Cali. Then it's back to Siloé. The gondola gives them some hope of getting home to take care of their families without getting robbed."

"Sad."

"Yeah. It just amazes me, though."

"What does?" Kate asked.

"What mothers will do for their children."

Kate couldn't have said it better, but her mind raced beyond the point of mere agreement.

I did it for Kate.

She glanced again at the women in line. Diego made another left turn, and as they continued down the street, heading straight toward the gondola rising toward the moon over the hilltop, Kate shook off the confusing thoughts of her mother's death. She was instead thinking of Sandra Levy.

I did it for Megan.

Kate had at first dismissed Sandra's words as a snarky comment about her mother's suicide note. Something else was afoot, and her father's explanation of the scraping tool behind Naïveté II was bringing it all into focus.

The bottom line is that it's a tool for outsiders to harvest data from platforms like TikTok, Facebook, Instagram, and all the other places where users give up way more than they should.

It was well known that the "users" who gave up the most on social media were between the ages of thirteen and twenty—and female. Studies proved it. Facebook, TikTok, and the other platforms admitted as much. Self-esteem, self-confidence, and self-worth were down; anxiety, depression, and suicide were up. The victims were mostly girls—daughters with mothers who would do anything to protect them.

Kate reached for her phone and was about to call her father when it vibrated with a text message. It was from Enrique on the inside.

They just sat down. Asian guy with the girl.

Kate put her phone away.

"Diego, turn up the volume on the audio feed," she said.

"If I turn it any louder, there's too much static from the background noises around them."

Kate put her ear to the car speaker. As they made their third trip around the block, she listened to the conversation at the table inside Club Siloé.

Chapter 62

L iu entered Club Siloé with a beautiful woman on his arm. If Olga was going to accompany him, she had to look the part. A backless dress would have been sexier, but Javier's knife had done its own brand of salsa dancing there. She looked hot enough in his second choice. Red was her color. A little makeup went a long way to hide the worry lines of captivity.

"Say nothing," he reminded her, as the hostess led them to the Cruz booth.

Liu had reserved this particular booth with purpose. Its proximity to the fire exit, an avenue of escape, had made it narcos' table of choice in Cali's drug-trafficking heyday.

"Speak only if *I* ask you a question," he said. "Understand?"

"Yes."

Ten steps from the booth, he made eye contact with Peel. He didn't recognize the man beside him, but his instructions had expressly allowed for "one bodyguard," and he had no doubt that Peel had chosen a capable one. The hostess placed two more menus on the table. Liu slipped her a hundred-dollar bill and said they wanted to be left alone. She smiled and stepped away.

"Don't sit," said Peel, before they could slide into the booth. "Your old friend here hasn't seen you in a while. He wants to give you a hug."

The bodyguard rose and embraced Liu. It was a pat-down, in actuality, and Liu went along with it.

"Great to see you again," said the bodyguard, satisfied. He returned to his seat. Olga took a seat directly opposite Peel. Liu followed, sitting across from the bodyguard.

"Doesn't Olga look terrific, Jeremy? All grown up, just for you. I mean *dressed* up. Freudian slip."

"Can we get on with this," said Peel. "We agreed on ten minutes. I've been waiting at least that long. You're lucky I didn't leave."

"And you're lucky you're still alive," said Liu, and then he addressed the bodyguard. "Just so my old friend here is in the loop, this is our second go at this transaction. The first time, we paid in full, but Mr. Peel didn't deliver in full. He left something out. Patrick Battle calls it Code Six. I don't know if that's a real name or not. But whatever was missing the first time better be on the flash drive the second time."

"Don't threaten Mr. Peel," said the bodyguard.

"What're you gonna do, shoot me? Then what, genius? You keep the girl, and nobody ever sees or hears from Patrick Battle again? Tell him, Olga. Even if your life depended on it, could you find your way back to Patrick?"

She hesitated, as if making double sure she was allowed to answer. "No. I couldn't."

"There you have it," said Liu. "That's why I'm not afraid to come here unarmed. And why you, pea brain, shouldn't even think of reaching for that pistol you have strapped to your ankle."

Peel and his bodyguard didn't deny he was armed. "Let's all just take a breath and relax," said Peel.

"How 'bout the two of you shut up and listen," said Liu. "Here's the deal. You give me the flash drive. Olga stays here. I take the flash drive to Patrick. If he can show me it's real, I let him go, and all is cool. If it's bullshit, I come for you, Jeremy. And next time, I plan to bring my benzene, gasoline, and plenty of Styrofoam cups."

"Bring *what*?" asked Peel.

"Homemade napalm," said his bodyguard.

"I fucking burn you alive," said Liu. "Not a pleasant way to go. Hurts just to have all that gel smeared on your skin. Right, Olga?"

A moment of hesitation, and then she responded. "Yes. It hurts a lot."

"Especially around the eyes," said Liu. "After a few minutes, most people end up begging me to light them up just to get it over with."

Peel laid the flash drive on the table but kept it close, covering it with his hand. "I'm not betting my life on Patrick's ability to convince you this is real."

"Because it's *not* real?" asked Liu.

"No."

"You screwed me once. Why should I believe you this time?"

"I didn't screw you. It was a mistake."

"A mistake? Hardly. You took our money and changed your mind."

"You got what you bargained for."

"What we bargained for was the same set of tools you delivered to the CIA. What happened, Jeremy? Did you suddenly get patriotic? Oh, sure, it's okay for Uncle Sam to scrape the digital world and build personal-sentiment profiles on each and every American who uses social media. But put that same power in the hands of a foreign government? No way. That's where Jeremy Peel draws the moral line."

"That's enough," said Peel.

"It was pointless to screw us, Jeremy. You said it yourself. If you didn't sell it to us, we'd steal it from you."

Peel wrapped the flash drive in his fist. "Fuck you. The deal's off."

"Don't make us steal it, Jeremy."

"You're gonna have to."

"Suit yourself."

In a sudden blur of motion, Liu reached under the table, grabbed the pistol he'd fastened to the underside with Velcro an hour earlier, and squeezed off two quick shots. The first hit the bodyguard, and the second was for Peel. The silencer muffled the gunshots, and before Olga could scream, Liu covered her mouth with his hand.

"Scream and you die."

Out of the corner of his eye, he saw a man running toward him like a charging bull, and Liu quickly surmised that Peel had violated the "one bodyguard" limit. He pulled Olga out of the booth, used her as a human shield, and fired a shot that dropped the charging bull in its tracks. The silencer kept the matter quiet, but the splatter of blood on the dance floor triggered screams of panic. The salsa music continued as men and women ran for their lives, stampeding toward the exit. Liu grabbed Olga by the arm and ran to the fire exit, setting off the alarm as they pushed through the door.

"I'm hit!"

Enrique's words came loud and clear over Kate's phone, hitting her like a punch to the gut. "How bad?" she asked.

"Got me in the shoulder. No major organs. He took Olga down the fire escape. Red dress. Alley behind the building. Go!"

"Are you sure you're okay?"

"Yes, go! Don't lose them! If they make it to Siloé, even the police won't follow!"

Diego hit the gas, and as the car whipped around the corner, a topless Jeep shot out of the alley in front of them. Olga's red dress was unmissable.

"That's them!" shouted Kate.

The Jeep sped up, and Diego was in pursuit.

"They're heading for Siloé," he said.

"Just like Enrique said they would."

"You have to decide right now, Kate. Let them go, or stay with them."

The Jeep continued toward the hillside barrio, speeding along a narrow street that ran beneath the gondola to Siloé.

"Follow them!" said Kate.

Chapter 63

Patrick was starting to lose feeling in his fingers.

Picking a padlock behind his back was much harder than picking his bicycle lock. At least a dozen times he'd felt on the verge of success, only to find repeated disappointment. He recalled Javier, back at the freighter, telling him not to "get all Houdini" on him and try to escape. He was beginning to wonder if the Great Houdini himself could have picked a lock with a bent welding rod and his hands bound behind his back.

Patrick opened and closed his hands several times, working out the cramps in his fingers, and then made a fresh attempt. Tension rod in the widest part of the hole, like the base of the key. Raking rod in the narrower slot, like the jagged edge of the key. Rake the pins from deepest to shallowest—and turn.

Click.

"Yes!"

The open lock dropped to the floor, and Patrick shook free of the chains. That first taste of freedom made him almost giddy with excitement. He climbed to his feet, ran to the side door through which Liu had taken Olga, and pushed at full speed. It opened a crack but no more, and Patrick was knocked to the floor by his own momentum, feeling as though he'd run smack into a wall. The door was padlocked on the outside. He jerked his shoulder back into place and searched for Plan B, his gaze sweeping the warehouse.

No windows. No other door, except the main garage door. It, too, was probably locked from the outside. But he had to try. He hurried past the line of chopped vehicles to the front of the warehouse. An electric garage door opener would have been nice, but there was just a rope hanging from the track above him. He pulled hard. The door jerked upward an inch, but it caught on the latch. Locked.

"Shit."

He released the rope and reassessed. He knew from the last call with Kate that Liu was coming back to the warehouse after getting the flash drive. Patrick had to either be gone by then or be able to defend himself. But with what? He counted nine cars, at least one of which had to have gas left in the tank. But a fire was risky. He could end up burning himself alive, trapped in a warehouse. And a Molotov cocktail was no answer to the pistol Liu was packing, only slightly less stupid than the old joke about the knucklehead who brings a knife to a gunfight. Patrick needed equal firepower. It seemed like wishful thinking, but not really. Chop shops were never in the nicest part of town. To be on the wrong side of Cali meant survival of the smartest, and anyone with a brain knew better than to cruise through the Warehouse District of Cali without protection. There had to be a gun in one of those cars.

Patrick started down the line of vehicles, throwing open the passenger-side door and popping the glove box. Nothing in the first. Or the second. Or the third. The fourth box was locked, which got his heart pumping. He ran to the work bench and grabbed a screwdriver, which made quick work of the shitty little lock. The box popped open.

Pay dirt.

Patrick smiled as he wrapped his fingers around the butt of the pistol. It was just like the one his father had taught him to use at the range. He released the magazine. Fifteen rounds of 9-millimeter ammunition. He had all the firepower he needed.

There was a noise outside the warehouse, the sound

of a vehicle pulling up in the alley. The engine stopped, and the door opened.

Liu?

A second door opened. Someone was with him, which confused Patrick. The deal was that Olga would stay if Peel delivered the flash drive.

Something went wrong.

Patrick crouched behind the car, switched off the safety on his pistol, and waited for the door to open.

Kate's wild ride into Barrio Siloé was uphill, a race past one redbrick building after another along narrow streets. Most of the streetlamps were unlit, either burned out or broken, but there was enough moonlight for Kate to read the endless string of graffiti messages on the walls, fences, and shuttered doorways along the way. One word caught her eye. It was eight feet tall and painted in the Colombian colors of yellow, red, and blue: *Orgullo.* Colombians truly were a proud people, even in the darkest corners of Siloé.

"They turned into that alley," said Kate, pointing from the backseat.

Diego steered to the curb and stopped the car just short of the alley entrance. The entire street was nothing but warehouses, not a pedestrian in sight. Directly overhead, a good fifty feet in the air, were the moving cables that carried the commuter gondolas up and down the hillside. Two blocks ahead, Kate could see the elevated platform for the nearest station. Not a soul on it.

"I don't feel safe here," said Kate.

"We're not," said Diego.

"What's the plan?"

"If I was alone, I'd find my way into that warehouse and do what needs to be done. But I can't leave you here."

"Then I'll go with you."

He shook his head. "Not gonna happen. The best we can do is call the police and circle the block until they get here."

"But you said the police won't come into Siloé."

"I have a few friends in the department."

"Friends who would come here?" she asked.

"How much would your daddy pay for the cops to show up right now?"

Kate stole a quick glance of the neighborhood. "Honestly, whatever they asked for."

"Perfect," said Diego, dialing. "Your old man's about to make a very generous donation to Colombian law enforcement."

"No," said Kate.

"What do you mean, no?"

"Patrick is like a brother to me. If your little brother

was in that warehouse, would you drive around the block and wait for the police, who may or may not come?"

Diego lowered his phone. "No. I wouldn't."

"Then don't ask me to."

Their eyes met in the darkness. "All right," he said. "We're going in. Check your weapon."

Kate opened her purse and removed the pistol Diego had given her. "Loaded, safety on," she said.

"Keep the gun pointed at the ground, and stay at least ten steps behind me at all times. Stop when I stop. Move from a position of cover only when I wave you forward. When we get to the alley, remove the safety."

Removing the safety had never been a big deal in target practice. Outside a dark warehouse in the heart of Siloé, however, her heart pounded at the mere thought of an active lethal weapon in her hand.

"Ready?" he asked.

Kate swallowed hard. "Ready."

The car doors opened, and they stepped into the night.

Patrick pointed his pistol straight at the side door to the alley. He was on his knees, with his arms fully extended and the butt of the handgun resting on the hood of the car to steady his shot. He knew he had just a few seconds to act. The pole to which he'd been chained would be in Liu's plain view, and Patrick's escape would be immediately obvious. His plan was to take the first open shot as soon as Liu walked through the door.

A clanking noise came from the other side of the door, which sounded like the padlock coming off. Patrick took aim. He had enough experience with guns to know that he was a better shot using the dominant-eye method. The pistol had standard iron sights, front and rear, which he'd been taught to think of as a teed-up football in the front and the goal post in the rear. The goal was to get the football squarely through the goal posts. He closed his left eye and, using only his right eye, aligned the sights, making sure the front sight was directly in the center of the rear sight notch. His target was an imaginary bull's-eye, chest high in the dead center of the door. He focused on the rear sight, leaving his target slightly blurry, which he knew was right. His finger covered the trigger, and Patrick took a deep breath. The door opened. Patrick applied a small amount of pressure to the trigger but held his fire.

Olga was squarely in his sights.

Liu was behind her. Patrick had no shot. His heart was pounding. Precious seconds were being lost. A more skilled marksman might have taken a shot, but as much as Patrick had loved the movie *American Sniper*, he was no Chris Kyle.

Two steps into the warehouse, Liu stopped and suddenly pulled Olga back against his body like a human shield, pressing his pistol against the base of her skull. He'd obviously spotted the loose chains around the poll. He knew Patrick had freed himself.

"Dumb move, Patrick!" he shouted.

Patrick wanted to squeeze the trigger but had no opening. Liu backed his way out, through the doorway, pulling Olga with him into the alley.

Patrick didn't hesitate. He jumped to his feet, ran to the door, and stopped, planting his back to the doorframe. Running blindly and with abandon into the alley was a good way to get shot, but if he lost sight of Liu he'd forever lose Olga. He pivoted, using the doorframe to protect his body, and peered down the dark alley.

A shot pierced the darkness, and Patrick hit the ground.

Chapter 64

Kate was at the entrance to the alley, ten feet behind Diego, when the shot rang out.

"Down!" he said, in a hushed but urgent voice.

Kate hurried to the brick wall and hid behind a tall stack of freight pallets. The warehouses were much deeper than wide, nearly the length of a football field from front to back. The alley was barely wide enough for two vehicles, and as far as Kate could tell, the only way out was the way they had come in. There was no streetlamp, or at least not a working one, and the moonlight did little more than create confusing shadows in what seemed like an endless black tunnel. But as Kate's eyes adjusted, she could make out Diego's silhouette ahead of her. He was hiding behind a Dumpster, pistol at the ready. He signaled for her to be quiet, which made her even more aware of how heavily she was breathing.

Kate calmed her nerves and listened. It had sounded as though the gunshot had come from the alley, outside the warehouse, but it wasn't easy to pinpoint a single gunshot. Diego signaled her forward with a wave of his hand. His hiding spot behind the Dumpster was better than hers, and she eagerly came to join him, moving as quickly and keeping as low as possible.

"I want you to stay right here," he whispered.

Kate nodded in agreement.

Diego raised his pistol and stepped out from behind the Dumpster. Through an opening between the wall and the Dumpster's edge, Kate watched him move deeper into the alley, his every move like a trained law enforcement agent. Roll-down steel shutters covered the windows and doors that faced the alley. Corrugated boxes, flattened and stacked for disposal, one on top of the other, rose in cardboard towers. Diego took cover behind one of the stacks about twenty feet ahead of Kate. He listened. Kate listened harder. There was only silence. Diego stepped out carefully from behind the cardboard tower and started forward.

A shot rang out. Diego went down, dropping to the pavement somewhere on the other side of the stack of crushed boxes. He was completely out of Kate's line of sight, making it impossible for her to know if he was alive or dead. Kate had to make a decision, but the possibility that Diego was only wounded, in need of help, eliminated one option.

She couldn't turn and run.

With her back pressed to the brick face of the building, Kate poked her head around the corner, peering cautiously down the black alley. She took another step forward, then stopped. There was a noise from the other side of the stack of flattened cardboard boxes, where Diego had fallen. If Diego was alive, she couldn't tell; and if his shooter was lying in wait on the other side, she couldn't tell, either. She took cover behind the stack, her heart pounding.

A chorus of sirens whined in the distance. Police were on the way. Diego must have called. That meant he was alive on the other side.

Two more quick shots rang out, which popped in the stacked cardboard. Kate hit the deck and saw a man running away from her. The woman in the red dress was with him. He turned and fired again in Kate's direction, still running. Kate log-rolled across the alley, and she didn't stop rolling until she bumped right up against Diego's body. She was looking directly into his eyes.

"How bad?" she whispered.

He tried to speak but didn't answer.

Kate checked his pulse. Weak, but still beating. The wound was to his upper thigh. He'd had the initial presence of mind to rip a rope-like fastener from the stacked boxes and make a tourniquet, but the blood loss had pushed him into near unconsciousness. Kate checked the tourniquet. Another gunshot pierced the darkness, the bullet whizzing overhead. Kate braced for more gunfire, but she heard only the echo of footfalls on asphalt. The shooter was making a run for it.

"Go," said Diego.

"I can't leave you here!"

Ahead, in the darkness, a stack of boxes toppled to the pavement. Kate took aim with her pistol, ready to fire.

"Kate?"

She recognized the voice, and Kate's heart leapt into her throat. "Patrick?"

He hurried toward her and immediately saw the gravity of the situation.

"It's my friend Diego," said Kate. "He's hit but alive."

The police sirens in the distance grew louder.

"I chased Liu toward you," said Patrick, using the name he'd given him. "But I never fired a shot. He has Olga."

"No one ran past us," said Kate.

"There's no other way out of this alley, except—"

They raised their eyes toward the sky at the same time. Liu was four stories above them on the fire escape ladder. Olga was with him.

"You stay with your friend until the cops get here," said Patrick.

"Patrick, you can't—" she started to say, but the look in his eyes said the matter was not debatable.

"I promised Olga I wouldn't leave without her," he said.

Kate squeezed his hand, so proud and yet wanting to tackle him and make him stay put.

"Please be careful," she said, and he was on his way.

Chapter 65

Patrick ran to the fire escape ladder, grabbed a rung, and started climbing the warehouse wall. As he stared up into the night sky, with countless rungs to go, the long and narrow ladder triggered a childhood memory of a picture book Kate had read to him as a toddler, *Papa, Please Get the Moon for Me*. For one scary moment, he wondered if his life was flashing before his eyes.

He was halfway up. Liu was at least three stories above him, and Patrick looked up just as he pushed Olga up onto the roof of the building. Patrick kept climbing. Liu fired a shot from the top of the ladder. The bullet skipped past Patrick against the brick wall. He pressed his body as close to the ladder as possible and looked up. No sight of Liu. The moon was above him, but this was definitely no children's book. Patrick shook off the distraction and summoned the courage of the U.S. Army Rangers who stormed the cliffs at Pointe du Hoc in support of the Omaha Beach landings on D-Day in the face of enemy fire.

Patrick, lead the way! he told himself, borrowing the Rangers motto he'd heard a thousand times in his Call of Duty video games.

Holding a gun was slowing his climb, so he tucked it in his belt. Hand over hand he ascended the ladder, reaching the top in a minute or so, stopping just below the roofline. Only at this height did he realize that the back of the building was built on the edge of a steep gorge in the hillside. Death was likely if he fell from the ladder into the alley; it was an absolute certainty if the fall were from the roof into the ravine.

Patrick removed the gun from his belt. With pistol in hand, he slid himself up and over the top rung, slithering onto the roof on his belly to avoid making a target of himself. The roof was flat and barren as a desert, save for a few exhaust vents and pipes protruding from the tar-and-gravel surface. His gaze swept the entire roof, or at least as much as he could see from his worm's-eye perspective. He saw no sign of Liu or Olga. Slowly, he raised his head for a better look.

The roof was tiered, he discovered, with two levels,

both flat. He was on the lower tier, alone. Another ladder led to the higher tier, toward the rear of the building—where Olga had to be with Liu. Patrick jumped to his feet and ran to the second ladder. He kept his gun in hand this time, climbing as quietly as possible. There were only ten rungs, and he stopped when his eyes were level with the second-tier roofline.

"That's far enough," said Liu.

Patrick froze. The elevated tier of the roof ran the entire width of the building, but it was a mere ten feet from Patrick's place on the ladder to the back of the building. Liu was standing at the very edge of the roofline. Olga was in front of him, looking terrified with the barrel of his pistol burrowing into her right cheek.

"Hurting Olga gains you nothing," said Patrick.

"Lay your pistol on the roof or she gets a bullet."

"Don't!" shouted Olga. "He got what he wanted! He got the flash drive!"

Patrick didn't move.

"Now!" said Liu, as he pressed the gun harder against Olga's face.

The utter terror in her eyes left Patrick no choice. He rested his weapon on the roof.

"Let her go," said Patrick. "Keep the flash drive and go. I won't stop you. I don't care if you get away."

"You and I both know that whatever is on that flash drive is worthless."

"That's not Olga's fault."

"No. It's yours."

"I had nothing to do with what Mr. Peel delivered on that flash drive."

"You're the one who said to bring Code Six as ransom. Code Six is made-up bullshit, isn't it, Patrick? You *told* him to deliver bullshit code."

Patrick was silent.

"Don't get me wrong," Liu said with sarcasm. "I can see why you'd want to play hero and keep the real code out of the hands of the Chinese government. As if it's any less dangerous in the hands of your own government."

"You're never going to get it," said Patrick.

"Not from Peel, that's for sure."

"Not from anyone," said Patrick.

"That's where you're wrong. Like I told Jeremy: we could buy it, or we could steal it. Might as well make a buck."

"Your logic may have worked with him. But I'm not for sale."

"That's a shame."

The police sirens he'd first heard in the alley were getting closer. All he had to do was keep the situation stable for a few minutes more.

"Just let her go. Please."

"I have every intention of doing so," said Liu. "And in case anyone asks, be sure to tell them: I did it for Kate."

Before Patrick could react to those words, Liu pivoted, flung Olga around, and pushed her off the building.

"Olga!"

Patrick pulled himself up over the top rung and grabbed his pistol. Liu took one last look at him, and Patrick braced himself for the explosion of gunfire, but there was no sound at all. Liu turned and faced the deep gorge in the hillside behind the building.

And then he jumped.

Patrick ran to the roof's edge. The gorge behind the building cut even deeper into the hillside than he'd thought—so deep that the warehouse roof was actually above the moving cables that ran the gondolas. Another hundred feet below the cable, at the very deepest point of the rocky ravine, beneath the glowing lights of a passing gondola, Patrick caught a glimpse of a red dress. His heart ached, and he could barely believe his eyes. Slowly, his gaze shifted to the gondola that had just passed below the roofline, and he saw the most sickening sight.

Atop the car, riding to the safety of the next gondola platform, was a cold-blooded killer who deserved to die.

Chapter 66

Kate rode with Diego in the back of the ambulance to the emergency room.

Imbanaco Grupo Quirónsalud clinic was ten minutes away from Siloé, so the hospital's surgical staff and seventeen operating rooms were no strangers to gunshot wounds. Enrique was coming out of surgery as Diego was going in. Kate called her father from the hospital waiting room. She told him that she and Patrick were safe, that Peel was dead, and that Enrique was on the mend. He had just one thing to say.

"I want you on the first flight out of Cali."

"I'm already booked. It leaves at eight a.m."

"That's not soon enough. I'll hire a private jet."

"Dad, it's almost eleven o'clock here."

"I can have you out of there by midnight."

Kate hesitated. "I can't leave yet. Patrick is still at the morgue. He wants to say a proper goodbye to Olga."

"Fine. Then he can stay. You're coming home."

"Said the father to his eleven-year-old daughter."

"I just want you safe," he said.

"I risked my life to come here and get Patrick. I'm not leaving without him."

"This is getting silly. All this for a prostitute?"

Kate swallowed her anger, but not entirely. "She was a victim of sex trafficking. A victim of *your* ex–business partner. So I'm going to hang up now, Dad, and try to forget what you just said. I'm flying home tomorrow with Patrick, after he says goodbye to Olga."

"I'm sorry, Kate."

"Good night," she said, and the call ended.

A text message came a few minutes later. Patrick had left the morgue and purchased a prepaid cellphone so that Kate could reach him. Diego was just about to come out of surgery, but with the general anesthesia, both he and Enrique would probably sleep through the night. Kate was exhausted and had yet to check out of her hotel. She texted Patrick back to let him know that Enrique's adjoining room was available, if he wanted to catch some sleep before their flight in the morning. He swung by the hospital via Uber, and they shared a ride to the hotel.

"I'm so sorry about Olga," said Kate.

He was casting an empty gaze out the car window. "Thanks."

Kate wanted to say more, but she remembered all too well how she felt after seeing her mother at the morgue. She decided to let him bring it up, but he didn't. At least not directly.

"Have you figured out what Project Naïveté Two is?" he asked.

"I know it includes a scraping tool to collect personal information."

"Not just information. It collects virtually every form of human expression, verbal or nonverbal, and translates it into code. The code is personalized to every technology user and becomes a personal sentiment library. The goal is to have a personal sentiment library for every person under the age of thirty who uses technology."

"For what?" she asked.

"Somewhere in those libraries is the future CEO of Buck. The future chief justice of the Supreme Court. The future president of the United States. And on and on."

"So the idea is, what? Blackmail these people when they grow up and reach positions of power?"

"This isn't about extorting or embarrassing someone for something stupid they did as a child. We're talking about knowing what that person fears. What that person values. What makes that person tick. That kind of window into the adult psyche starts by building a personal sentiment library in the formative years."

"Let me guess: the more expressive a user is on social media, the more robust his or her personal sentiment library will be."

"Yep."

"And we all know that the more expressive user isn't going to be a '*him.*' It's a '*her.*'"

"That's a fact. Teenage girls, especially, are way out in front of boys in sharing what the industry calls sentiment data."

Kate was beginning to connect the final dots, but it wasn't easy to say it. "After my mother died, I visited Sandra Levy to find out why she was trying to steal code. If I were to tell you she said she did it for her daughter, what would you say?"

"I'd say she told me the exact same thing."

"When?"

"Right before she was arrested. She knew the FBI was closing in. She needed to line up someone on the inside to take the baton from her and stop Naïveté Two. She chose me."

"How did she expect you to stop it?"

Patrick turned his gaze away from the window and

looked at her directly. "Expose it. Give people hard proof of how their own government intends to handle the next generation of leaders. Make them understand how it would be even worse in the hands of a hostile nation."

"Do you think Peel was on to you? Is that why he sent you to Colombia?"

"Probably. My only regret is getting your mother involved."

The car entered the hotel motor court and stopped. "What did you just say?" asked Kate.

Patrick climbed out of the backseat. Kate followed him into the lobby and to the reception desk.

"Getting my mother involved in *what*?"

"This mess."

The receptionist gave them an extra key to Enrique's room, and Patrick started toward the elevator. Kate continued after him.

"Patrick, you're not nine years old, and I'm not your teenage babysitter. You can't just drop a bomb like that and walk off. Talk to me."

He stopped midway through the lobby, looked at her, and spoke in a voice mixed with anger and apology—but the anger was at himself. "I screwed up, Kate."

Kate wasn't sure she could handle what he was trying to say, but this was Patrick, and she forced herself to be patient. "Tell me what it is. Nothing is unfixable."

"It's not that I wanted to hide anything from you. It's like I'm figuring out I screwed up in real time—as I'm talking to you right now."

Kate was about to lose it. "Patrick, just tell me."

"I was in a tight spot," he said. "To stop Naïveté Two, I needed the highest credentials in the company. I could think of only one way to get them."

"You stole them?"

"'Borrow' was the word I used with your mother."

"My mother never had any credentials to borrow."

"I know. I figured that if your father's mistress was able to access his credentials, so could his wife."

Kate looked away in disbelief, then back. "There's so much wrong with what you just said. First of all, my father didn't have credentials to Naïveté Two. And Sandra Levy was *not* his mistress."

"I know that now. That's where I screwed up. I went to your mom. I told her what I *thought* was going on."

"Told her *what*? I want to know exactly."

Patrick struggled, then answered. "I told her that Sandra was using your father's credentials to access Naïveté Two."

"Oh, my God. You made her think my father was sleeping with Sandra Levy."

"I'm sorry. Sandra told me she got the credentials by 'playing the boss.' I assumed she meant your father."

"She meant Jeremy Peel."

"Yes. We all know that now. But back then, I was just thinking the same thing everybody thought about Sandra and your father."

"That they were having an affair."

"Yes. I didn't even realize what I'd done until *now*. That's not an excuse. You have every right to be furious with me. But I want you to know that your mother was so brave, Kate. I told her how awful this project was, especially for girls and young women. I told her Sandra was doing it for her daughter. And you know what she said?"

"What?"

"She said, 'Well, then, I'll do it for Kate.'"

Kate's knees nearly buckled. "I have to sit down," she said, and she found a couch. Patrick sat beside her.

"Here's the weirdest thing," said Patrick. "When Liu pushed Olga off the building, he said the same thing. 'I did it for Kate.' How could he possibly have known that's what your mother said to me—'I'll do it for Kate'?"

"He got it from the note my mother left: 'I did it for Kate.'"

"Don't take this the wrong way, but that's a really strange suicide note."

Kate's expression turned very serious. "That's because it wasn't actually a suicide note."

"Then what was it?"

"I think my mother wanted it to look like a suicide note. But she chose those words so that you would recognize them and know that it wasn't."

"Why?"

Kate hesitated to say it, but it was where her thoughts had led her. "Maybe it was her way of letting us know her death wasn't really a suicide."

"Whoa."

"Yeah. Whoa."

Kate rose. Patrick joined her in the walk to the elevator, and they rode up together.

"When's the last time you showered?" she asked.

"I don't remember."

"Get cleaned up in Enrique's room. I'm sure he has clean clothes that will fit."

The elevator doors parted, and they stepped off at the seventh floor.

"You're acting funny," said Patrick.

"I just discovered my mother may have been murdered. How do you expect me to act?"

"What are you going to do?"

"Call my father. He needs to know all this."

They stopped outside Patrick's room, next to Kate's.

"What if he already knows?" asked Patrick.

"Knows that she was murdered?"

"Yeah. I mean, what if—"

"I know exactly what you mean."

"Don't be mad. I'm just thinking out loud."

"My head is spinning."

"Mine, too," said Patrick. "I'm going to shower. If you need anything, I'm in the next room."

"Thanks. Be ready to leave for the airport at five a.m."

"No problem. I'm dead tired, but I'll be shocked if my mind shuts off long enough for me to actually fall asleep."

"You and me both," said Kate.

Patrick disappeared into his room. Kate dug her key from her purse, the light on the electronic lock flashed green, and she opened the door.

Kate knew perfectly well what Patrick had meant, and the thought of her father having some connection to her mother's death—her *murder*—had her stomach in knots. It seemed impossible and contrary to everything she believed about him. But what if her mother's call to 911 wasn't a revenge call? What if Patrick knew something she didn't? It was too much to think about. She closed the door and stepped inside.

The room was a typical hotel layout with a short entrance hallway, and Kate passed the bathroom on her right and the closet on her left before entering the bedroom and living area. She switched on the light and froze. The sliding glass door to the balcony was open, and the way the lace curtain moved in the breeze was eerily reminiscent of that horrible moment of discovery in her parents' penthouse.

A hand came over her mouth, and she felt the cold barrel of a pistol beneath her chin.

"Not a peep," a man said.

Chapter 67

Kate recognized his voice as the one she'd heard through Diego's phone while circling the block around Club Siloé. It was the man who'd shot Jeremy Peel, his bodyguard, and Enrique. The man who'd pushed Olga off the roof and said, "I did it for Kate." The man Patrick called Liu.

"Is that your mother's perfume I smell?"

Kate wasn't wearing any, and she knew he was messing with her, but she returned the volley. "How do you know my mother's perfume?"

"She just couldn't leave well enough alone, could she, your mother?"

The anger wasn't just in his voice, but in the way he shoved the gun up under her chin. Kate was afraid to say the wrong thing and set him off.

"I don't know what you mean."

"Even Sandra Levy stopped at the point of finding out that the CIA was behind Naïveté. Your mother got dangerously close to finding out that Peel was about to sell it to the Chinese. Sandra got jail. Your mother, of course, got worse."

"My mother took her own life."

"Did it ever occur to you how easy it is to climb from the balcony of your apartment to the balcony of your parents' penthouse?"

It was two stories. And a way to avoid security.

"What are you saying?"

"You know what I'm saying. I brought my own vodka, which was totally unnecessary. That should have been clue number one to you that something wasn't right—that she was dead drunk and hadn't touched the vodka from her florist."

"You made her drink?"

"I didn't make her. I gave her a choice. She could drink up and jump. Or the two of us could sit there and wait for you to show up. And then I'd toss you both over the railing. She made the right choice. I even let her leave a note."

Kate nearly gasped at the realization.

I did it for Kate.

"What do you want from me?"

"The code on Peel's flash drive turned out to be shit. So you're going to text Patrick and tell him to come over."

"He won't give you the code you want."

"He risked his life to save a whore. Imagine what he'll do to save you. Where's your phone?"

"In my purse."

"I want you to remove it, nice and slow. And then you're going to text exactly what I say. Got it?"

Kate swallowed her fear. "Got it."

Chapter 68

P atrick stared at his image in the bathroom mirror. Even in periods of raging hormones, he had about as much facial hair as a teenager, but he hadn't shaved since setting foot in Colombia. The last time he'd needed a shave this badly he was a teenager with a caterpillar on his upper lip. He borrowed Enrique's razor and hoped he wouldn't mind.

Kate's room was directly on the other side of the bathroom wall. He didn't mean to eavesdrop, but the hotel was far from soundproof. He couldn't make out what was being said, but he definitely heard voices—male and female, not just Kate's. If she was talking to her father on speakerphone, it was none of his business. But to be curious was human, and Patrick's time in captivity had made him an expert at overhearing conversations in the next room. He leaned closer to the wall and listened. The man was talking, and the voice chilled Patrick so deeply that he nicked his chin with the blade. It sounded strangely like Liu.

No way.

Patrick wondered if this was the first sign of PTSD and of many sleepless nights to come—hearing the voice of his captor when it couldn't possibly be him.

As he dabbed away the blood, his burn phone chimed with a text message, which was odd, since the only person who had his prepaid number was Kate. He checked the display:

Need to talk now. No phones. Come to the hotel. IMPORTANT.

Another chill came over him, but it was no harbinger of PTSD or other psychological trauma from the kidnapping. This time, the fears were grounded in real and present danger. Kate was in the next room. Why would she text him? Why would she tell him to come to the hotel? Why wouldn't she just knock on the door that connected their rooms?

Why did that man's voice on the other side of the wall sound like Liu?

Patrick hurried from the bathroom, went to the door that connected his room to Kate's, and stopped.

The lock on his side of the door was bolted. He assumed there was also a bolt lock on the other side, allowing either occupant of the adjoining rooms to keep the other out. Patrick stared at the doorknob and wondered:

Did Kate have the bolt on?

As things stood, Liu was expecting Patrick to come to the hotel and knock on Kate's door. The side door offered the element of surprise, but all advantage would be lost if his entry weren't sudden and overwhelming. There could be no fiddling with locks to tip off Liu.

Quietly, Patrick stepped to the opposite side of the room and braced his foot against the baseboard. His last attempt at busting down a door had not gone well, but this was not a steel-encased warehouse door with a kickass padlock. Even so, he grabbed a pillow from the bed for the benefit of his shoulder.

The risk was high, and the probability of success was low, but the options were few. He was certain Liu was in the next room. He'd stood and watched as Liu threw Olga off the building. He wouldn't make the same mistake twice. Liu might have something even worse in store for Kate, as witnessed by his fascination with burning flesh and his homemade napalm concoction. Kate had put everything at risk to come to Colombia and help him. He had to act, and quickly.

On the mental count of three, he pushed away from the wall and charged at the door with all the force he could muster.

Chapter 69

The side door flew open. Splinters of wood from the shattered doorframe sailed into Kate's room. It sounded like an explosion, and almost simultaneously, Kate felt Patrick's body slamming into her side. The impact took her down and Liu with her.

A gunshot rang out, shattering the full-length mirror on the wall. Kate wasn't hit, and she managed to extricate herself from the tangle of flailing arms and legs rolling across the carpet. The two men were suddenly on their feet, and in a sudden burst of motion, Patrick slammed into the flat-screen television and Liu pointed his pistol. Maybe the gun had jammed, or maybe Kate had actually reacted that quickly, but before Liu's trigger finger could squeeze off a shot, Kate kicked the pistol from his hand and sent it flying out of the open sliding glass door onto the balcony.

The men sprinted to the gun, pushing and shoving each other, and knocking the sliding door from its track on their way out. Shattered glass showered over them, as the struggle for the gun continued out onto the balcony. Kate felt like she was watching in slow motion, but even in her surreal frame-by-frame view, the two men only seemed to gain speed, like a boulder rolling downhill, as their momentum carried them across the balcony and into the aluminum railing.

Kate screamed as the railing gave way.

Liu went over the edge with the first section of battered aluminum balusters. Then Patrick.

"Patrick!" Kate cried, and she ran to the balcony's edge.

Patrick was hanging on by one hand to a piece of metal railing that was still fixed in the concrete floor of the balcony. His feet dangled in the air, high above the motor court below. Patrick had managed to grab Liu on his way over the railing, and his left hand clung to Liu's forearm.

Kate was standing at the balcony's edge, looking down. Liu looked up, and their eyes met. He was twisting in midair like a kite tail, his life literally in Patrick's grip.

"Tell him to pull me up!" shouted Liu.

Kate said nothing.

Patrick said something. He spoke in a soft voice, as if his words were not intended for Kate, Liu, or any other living person. It was possible, Kate would later tell police, that Patrick was running out of strength and said something like "I can't hold on any longer." But the more likely scenario would forever remain a secret between her and Patrick.

"I did it for Olga," was what Kate heard.

Liu slipped from Patrick's grip, his scream piercing the night until his body slammed into the pavement below.

Chapter 70

January. A blanket of white covered Washington, D.C. Kate had butterflies in her stomach. Giant butterflies. Pterodactyls, even. She hoped that snow on opening night was the theatrical equivalent of rain on a wedding day, a sign of good luck.

The theater held about two hundred, and every seat was taken. Kate chose to sit among strangers, not with family or friends. She preferred to surround herself with the unvarnished reactions of real theater goers, not the obligatory praise of folks who were kind enough to come but probably hadn't seen a live play since their middle school's production of *Annie*.

Patrick was seated a couple of rows behind her. He'd brought a date, which Kate was happy to see. Her father was seated on the aisle in the next section over from her.

Minutes before curtain, she received a text message from Irving Bass.

Break a leg.

She smiled to herself and texted back. Wish you were here.

It was unusual for the director not to attend opening night, but the production of *Code 6*—she finally had a title—had been anything but "usual." It had felt rushed from the beginning. A completely rewritten script. Casting before the script was even finished. Irving's collapse and hospitalization. Hers should have been the first play of the coming season in September, not the first play of the new year in January. Not until December did Irving come clean with her and explain the fast track.

"I have pancreatic cancer, Kate. There isn't going to be a next season."

At first, she'd refused to believe it. Half joking, she'd even accused him of stopping at nothing to get her to accept his revisions to the script. But he was seriously ill, and the fact that her play would likely be his last became their secret. They drew closer over the following weeks, though disagreements were still intense. Irving had even thrown her out of rehearsal one afternoon in front of the entire cast. And, for the most part, Irving did get his way, including his "non-negotiable" item: one act, ninety minutes.

Kate watched the first seventy-five minutes with fingernails digging into the armrest. Some of the "humorous" lines she'd absolutely refused to cut from the script had fallen flat with the audience; Irving had been right, after all. Nonetheless, the audience seemed to be enjoying it. The real test was the final scene—the volcanic point of conflict between an aging Thomas J. Watson, Sr., and his up-and-coming son.

The setting was the 1950s. Watson was grooming his son to replace him as CEO. It was the dawn of the computer age, and IBM was transitioning from electromechanical technology to fully electronic. It was also the height of the McCarthy era, and Tom Junior had made the mistake of speaking out publicly against it. His father had harsh advice for him, leading to another one of their epic confrontations after work at the Watson town house on the Upper East Side.

"A businessman sticks to business," said Watson.

"That's the most narrow-minded view of the world I've ever heard."

"'Shoemaker, stick to your last.' It's the best advice I ever got."

"Which explains how you kept quiet and just kept making shoes, even as German boots were trampling all over Europe."

"You're such a smart-ass, Tom."

"You're such a coward."

"I am not a coward!"

"You don't know what courage is. Did you not learn anything from the way Hitler played you? Spineless suggestions that he follow the Golden Rule didn't exactly do the trick, did they?"

"I did more than any businessman in America to keep war from coming."

"You did more than any businessman to treat Nazi Germany like a business problem. It wasn't. You can't appease men like Hitler and just hope they'll come to their senses."

"I haven't appeased anyone!"

"If you don't work against them, you're appeasing them. A flat condemnation of Hitler could have made a difference."

"You have no idea what you're talking about. One wrong word from New York and the Third Reich would have nationalized Dehomag. What would that have accomplished?"

"You would have taken a stand. It would have shown the world that 'world peace through world trade' wasn't just a catchy slogan."

"You're never going to let that go, are you?"

"No. You can retire and turn the page. I have to

deal with this for the next ten, twenty—who knows how many years. I've only been president since January, and reporters are already breathing down my neck, trying to get records from Europe."

"Records of what?"

"The Nazis' use of Hollerith machines and punch-card technology."

"Why is that a story? Herman Hollerith licensed his patents to Willy Heidinger in 1910. Punch cards were part of the German economy long before the Nazis even existed."

"The story isn't about the German economy. It's about Nazi concentration camps."

"Then it has *nothing* to do with IBM."

Tom paused, his gaze tightening. "Who is Harold J. Carter?"

"Carter? The name doesn't ring a bell."

"I'm told he visited IBM headquarters in July 1943."

"Carver, you say?"

"Harold *Carter*. Damn it, Dad. Don't pretend like you don't know! He's an investigator with the Economic Warfare Section of the Department of Justice." Again he paused, and then he asked in a louder voice, "Did he visit IBM headquarters in July 1943?"

Watson breathed deep, then answered. "Yes. He was here."

"And I have to hear this from a newspaper reporter," Tom said with an angry chuckle. "You didn't think to tell me?"

"Nothing came of it."

"What was the Justice Department investigating?"

"Our German subsidiary."

"What about it?"

"Making sure we played no part in our subsidiary's support for the German military."

"In other words, making sure we weren't in violation of the Trading with the Enemy Act?"

"And we weren't," said Watson.

"That's not the point! Why didn't you tell me about this?"

"It wasn't even an investigation. The Justice Department looked into dozens of companies during the war. Companies as red, white, and blue as Standard Oil."

"There's a difference. Oil isn't refined to process personal information. Hollerith machines were invented for that very purpose—for the Census Bureau."

"It was a big nothing! Harold J. Carter visited and left. He never came back. *Nothing* came of it."

Tom faced his father squarely and assumed a more challenging posture. "Let me ask you a simple question: When did it occur to you that the Nazis might use Hollerith machines against Jews?"

"I—I don't know if it ever occurred to me."

"Hitler's election in 1933?"

"It never even crossed my mind in 1933."

"The Nuremberg racial laws in 1936? Kristallnacht in 1938? Hitler's invasion of Poland in 1939? The creation of the Warsaw Ghetto in 1940? When, Dad? *When?*"

"I don't know when."

"You must know! When did it finally dawn on you that Hitler might use Hollerith machines against Jews?"

"What do you want me to say, Tom?" he asked, shouting.

"After our German subsidiary went from three hundred employees in 1930 to *three thousand* in 1940? After the record profits of 1939?"

"I said I don't know!"

"You do know! When did you know?"

"When it was too late!" he said, his voice booming. "All right? Is that what you want to hear me say? When it was too *damn* late!"

There was utter silence. Father and son were completely still.

The stage lighting changed. Kate glanced across the auditorium in her father's direction. He looked back with an expression that asked the question Kate should have expected:

Is that what you think I am? A coward?

She wanted to explain, but she wouldn't get the chance. At least not that night.

He got up from his seat and left before the final curtain.

Epilogue

I rving Bass died a happy man. His final world premiere was a sellout.

The reviews were not what they had hoped for, but if Kate had gained anything since her mother's death, it was perspective. "An ambitious effort from a promising young playwright," one critic wrote, "but a story too big for the stage." Kate would never say Sean the Snake was right, but she was getting serious interest from Hollywood. "Send me ten pages," an agent at CAA had told her. Thanks to Irving Bass, she didn't have to ask what made a great ten pages.

Do you want to get to page eleven?

The big story was Jeremy Peel. He'd fallen from "boss of the boss"—Buck's chairman of the board, to whom CEO Christian Gamble reported—to working for a foreign boss, better known as the Chinese Ministry of State Security. The man Patrick called "Liu" was identified as an agent of the Chinese state-sponsored cyberespionage group Red Apollo, acting under the direction of the Tianjin field office of the MSS. The DOJ cybersecurity audit, led by Noah, confirmed that Peel never did transfer the key code to the Chinese, though it was up to Swiss banking authorities to reveal how many millions Peel had taken before reneging on the deal. It was unquestionably Peel who had hired Javier to keep Patrick out of the country until the DOJ's audit was over. It was Patrick's theory that "Liu"—*el jefe del jefe*—then hired Javier to push him off the mountain and connect Peel to Patrick's murder, placing him firmly and forever under the thumb of the Chinese government. The world would probably never know if Peel double-crossed the Chinese because he found patriotism, or because even he couldn't find a way to sneak Buck's most secure code out the door without exposing himself as a traitor.

Strangely, what Kate considered the most important part of the story was, to everyone else, a nonstory. It brought to mind her research trip to see the Hollerith machine, Irving's hundred-year-old aunt who'd survived the Nazi concentration camp at Buchenwald, and his warning about "Holocaust fatigue." Social media was newer to the planet than Kate, or even Patrick, but already the world was suffering from Big Data fatigue.

"Privacy, schmivacy," to coin an Irving-ism.

But Project Naïveté II wasn't just another story about the loss of personal information. It was the CIA's use of taxpayer dollars to fund Buck's development of technology that capitalized on all that was wrong with social media. Its "stealth" scraping tool—the key code that Peel withheld from the Chinese—could scrape (read: steal) data from every imaginable source, without detection by Google, Facebook, or other platform that collected the data in the first place, and package all that disparate and disconnected information into a single and ever-evolving personal sentiment dossier on every American who didn't live under a rock. Jeremy Peel showed how easily that top-secret technology could fall into enemy hands. Perhaps the wake-up call would come twenty years down the road—"Too damn late," as Kate's Watson had put it—when the president of the United States was eyeball to eyeball with a foreign dictator, world peace hanging in the balance, and America's enemies could calculate that her tough talk was merely a bluff, thanks to the personal sentiment data they'd been scraping from her every encounter with both on- and off-screen technology since she was a child. Some members of Congress were calling for an investigation. Change was possible, but Kate wasn't holding her breath.

One change was immediate: the stated manner of death for Kate's mother was no longer suicide. Elizabeth Gamble was officially the year's twelfth homicide victim in Fairfax County, Virginia.

"I think of her as a hero," Kate told reporters. A hero with baggage.

The funeral service for Irving Bass was small, in accordance with his final direction. It was a cloudy day, which all agreed Irving would also have wanted, cold enough for conversations to vaporize in the air, but just warm enough for some of the fallen snow to begin melting. Kate was one of about a dozen invited guests at the mausoleum. Kate's father was not invited, but as Kate walked to her car after the service, he was waiting on the shoveled walkway that led from the mausoleum to the parking lot.

They hadn't spoken since opening night.

"I've been thinking a lot about your play," he said.

She stopped. They were standing near a seventy-year-old gravestone, beneath a seventy-foot blue spruce that was the same age.

"Dad, I don't want to get into it here."

"It was terrific."

"Oh," she said. Not the words she'd expected.

"You were right," he said. "I did turn a blind eye."

"That wasn't the point of my play."

"Isn't that the point of *any* historical work—that history repeats itself?"

She hadn't really thought of that. But he had a point. "I suppose."

"Tell me again. What was the name of the president of IBM's German subsidiary?"

"Willy Heidinger."

"Heidinger, yes. I remember his line: 'Might as well do business with the Nazis, because if we don't, they'll just nationalize the company and take it, or get it from someone else.'"

"I don't know if he actually said it. But that was pretty much his approach, at least in my interpretation."

"It made me think of Jeremy."

Kate couldn't disagree. "Not a bad comparison."

"Watson made me think of me."

Kate glanced back at the mausoleum, recalling how her interpretation of Watson had clashed with Irving's. "It all depends on how you think of Watson."

"I think he lived with regret."

"That's one interpretation," said Kate. "Others would say he was too much of an egomaniac to admit a mistake, even to himself."

"By 'others,' you mean his son?"

Again, she glanced toward Irving's final place of

rest. Visions of red ink came to mind, the felt-tipped pen shaking in a hand that grew weaker with each passing day. *Conflict, Kate! We need more conflict!*

"Like I said. It's all a matter of interpretation."

Silence hung between them. Kate knew what he was wondering, and she hadn't prepared to discuss a certain daughter's interpretation of her own father. But in some ways, she'd been preparing all her life.

"You know, I still think Irving had it wrong," said Kate.

"Had what wrong?"

"Tom Junior didn't hate his father. The old man infuriated him to no end. But he didn't hate him."

"So he tolerated him?"

"More than that," said Kate, looking him in the eye. "I think he loved him very much."

The air around them seemed to lose some of its chill.

"Hmm. That's an interesting view."

"People don't have to agree all the time in order to love each other," she said.

"Right. They can agree to disagree."

"Of course, it helps if they agree at least some of the time."

He smiled a little. "I agree with that."

The wind blew, and a few needles from the blue spruce dropped to the snow around them.

"Hey, you want to get a cup of coffee?" he asked.

"Sure," said Kate. "I'd like that."

They started walking toward the parking lot together.

"Capitol Roasters is pretty close," he said.

"Mmm. The coffee at White's House of Bagels is so much better."

"Okay, if we're talking quality, not convenience, then we should go to Brews by Benjamin."

"Ugh! Really, Dad? How do you drink that stuff?"

Acknowledgments

The legal disclaimer says "any resemblance to actual persons, living or dead, is entirely coincidental." It's in all of my books. This time, there's a twist.

The friendship between the Battle and Grippando families goes back more than two decades, predating the birth of Patrick Trowbridge Battle, Jr., in 2002. To his mother and all those who knew him in diapers, he was "Baby Patrick." Patrick received a cancer diagnosis in 2017, and despite the love, prayers, and optimism of the "Battle Strong" movement, he passed away on December 11, 2018, at the age of sixteen. In a moment of love, compassion, and perhaps temporary insanity, I promised his parents I would write Patrick into one of my novels. A seamless appearance of a teenage boy in a Grippando novel would be no easy task, and I came up empty in my next two releases—no Patrick. Then, when the seeds for *Code 6* were just taking root, it occurred to me that by the time the book would be in bookstores, Patrick would have been a young man in his twenties. It was a lightbulb moment: I would age Patrick in real time. I owe a huge debt of gratitude to his godfather, Walter Strump, for helping me imagine Patrick as a twenty-something-year-old whiz kid in the tech industry. Walter, your input was invaluable, and your endless love for Patrick is inspirational.

I am also deeply grateful to GableStage and its founding artistic director, Joseph Adler. Joe developed and directed my first play, *Watson*, which made its world premiere at GableStage in 2019. Based on events in the life of IBM founder Thomas J. Watson, Sr., *Watson* is the story of the Nazis' exploitation of IBM technology during the Holocaust and the world's first personal information catastrophe: the systematic identification of Jews for extermination. Sound familiar? If you're wondering how Kate's play turned out, check out *Watson*.

Thanks also to my editor, Sarah Stein, for helping me stretch myself as a writer and create something special for my thirtieth novel, a play within a novel. Thanks also to my agent and friend, Richard Pine, who has been at my side for all thirty creations (thirty-one, if you count the one that crashed and burned), and to my beta reader, Judith Russell, pinch-hitting for her friend Gloria.

Finally, my biggest thank-you is to my wife, Tiffany. Thirty rides on a roller coaster is a lot to ask. You don't even like roller coasters. Thanks for keeping it fun. Thanks for laughing even when it wasn't fun. Thanks for *not* laughing every time I thought I could throw my hands in the air and ride standing up. I'll be loving you . . . always.